Wapsipinicon Summer

Wapsipinicon Summer

By

Jay Soupene

This is a work of fiction. All of the characters, organizations, and events portrayed in this novel are either products of the author's imagination or are used fictionally.

ISBN: 1493731890

ISBN-13: 9781493731893

This Book Is Dedicated To Our Veterans
Past, Present, and Future

A LONG TIME ago, a Fox Tribal Chief told his son this story:

"There is a river to manhood that we all must travel. On this journey, you will come to a great fork in the river where you will make a choice. At the river head, both streams will seem the same, but at the great fork, they will go their own direction. In the end, their mouths will tell of entirely different journeys. One will take you to a land rich with life, light, truth, confidence, peace, love and joy, and the other will take you to a desert that is dead, full of darkness, lies, anger, fear, and hate."

His son asked, "How will I know which one to choose?"

His father answered, "This world will deceive you—keep your eyes on heaven, my son. Let the stars in heaven fill your heart with truth, wisdom, strength, and courage. They will guide you on this journey and will show you the way."

Prologue

ANDY CRAWFORD GOT the phone call seven hours ago. He was riding the Metro, on his way to Charles Center in Downtown Baltimore, when his phone vibrated in his inside breast pocket.

Prior to the call, Andy had been distracted by the nuances of an ongoing project at work; not with the project itself, but mainly with the people involved. He loved his job as an engineer for a defense contractor and marveled at the capabilities he developed for those who dared to enter harm's way. However, today would be another day of struggle, trying to convince coworkers of what was in their best interest and that of the company. Dealing with people who were stubborn, ignorant, lazy, or a combination of all three was simply exhausting.

Andy's mind had drifted to thoughts about his wife, Susie. He didn't know how she raised their two children, served as a partner in a law firm, ran their home, and balanced everything so seamlessly. He smiled, realizing how fortunate he was—the love of his life was simply an amazing woman.

When Andy saw her ID pop up on his cell phone, he patted his back pocket, sure he'd forgotten his wallet or something else he would routinely leave on the dresser.

However, this time something was different.

"Andy?" Susie's greeting was followed by a pause and an immediate tone in the silence. Rarely had she called him by his first name—unless it was serious. Something had to be wrong. His thoughts raced to their children, and his stomach dropped in anticipation of what would come next. And then Susie let it out in a choked whimper. "Dad's gone."

He flinched back, confused. Her words made no sense to him. Susie's dad had died eleven years ago. Andy opened his mouth to respond when at that moment, the truth cut through him, and he realized *his* father was gone.

Nothing else was said for what felt like an eternity.

Andy stood on the train, numb with shock, surrounded by people reading newspapers and magazines with their ear buds in and tuned out to everything around them. He looked at their empty faces. Nobody seemed to care. Their blank stares offered no solace and were suffocating. He was stuck with them on that crowded car, moving forward—the rhythm of the tracks clicking to the beat of a world that kept moving forward where everything appeared the same. Yet in his world, life as he knew it had permanently changed.

Andy was suddenly struck with an overwhelming wave of panic and needed to get off the train. His knees buckled, and his head grew dizzy. Thinking he might vomit, he needed fresh air.

Everything whirled about him as his mind fought to accept the words he'd just heard. Andy had talked to his father two days earlier. The conversation had been like all the others they'd had. His father had mentioned struggling with a bad cold that he couldn't shake. Other than that, he had sounded fine.

But now, now he was gone. Gone from his life forever.

The world would never be the same now that his father,

John Crawford, was gone.

ꕥ

The phone call had come seven hours earlier. Since then, the day had been a whirlwind of confusion and contradictions, of funeral details and memories, and of changes to family and work schedules. In an instant, Andy's life had permanently morphed into one he had not come to peace with; yet, without hesitation, he dropped everything to catch his flight to Iowa.

Now sitting on the plane, he was numb with exhaustion. The sadness had not come yet. It wanted to, and Andy could feel it creeping into him at his edges. Not yet. He needed to stop the emotions and just think. Just think for a while. This was the first time he had been able to really take everything into account.

As the plane descended below the cloud line, Andy was startled awake from his daze. He peered from the window on the last leg of the short flight from Chicago's O'Hare to Cedar Rapids, Iowa. The rich farm fields and rolling shades of green greeted him, and he smiled. Summer in Iowa. It was simply beautiful with the fields of green intermixed with the darker, rough textures of deep woods.

Sprawling north to south, the Mississippi River was easily identified. Even at this altitude, Andy saw the locks and the barges pushing loads on the chocolate brown water. And then he saw the Wapsipincon River cutting through the hills from the northwest and meeting the Mississippi just north of Interstate 80 and the Quad Cities.

The plane took a deeper pitch toward Cedar Rapids, yet beyond the city, Andy could still see the Stone City Quarry along the banks of the Wapsi. As he looked north toward the river, it was as if he could see one era attempting to swallow another. The yellow escarpment of the large quarry, rich with history, stirred nostalgia for simpler and slower days long gone. All the while, the urban sprawl of Cedar Rapids continued to grow unimpeded, faster and faster, out from the city, devouring miles of farmland in the process.

Andy glanced out to the river once more and found peace. Despite all of the urban growth, nothing had changed.

This was his home.

Andy believed the river possessed a mysterious depth that defined the land and its people. Flowing southeast to the Mississippi, the Wapsipinicon River cut through the region and exposed its core. It shaped the farmland, the wild rolling hills and the fields, and covered them with a thick blanket of rich black soil that was darker and more productive than any other in the world. The river brought life to the deep woods of massive, towering white and red oaks, black and silver maples, hickory, elm, and cottonwood trees. It pulled on the transportation arteries, the junctions, and the communities and tied them together. Andy smiled again and pondered the impact the river had on the people and the land.

Glancing down to his phone, Andy saw over thirty new emails in the last six hours. He looked back out the window to the river now blending into the horizon. For centuries, it had been the lifeblood of this agricultural area, and today it still was. The river appeared so peaceful from the air, but from time to time, it could unleash its strength—at some point in the future, the pendulum would shift, and its flood waters would turn destructive with an unforgiving force. It would remind Iowans that it still brought character to the land—struggle and strength, fear and perseverance, hope, despair, and courage to the people.

Andy looked back down at his phone and scrolled through the last pictures taken of him and his father together. Tears welled up in his eyes, and he tried to smile at how blessed he was to have had him as his father. He peered back out the window one more time as they began the final descent. He was born and raised here in Eastern Iowa. On this river, he had learned what it was to be a man—to truly love, to find courage, understand strength, and to dream and to believe.

Everyone has periods in their life that define who they are. The summer of 1966 was one of those crossroads for Andy. For seven weeks during that summer, he had been fortunate enough to be surrounded by a handful of amazing people. Seven weeks that had changed his life forever.

Andy's mind was flooded with memories from all those years ago—of loved ones, of wounds healing and scars left behind, of choices in life and their consequences, of love and sacrifice, of forgiveness and redemption, and of the friends and family who made him what he was today.

This is their story.

Part One

David

July, 1966

I

"I AIN'T NEVER seen anything like it." Dave raised his voice. "The night the Old Man took his stand and paid the price. Paid the price for all of us, he did. Things weren't quite right that night." He clutched the beer in his hand. "Laying there in the shadows around Djebel Lassouda. I remember an anxious anticipation, just feeling undone and an uncomfortable heavy silence in the shadows. First came them Panzers. We was low on ammunition and didn't have much to fight them with, so we stayed down in our holes. The ground shook us up as those tanks grumbled past our positions. The vibration rattled my chest, and my knees shook with fear. But that wasn't the worst of it. Their infantry followed, and everything went to hell in a hand basket."

Andy looked up at his father and his Uncle Dave. The darkness of the summer evening had closed in around them, but out on their back porch, he could still see his uncle's ghost-like expressions in the moonlight. His uncle's face seemed so sad, so solemn. Andy felt an awkward twinge of guilt, but he didn't want Uncle Dave to stop telling his story.

Dave looked away. "It all went from bad to worse, and I probably wouldn't be here if not for what the Old Man done. I think he knew it, too. He knew what was wrong and what needed to be done. He had that way about him."

Dave sipped his beer. "We called Captain Sterling the Old Man with pride. Although he wasn't much older than any of us, he seemed older. He had that special touch with people. He knew how to lead. A kind word, a hard look, or just his own personal example, he always knew how to get the best out of us. I rarely heard him raise his voice, and I never heard him cuss. Sometimes he was our father figure, other times our brother. Every now and then, he was our preacher, or our teacher, or our counselor. But even when he was tough on us, somehow we knew he was our friend. He never got too close to anyone; it weren't professional. But he was always there for us, willing to listen and ready to make things right. He was fair, but he was also firm."

Dave's lip curled in a small smile as he glanced at Andy, and his voice tapered. "I think about him often, and why we all loved him so much. More than anything, it was probably his humility. He served us. He loved us. He never asked us to do anything he wasn't willing to do himself." Dave paused and stared at the label on his beer.

John laid his hand on his brother's arm. "You don't have to…"

"Captain Sterling could see things most of us never saw." Dave raised his voice, ignoring his brother. "He could size up the problem and always knew what to do. I think he knew it when he done what he done. Must've figured it was the only way when he decided it was his turn."

Dave stared into the night and shifted his voice lower. “They were all around us. I could smell them in their leather and steel. Them Krauts were all over us, and the Old Man jumped headlong into the mass of them. We were overrun, but there he was in the smoke and darkness. I could see his silhouette in the shadows. He was shooting them point blank with his .45. Don’t think them Krauts knew what was coming at them, or maybe they was so surprised somebody would do something so crazy." Dave shook his head with a soft chuckle. "But there he was, shooting them down one by one till he was out of ammo. I heard his sharp high pitch scream as he swung wildly at them. His knife in one hand and his helmet in the other. I can still clearly see them two shiny bars on his collar flash in the moonlight as he fought them off. Killing three or four more of them until a mass of about twenty Krauts appeared out of the shadows and swallowed him up." He let out a deep sigh. "Then I didn’t see him no more, just those Krauts standing there weird. Seemed like they were in awe of him, almost a strange respect. Cold and quiet, a clump of them in the darkness."

Dave looked up at Andy. “About that time, me, Smitty, and Larson had just about had enough. Don’t know if I’ve ever been so angry and scared all at the same time. With our bayonets fixed, we poured out of our holes and charged headlong into the dark mass. I don’t remember anyone giving the order; it just happened. It wasn’t anything like we ever trained. It was worse. Pure chaos.”

He leaned back in his lawn chair, and Andy could no longer see his face in the moonlight. His uncle’s voice lowered to a whisper, but Andy could still hear him and hung on every word. "As we lunged forward from our holes, I yelled at the top of my lungs. I must've been out of my mind when all hell broke loose. It was like I was no longer in my body but watching from above. One thing I clearly remember, that I will always remember…the first Kraut I killed that night."

Dave took a drink of his beer and then he raised his voice. "As we ran into the mass of enemy soldiers, I lunged forward at one of them. I thrust my rifle with all my strength deep into his middle. Pushing my bayonet through, his hands wrapped around my rifle—we were locked together, both gripping my weapon. Everything slowed down, and it was just the two of us. There was this warm greasy wetness, and then I remember his eyes. They were young eyes. Just a kid. Maybe a few years older than young Andy here."

Dave turned to Andy's father, sitting next to him on the porch. "We were locked together through my rifle for what seemed an eternity. As his life was draining out of him, he stumbled to his knees, and an intense flood of shame washed over me. My gut retched with disgust in myself, and for an instant, I thought I was going to vomit."

Dave paused and looked out into the distance. "Then something smashed into my right leg, and the whole night lit up around us—like a hundred Fourth of Julys right on top of us. Next thing I remember was all of Bravo Company screaming across the field into the tree line. And the panic stricken screams of the Krauts as old Bravo poured over their position and massed our fires into them. I shot four more almost instantly.

They were all around me, and I couldn't miss. It couldn't have been more than five seconds, but it felt like the world had slowed down, and I could move in and around time how I pleased. Strange."

Dave took another swig of his beer and cleared his throat. "In those few seconds, everything was so clear. I sensed the whole situation and could do whatever I wanted. It was a weird powerful feeling, like I was super human. All powerful… Ain't never been that way before nor since. I shot each one of them right in the face, and they just dropped heavy, dead to the ground. Must've been all that training from Captain Sterling. He had been hard on us in our training, and sometimes we hated him for it, but now I know. We didn't understand what he was preparing us for. But that night in the desert, we understood." He set his beer down, and his voice dropped lower. "We understood all right, and it saved our lives."

Staring into the night, Dave seemed as if he saw it happening again. "I remember looking to my right and seeing old Bravo rushing ahead into the rock formations, and the quick fear that I'd be left behind by my brothers lit a match under me. I turned to run after them, but couldn't get my balance—my right leg was all wrong. My head was dizzy, and the night's darkness was spinning around me. I was sinking…sinking…slow at first, and then I fell. I couldn't stop it. I remember it all seemed silly. I fell. Fell flat down on my face…" Dave's voice tapered off to silence as his eyes gazed out beyond the porch, across the street somewhere toward the edge of the neighborhood.

Lightning flashed in the distance, but no thunder followed.

It was still too far away. It reminded Dave of artillery fire at night, and instinctively, he began counting. Flash to bang. Using the speed of sound, he could quickly calculate how far away the artillery was or in this case, the storm. In some ways, everything reminded him of that war.

"Looks like a storm may be coming on tonight," John said, interrupting the silence.

"We sure could use some rain," Dave replied. "The storm's still a ways off. Probably five miles or more."

"You're right. Still got time for at least one more beer. What do you say?" John suggested, standing up from his chair.

Dave broke his gaze and looked up at John. "Yeah, another beer would be great. Thanks, John."

John turned to his son. "Andy, you best be getting ready for bed soon. We got church in the morning, and you don't want your mother to…"

Andy interrupted his father. "Oh Dad, just a few more minutes. I want to hear the rest of Uncle Dave's story."

"Five minutes." John lowered his chin and raised five fingers, making sure Andy understood. "Just five more minutes, and then it's time for bed." John then stepped inside to get a couple beers for him and his brother.

A slight breeze picked up, and the trees in the backyard swayed back and forth. Dave felt the storm closing in on them. He tried to continue with his story, but his thoughts were jumbled. "Well, uh…well, like I said, the Old Man laid it on the line and gave us his best. He saved many of us. He saved his company. We was overrun. Rommel…that damned old wily desert fox out-smarted us that night. But Captain Sterling saved us. I don't know how, but he done it. We just followed. Somehow he knew, and we followed him."

The night closed in on their conversation, and Dave lowered his voice to a whisper. "There ain't a day goes by that I don't think about him. What he done for me…and I wonder. I wonder if I'm measuring up—if my life is worth his sacrifice, worth his respect."

Dave dropped his head, and Andy no longer saw his face. When John stepped back out on the porch, Dave cleared his throat as he prepared to continue his story. "Somebody must have pulled me for ten miles after that fight. It was daylight before we finally made it back to old Kern's Crossroads and were safely behind our line…"

"What about Larson and Smitty? Where were they?" Andy implored.

Looking in the far off distance and into the darkness of the summer evening, Dave tried to forget the ugliness, tried to forget the costs. Lightning flashed again, this time it was accompanied with the low rumble of thunder. "Larson? Smitty? Well uh…they uh…they didn't…I…I don't…"

John handed him a beer. "Here you go, Dave—a cold Old Style."

Uncle Dave sat there on the front porch, eyelids half open, looking off in the distance. Looking for something, remembering something, mumbling something to himself.

"Andrew, it's past eleven, and you best get in and get ready for bed. Your ma will have your hide if you're not in bed in the next thirty minutes. Besides, it looks like it's going to rain soon."

"Aw, Dad, do I have to? Uncle Dave never told me about these parts," Andy begged with a pout. "I want to hear more 'bout how he was a hero in North Africa."

"Your dad's right. You best get ready for bed. You got church tomorrow, and you don't want to get your ma cross with you. Especially if you want to go fishing tomorrow with your Uncle Dave." Dave smiled and ruffled Andy's hair with his hand.

Andy turned to his father. "Really Dad? I can go fishing tomorrow?"

"Yeah, sure, Son, but you best get to bed otherwise your ma may have something to say 'bout you doing chores instead."

Andy gave his dad and his uncle a hug and ran in the house. At age twelve, he was entering that awkward stage of growth both physically and emotionally. He was stretching out, growing faster than all the previous years combined. His voice had taken on a hint of deepness, and peach fuzz dusted above his lip. Andy was stepping up to the edge of manhood.

Dave turned to his brother. "Thanks. I don't know why I was talking about this. There's something in a summer evening that brings back those memories. I apologize for leading Andy on like that."

"Brother, you ain't got to apologize for nothing. Sometimes you just got to let things out a little. I didn't tell you this earlier, but I want to thank you for spending time with Andy this summer. It's meant a lot to Maggie and me. This guard schedule at the prison has been tough for all of us. You know better than anybody working up in the front office." John stopped for a moment and looked to his brother for his concurrence.

"Working on The Stone is a hard life for everyone." Dave let the words hang in the air.

'The Stone' was what everyone called the Iowa Men's Reformatory. Partly because the maximum security prison had the appearance of a massive stone fortress, complete with a thirty foot stone wall, bulwarks, towers, and even stone lions guarding the entrance. But also because serving in the prison, amongst some of the most hateful and violent criminals in the Midwest could turn a man hard and cold. It could turn a good man to stone if he let it. 'The Stone' had its effect on everyone whether you worked there or were a full-time resident.

John nodded. "By the end of August, I'll finally be able to come off working nights. This shift schedule over the past year has been hard for Maggie, but it's been really tough on Andy. Thought I'd get more time this summer if that damn schedule would've changed. But it ain't going to happen—at least not 'til August at the earliest. Won't see any change 'til the state hires on more guards."

"Brother, no problem. I know you'd be doing the same for me."

Dave gazed off into the distance. During July in Iowa, the nights exploded with life. The backyard sparkled with lightning bugs, sung with the siren sounds of locusts in the trees, and flickered with June bugs on the porch light as they sputtered and knocked into the front screen door. A big old raccoon dug into a trash can across the street in the Meyer's front yard, and the distant sound of Jimmy Barnes' screeching the tires of his coupe down on Main Street. All could be heard. With the humidity and the constant movement, the night was teeming with life.

A storm was blowing into town. The lightning picked up and was now accompanied by thunder. Strangely, it reminded Dave of the nights that would never end—all those years ago in the shadows, in the awkward clumps of men, in the heat and confusion, in the steady stream of chaotic noise, in the constant din of a battlefield in North Africa. And now in the heat of the summer evening in Iowa, he still struggled with the shame of all those things he had to do.

A storm was blowing indeed. The brothers, Dave and John Crawford, felt it coming on. This was the heavy calm before the storm.

"How about one more beer before we call it a night?" John asked.

"Now you are talking, brother. I sure could use one more," Dave replied.

II

THE LIGHTNING FLASHED in the distance. Eddie Gruber shuddered as the storm closed in on him.

"Damn it," he said to himself. The rain would ruin his night of catfishing out on the Wapsipinicon River. He often talked to himself when he was alone. "I can't seem to catch a break," Eddie mumbled as the thunder rolled overhead.

This was just his luck. Rain. All he had wanted was a little time on the river. He'd had a hell of a week and needed a break. He needed solitude and some time to think.

He had looked forward to Saturday night. During the summer, he could be found every Saturday evening out on the river, fishing. His favorite fishing hole was at the point where Buffalo Creek entered into the Wapsipinicon River. He would fish into the early morning and sleep through the next day. Under the stars and with the river was his time away from his troubles and from everyone. This was Eddie's time to think. Right now, he had a lot on his mind.

Things in his life had not gone as planned. The truth was, he'd never had a plan. He had graduated from high school three years ago. Since then, he'd been living in a fog—aimless, bumping along, looking for something better. He'd held down a handful of jobs, cutting grass, bailing hay, shoveling snow, and working at the grocery store, but for the most part, he was lost.

He really had no idea who he wanted to be in life.

Eddie still lived at home, and his parents continually pestered him to get on with his life, to grow up, and be someone. College, the military, or work outside of the state—they didn't care as long as he did something, anything to get out of their house and get on with his life.

Eddie hated these damn crossroads. He wondered why he always had to make these kinds of decisions. In this case, indecision was his decision. The thought of having goals, of having a direction, or of having something to work toward hadn't ever interested him. His aimlessness was at the heart of the problem. He didn't want to be anything. He was happy doing odd jobs, living in his bedroom, hanging out with his friends, and fishing all night. His simple routines had gotten him this far, and up until a few weeks ago, he was content.

"Snake in the grass," Eddie mumbled. He was thinking about Joe Matsell. Joe reminded Eddie of a snake. Joe had something deceptive about him, possibly even evil. With Joe, Eddie always had the feeling of something under the surface, something dark, something he couldn't trust. Eddie often found himself wanting to trust Joe. At times, Eddie even went along with him, knowing in the back of his mind it would all come to loss.

"Damn gambling. Why the hell did I ever start playing blackjack in the first place?" Eddie said under his breath.

Up until a few weeks ago, his life had been pretty simple, but now he was in over his head. He felt like he was drowning. He had been lured in by Joe and was now playing cards almost every night. At first, Eddie had been successful at the table. He had been up almost a thousand dollars. A thousand dollars. He liked the taste of winning, of money coming in—something he never had before.

But in the last ten days, Eddie's luck turned. No matter how hard he had tried, he couldn't win. Nothing would go right. Now he owed Joe Matsell over five thousand dollars. Five thousand dollars. He could never come up with that kind of money.

Eddie had one chance. He had made Joe an offer he hoped Joe would accept. Really, it had not been an offer. Eddie had given him an ultimatum. He was the only person who knew about Joe Matsell's business—not the tavern he managed, but his other business in Cedar Rapids and Iowa City. Joe Matsell was heavily involved with selling marijuana to college students. For some reason, Joe trusted Eddie, and he had Eddie with him during several sales transactions. In fact, Joe had given Eddie the responsibility of closing a few deals.

For the first time in his life, Eddie felt empowered. The drug business had given him some authority. The money had rolled in, and he had earned over two thousand dollars in a month. That was more than he had ever seen working at the grocery store. But now that money was gone. Joe had won it all back at the blackjack table. Not only had Eddie lost the money he had earned, he now owed Joe money he didn't have. A lot of money.

Two days ago when Joe Matsell had made Eddie the offer, Joe had told him he felt horrible about the gambling debt, and he wanted to help Eddie out. Joe had explained that he had a major deal he was working on with a group out of Chicago, with a lot of money at stake. Joe would have to put down over twenty-five thousand dollars for the marijuana. He had the cash. That wasn't the issue. He and Joe both had known what the problem was; that much money made people unpredictable. Eddie knew exactly why Joe wanted him to close the deal. The supplier might rob him or do something worse.

To Joe, the risks were worth it. This deal would be a huge investment and could potentially set him up for future business in other parts of the Midwest. Joe had told Eddie that if future sales went well, he might actually pay off his debt and come out ahead in all of this.

Eddie had known it was risky. Too risky. He didn't mind gambling, but he didn't like risks. Even though Eddie had never planned for his future, he had figured any path would get him there. But he wasn't a criminal, and he didn't want to get wrapped up in all of this—drugs, jail time, possibly something worse.

The stakes were too high. Eddie would have to fold on this deal, but he felt trapped. He knew too much, and Joe had him cornered.

With nowhere to turn, Eddie had gambled one more time, and had countered Joe's offer. Eddie told Joe he would turn him into the authorities for all the business Joe was doing. Unless of course, Joe would lift the gambling debt Eddie owed him.

Eddie hadn't been sure how Joe would respond. They'd been alone at the tavern when he made the offer. Eddie had feared Joe might get angry, possibly even violent, but he hadn't.

He'd just smiled. He'd said something about this not being personal but a business decision that would benefit them both. Joe had told Eddie he would have to think about his offer and would let him know soon.

That was twenty-four hours ago, and Eddie hadn't heard anything. Nothing. He had stayed clear of Joe's bar, but he thought he might have heard something by now.

Eddie needed to think. Fishing gave him that time. What would Joe do? Eddie wished he had never sat down at that damned blackjack table.

Eddie looked out across the river and then to the stars above. It was so peaceful. Lightning flashed off to the west, and he watched the storm front drifting toward him.

"Damn storm's going to ruin everything," Eddie mumbled as he picked up his fishing pole and cast his bait out into the dark river.

ຽຌ

Eddie waited as long as he could with hopes of catching something. Even though he had watched the front coming in, it still caught him off guard. The wind picked up, and the storm hit him with such ferocity he thought he would be blown into the river. The rain came down in heavy torrential waves, and Eddie scurried on the bank as he tried to load up his tackle box.

The lightning flashed, and for a moment, he thought he saw someone at the top of the hill, looking down on him. In daylight, the cemetery, on the bluff overlooking the river, was a beautiful setting. At ten o'clock at night, alone in a thunderstorm, it was something altogether different. A strange wave of fear shot through his body as he felt someone watching him. He wiped the rain from his eyes and tried to focus on the hill above. When the lightning flashed again, Eddie didn't see anyone there.

Ghosts. That was the first thought that entered Eddie's mind. He must have seen a ghost. He wiped the rain from his face again and peered up the hill into the darkness. Lightning flashed and again, no one was there. Eddie was not a superstitious person, but he had seen enough over the years on the river that made him wonder about the unseen forces of nature. He had come to believe there was more to this world that couldn't be explained.

Another wave of fear trembled through Eddie's body. He tried to convince himself he was seeing things and hurried to pull all of his gear together. Something in the back of his mind told him he was not alone, and this made him move even faster. The rain came down harder. Eddie suddenly slipped as he reached down for his fishing pole, and his foot slid off the river bank and into the water.

"Damn it!" Eddie cursed as he found himself on his hands and knees in the mud and his right foot soaked from the river. Climbing to his feet, he cursed again and turned to pick up his fishing pole.

At that moment, a heavy force crashed into him from behind and lifted him from his feet, sending him sailing into the river. Eddie plunged under water and couldn't breathe. He was not alone. Someone massive was on top of him. Someone with incredible strength pushed him down. Eddie reached up and clawed at whoever was on him. With all of his might, he kicked with his legs and swung his arms at the force holding him down. Adrenalin surged in Eddie's veins. He clenched his fists and beat against the bulky figure.

For a brief moment, Eddie broke away. He reached the surface and gasped for air. Then without warning, enormous arms wrapped around his neck from behind and pulled him back into the water. Eddie kicked his feet frantically as he went back under. He violently thrashed against the heavy force behind him, but it was no use. He couldn't break free.

Eddie panicked with fear. He had no way out. He kicked and clawed in one last effort, but he couldn't get away. As he struggled, his head pounded as if his brain would explode. He gasped, and the water poured into his lungs. Eddie's throat tightened and darkness closed in around him. He floated in a fog as he began to drift out of consciousness. Eddie was falling, falling deeper and deeper into an abyss. His mind raced as he sank. He thought about his parents and their disappointment. He thought about crossroads and indecision. As he blacked out, his last thought was of the peace in the stars above.

III

MAIN STREET ON Sunday afternoon was quiet. Lined with two-story brick buildings constructed in the late 1800s by industrious Germans, English, and Irish that settled in Eastern Iowa, the street was a central economic and social symbol in Anamosa. Many of those descendants still lived in this area of the state. Multiple families with names like Eilers, Shaw, Schmidt, Ford, Zimmerman, Booth, and Meyer could still be found in the phone book. Several of the buildings were adorned with their names permanently carved into the stone and brick at the top of the ornate building fronts. These buildings, once banks, general stores, or hotels, now served the needs of the people of the community with services that ranged from beauty salons, women's clothing stores, to hardware stores and taverns.

Other than the cars from the after-church crowd in front of Buddy's Café, the half mile street was empty. Dave and Andy turned onto Main in Dave's rusty 1951 pickup truck and drove south toward the cemetery.

"What we got for bait today, Uncle Dave?" Andy asked.

"Got us some chicken livers from Hargrave and Johnson's Meats. Also got some night crawlers from Old Man Gelkie's General Store. The old fart charged me a dime more for a dozen than what he charged me last year," Dave cursed.

"Where we going to fish?"

"Think we'll throw our lines in right below the point where Buffalo Creek enters into the Wapsi. A tree came down last fall, and I think there's a pretty good catfish hole there."

"I love catfish'n. Dad didn't take me out last summer at all. He was working nights at the prison. And this summer's the same." Andy had a hint of disappointment in his voice, but without missing a beat, he asked, "Do you think we can go swimming if we don't catch nothing?""

"Not on your life. Not in the Wapsi," Dave said curtly.

"Aw, why not? Molly swims all the time with her sisters up by Stone City," Andy pleaded.

"River's different here. The Wapsi flows deep down here below Buffalo Creek. Ain't meant for swimming. The water's dark and seems slow. The mud-covered bottom creates a murkiness that makes it hard to judge. The river ain't what it seems. The water on the surface moves slow and calm, but below the surface, there's a lot of undergrowth, strange currents, and deep pools. This part of the river can be dangerous…it's got too many unknowns, too much that can't be seen."

Entering into the cemetery, Dave steered the old pickup past the gravesite of Anamosa's famous son, Grant Wood. He was now considered an artistic genius for his masterpiece, *American Gothic*. But when he lived in Eastern Iowa, he was not accepted and was odd to most locals. In fact, rumors of his homosexuality and a bizarre life of sin in his art colony ran rampant, a standard of living overtly repulsive to the majority of the ironclad Lutherans and Catholics in the area.

Most had never really known him. He had served in the

army during WWI, and he had turned away from the locals and tended to socialize with folks from Cedar Rapids and Iowa City. Despite his questionable reputation in the community back in the 1930s, Grant Wood was arguably one of the greatest American painters of the Twentieth Century. This fact had not been lost on the locals, and Grant Wood was now a symbol for the county. In death, any earlier shortcomings were easily overlooked as the community commercialized the figure of Grant Wood in an effort to draw tourists and business to the sleepy Iowa town.

His art was now internationally renowned and largely recognized, not by locals from Anamosa, but by the college people from Iowa City and even the urban elite of Chicago, St Louis, and Minneapolis. Every summer, artists, educators, and students flocked to the small, quarry town of Stone City for Grant Wood Days. Three miles outside of Anamosa, the weekend-long backwoods festival combined liberal politics, music, art, sex, and marijuana. It was a major event that had set the stage for some interesting events that didn't normally occur in this part of Eastern Iowa or even in the Midwest for that matter. The most profound aspect of having the famous artist as a hometown favorite son seemed to be the titillating gossip for the locals at Buddy's Café on the Monday after the festival. This was where one could always find the loud and obnoxious Jones County Sheriff, Jim Barton.

Jim Barton was not one to hold back his tongue, especially when he was the center of the conversation as he talked of the trials of maintaining stability when all the college folk came to town. His stories ranged from mass groups of adults skinny dipping in the river, to drunken students arrested out at Mount Hope for doing God knows what, to long-haired hippies leading peace marches down Main Street. Car races out on the old Ridge Road between Stone City and Anamosa were common during the art festival—at least one car would always be pulled out of the ditch near one of the dangerously sharp curves. These types of events had been common for Grant Wood Days.

Dave Crawford, like most Anamosans, didn't have much time for art. He didn't see the point since nothing good ever came from it, nothing that mattered anyway. Hunting, fishing, and sports were what mattered to most in Anamosa. Talk at Buddy's Café generally revolved around the Friday night football game, the best lures for bass fishing, or the anticipated start of deer hunting season. These were the activities most folks lived for.

Eagerly looking out the window as the truck slowly turned down the narrow road in the cemetery, Andy caught his first glimpse of the Wapsi. The dark brown, slowly moving waters had gotten Andy excited with anticipation of catching fish. He could see more of the river as they got deeper into the cemetery. The old oak trees hung at awkward angles, bent over the river. Some touched the water while others stood proud, reaching for the sky. The shadows from the trees and the coolness of the shade made a prime area for catfishing, and Andy bounced in his seat, barely able to contain himself.

Parking the truck at the edge of the cemetery, above where the Buffalo and the Wapsi met, Dave got out and pulled at his fishing poles in the back of the truck. "Andy, I need you to get up there in the truck and grab the tackle box and bait."

"You got it." Andy jumped out of the truck with a hop in his step.

Andy knew he would have to carry most of the gear from the truck to the river. The hike was a good hundred feet down a pretty steep incline, and Uncle Dave always walked with his cane. At age forty-three, he still dealt with his injuries from the war as he limped toward the sharp incline down to the river. Even though it was almost twenty-five years ago, that old wound from North Africa never properly healed. The bullet shattered his femur, and he lost much of his muscle in his thigh. Sergeant Dave Crawford had spent three months in a hospital in Morocco, getting healed. Initially, all Grandma and Grandpa had known was that he was missing. Over time, they had received conflicting bits of information that could not be confirmed. For all they knew, he was either missing, captured, or had been killed. This had been early in the war, and information hadn't always gotten back home correctly. It wasn't for another two months before they had learned he was alive.

Andy's father and uncle grew up in Red Oak, Iowa. The boys from Red Oak had all gone to war together. Most of them had been in Bravo Company of the 168th Infantry Division and had fought in both North Africa and in Europe. It had been well known in Iowa during World War II that Red Oak, Iowa had suffered more casualties than any other American community. Most of the boys had never come home from that war. Those that had were changed forever.

Prior to the war, Dave had been the captain of his football

team and class president. He had once been sociable and well known in the community. After he returned, he was different and became a loner. The once ambitious and lively youth had changed in a serious sort of way.

Dave rarely talked about it, but Andy gathered from his dad that his uncle was living with considerable guilt. Andy remembered overhearing his mother talking to his father out on the front porch one evening. She had said that the war took everything. It had taken everything from him and his brother. It had taken the best from them and gave nothing back but scars. Andy remembered her words. She had said they were both shells of the men they were before their wars. The man she had married and the man she was living with now were not the same.

Andy looked up to his uncle with admiration. Once he had overheard his father say that Uncle Dave was one of the few that had returned from the war, and it was difficult for him to face the Red Oak families who had lost loved ones. It was too hard to remember it all, to be constantly reminded. He could hardly walk down the street without seeing somebody who lost someone. It was too hard. The guilt was too heavy, suffocating him. In the end, he had to leave Red Oak. That was when Uncle Dave had moved to Anamosa and found work at the state reformatory in administration. He rarely ever returned to Red Oak. Anamosa was his home now.

In 1945, Andy's father had just turned seventeen. He was five years younger than Uncle Dave, and by the time he had enlisted, the war was over. His dad had served in the famed First Cavalry Division in Japan and fought in Korea, but he had never said a word about it. Andy only knew he had fought in the war because he found a medal in his ma's jewelry box—a silver star. When Andy had asked whose it was, his mother said it belonged to his father and that he got it in Korea. Nothing else had ever been said about it.

"I got the chicken livers and night crawlers," Andy said.

"Grab the stringer in the cab under my seat—I got a feeling we're going to need it today," Dave said as he pointed toward the cab. Andy did as he was told and proudly held the bait.

Stepping away from the truck, the two started down the narrow trail toward Buffalo Creek. The incline proved to be steep. Andy carried the tackle box and poles, and Dave leaned heavily on his cane, carefully moving downward to the base of the embankment. The trail was still slippery from the thunderstorm the night before. Thick, wet mud caked to their shoes, making the journey even more difficult. After five minutes, they safely reached the bottom. Breathing heavily, Dave pulled out a handkerchief and wiped the sweat from his brow.

"It's a beautiful day for fishing." Andy glowed with excitement.

Still catching his breath, Dave stood on the bank of Buffalo Creek and looked upstream. "Quite a storm last night, but today is beautiful. It's going to be a great day of fishing." Dave paused and leaned on his cane. "Every day is a great day for fishing, Andy. The key is to figure out where the fish are and what they're eating."

"Uncle Dave, is this the fishing hole?"

"Nah, there ain't much in the Buffalo, except for a handful

of carp here and there. We're going to follow the creek down yonder to the Wapsi. We get to the river, and the catfish hole is down the way from where the Buffalo flows in."

Turning toward the Wapsi, the two began the final leg of their journey. Andy picked up the pace with eagerness as they got closer.

"Take the trail over to the left. The point up ahead, where the Buffalo enters the Wapsi, is over fished. I know a good hole a few hundred feet downstream," Dave explained as they veered away from the point, and he guided Andy down the trail.

Reaching the Wapsi, Dave took a knee, and Andy crouched down beside him. Dave pointed toward the river. "Now look out there. See how the river flows?"

Andy was quickly overwhelmed by the immensity of it. He had been fishing on this river many times, but never with Uncle Dave alone. And he'd never gotten down on a knee to "recon the river" as Uncle Dave called it.

Dave turned to Andy, and in a whisper, he showed him how to read the river. "You see how the Buffalo meets the Wapsi upstream? How it seems to pick up speed out there? All that water pushing in? Ain't nowhere for the water to go, so it pushes further out to the other side of the river. It don't look like it from here, but that there is a fast current. If you get down and look close, you can see where the water flows over large objects. Look how the water swirls up and out. That current is strong, and it is flowing over something pretty big."

"Is that where we want to fish?" Andy asked, matching Dave's whisper.

Quietly, Dave replied, "Nah, moves too fast for catfish. Too much work for them to feed in. The current is slower over here along this bank—that's where we'll drop our lines. You see down over there, where the tree has fallen into the river? Look how the water slowly collects behind it. How leaves and sticks flow into it and stop. What that is, is a steady source of food for the catfish, and they don't have to burn too much energy to get it."

The two slowly crept up toward the fishing hole. Reaching the site, they stood back from the bank and crouched down.

In a whisper, Dave instructed Andy. "Get the poles ready. I already got them strung up with treble hooks and two split shots. Grab two of the bobbers out of the tackle box and put them 'bout five feet above the hook. I'll get the bait ready."

Andy complied, and Dave opened the chicken livers. Dave had them sitting out for two days, and when he lifted the lid, the putrid smell of spoiled blood filled the air.

"Oh yeah, just right. Mr. Whiskers down there on the bottom is going to like this," Dave said as the strong odor filled his nostrils.

The foul odor turned Andy's stomach, but he smiled and shook his head approvingly because nothing was better than fishing—especially with his Uncle Dave. Dad was a great fisherman. He always caught fish. But Dad claimed that Uncle Dave was a fishing master and that a boy could learn a lot from him in one day on the river.

Dave grabbed hold of the base of the treble hook with his left hand and with his right reached in to the livers and pulled up a mushy chunk of reddish-brown, bloody, dripping slime. He slowly pressed the liver into the prongs of the hook and wrapped it securely around it.

"We going to use night crawlers?" Andy asked, his eyes widening.

"Not yet. We got to get their attention first."

Getting the second hook baited, Dave turned to Andy. "Now look out there where the tree goes under the water—'bout fifteen feet out. What I want you to do is slowly cast your line there. Nice and easy. You don't have to hit a homerun with it. You got to put it right there...nice and easy."

Andy complied, and with a near perfect cast, he dropped the bobber exactly where Dave directed.

"Now reel in a little till it clicks and loosen up your drag. You want him to be able to take it. Don't need to fight him yet. You can let that hook do the work for you."

Getting the second line in a little closer to the bank, Dave then walked about thirty feet downstream from the fishing hole. Andy tended to the poles while Dave washed all the blood off his hands and then rounded up a couple of sticks. Returning with the sticks, Dave broke them down into Y-shaped stands and pulled out his buck knife and started whittling. Sharpening the ends, he pushed them deep into the ground and rested a pole on each stand.

"How we doing, Andy?" Dave whispered.

"Nothing yet. Not even a nibble."

"Patience, Young Andy. Everything is set. Old Mr. Whiskers is down there, and he'll come when he's ready."

"You think Mr. Whiskers is really down there?"

"I am sure of it. I bet he's down there with a couple of his friends. Just need to be patient, is all. They'll come."

"The river sure does seem slow and calm today," Andy stated as if he was already getting bored.

Gazing out over the river, Dave whispered, "Yeah, you can't really tell too much by looking at it—you got to study it. So much that you're looking into it, seeing the layers, understanding the depth. There's a lot going on out there—a lot more than you may think. The river moves; the river changes. It ain't what's on the surface that matters. On the surface you see things. You might see tiny whirlpools and the water swirling upwards. These are just indicators, and they might not be at all what they seem. A good recon of the river makes all the difference between catching fish and standing on the bank, wasting your time. You got to get to the why of the river. You got to study it in parts and put it together and then test it to see if it is what you think. Only by doing this can you really get at the truth of it. Your dad and I have always said that you can learn a lot by studying how a river runs. It's what's under the surface that really matters… That's what makes all the difference."

"Uncle Dave, I think I got a bite!"

"Slow down there, Young Andy. I think Old Mr. Whiskers may have decided he's ready. Stay calm," Dave whispered.

The bobber bounced. Still in a whisper, Dave instructed, "Slowly pick up the pole without moving your line, Andy. You don't want to scare him. When your bobber slowly goes under and stays under, I want you to firmly pull up on your pole. Don't jerk it, just firmly pull the end upward. Let the hook do the work for you. That should set the hook."

"Uncle Dave, my bobber's moving! I can feel him pulling on it! My bobber's moving!" Andy shouted excitedly.

"Hold it…steady…steady…wait on him, Andy."

The bobber moved toward the sunken tree and then bounced back toward the bank. Andy could hardly contain himself as the catfish on the other end of the line toyed with the bait. The bobber moved and then stopped. It moved and then bounced back again. Then the line went slack, and there was nothing. Andy could feel that there was no life on the end of the line…nothing. The bobber slowly spun in small circles with the current and turned over on its side.

"Aw, shucks!" Andy cried. "I think he's gone. He robbed me blind and took my bait."

"Maybe, Andy. You got to wait on him. I want you to slowly bring in your line two turns on your reel."

Andy did as instructed, but there was nothing on the end of the line. With the slack line came an aura of hopelessness. Andy had been so close—he could feel the catfish on the other end, full of life, full of vigor. And Andy was ready for the challenge. He was ready to tussle with Old Mr. Whiskers. He was now resigned to the belief Old Mr. Whiskers was gone. Andy had missed him, and he may not catch any fish today.

"I think I'm going to need more bait and…" Andy said when he was completely stopped in mid-sentence by the violent tug on his line. The bobber disappeared and the line was tight, running out under the sunken tree.

"Loosen your drag! Andy, loosen your drag!" Dave coached

excitedly.

Whatever was on the end nearly yanked the pole out of Andy's hands. Andy fumbled with the rod as he tried to adjust the drag on the reel.

"Should I yank on the pole?" Andy asked as he struggled with the fish.

Standing to his side, Dave coached, "No, you got him hooked pretty good. From the looks of it, I think he's got to be at least five pounds. Keep the line tight so that you're providing constant pressure on him. But not too tight or you'll snap the line. He'll tire out soon. As he wears down, reel in a little line at a time, but keeping constant pressure on him."

Andy continued to struggle with the fish—he could feel the fish's strength on the other end of the line. It was a force he had never felt before. So much life, so much strength. He admired the creature under the surface of the water. In a strange way, Andy felt connected to the fish. The fish would pull and stop, pull and stop, each time a little less. Uncle Dave was right. The fish was tiring, and with each passing second, he put up less and less of a fight.

"Do you think it's a catfish?"

"I reckon so, and a pretty good sized one from the way he put up a fight. Just hang with him. Keep the line tight. Keep the pressure on him. He'll surface soon."

The fish was getting closer to the bank. As he got closer, he moved slower and slower. Then there was a violent splash, soaking Andy as the catfish surfaced near the bank. Andy shouted in exhilaration as he caught his first glimpse of the fish's dark brown skin and yellow underside as it rolled and splashed with the line on the surface of the water.

"It's a catfish! It's a catfish!" Andy shouted and jumped up and down with excitement.

"Sure is, and much bigger than I thought. That old boy is enormous, weighing anywhere from twelve to fifteen pounds," Dave said.

"Holy cow!" Andy shouted as his eyes widened in pure amazement at the monster that had risen from the depths of the mud bottom river.

"Hold him steady right there, Andy. I need to get this net underneath him, scoop him up, and pull him onto the bank."

Andy did as he was told, and Dave slowly reached out with the net and maneuvered it underneath the catfish. Dave quickly scooped under the massive fish, pulled up on the net, and strained to lift him from the water. Squatting now, Dave had to reach down deep to get leverage to pull the catfish out. Then, in one quick movement, he lifted upward and lobbed the fish onto the bank.

"Holy Macaroni!" Andy's mouth fell open and then curved in a huge smile.

The catfish was a monster, a good catch for this part of the river. Dave had caught a number of thirty to forty-five pounders below the dam but never anything this size in this part of the river.

"Andy, that's a fine looking catfish you pulled in," Dave congratulated, patting him on the shoulder. The catfish sat on the bank, whiskers twisting in the dirt and tail flailing in the grass.

From head to tail, he was about thirty inches long. "Yes sir, that there is a fine looking catfish. Nice work, Andy."

Andy sat there in disbelief. He had caught good sized channel cats before—the biggest usually around three to five pounds. And once when he was with his dad, his dad had pulled in a mud cat that was about seven pounds. But Andy had never seen anything this size before. The head of the fish was as big as his uncle's hand. Andy was dizzy with emotions as he watched his uncle hook the fish on to the stringer. The whole thing had been exhilarating, but now he was absolutely exhausted. He could not wait to take the fish home and show his mom and dad.

Dave nodded with a hint of pride in his eye. "Based on my scale here, he weighs 15.4 pounds. One heck of a nice catch, Andy."

Dave slowly set the catfish into the water and tied the stringer to a tree root on the edge of the bank. "Grab me the night crawlers."

Opening the foam container of worms, Andy looked down into the soft dirt and saw the ends of several of the night crawlers. "We going to switch to night crawlers now?"

"We're going to mix it up a little. Hand me your rod, and I'm going to bait your hook with one of these fat old night crawlers. I'm going to keep my pole out there with the chicken liver. The livers should attract their attention, and your night crawler will give them something to go after," Dave explained as he hooked the bait.

Setting their lines out, Andy and Dave sat in the sun and mused about the incredible catfish they had pulled in. "The key to being successful is you got to recon the river and figure out how it works. This part of the Wapsi is tricky, so it's always best to stay close to the bank. There's too much going on out there in the middle, too unpredictable, and too much that can't be seen."

Dave gazed out across the water. Andy saw the same look in Dave's eyes he had seen the previous night out on the porch. It was a terrible look of loss and sadness. Andy wondered what he was thinking about.

Dave picked a long piece of straw and put it in his mouth. "In fact, legend has it that it was from this stretch of the river for which it got its name."

"Really? Right here where the Buffalo flows into the Wapsi? What's so special about this stretch of the river?" Andy asked, hoping his uncle would break into one of his stories. Dave was an amazing storyteller. He knew so much about history, about people, and why things were the way they were. He could always tell them in such a way that Andy never knew he was learning something and actually enjoy it.

Turning to Andy, Dave began the story. "This area of Iowa was once occupied by the Sauk and Fox Indians. They lived in this area before the Black Hawk War of 1832. They were mainly hunters that lived in the rich, rolling hills and deep woods along the Maquoqueta, Cedar, and Wapsipinicon Rivers. This area has always been teeming with life—over 100 years ago, deer and buffalo were plentiful, even bears were seen down in this area. The Indians lived amongst them along these rivers. All of which run southeasterly and flow into the Mississippi.

"Legend has it that the Wapsipinicon River is named after

two of these Sauk Indians—Wapsi and Pinicon. Pinicon was a great hunter, who, at an early age, had proven to be a brave young warrior. On one occasion, a black bear entered into his tribe's village—the men were all gone on a buffalo hunt. The bear tore through their living area, ravaging the women and children. As the story goes, Pinicon struck down the bear with a large stone then killed him with his knife. When the men returned from their hunt and saw what Pinicon had done, they cut out the heart of the bear, and Pinicon ate it. From this bear, the people believed that Pinicon gained incredible strength, bravery, courage—and they say—even immortality. Seen as a hero in the eyes of everyone in the tribe, Pinicon was believed to be above the harm and pain of this world and was to become a great leader for all the Sauk Tribes.

"For all of his strength and courage, Wapsi matched him with her striking beauty. There were none in the region as beautiful as Wapsi—she and Pincon had been in love since the moment they met. Never had a love between two Sauk been more strong and true. Their special love was recognized by the elders, and they were to be married. As the legend goes, while Pinicon was gone with the men hunting buffalo, Wapsi drowned right here on this very spot where the Buffalo enters the Wapsi. They called this spot Buffalo Forks. It was here where several children were swept away in the current, and she had tried to save them. The current was too strong for her, and she didn't make it."

Dave reached down, picking up another piece of straw, and stuck it in his mouth. "Amongst the Sauk, never had there been a love more true than between Wapsi and Pinicon. For all his courage, for all his strength, Pinicon was a tender warrior—and when he lost Wapsi, he lost all hope—it was as if his heart had been ripped from his chest. With the loss of hope, the river took away all reason for living. He was a great hunter, a fearless warrior, and no one could take Pinicon's life…except Pinicon himself. Realizing he couldn't live without his beloved Wapsi, a grief-stricken Pinicon is said to have jumped to his death off the cliffs down the river. Most folks today call it Pinicon Ridge down below the dam."

Andy turned to Dave with a serious look. "Is this really true?"

"That's the legend, passed on from the Sauk Indians to the settlers of this area," Dave's eyes crinkled as he twisted the straw in his mouth.

"I ain't never heard of anything so sad." Andy sighed, looking down.

"Sad? Yes, very sad. But in a strange way, also wonderful."

Andy looked puzzled at him, questioning. "What do you mean?"

"Wonderful in that they were able to experience a true love for one another. They were so fortunate to find it, to have it, to enjoy it, if only for a little while. Most never find it, Andy. Kind of what Preacher Jones calls agape love, a love that transcends this world. A love that endures all hardship. A love that's unconditional. A love that's given, even when a person doesn't deserve it. A love so rare that most never understand it."

Dave cleared his throat and gazed out at the river slowly

flowing by. "Yet, if this legend is true—and I'd like to think it is—they shared it, they held it, and they couldn't live without it. I think it probably consumed them. It was the type of love that defines a person to the depth of their soul. It was a love that was interwoven through the core of their existence. It was the type of love for someone that one would give their life up for. To lay down your life for someone—that type of love, Andy, is uncommon. It's truly a gift from God. It's a gift we can only marvel at. But when it's gone, there's nothing else to live for."

Andy listened to his Uncle Dave. He enjoyed hearing his uncle's stories and his explanations of things. There was always a depth to their discussions. A day with Uncle Dave was a learning experience, the kind Andy liked where he didn't know he was learning anything until the day was done and he reflected back on his time with his uncle.

Suddenly Andy felt something hit his bait, and he instinctively jerked his pole upward.

"I think I've got another one!" Andy shouted as the line went tight and his pole arched downward.

"Hold it steady, Andy. Is he making a run for it?"

"I don't know. He feels heavy, really heavy. I think this one's a lot bigger than the first one!" Andy grimaced as he tried to pull in whatever was on the end of his line.

"Is he moving?"

"He was. It felt like he hit the bait and then just stopped. I thought I felt him moving, but I don't know now." Andy was puzzled.

"You might've snagged something. You mind if I take the

pole for a minute?" Dave put his hand over Andy's.

Taking the pole from Andy, Dave felt something heavy on the other end of the line. At first, he thought he hooked into a large log, but there was a strange movement to it. Something he had never felt on a line before. He lifted the pole high in the air, and something tugged on the line. Whatever he hooked into could be moved. He pulled as hard as he could, and it move toward him. Suddenly, it stopped as if it was hung up on something.

"Do you think it might be a snapping turtle?" Andy asked, peering out into the river.

"I don't know. Don't think so. It's bigger than any snapper I've ever caught."

Dave pulled it as hard he could, and he worried he might snap the line. The dead weight moved again. Dave lifted the pole above his head again and pulled with everything he had. It moved slowly toward him, this time a little easier. The water in the fishing hole churned up with all kinds of mud and debris.

"Whatever it is, it sure is big," Dave said, struggling with the line.

"It's getting closer! Just a little more, and I think it'll surface!" Andy shouted with excitement. The water swirled, and the large object neared the surface.

Dave yanked with every ounce of strength he had. Something didn't feel right. He wasn't sure what it was, but whatever was on the end of the line was cumbersome and strange.

"Just a little closer, Uncle Dave. It's almost here!" Andy

leaned down over the bank and stretched out his hand toward the line in the water.

The heavy mass on the end of Dave's line slowly rose to the surface. Suddenly, a tremor of fear shot through him. His instincts told him he didn't want to see what was coming up on the end of his line. He remembered stories about great snapping turtles pulled from the river, and he pushed that thought out of his conscious. If it was a snapping turtle, Dave knew how he would deal with it. Then with everything he had, he lifted up on the fishing pole.

Suddenly the line snapped, and Dave slipped backward, falling to the ground.

"Well I'll be damned!" Dave shouted with disgust as he sat on the bank, defeated.

"What happened?" Andy asked, knowing the answer as the words flew out of his mouth.

"Damned line snapped." Dave looked down at the water. "Whatever it was, was bigger than anything I've ever hooked before on this river."

Both Andy and Dave looked down into the churned water, puzzled at what it could have been. Dave couldn't shake that something wasn't right. "I think it would be best if we move a couple hundred feet further down the river. There's another good hole down a ways, and I'm sure we'll find more fish there." Dave turned to pick up the tackle box. "Besides, after we churned everything up in this hole, I'm sure we've scared all the fish away."

Andy nodded as he picked up the bait before following his

uncle along the river bank to the next hole.

They spent the rest of the day on the bank of the river and caught three channel catfish that all weighed from two to five pounds. Their afternoon had been an incredible day of joy for Andy. Spending time together, sitting on the river bank, talking like men, and being treated like one simply made for a great day of fishing and spending time with his uncle.

That night, as Andy crawled into bed, he talked to his mother. "Ma, do you love Dad?"

"Of course I do, sweetie. What kind of question is that?" Maggie asked, tucking the sheets and sitting on the side of the bed.

"I don't know. I was just thinking," Andy said, deep in thought. "Ma, one more question?" He looked up to his mom in curious wonder. "You ever want to jump off a cliff for Dad?"

"Ah, I can't say as I have. What in the Sam Hill have you got floating around up in that noggin of yours?" She asked, tapping his head.

"Aw nothing, Ma. Just thinking about what a great day I had fishing with Uncle Dave." Andy rolled on his side and tucked his hands under his pillow. "I love you, Ma."

"I love you too, Andrew. Now get some sleep." Maggie's heart warmed, and she kissed his forehead.

Andy smiled as he pulled the blankets up around his shoulders. His mind was filled with wondrous thoughts about catfish, Wapsi and Pinicon, reading the river, and the amazing day he had fishing with his Uncle Dave.

IV

"TURN OFF THE radio, Andrew," his mom called from over her shoulder.

Andy and his father were standing at the kitchen counter, huddled around the radio listening intently to the sportscaster.

Both father and son turned in disagreement toward the head of the kitchen. "Aw, Ma, just a couple more minutes. It's the top of the ninth against the Pirates. The Cubs are up five to four with Jenkins pitching. Can you give us a few more minutes?"

In 1966, the Cubs were having an abysmal season. With twenty-eight wins and fifty-eight losses, they were over halfway through the painful summer. But despite their record, everyone loved Ernie Banks—he had been with the Cubs since his rookie debut in 1953. Since then, he had four seasons in which he hit over forty homeruns, and he had five grand-slams in one season. Anything could happen when Ernie was on the field at Wrigley.

Their beloved Cubs were on the radio almost every afternoon in the summer. However, the games always ran up against the boundaries of dinner time. This was a boundary that neither Andy nor his father dared to cross with Maggie. It was the same challenge almost every evening. Maggie would finish up cooking dinner while Andy and his dad sat glued, listening intently to the Cubs game. Tonight would probably be no different.

Maggie wiped her hands on her apron and turned to her boys. "I've got to finish frying up these potatoes in the skillet, but when I'm done, it'll be time for dinner, and that radio is going to be off." She gave her son and her husband a look that said, "I am giving you a little more time, but don't you dare ask for a second more when it's time to eat."

The kitchen was always a central place of activity in the Crawford household, especially at dinnertime. In the summer, the windows were open, and the steel fan hummed as it rotated back and forth, blowing the air to reduce the impact of the humidity. Maggie sliced fresh tomatoes and green peppers from the garden. Then she pulled out the cottage cheese, and dinner was almost ready.

"Yeah!" Andy and his father simultaneously shouted. The game ended with a strikeout, and the Cubs won the game. Andy immediately turned off the radio and washed his hands in preparation for dinner.

Sitting down at the table, the family joined hands, and Andy's father said grace. "Dear Lord, thank you for all of your blessings. Thank you for this fine dinner. Give us the strength to do what is right in your eyes, to follow you in your way, and to do your will. In Jesus' name we pray, amen."

Before their eyes were open, Andy reached for the food. "Pork chops and fried potatoes, my favorites."

"Slow down, Andy. There's plenty to go around for all of us," his father gently admonished.

"Heard today from Jimmy Ray that they finally found Eddie Gruber." As he cut through his pork chop, Andy tried to change the subject to the topic that was the talk of the town. "About a half mile down from the Buffalo."

"Poor folks. I feel horrible for George and Bonnie Gruber. To lose their son…" Maggie placed her napkin on the table and shook her head. Tears formed in her eyes and she was overcome with emotion as she thought of Eddie Gruber's parents.

John and Maggie Crawford had been following the event in the news. Gruber had been missing for a week. The only trace left had been his fishing pole and tackle box on the river bank at the point where Buffalo Creek entered the Wapsipinicon River. An initial investigation by Sheriff Barton had not revealed anything suspicious, and the event was being treated as an accidental drowning. The authorities had been dragging the river for most of the week when they had finally found his body wrapped up in submerged tree branches in fifteen feet of water.

"That boy never had a lick of sense," John said indifferently, slicing through the pork chop with his knife. He pointed his fork toward Andy. "To be out fishing last Saturday night in a thunderstorm? Not a lick of sense."

"It's all just tragic. Just a horrible affair." Maggie raised her voice to her boys. The fact that Eddie Gruber lacked good judgment had nothing to do with the degree of tragedy in the Gruber household.

"From what they're saying, he must've slipped and fell in," Andy added as he searched his parent's faces for acceptance. It was rare for him to enter into a conversation with them that wasn't about school or chores.

"Let this serve as a lesson to you, Andy. Never fish alone,

especially at night when there's a storm brewing." Andy's father's statement hung in the air. "Bad things can happen on that river, especially when you're alone."

Maggie didn't like the direction the dinner conversation was going, so she switched lanes quickly. "Was talking to Sarah Jacobs today. Ran into her down at Wilson's."

"That so? And what bits of gossip did Sarah have today?" John responded as he bit into his pork chop.

"She said that Billy West got back this week." Maggie waited for John's reaction.

Andy's father stopped eating and took a sip of his iced tea. Suddenly a serious look settled in his eyes. He usually didn't react to any of the gossip that Maggie brought to the dinner table, but this was different, especially if it was true that Billy West was back in town.

Over the past couple years, Billy West had become a well-known name throughout Eastern Iowa. Billy had been the quarterback of the high school football team, and he had led them to a state championship in 1963. As an all-state pitcher, he had set just about every pitching record in the WaMaC Conference. The University of Iowa and Iowa State had extended offers for him to play both football and baseball at their institutions. Billy had also tried out for their beloved Chicago Cubs and had been selected to pitch for their minor league team in Waterloo.

Andy had high hopes that someday Billy would take the mound and lead the Cubs at Wrigley Field. But something had happened, something nobody had seen coming. Upon graduation in 1964, Billy had turned down all the offers from the Cubs and from the colleges. Instead, Billy West had joined the army, volunteering for the infantry. The army had assigned him to the First Cavalry Division that subsequently deployed to Vietnam. Now nearly two years later, Billy West had returned home.

"That so," Andy's dad said. This was more of a response than he had ever given to any of the dinner table gossip.

"Sarah says he got home and went straight out to their farm in his uniform to see Anna. She said he looked so handsome with all his medals." Maggie loved young romances and had a sweet smile on her face as she cut her potatoes into tiny morsels.

"Hmm," Dad answered in a low tone as he often did when eating at the dinner table.

"She thinks Billy's finally going to propose to Anna. She said she could see it in his eyes."

"Hmm," Dad responded again as he chewed his pork chop.

Billy West and Anna Jacobs had dated all through high school. She had been the homecoming queen, and he had been her king. They had always been the perfect couple. Even back then, they had been meant to be together.

Many had thought he would go on to play professional baseball, and she would follow. But when he had enlisted in the army, she couldn't follow him to basic training. Not long after his training, he had gone off to Vietnam. There had been little time for them to expand the love they had shared in high school. Based on Maggie's enthusiasm at the dinner table, she and Sarah Jacobs clearly wanted the courtship to continue.

"Jimmy Ray says that Billy West is a no-good dreamer,"

Andy interjected and looked to his parents for approval to go on.

"He may be a bit of a dreamer, but there isn't anything wrong with dreams. He's a dreamer with amazing talent," Andy's mother defended, shooting her son a little glare.

"Jimmy Ray says that Billy's a no-good loser like his dad, the town drunk," Andy said before stuffing his mouth with fried potatoes.

"Well I don't care what Jimmy Ray Johnson has to say. What do you say, Andrew?" Andy's mother was surprised at his comments and pointedly questioned her son.

"I think Billy West is the best athlete Anamosa ever produced," Andy answered, wiping the milk off his mouth. "I wonder when he's going to come back to play ball for the Cubs. I wish he'd never joined the army. We could be listening to him right now on the radio, pitching against the Pirates."

At that point, Andy's dad dropped his fork and looked square at Andy. "Well, Son, his dreams aren't necessarily your dreams, or Jimmy Ray's, or this town's. A man has to decide what's important to him and choose his path accordingly—others with less courage will sit back and criticize from their corners. Billy West has always been different. He was the best pitcher I ever saw, and I think he could play in the majors, but he always had his eyes on something more. Something bigger than the game."

Andy sat in silent shock. This was the most he could ever remember his father saying at the dinner table. There was a heavy silence in the kitchen as his father lifted his fork and continued to eat his dinner. Andy sat there, stunned, trying to soak up what his father had just said.

"I reckon you're right, Dad. I don't see why anyone would turn down playing in the big leagues." Andy reached for another helping of fried potatoes.

His mother and father didn't respond. They continued eating their dinner, deep in the heavy silence that held too many questions about Anamosa's favorite son.

V

BILLY WEST ENTERED Gus's Tavern. Standing in the doorway, lean and muscular at 6'3" with his piercing blue eyes, he was greeted with the pungent odor of urine and vomit. The inside wasn't much better, smelling of stale beer and old fried food. Cigarette butts, beer bottle caps, peanut shells, bits of popcorn, and other pieces of assorted bar food littered the dirty floor. About a dozen people sat at the tables, eating lunch, and a handful of young men were at the bar, drinking beer.

Gus's son, Big Joe Matsell, tended the bar with an audience of young men huddled around him on their bar stools. Benny Moore, Dicky Moss, Ronnie Wilson, and Sam Weers all turned at once and looked toward Billy.

Billy had known all of them in high school. They hadn't been athletes, or scholars, or involved in school extra-curricular activities. No, these four had run in different circles than Billy, and they were almost always connected to some kind of trouble.

"Well look what the cat drug in," Big Joe sneered. "Anamosa's prodigal son."

"Hey Joe, how are you?" Billy asked directly as he took several steps closer to the bar.

Something was said between the guys at the bar, and all four erupted in laughter. Billy knew they were heckling him, but he ignored them.

"Doing great, Billy. It's been a couple years since you been around—I got this place back up and running and business is looking up." Big Joe squared his shoulders and responded with a slight tone like he had something to prove.

Big Joe Matsell had inherited Gus's Tavern following the death of his father, Augustus Matsell, Junior. The bar, situated halfway down Main Street, was a dilapidated mess. The establishment never had any golden years. It had always been a dump and in a state of disrepair. In over twenty-five years of shoddy service to the Anamosa community, it always seemed to attract the local dregs of society. During its quarter century of existence, the bar had been the center of illegal happenings on more than several occasions. Bootlegging homemade liquor, illegal gambling, and prostitution were a few of the activities rumored to have occurred since its doors opened in 1940. There had been no less than three separate murders in the tavern. Even now, on any given weekend, there was the potential for a knock-down, drag-out brawl.

Yet for some god-awful reason, the doors managed to stay open. In spite of its notorious reputation, the police stayed clear of the place—showing up late, after the fights were over and the dust settled. The rumor all across town was that ole' Augustus Matsell had something on the former Jones County Sheriff. Seems Sheriff Earl Brown had a real hankering for poker, and it was said he used to sit down at the table with Gus at least once a week. Some said the sheriff owed Gus five thousand dollars, others said he owed fifty thousand dollars. No one ever knew for sure. One thing was true, though—despite the police department only being a block away, the cops always showed up at the bar long after the messes had been cleaned up.

Gus's Tavern stood as a landmark in Anamosa for local tragedy. Augustus Matsell, Junior had been the grandson of a somewhat famous historical figure. Ironically, his grandfather, George Washington Matsell, had been the first Police Chief of New York City. George Matsell had been a towering figure in the middle of the Nineteenth Century in New York. Well known as the "Big Chief", he had stood over six feet tall and weighed approximately 300 lbs. He had been well respected by lawmakers, politicians, businessmen, and the like. As the first Police Chief, he had organized a uniformed force of over 800 police officers and established procedures used well into the Twentieth Century.

In the 1850s, while serving as the Police Chief, George Matsell had ventured west to establish a summer home and country estate. He had purchased over 3,000 acres on the Wapsipinicon River, outside of Anamosa and north of the small farming town of Viola. By 1856, his luxurious twenty-five room mansion was finished. Complete with a veranda and fashioned in the spacious Hudson River tradition, all of the rooms had fireplaces and high ceilings. The opulent structure included a kitchen and pantry, multiple dining rooms, living rooms, and parlors, as well as magnificent balconies overlooking the river. Furthermore, the mansion was comprised of separate sections for the corps of male and female servants who had been required at the manor to tend to Chief Matsell's daily affairs.

Few local Iowans ever stepped foot onto George Matsell's estate, but the rumors about the estate permeated Eastern Iowa and even got the attention of many of the Cedar Rapids' elite. The mansion had been modeled after George Washington's Mount Vernon home on the Potomac, and there were even rumors that Matsell actually had a number of Washington's items in his possession. Matsell had been a collector of the extraordinary—the manor was complete with magnificent furniture, tapestries, silver serving sets, vases, statues, pictures, chairs, tables, and ornate curios from all over the world.

George Matsell had died in 1877, and his estate had been handed down to the four children. Augustus Matsell, the youngest of the four, had survived the entire family. At the turn of the century, Augustus had owned half of Main Street. Tragedy had struck when his wife died giving birth to their only son, Augustus Jr. Misfortune had followed tragedy as Augustus Senior lost most of his fortune when the stock market crashed in 1929. Forced to sell the family estate, as well as most of his businesses in Anamosa, Augustus Senior had died broke, leaving only the building that would become Gus's Tavern to his son.

In 1940, Augustus Junior opened the bar, and it had been open almost every day since. The bar stood as a tragic reflection of the first Police Chief of New York City. The rundown tavern was all that remained of the iconic figure who rose above the corruption in the City, who was friends with several U.S. Presidents, and who was one of the original elite of Eastern Iowa.

And now three generations removed from the great George Matsell, the tavern was under the management of Augustus Junior's son, Big Joe Matsell. The only similarity between Big Joe and his great grandfather, George, was his size. Big Joe was called Big Joe for a reason. He was about 6'5" and weighed over 270 pounds, and he was strong as an ox.

Big Joe Matsell was four years older than Billy. He had been a great athlete once and had set most of the football records that Billy later broke. Joe never went anywhere after high school. He had stayed in Anamosa and had picked up his dad's business of running the tavern. Here, in this place with the locals, he lived out whatever past glory he thought still existed where he would always be Big Joe Matsell.

Big Joe was also a big bully—always had been. He used his size to ridicule others. He had been doing it for years—for as long as Billy could remember. Joe liked playing the angles. There was always an angle with him, and nothing was ever what it seemed.

Billy knew Joe was a man that could never be trusted. He never liked Big Joe and was already annoyed after a few seconds of time with him. Joe was trouble, and from the looks of it, he had not changed much. He was a man that got things done through fear—a hard-headed bully living through his reputation. Big Joe had the propensity to be dangerous. If his reputation was threatened, he would be forced into a corner, a place with few options.

Billy often wondered why men did what they did. What made a man turn toward evil? Billy's dad used to tell him that all men were the sum of their choices, and after only a few years away from home, Billy had found this to be true. To him, it all came back to having a firm foundation of what he believed in. If this foundation was not strong, he knew the world was too hard of a place, and one could easily find themselves on a slippery slope to ruin.

Walking into that bar, Billy knew in his gut that Big Joe was somewhere on that slope right now. Behind the bar, Joe was a big fish in a little pond. He had a few athletic scholarships and could have gone to college, but he had never left Anamosa. Billy reasoned that it was probably because he didn't need to. Here in this town, he could bend people and manipulate them to get what he wanted.

Looking at Big Joe, Billy could see the wear that life in a small town running a bar was having on him. He was still big and probably very strong, but he looked sloth-like, a little jowly in the face, his hair had thinned, and his eyes drooped tired. He looked older, much older. All the beer he'd been drinking was having its lasting, aging effect on him.

"Hi Billy." Sally Mayfield walked out from a backroom and cleaned one of the tables. She smiled at Billy. "Can I get you something to drink?"

"No thanks, Sally," Billy answered, looking around the bar.

Sally Mayfield was a year older than Billy. He had known her from the old days, growing up in the same neighborhood together, but she was Joe's girl, always had been. From the looks of it, she still was. She had been pretty back in high school and had a spark that made others smile, but now something was lacking. She looked tired with a settled dullness that clouded her. She had also gained some weight. Maybe it was her dingy clothes, or the fact that she had no makeup on, or that her hair was frazzled, but Billy had a feeling of sadness as he studied her—he thought she looked like she had stopped trying. Her spark was gone.

Something was mumbled again by Dicky Moss at the bar, and the four men looked at Billy and once again erupted in laughter. Billy was getting annoyed. He clenched his teeth, flexing the muscles in his angular, muscular jaw. He did not respond to their banter but stared them down with his intense eyes.

"Have you seen my pop around?" Billy asked, turning to Sally.

"Your pop? He ah…he…" Sally stammered.

"Your pop owes me quite a bit of money," Big Joe interjected from behind the bar. He sat with Ronnie Wilson, playing a game of chess.

Billy's father, Butch West, was a drunk—not just any drunk, but was well known as the town drunk. He had spent much of his time in the Jones County Jail, getting sober, working odd jobs, or panhandling the streets to support his need for alcohol. In the past ten years, he had been admitted to the mental hospital at Independence several times. On each occasion, he would spend thirty days at the hospital, getting sober, getting help, and then he would be released. But trouble always followed Butch, and he could not shake his life free of the demons plaguing him for so long. Within weeks of his release from the hospital, he would fall off the wagon and could be found passed out in a bar, curled up on the sidewalk on Main Street, or laid out cold, asleep in the cemetery.

It had not always been this way. Butch used to work for the

state prison, was married, and owned a nice home. When Billy was twelve years old, his mother, Amanda, got seriously ill and died. With her passing, everything had changed. When his mother was alive, Billy never saw his pop drink a beer—there was no alcohol in the house. But with Amanda's passing, Butch had started to drink and had really never stopped. His drinking had cost him his job, his social standing, his role as a father, and his self-respect. Butch still owned the house, but the years had passed with little care to it. It was now a run-down, dilapidated structure—much like the West Family.

For Billy, losing his mother had been a horribly traumatic event. It had an enduring effect on his life, but he had dealt with it differently. While his pop had turned to the bottle, Billy had turned his energy to sports. Baseball, football, basketball, track, he had excelled at everything. Billy was gifted, but the loss of his mother had given him an uncommon, intense drive. He had pushed himself harder and further beyond where most would ever go or even thought possible. Billy went well beyond physical and mental exhaustion with an amazing intensity; always pushing, always stretching the limits. And on the playing field, his efforts had paid off—he had carried his high school teams to conference championships in baseball and basketball and to a state championship in football. The loss of his mother had propelled him to go harder, faster, and to be stronger than everyone. In sports, Billy left his mark on Anamosa. That was two years ago, but Billy wanted more—something deeper, something more meaningful in his life.

"How much does my pop owe you?" Billy asked,

unintimidated by Joe.

With a gleam in his eye, Big Joe looked at the boys at the bar and sneered at Billy. "Bout five hundred."

Billy glared at Big Joe, knowing he was lying. That was what Big Joe was, a liar—nothing changed with him. Billy quickly realized the direction this was going to go. In an instant, he played it out in his mind. He knew Joe had already sized him up, was working an angle, and trying to bend him. Billy had to get ahead of Joe, and it would be hard to do on his territory. He realized he had to hit Joe when he least expected it. He had to leverage the element of surprise. Billy had to confront Joe head-on, right here, right now, in his comfort zone. Joe played the angles, but he wouldn't expect this. He didn't have the imagination for it.

Clenching his teeth, Billy stared down Big Joe. "Where is my pop, Joe?"

"Like I said, he owes me money. I got him out and about doing some errands…and other things." Big Joe smiled at the boys at the bar, and they all laughed again.

Ignoring Billy, Joe moved his rook on the chess board, and then looked up at Ronnie Wilson. "I've got you in check."

Billy took a step forward and pointed his finger directly at Big Joe, interrupting his game. "I'll give you five minutes to have my pop out here. Now go get him."

Billy had sized up Big Joe. He was strong but not very agile. Billy could drop him with a couple of punches. As for the other boys at the bar, there was some risk. He could take two or three of them, but four? That could be tough. He calculated the risk and estimated that when he took out Big Joe, the other four would quickly skedaddle out of the bar. Big Joe had pushed others around for a long time. His day had come—his days of ruling others as a bully were over. It was now his time to pay up.

Big Joe smiled, but there was a little twitch in his right eye. Billy sensed his surprise and likely even fear. Big Joe glanced at the boys sitting in front of him and then walked out from behind the bar. Posturing in front of the losers, Big Joe mocked, "Young Billy West, who went away to join the army, has come back with a set of balls. Unfortunately, like your drunk pop, you ain't got a lick of sense."

The boys at the bar laughed in support of Big Joe. They were excited to watch Big Joe beat the crap out of somebody as they had seen him do so many times before. Smiling confidently, Big Joe moved with this new momentum away from the bar toward Billy. "You think you can march on in here with your army haircut and big attitude and start bossing me around like I was one of your soldiers? Not in my bar and not in my town! Guess they didn't teach you everything in the army, and now I'm going to have to teach you a little lesson. Billy, Billy, Billy, what have you learned since you've been away? Obviously not too…"

Big Joe never finished the sentence. As he closed within four feet from Billy, Billy quickly lunged forward with his fist and sent a crashing right hook down on Big Joe's temple. Big Joe stepped into the full weight and power of Billy's fist—the right hook whipped his head back and to the side. Big Joe teetered back a step, looked wildly stunned, and then his knees buckled. He fell face first on to the dirty bar room floor. He never saw it coming, never knew what hit him. Billy was postured to hit him one more time to put him down, but it wasn't necessary. The power from Billy's right hook came from his core strength, from his hips, from his legs all working together to deliver one powerful blow. One punch and Big Joe was out cold. His time was over.

Tasting the adrenalin, Billy turned toward the four boys at the bar and spit on the floor. "You boys want some of this? Come on, bring it on, bring it…" The four boys sprang from their bar stools. Billy had calculated correctly, seeing the fear in their eyes. Billy verbally taunted the four men as he chased them toward the door. They quickly ran out of the bar while Billy stalked them.

Looking around the bar, Billy realized it was just him, Big Joe on the floor, and Sally Mayfield in the middle of the room. The rest of the patrons sat at their tables, frozen in awe of what they witnessed. Sally stood with her mouth open and tipped her head to the side, stunned by what had happened.

Sally had known Big Joe a long time. He was strong and could even be brutal to others. He was abusive and often cruel, but still, she was drawn to him. She didn't agree with how he treated her or others, but she accepted it. She tolerated it because she hoped that one day he would grow out of it. She was drawn to his strength, to his power, and although it was misunderstood, she loved him for it. She stood, clutching her neck in a near state of shock. She had never seen anyone do to Big Joe what Billy had just done.

Billy turned to Sally. "Where's my pop?"

Still bewildered, she looked at Billy and mumbled, trying to get the words out. "He's…he's in the…in the back…in the back room of the bar, doing dishes."

Billy immediately moved away from Sally and stormed through the door to the kitchen at the back of the tavern. His father stood bent over the sink, washing dishes. He had not seen his father in two years, not since the day he had left for basic training. Now staring at him, Billy saw the effect time, booze, and grief had had on his father. Although he was fifty-one years of age, he looked more than old. He was beyond old. He was hunched wearily over the sink in a dirty, stained, white T-shirt. Billy could see the dark blue, smudged Semper Fi tattoo on his weathered right arm as he scrubbed the dishes. Barely readable, the old blue tattoo had lost its definition. It had been there for as long as Billy could remember but now was some foggy reminder of something important long ago.

When Billy returned to Anamosa two days earlier, he stopped by his home before heading to see his girlfriend, Anna Jacobs. The house had been empty. In fact, it had looked as if it hadn't been lived in for months. Walking into the dilapidated house had confirmed what he had suspected. His father had been drinking again, drinking hard. Billy had known that his father wasn't well. Billy had been writing him letters from the hospital at Fort Benning, but it was rare for Billy to get one in response. And when he did, what he had gotten was not much of a response.

Over the past couple of months, Anna had grown increasingly concerned about Butch. She would rarely see him, and there had been a number of rumors floating around town. After a couple days out on Anna's farm and a number of discussions with locals, he had come to understand the demise of his father.

There in the kitchen in the back of the dingy tavern, Butch West looked like the vague shell of the man Billy once remembered him to be. Billy still remembered with great fondness the times they would spend in the yard, playing catch with the football or the baseball—just the two of them out in the front yard connected through sports. That was so long ago. So much had passed since then—his mom's death, the pain and the loss. Looking at his father, he could now clearly see how it had all added up.

Billy put his hand on his father's shoulder and got his attention. "Hey, Pop." Those words came from his mouth just as they had when he was ten, when he was fifteen, and now, at the age of twenty.

His father peeked up from the sink, slightly startled, and then instantly recognized his son. The sound of Billy's voice cut deep through all the pain in his life and instantaneously filled his heart with joy. He looked up with the love only a parent could have for his child. He briefly smiled. Then his face turned to sad shame, and his eyes moistened with tears. He groped forward, falling into his son. Billy caught him in his strong arms. There was a moan and then a muffled sob as Butch was cradled in his son's arms.

There, in the grease and dinge of the backroom of the bar, they held each other. Butch sobbed quietly, pressed against Billy's chest. Deep painful heaves shook his body in a slow, rhythmic convulsion then after a minute, slowly subsided.

Finally Billy pulled away from the embrace and peered directly into his father's eyes. Both men's faces were stained with fresh tears. "Hey Pop, let's go home."

Butch West looked up into his son's eyes. His eyes stung with tears. It had been a long time. When Butch saw his son off to basic training, Billy was no more than a boy; now he was a man. Butch was embarrassed for what he had become as a father and as a man, but he was so proud of his son. His son had grown in maturity, and Butch saw it in Billy's eyes. He could see it in the way his son carried himself, in the steel strength of his hands, in his angular shoulders ready to carry the world, in the force of his voice—confident, direct, and strong. The army had made him a man.

"Sonny, it's been a long time," Butch said feebly, pulling at the hem of his T-shirt. Nobody but his pop called Billy by that name. Looking at his father, Billy calculated the smallness—Butch was a shell of a man, wiry and tired—probably no more than 120 pounds. Butch raised his voice. "When did you get home, Sonny?"

"Got back two days ago and spent most of my time out on the Jacobs' farm with Anna. Stopped by the house yesterday and today. You weren't there, so I figured you might be down here at the Tavern." Butch looked down, embarrassed at his surroundings, at what he had become. Billy sensed his father's shame and put his arm around his shoulder. "Let's get out of here, Pop."

The two turned and walked out through the bar. Big Joe was still out cold on the floor of the tavern. Sally was at his side, trying to wake him up. Billy dropped a fifty dollar bill at Big Joe's feet and told Sally that this business transaction between him and Big Joe settled his father's debt. And furthermore, if Big Joe had a problem with this, he would be back to make it more clear for him. Butch looked down at Big Joe, amazed at what he saw and could imagine the events that had taken place.

"Pop, stay out of Gus's Tavern. You ain't welcome here anymore," Billy warned his father as they stepped over Big Joe and walked out of the bar together.

VI

"NEVER THOUGHT I'D see it with my own eyes. One punch. Just one punch and Big Joe Matsell was out like a light," Benny Moore said to Ronnie Wilson and a small audience around him at a table in the café.

"Another cup of coffee, boys?" Mabel Lewis asked, interrupting the young men in their excited dialogue.

"Please, Mabel, all of us will need a hit to top off our cups," Benny said, looking up at the waitress.

There in Buddy's Café, Benny Moore and Ronnie Wilson shared the story of what happened the day prior at Gus's Tavern. In fact, the whole café buzzed with gossip about it. Billy's name had not been mentioned in there for over a year. When Billy abruptly left Anamosa after high school, many had thought he had gone to play professional baseball or to college to continue his athletic endeavors. However, he had surprised (and disappointed) all of them when he had joined the army instead. His incredible feats on the playing field had often been the center of many discussions at Buddy's after a Friday night high school football or basketball game.

Buddy's Café was not only a social center for juicy gossip, it also served as a portal down memory lane. Pictures and sports memorabilia dating back to the 1920s adorned the walls and filled the corners of the café. Photos of conference champion teams, players in action on the field or the court, little league baseball teams, linking together generations from over the years, covered the walls from corner to corner. Old leather footballs with faded signatures as well as basketballs marked with winning seasons and championships were proudly placed on display.

In the center of the back wall was a monument to Billy West. There were photos of him leading his basketball team to a conference championship, leading his baseball team as an all-state pitcher, and winning the football state championship. Billy had captained all of these teams—and he was singularly recognized in the café more than any other athlete.

But over the past two years, Billy's name was seldom mentioned. Most of the rhetoric in the café had an air of cynicism and focused on people still a part of the community—not those who left Anamosa. A strange sense of jealous contempt followed those who had gone away. In leaving, they had betrayed those who had remained. No one ever said it, but in many ways, those who stayed believed former residents had given up their right to claim to be a native Anamosan or even an Iowan. However on this bright summer morning at Buddy's, these feelings were mostly lacking from the conversations. Billy West was again the talk of the town.

Mabel floated from table to table, filling coffee cups and serving her patrons. At every table, there was talk about Billy.

"That settles it. There's no question," Ronnie Wilson said. "Billy's clearly the better athlete. Probably the best athlete Anamosa has ever produced."

"Ah hell no! You got to be crazy. That was a lucky sucker

punch—if anything, it proves Billy's as crooked as his old, drunk father."

Mabel overheard a different discussion about Billy from another table. "I got it from Ben Jacobs that Billy had been decorated for bravery in Vietnam. Some place called Yahh Drang and is back here on leave," Old Man Gelkie said. The old men at the table nodded their heads slowly and sipped their coffee, but none could prove or disprove the information. If it was true, nobody had ever heard of this strange sounding place before. To them, "Yahh Drang" didn't have the proud ring they were familiar with—not like Iwo Jima, Normandy, or Bastogne.

Mabel continued to weave her way around the tables, and she overheard loudmouth Jones County Sheriff Jim Barton ranting about the incident at Gus's Tavern. "That is damned aggravated assault. I won't tolerate such lawlessness in this town," the young sheriff declared as he stuffed another wad of pancake in his mouth. With syrup dripping down his chin, he announced or sputtered his plan to begin an investigation immediately.

Mabel smirked. She knew Jim Barton had never done anything in his entire life immediately, if ever at all. As she had often said, Jim Barton could talk the talk, but he had never been much for walking the walk. He had pretty much always been full of hot air…and pancakes.

"So you finally found the Gruber Boy," one of the men at the table interjected.

"That was quite the ordeal. Those damned currents in that part of the river are some of the most unpredictable I've ever seen. Took us four days, but we finally found him about a quarter mile down from where he was fishing."

Barton took another massive bite of pancakes, washed it down with his coffee. "That river is damned dangerous. And to be out there fishing alone, at night, with a storm blowing in. From the looks of it, he must've slipped and gotten pulled away by the current. Hard to say for sure. That storm blew in and washed away everything. There's no evidence of anything. The reason we even knew he was there was his pole and tackle box were found on the river bank."

"Just another tragedy on that river," another at the table added.

Barton took another sip of his coffee. He didn't want to talk about work. He had had a long week and was tired. First the Gruber Boy drowning and now the fight at Gus' Tavern. There was always something.

Sheriff Barton changed the subject. "Did I ever tell you about the time I was the starting center for Big Joe back in '59? Went nine and four that year. Almost beat Maquoketa in the playoffs. I remember it was late in the game, fourth down with three yards to go. Big Joe took my snap and followed my blocks. Then out of nowhere, he got sideswiped by their all conference linebacker. Bam! Never saw him coming. We was so close." Barton took a drink of his coffee. "Just missed short of getting a first down by inches. So close. Well, that's how it goes sometimes. Now that was a great team, Big Joe up front leading us to victory," Jim Barton, gazing across the room, sticky syrup dripping down his chin, remembering his near-glorious moment on the football field.

The men at the table had heard the story before. They had heard the story about every Saturday at the Café for the last seven years. Jim Barton was no athlete. In fact, growing up in the sand lots and backyards of Anamosa, he had been the type of kid who was picked last for a team, and he had almost always been the wimp on the playground that got picked on.

In the history of sports in Anamosa, as fate would have it, Jim Barton had started one game as the center, and it had been the conference championship game against Maquoketa. But everyone knew that having him on the offensive line to replace Fred Droogen, who was out with an injury, was a mistake. A mistake that most who'd seen the game knew cost them the conference championship. But even though Jim Barton was full of hot air, grating, and basically annoying as hell, no one had the heart to tell him his one shining moment in the history of Anamosa sports cost the team their season.

The true miracle was how Jim had gotten selected to be the sheriff of Jones County. He could barely lead himself to the bathroom let alone manage law enforcement in Jones County.

Rumor was that his uncle, Earl Brown, who served as the sheriff of the county for over thirty years, fixed it so his nephew would be sheriff. His uncle had ties to the state governor and was still active in politics. No one could say for sure how he did it, but there had been plenty of talk when Jim Barton pinned on that sheriff badge.

Seeing how the most illicit activity was smoking marijuana and firing off illegal fireworks smuggled up from Missouri, most had agreed having young, eager, and mostly annoying Jim Barton as a sheriff was a risk they could accept. He could be steered in the right direction and controlled when it came to important decisions. Plus, no one else wanted the job.

"No siree, the apple never falls far from the tree," Sheriff Jim Barton said, referring to Billy and his drunken father. "I ain't going to stand for it—I will hunt down Billy West right after I leave here and get to the bottom of this. Don't care what he may have done in the past or how many pictures he has on these walls. He's been out of town for a while, and as I see it, he's brought back some of them out of town notions with him. This may be how they solve problems in the army but not here in Anamosa, not under my watch."

Circulating to the back of the café, Mabel filled up Ginny Ford's cup as she shared the latest with Laura Lee Meyer and Julia Mayfield. "Anna told her mom, who told me, that Billy's going to propose while he's home on leave from the army. I just can't believe it. After all this time, Billy West and Anna Jacobs getting married," Ginny gushed as the fresh information spewed from her mouth. The women listened intently and slowly nibbled on their cinnamon rolls. There was nothing better than good gossip on a Saturday morning, and they were going to savor every second of it. Billy had been gone for some time and this proposal idea came out of nowhere.

The three women all secretly wondered if Anna Jacobs was pregnant. This past winter Anna had visited Billy at Fort Benning *alone.* They were appalled any parent would allow their daughter to get on a bus and travel half way across the country to pay a visit to a soldier at his base. There was definitely the possibility she had gotten pregnant. Not that they wanted her to be, but it would make for a juicier topic of discussion. Secretly, they did want Anna to be pregnant, especially because of her goody-goody mother, Sarah Jacobs.

Anna's mother was always seen as holier than thou, and the ladies were almost ecstatic that Sarah "Squeaky Clean" Jacobs would have to deal with the disgrace of her perfect daughter's pregnancy. The joke among the ladies was that from a block away, they could hear the high pitch squeak of Sarah Jacobs' tight ass rubbing together as she walked. They mused that one could polish a bag of nickels in between her squeaky clean butt cheeks. But nobody wanted Anna Jacobs to be pregnant, at least not openly.

Standing back at the main counter in the café, Mabel organized each table's tab and passed new orders back to the kitchen. Dave and John Crawford sat on stools at the counter, quietly sipping coffee and reading the paper.

Mabel asked, "Can I get you fine gentlemen another cup of coffee?"

Both looking up from their paper, they said in unison, "Thank you, Mabel."

The Crawford brothers came in for breakfast every Saturday morning and sat at the same place at the main counter. Both were normally quiet and pleasant, but today it appeared to Mabel that they were agitated with all the talk and noise in the background. On several occasions, both turned and glared at various yappers in the café. Their eyes communicated to each of the loud mouths to shut the hell up. They would look, turn back around to their newspapers, sip their coffee, and then just shake their heads. Mabel topped off their coffee then continued sorting through each table's tabs.

Mabel Lewis was born and raised in Central Texas. She was an outsider, and her opinions were not always accepted, especially when it came to discussions about a native Iowan. Her husband, Buddy, was from Anamosa, and they had met when he was in the service, stationed at Fort Hood. When he had returned to Fort Hood from Korea, they got married. After he got out of the service, he'd brought Mabel to his hometown. Her husband had warned her many times that when it came to criticism, some Iowans could be as cold as a witch's tit and as cynical as a clear, bitter cold night in February. This morning in the café, she had to agree with him. She couldn't help but notice the level of noise was several octaves higher than usual. The cacophony of gossip was almost deafening. In fact, it was louder than she could recall in years, even louder than after their state championship back in 1963.

As Mabel had made her way from table to table, she felt her head spinning. She heard bits and pieces of conversations—all revolving around Billy West.

"Never falls that far from the tree."

"Yahh-Drang, where in the Sam Hill is that?"

"Married next month? I may need to pick out a dress."

"I tell you it was a cheap sucker-punch—hit him right in the eye."

"Billy lost his eye in Vietnam? How many medals did he

get?"

"That Anna Jacobs is such a doll. Don't know what she sees in that Billy West. Looking at his dad, he can't be nothing but trouble."

"You don't say. Yahh Drang? Never heard of it."

"Big Joe's bar is closed for the week."

"It's a shame. Thought that Anna Jacobs came from a God-fearing family."

"You know what they say about apples."

"Big Joe told me he had some business to tend to up in Cedar Rapids for the next few days."

"Did I ever tell you about back in '59 when I was the starting center for Big Joe in the conference championship?"

"The wedding may be in August. That seems awfully quick. If she's able to wait and gets married in the spring, I should be able to wear my Easter dress."

"Mabel, can I get some more syrup?"

"Two silver stars, you don't say. And he lost his right eye to shrapnel?"

"Big Joe was a much better football player. He just didn't have the offensive line Billy West had."

"You don't think Anna's pregnant, do you? She's such a good girl and comes from such a good family. But you never know with that West boy."

"Vietnam? Never heard of it. We got troops there?"

"Never fall far from the tree."

"She could be pregnant. Can you believe her parents let her visit him at Fort Benning this past winter? What in Sam Hill were they thinking?"

"I've got a lot on my plate today, so I probably won't make it. I'll try to stop by Billy's house later this week for questioning… Mabel, can I get another order of pancakes?"

"Gail Lawrence said she saw Anna last week. Now that I think about it, she did say that she thought she might've put on some weight."

"It was a sucker punch if…"

Suddenly the room went almost completely silent. The ladies froze in unison and stopped sipping their coffee. Their eyes scanned the room from behind their cups. The only sound heard was the fork drop onto a plate as Jim Barton, with a wad of pancakes crammed in his mouth, stopped eating and talking simultaneously. He looked to the men at his table with a disturbed and stupid expression, a stringy mixture of drool and syrup hanging off his chin.

Billy West opened the door for Anna Jacobs, and the two walked up to the counter. "Hey, John. Hello, Dave." Billy tipped his head to each of them and turned to Mabel. Billy had been in this café many times over the years, and it had always felt good, like home. "Mabel, table for two, please?" Billy requested confidently.

"Got one for you guys over in the corner. I'll be right there with a couple cups of coffee and some menus."

"Thanks, Mabel. Gentlemen." Billy tipped his head again in respect to the Dave and John.

Billy and Anna stepped away from the counter and moved around the tables across the café. Anna was dressed, leaving little to the imagination. In tight denim shorts and a button-down shirt tied up high at her waist, she showed skin from below her navel up to her breasts. Despite her provocative attire, she glowed like a beam of sunlight and lit up the room. She caught one's eye with her simple beauty and joyful disposition.

The café was quiet now. The men sat stunned, gazing upon every inch of Anna. Every single male gave her the complete vertical and was pleased with the incredible image emblazoned in their heads. The image and subsequent fantasy brought a visible smile to several of their lips. Everyone saw her except Jim Barton. His back was to the door, and he was unaware of who had just entered the café. He studied the faces of the men around the table with mouth open and a mashed up soggy pancake, visibly slopping around in his mouth.

Crusty Old Man Gelkie, who twisted his entire head around to see the spectacle, turned back to the other old men at the table. He felt a tingle of shame as heat crept up his neck, and his ears turned red. He realized all the men at his table had a red face and tried to act as if they had not just checked out a girl younger than most of their grandchildren.

Ginny Ford, Laura Lee Meyer, and Julia Mayfield also gave Anna the full vertical—all looking disapprovingly at what they considered a scantily clad, attention-seeking vixen whose purpose was to tempt the male population with indefensible sin. In reality, the three women secretly wished they still had that effect on men when they entered a room. Truth be told, none of them ever had that effect on men to begin with.

Ginny turned to Laura Lee and whispered, "She don't look

pregnant to me." Laura Lee nodded her head in disappointed, quiet agreement.

ꕤ

Billy pulled out the chair and seated Anna. Moving his chair close to her side, Billy whispered in Anna's ear, "Did I tell you today how absolutely, stunningly beautiful you are?" Anna's nose crinkled and she shied away, blushing.

The two sat in the café, chairs close, whispering wonderful, loving words back and forth. They held hands, stared in each other's eyes, and kissed. They were oblivious to those around them salivating in their pancakes and gossip.

Anna Jacobs was in love. She had been in love with Billy West since she was thirteen and he was fourteen. They had met at the Pumpkin Fest Street Dance on Main Street. It had been the first social event she had been permitted to go to in town. She had come in from the farm with her older sister and her mother. They'd only been in town for two hours when she saw him standing across the street, looking cocky and confident, leaning against a stack of bales of hay with a group of boys. Feeling her cheeks flush red with an exciting new crush, she had immediately fallen for him. Even there on the street corner, it had been clear to Anna that Billy West was a leader with an entourage of a half dozen other boys following him around.

That had been seven years ago, and there had never been anyone else. Anna never thought about love at first sight. It had only ever been Billy. He was all she needed, her love, her true north. She had always been true to Billy—he filled her heart with a love no one else in the world could.

Now, he was back from Vietnam, back from a battlefield he didn't want to talk about. He was finally home on leave and back in her life, and their love was deeper, richer, stronger, and more intense than ever before. Billy had been home for a couple of days, but he had already hinted at their life-long future together, about the possibility of marriage.

There was more now, more in Billy's eyes—a depth, a sadness, a place outside of Iowa. A place Iowa could not touch, and it left a subtle dullness in his eyes most couldn't recognize. The army and the war had changed him and made him different. Before Billy left, he was lighthearted and so full of life. Now that shiny glimmer was gone. Despite the sadness in his eyes, in most ways, the army had made him a better man. He was more aware, more confident, more assertive, and more certain about what he wanted. He had a vision spanning beyond the next five, ten, twenty years, and it included her in his life.

Anna and Billy had maintained intermittent contact throughout his tour in Vietnam. Initially, she had received letters every week from Billy. But after December, something had changed. The letters had slowed. One per month, then one every couple of months. Toward the end of his tour, there had been next to nothing. She had worried about Billy. His letters had been so positive initially. But December had been a tough month for him, and everything had changed.

He had been in the Ia Drang Valley, and there had been heavy losses. He wouldn't really talked about it in his letters nor in these first days home, but back in December, it had been in all the newspapers. Anna had actually seen Billy on TV one night during one of the reporter's live footage. She had held her breath and clutched her father's arm, watching Billy talk to a reporter and then lead several soldiers in a dark, thick jungle. During the broadcast, gunfire broke out, and casualties were seen.

That was the first and last time she had seen Billy on the news. She'd never forget it for as long as she lived. It had scared her. She couldn't wrap her mind around Billy being in a dangerous place, doing all those things—where he had to fight and where people died.

Several weeks after the broadcast in December, Anna had received a letter from Billy—it had not mentioned the reporter or the fighting. It had confirmed he was all right. In fact, the letter hadn't said much of anything, but she had sensed, in the spaces between the lines and in the nuances of his words, this war had changed her Billy.

Sitting in the café, she held his hand, lacing her fingers with his. She loved how perfectly they fit together, but she still could not believe that with these same hands he could do the things he did over there.

She saw it in his eyes. Over the past few days since he had returned home, they would be talking about something, and she would see, in his far away stare, that he was lost in his thoughts, someplace horribly sad. His youth had been stripped away, and now he wasn't quite complete—he was marked with a sad, dull reflection in his eyes.

Anna never worried if Billy had been true to her. He'd said he was, and she knew it to be true. No, this change had nothing to do with her. He loved her; she knew that. But something in that war had taken a part of him away from her, something in his heart she couldn't touch. Something was missing. Something had been ripped from his heart and replaced with a tragic darkness. He had left a part of him behind in that jungle in Vietnam. She quietly wondered if she would ever know what it was. She wondered if she would be enough to fill and mend those cracks in his heart.

She ran her thumb over his and stared at the menu she had memorized. Her thoughts were back to the day when she had to say good-bye to him at the bus station in Cedar Rapids when he left for basic training at Fort Benning. Agonizing pain had enveloped her, and her days had dragged, during the long, slow, suffocating summer that followed. It was a distant memory, but the cruel piercing pain was still real.

She drove with Billy's father to Cedar Rapids to see him off—the three of them sitting side by side, tight in the cab of their old truck. She looked down, studying the lines in Billy's hand as she held it in hers. With every passing mile, her heart screamed stop, stop this truck and turn it around and take her Billy home.

But then, in her pain, she looked up at Billy's eyes. They were confident, forward looking with an air of excitement for his future in the army. He had always wanted to serve his country. She never understood it and didn't think she ever would. All she wanted was to stop that truck and turn it around, to stop the pain in her heart, to stop the madness. But she dared not say a word about what she felt. No one could stop Billy when he went after something. He had the amazing ability to get others to go along with what he wanted. Not just go along, he could persuade people to honestly believe in what he was doing and to do everything in their power to help him get there.

This adventure in the army was something he had wanted. He not only wanted to be a soldier, he wanted to lead them. He was an amazing athlete, and the trophy cases and record books proved his abilities, but this desire was different. This was something he had wanted long before he had made his mark on the playing fields. Anna knew this. In her heart, she had never agreed. Her heart begged her to say something, anything that would stop the pain, anything that would change his mind. But when she looked into his eyes and held his strong hand, she knew this was what he wanted, and she could not stop him.

Anna hated good-byes, and she hated bus stations. In her memories, they were one and the same. Once, she had seen her uncle off at the same bus station when he went to college in New York. But this time with Billy, it was so much more real. The pain was permanent. Something left her when she kissed him before he turned away and got on the bus. Something she wondered if she would ever get back. No, bus stations brought nothing but loss.

Then came February, and the darkest of days were permanently ingrained in her memory. The phone rang. Billy's father was on the other end of the line. Billy had been wounded in Vietnam. His condition was stabilized, and he had been sent to a hospital in Japan. Subsequently, he had been evacuated to the hospital at Fort Benning.

Anna found herself there again, at the same bus station, waiting for a bus. She fought off the terror that she might lose Billy. With all her strength, she gathered up the courage to face whatever waited for her on the end of her journey. Nothing else mattered to her other than the fact that Billy was hurt, and she had to be there for him.

Within twenty-four hours of discovering that Billy was in a hospital in Georgia, she got on a bus to be with him and endured the thirty hour bus ride to Fort Benning*. Everything was like a murky dream. She was confused and had so many questions about Billy's condition. The information she had was that he had been hurt and she needed to be with him. The memory of the bus station was a painful, confused dream now.*

What was clear were her feelings when she first laid eyes on him at the hospital. She walked into his room and found him asleep, almost entirely hidden under heavy blankets. Billy looked small and frail. His face was uncovered with tubes in his nose and another one coming out of his mouth.

Immediately her heart flashed from disbelief, to shock, to a fearful level of despair. The next thing she knew, she fell on her knees with her head buried on the edge of the bed, sobbing uncontrollably. She surprised herself as a deep groaning pain wailed out from deep inside. She never felt such pain, radiating from somewhere deep inside, from a place she didn't know existed. She was lost. She was lost in the pain. What had happened to her sweet Billy? He had always been so much larger than life, larger than anything in her world. She cried in wonder of what could have done this.

And then Billy's fingers lightly grazed her hair. Startled, she immediately pulled back and looked down at Billy's smiling face and slightly opened eyes. His mouth slowly moved. No sound came out, but it didn't need to. She knew what he said.

"Hello, My Sweet Angel" was how he had always greeted her after being apart. He was the only person who had said those words to her. Instantly bursting into tears and falling forward, she then wrapped her arms around his now glowing face.

She held him, tears streaming down both their cheeks. No words were spoken, but she looked at Billy and despite the tears, he was smiling. That was all she needed.

She didn't remember how long she held him, but she did remember being startled when a doctor entered the room. "Miss, visiting hours will be over in thirty minutes, and I have to re-dress Sergeant West's wounds."

Anna smiled at the doctor and nodded. It did not matter, she had her Billy. She felt complete. So many months apart, but at his side, the pain was gone. She held his hand, knowing things would get better. Billy would get better. She would be there for him and would do everything she could to help him.

Billy looked into her eyes, flooded with tears. His mouth continued to move slowly. There was no sound, but his lips formed the words she had heard so many times before, words she had not heard in months. "My Sweet Angel, my Sweet Anna Angel." She held him in her arms, covering him as if now protecting him from the world, swirling around them. Yes, she would be his protector. She would love him like no one in the world could.

In the following days, she spent every possible second at Billy's side in the hospital. His wounds healed far better than the doctors had originally estimated. They were amazed, but Anna wasn't. This was Billy West, and in her life, he could do anything.

Billy's upper left torso and left arm had absorbed the blast of a rocket propelled grenade. Shrapnel had torn into his left shoulder and his left side. Shards of metal had peppered the side of his body. Fortunately, his organs and his main arteries had escaped the blast unscathed. The doctors, however, had still been concerned about infection and had spent hours in surgery, removing the shrapnel from his body. Despite the potential for complications, Billy's condition rapidly improved.

But she still worried about him. He seemed different. He was healing, but something was lost.

One night in the hospital. He was asleep but mumbled the words, "zulu, bravo, tree." Later, when he was awake, she asked him about it. He immediately reacted defensively and turned white. He denied remembering anything about it. She knew it wasn't the truth. He had something inside he wouldn't let out, wouldn't show her, and wouldn't let her try to heal.

Anna stayed at Fort Benning for a week. During that time, Billy's recovery was nothing short of miraculous. The doctors warded off the possibility of serious infection, and Anna spurred Billy's spirit—he would stop at nothing short of a complete recovery. In only four days after her arrival, Billy was up and out of bed, hobbling around on crutches. By the time she boarded the bus back to Iowa, Billy was able to walk on his own to and from the latrine.

She had never seen Billy challenged like that. It frightened her to see him so vulnerable. He would not admit it to her, but he needed her—physically, emotionally, and spiritually. And all of this made them stronger. He leaned on her, and she held him up.

The time together in the hospital took their love to a new depth, to a new level. He wanted her, and she yearned for his touch. However, it was impossible for them to be intimate. His injuries prevented him from acting on his deep seated needs. Yet their time together was so much more. It was deeper. Out of this tribulation came a deep level of trust she and Billy had never felt before—an all-encompassing trust reaching to the core of who they were.

Looking back, it had been like a bad dream. But that had been February when winter had filled their lives. Now it was July, and they basked in the warmth of summer. Billy's scars had healed, and he was home, at her side where he belonged.

Now holding his hand at the table, she closed her eyes

tightly, reminding herself the war was behind them, and today was a beautiful July day in Iowa. Their life together was alive with love, alive with hope for the future. Despite his momentary lapses back to a battlefield in Vietnam, Billy was coming around. He was changing with each passing hour—more responsive, more connected to her emotionally and physically.

Billy complimented Anna on her beauty, and she smiled broadly, savoring every word of it. Billy was no longer the boy she remembered, He had come home from Vietnam a man. Their lovemaking was a completely different experience than it had been two years ago before he had joined the army.

She had always wanted him to be her first, and as his time prior to basic training wound down to a matter of days, she knew they only had a few opportunities to do this. Billy had always wanted her but was never pushy. He had respected her. He had loved her too much to put her in a compromising position. This had to be her decision. And when she made it, and they had the conditions set to make love, Billy had treated her with complete respect for the gift she was giving him.

In the days prior to his departure to Fort Benning, Anna had given up her virginity to Billy. The first time, he had been gentle and patient with her, taking it slow, ensuring she was ready and comfortable with every movement however overt or subtle it may have been. Despite Billy's efforts, she hadn't found any pleasure in it. Instead, it had been painful, and when he had finished, she cried. Billy had held her in his arms, consoling her, caressing her, bringing comfort to her in return for the love she had given up for him.

They had made love three more times. Each time had been marked with a little less pain and little more comfort between the two of them. She had not seen Billy naked before, and she'd been self-conscious about her own body. But each time they made love, she had become more familiar with his body and more confident with revealing herself to him.

But things were different now. Fort Benning had made them stronger, and she wanted her man more than ever. She had been loyal to him. Several boys paid her unwanted visits, and she had gone on a couple of blind dates with her friends, but those had been purely social events. There had been no one who could fill her heart but Billy.

At 20 years old, she was a woman, and she knew what she wanted. She wanted him. The day Billy returned home, they'd made love on a blanket under the stars out at the timber on her farm. When they'd made love, he had filled her with a pleasure she had hungered for. She was awakened with needs, and Billy was the only man who could please her. That night, she had let go, and he had taken her over the edge…falling, falling in his arms, into a wonderful state of bliss.

Now sitting in the café, she could still feel him. She slightly blushed as she thought about how she wanted him and the amazing pleasure he brought to her. No longer kids, they made love confidently. He had a new knowledge of how to please her, and she was able to open herself up and let him do it. She smiled at the table as she remembered the other night, out in the timber on a blanket, and how the stars fell from the sky as she had drifted away, numb with pleasure. She had never felt surer of herself and more confident about her love for him. Billy was her man, and she loved him.

"I love you, Anna Angel," Billy said, looking directly into her eyes. She gazed into his deep blue eyes, brimming full of tears. He had told her this many times before but never with so much emotion and she knew he meant it to the core of everything he was. There was a sadness in his eyes, too. Something there, faded, hurting, needing to be repaired. She would repair it. She would fix whatever was bringing pain to Billy.

"I love you, too." Anna smiled and leaned forward to kiss him.

"You kids going to be able to pull yourself apart to order something?" Mabel Lewis interjected as she prepared to take their order.

"Thanks, Mabel. We'll have two glasses of orange juice, and I'll have a Buddy Supreme Omelet. Anna, my love, what would you like?"

"Could I please have two pancakes?" Anna requested, sitting back in her chair unable to look Mabel in the eye.

"Got it, juice, supreme omelet, and two pancakes, anything else?"

Billy and Anna looked at each other, both good with what they ordered. "Nope, that should do it. Thanks Mabel."

Mabel turned and walked toward the counter. She smiled. It was clear that Billy and Anna were in love. Sitting at the table, they shared a magical aura between them—they were swimming in an amazing joy that only they could bring each other. Despite the crowd in the cafe, they were alone in their love. They didn't give a damn about what was going on around them and all the scuttlebutt gossip swirling between the tables. Mabel smiled and briefly remembered when she and Buddy were like that so long ago. It had been years ago at Fort Hood after he had returned from the Korean War. It was such a wonderful time in her life with Buddy. It was refreshing to see that same love, blossoming here in the café.

Billy and Anna sat, smiling and gazing into each other's eyes as they discussed their plans for the day and what they wanted to do the rest of the week.

"Ma wants to have a family picnic sometime in the next couple of weeks, and she said she thought it might be a good idea if I invited you," Anna said, reaching out with both her hands and coupling them over Billy's hand on the table.

Billy smiled. Since his return from Vietnam, her parents had been very receptive to his presence out at their farm, and they welcomed the relationship he had with their daughter. When he had been in high school, they didn't have the time of day for him and were very restrictive any time he paid Anna a visit out at the farm or whenever they went out on a date. Her curfew at midnight had always put a damper on their evenings together. Things had always seemed to get started around midnight, but now, she didn't have a curfew.

"Family picnic sounds good to me. I'll bring a blanket and maybe we'll be able to slip away into the woods." Billy smiled sheepishly at Anna. "I can see it now. 'Ah, Mrs. Jacobs, great fried chicken and don't mind us, we're just going to go for a walk in the woods. We're taking a blanket in case we need to stop and rest for a while. We should be back in about a half hour'," Billy said in a mocking tone.

"Samuel William West, you stop it. You're being silly," Anna said, swatting him on the arm while a warm blush touched her cheeks.

Only Billy's mother had ever called him by his full name. There was a strange feeling when it came from Anna, but it felt right. Everything with Anna was right.

"I may be silly, but you know it would be fun…until we got caught by one of your sisters or worse, your dad," Billy responded, wide-eyed.

"Samuel West, you have a one-track dirty mind! Now, I'm going to go to the restroom, and while I'm gone, I want you to get a grip on yourself." Anna playfully pointed her finger at him as she got up.

Billy leaned back and watched Anna walk toward the restroom. She looked absolutely incredible. She had developed into an amazing woman. Billy smiled at how lucky he was to be in love with such a fantastic person. And the wonder of it all was that she loved him as much as he loved her…completely. One thing was for certain, he was head over heels in love with her and could not see anyone else in his life. He had made up his mind. He was going to marry her.

"It was just a weak sucker punch and proves he's a loser like his father…" The words from a nearby table broke Billy out of his happy trance. Did he just hear what he thought he heard? He couldn't believe somebody would be so brazen as to insult him like that. He leaned forward, annoyed and fought off the temptation to be filled with anger. Maybe he had misunderstood what was said.

Benny Moore said something barely audible and Ronnie Wilson burst out in explosive laughter. Billy turned and saw Mrs. Ford and Mrs. Meyer shake their heads annoyingly and glare at the table where the young men were stirring up trouble. Billy turned back to his table. He was not going to get worked up over those boys. He could feel the anger burn inside and his jaw clench as he tried to maintain his composure. He was going to sit here—in control—and have a wonderful breakfast with Anna.

Anna returned from the bathroom. "What's the matter? You have a look on your face like you're really angry," Anna asked as she sat down in her chair.

"What? Me? A look? No, it's nothing. Just getting hungry. Hope our food gets here soon," Billy replied. He leaned back in his chair, and ran his hand over his thigh to calm his nerves.

"Me too. Say, what do you want to do today? I was thinking maybe we could drive over to Monticello and check out the new women's clothing store that opened last month." Anna smiled and reached forward to hold Billy's hand on the table.

"Monti? Shopping? Sure, sounds good. I'd like to check out Pearson's Sporting Goods Store. Haven't been there for a few years," Billy answered as he gently caressed Anna's hand.

"Seems like a waste to me. Such a pretty girl hanging out with somebody who ain't going to be any better than a no-good town drunk," Benny Moore said and Ronnie muffled his laughter.

Billy sprung from his chair with his fists clenched, then turned from the table. Anna looked at him, astonished by the flash of anger on his face. The deep fury in his eyes, and fearless, pinched expression transformed him into something she had never seen. Billy pivoted from Anna and walked purposefully as if he was stalking his prey toward the table where Ronnie and Benny were laughing with Dicky Moss and two other young men.

"I'm going to say this one time. Get the hell out of Buddy's, right now!" Billy said sternly in a low, menacing voice.

The café immediately turned to a startled, awkward silence. The boys looked at each other, shocked that anyone would dare confront them. Billy stood, hands on his hips. Like a stick in the mud, he was not going to move from their table until they left. The boys sensed he meant business. The smile on each of their faces quickly faded to a mixed look of anger and fear.

"Don't even think about doing anything stupid. I promise, you'll lose. I'm going to give you thirty seconds to get up, pay Mabel, and get the hell out of here," Billy demanded as he opened and closed his fists. All four boys looked at Billy like they couldn't believe what he was saying. They were astonished that one person would try to push them around like this. "Twenty seconds! If you aren't out that door, you'll soon wish you were." Billy pointed his finger at the door.

Ronnie shook his head and stood up. He briefly squared with Billy. Giving him a once over, Ronnie realized that Billy West had filled out and was considerably bigger and stronger than he had been in high school and more importantly, he was about to get his ass handed to him. Wisely, he turned toward the door. The other boys stood up uneasily, unsure what they should do.

"We can finish this now or later. I'm going to eat my breakfast. In thirty minutes, I'll walk out of this café without Anna. If you have the guts to face me like a man, I'll meet you around the corner in the alley. I promise you that if that's your choice, you'll lose. Now get the hell out of here!" Billy raised his voice and pointed at the door again.

Billy clenched his fists and postured to attack them. The boys jumped as Billy put the fear of God in them. All four were visibly rattled as they quickly threw cash down on the table and left. One of the boys stumbled over a chair, and picking it up, mumbled something in defiance as he walked out of the cafe.

After the door closed behind them, Billy turned toward Anna at the back of the cafe. Dave and John Crawford cut him off at Jim Barton's table.

John put his arm around Billy, and Dave turned to Sheriff Barton. "Jim Barton, is there an ounce of courage in those fat-covered bones of yours?"

Barton looked up, still slogging through a large bite of pancake, a wet spot of dripped syrup shining on the right breast pocket of his uniform. He swallowed his pancake and looked up at Dave. "I don't know what you are talking about, Dave."

John raised his voice. "Like hell you don't. You sit there talking all kinds of bullshit, and everyone in this room heard those boys insult Billy several times. Billy was finally pushed to where he had to take action. Jim, I'm disappointed in you. Not surprised, just disappointed." John looked around the café, and a number of the men nodded.

Still looking up in disbelief, the sheriff rebutted, "Now wait one minute here…"

"No Jimmy, you waited long enough. The point for you to do something has come and gone. Billy handled it himself. Just like he had to handle that no-good Joe Matsell."

"I don't know what you are talking about, John…" Jim quipped.

"Everybody and their brother knows what trouble has been brewing down at Gus's Tavern. Joe Matsell is nothing but trouble. Rumors are circulating about illegal drugs and prostitution at that bar. Unfortunately, it took young Billy here to come home on leave to try to set things straight. Just stop. Stop disgracing yourself more than you already have. If anything, you should be thanking Billy West here for bringing some order to this town." John stabbed his finger into the Sheriff's chest.

"John, it ain't nothing. Nothing I can't handle…" Billy shook his head as he tried to dismiss John.

"Billy, you shouldn't have to. No one should. You deserve better. We all deserve better." John raised his voice and looked around the restaurant as everyone stared back at him.

"Thanks John, but it's something I've just come to expect here in my hometown."

"But Billy you've…"

"I appreciate what you're doing and all but it ain't going to make a difference. From what I hear, it never does." Resigned, Billy forced a smile as he reached out and shook John and Dave's hands.

The café was dead silent. Jim Barton sat there, wide-eyed, looking at Dave and John. Amazed that he was being called out like this by a couple of locals, he could not bring himself to rise from his chair. He sat there and seemed to sink lower and lower as John Crawford accused him of being an incredible slouch. Mabel acted as if she was busy cleaning up the mess that the boys had left at their table. She was listening, as was everyone in the café, and enjoying every second of it.

Billy West walked back to his table and sat close to Anna. "Sorry about that, darling. Some boys just got to learn the hard way."

"It wasn't a big deal. I didn't even hear what they said." She had heard them but was proud that Billy stood up for her—that he faced four men to protect her honor.

"Nothing worth repeating. Just bad manners. They're a sad lot. I know their fathers, and I know they done better than that raising them boys," Billy answered as he leaned closer to Anna.

Anna reached out and grasped Billy's hand and looked into his eyes. "Most folks aren't really bad. They're just lost. Guys like Dicky and Ronnie are bouncing out there on the ocean like a ship without a rudder, turned whichever way the wind blows."

"You're probably right, but folks without any direction, without anything to live for, can be the most dangerous." Billy sat back in his chair.

John and Dave walked up to Billy and Anna's table. Still annoyed at what had transpired, John broke into the conversation and switched the subject. "Billy, it sure is good to see you again. It's been what, two years?"

Billy stood up from his chair and firmly shook John and Dave's hands. "Yes sir, two years last month since I went to basic training."

"Well Billy, Maggie and I would be honored if you'd come on by for dinner this Monday night. You can bring your pop, and even pretty Anna here is welcome. Although I think Maggie might get a little jealous at her youth and beauty." John smiled.

Anna blushed and buried her face shyly. Billy answered, "Why thank you, sir. Monday dinner sounds great."

"Okay, Monday it is. Six o'clock. We look forward to having you," John said, patting Billy on the back.

"Great, see you then," Billy replied with a nod.

Dave and John shook hands with Billy and turned to the counter, paid their tab, and exited the café.

"That sure was nice of them," Billy said as he sat down and turned back to Anna.

After Dave and John left the café, there was a steady stream of patrons leaving. Jim Barton's table first, then the old men's table, and finally Mrs. Ford's table.

It was just Anna and Billy now, happily sharing their morning. Finishing breakfast, Billy walked to the counter to pay his tab.

"Got my bill, Mabel?" Billy politely asked.

"No sir, your bill's been paid." Mabel smiled as she held up the tab.

Billy shook his head and smiled. Dave and John had footed the bill. It was good to be home. It was good to have true friends, men he could trust and had his back covered when he needed it. It was something he learned playing football—the importance of teamwork. A tight group of two, three, or four people could make all the difference. Even more so in the army, on a team that lived together—that sweated, laughed, cried, bled, and even died together. Loyal men could change the world. He caught glimpses of this camaraderie playing football, but he lived it in Vietnam. A small group of men in his platoon had changed his life, had made the impossible, possible. They would always be his brothers.

Anna stepped up to Billy's side and hooked her arm in his. "I'm ready to go."

Billy pulled Anna's arm close to his body and escorted her out of the café. Walking down the sidewalk, Billy glanced over his shoulder and saw that the alley was empty, just as he knew that it would be.

VII

"THAT WAS A great dinner. I don't remember the last time I ate so well." Billy sipped his iced tea and leaned back in his chair at the table.

"This has been our pleasure. We're honored to have you in our home," John Crawford answered in mutual gratitude.

"Thank you, ma'am," Dave said to Maggie as he, Billy, John, and Andy stood up from the table. The old screen door creaked open as the spring stretched and then closed behind them with a quick snapping crack. The men moved to the three old metal, motel rocking chairs while Andy sat on the steps, turning to his side to be a part of the men's conversation. Passing around their smokes, the men reclined with a collective sigh that only came with a cigarette after an amazing meal together.

They smoked Lucky Strikes, not because they were good. There were better cigarettes that could be purchased at the same price. They smoked them because that was what they smoked when they were soldiers. They smoked them with a quiet pride born out of a time when they moved mountains. Lucky Strikes were another badge they wore—that identified who they were, what they'd done, and what they believed.

The sun was setting and the locusts began their evening chorus as the men enjoyed their cigarettes. It was a still about eighty-five degrees, but the soft, summer breeze released the noose of the suffocating humidity.

The Johnson and Meyer boys were down the street playing ball, and Andy considered joining them. On any other summer evening, he would have, but tonight was different. Tonight he wanted to stay close to Billy. He wanted to spend time with the men.

These were men of few words, yet they were always meaningful with long, comfortable silences in between each one. Being near the men and listening to their talk was like being one of them—they didn't ask him or expect him to speak, but they didn't tell him to leave either. This was as good as being accepted. This made a twelve year-old stand up straighter, walk taller, and speak more confidently—it made him yearn even more to be a man, a real man of honor. And tonight, with Billy West in his presence, it was more than he could ever have expected.

Billy was a hero to just about every boy from Anamosa aged ten to eighteen. They all had watched him lead the Blue Raiders to championships in multiple sports. He was the talk of the town at most dinner tables and establishments in Anamosa, and he had been a hero in the newspapers every week. He was even recognized by the Des Moines Register as one of the few athletes with a promising future beyond high school. Andy aspired, like most boys, to be like him.

When Andy had found out that Billy was coming over for dinner, he was absolutely beside himself. He could not believe Billy West was actually going to be sitting at their kitchen table. Yes, tonight was different. Tonight there would not be baseball with the Meyer boys. Tonight Andy would be with the men—to include his hero, Billy West.

Over the years, Andy's father and his Uncle Dave had shared a special relationship with Billy. Not much was ever said about it, but from what Andy had gathered, it had started soon after Billy's mother passed away. As he understood it, they had gotten him a part-time job in the summers working as an assistant to the warden at the prison. Nobody knew it, but Uncle Dave and his father had also supported Billy financially when he was in high school, buying him quality sports equipment each season.

Andy remembered going to Monti with his Uncle Dave to pick-out a new Wilson A2000 baseball glove at Pearson's. He had later seen Billy on the mound pitching—with that very glove. When Andy had asked his dad about it, his father had denied it, stating he didn't know what Andy was talking about. It didn't make sense to Andy. These men did things for Billy and for several others in the community, but they never talked about it. It was as if they were living a different life.

"That Maggie is one fine cook," Dave said, exhaling a smooth cloud of smoke. "Just a damn fine cook."

John and Billy leaned back in their chairs, nodding, and relaxed as they inhaled the crispy taste of their cigarettes.

Dave smiled with a glint in his eye. "Damn fine woman, John. Unfortunately, there must be something unseen that is seriously wrong with her." Dave chuckled, tapping the ashes into the tray. "None of us were ever able to figure out what she ever saw in you."

"I can't say I disagree with you. I often wonder how I was

ever so blessed to share my life with such a wonderful woman," John replied, knowing there was truth to what his brother said.

The men shook their heads and smiled as they slowly rocked in their chairs and looked out across the front yard. As the sun dropped, the shadows stretched across the lawn, and the whir of the locusts grew louder. It was a beautiful evening.

"Those steaks were so tender tonight, and those grilled potatoes were out of this world." Dave patted his stomach, still savoring the amazing dinner.

"Yeah, that was fantastic. I'll be sure to let my pop know what he missed," Billy said in agreement.

Billy's father couldn't make it to the dinner. He had been admitted into the hospital again up at Independence. With Anna at Billy's side, they had spent the past three days up there with his father, getting him moved in and established. This time, he would be staying for three months. With some assistance from Judge Bob Swanson, Billy had been able to expedite his admission into the hospital. Billy had been on a tight timeline. He was scheduled to report back to Fort Benning in mid-August. Judge Swanson had recognized the urgency of the situation. With a letter of recommendation and a few phone calls, he had been able to cut through much of the red tape to get Billy's father the care he needed.

This was not the first time Butch West had spent time at the hospital in Independence. But this time was different. He was going at it on his own. He had become aware that with Billy in the army there was no one to take care of him, and if he didn't do something to get better, he wouldn't live much longer. To

Billy, it was as if his father had stopped living years ago after his mother had passed away. Something had died in Pop with the loss of his wife, and it had taken this long for his body to catch up. Billy didn't want to lose him. Other than Anna, Pop was all that he had. There was still hope for him.

It had been an emotional process for Billy. Sitting on the porch with the Crawford men had been Billy's first chance to relax in a week.

"I appreciate you guys, having me over for dinner. Just a fine gesture. I can't remember the last time I ate so well," Billy said, taking a drag on his cigarette.

In the background coming from inside the house, the clank and clatter of the dishes being washed could be heard. Short bursts of laughter came from the kitchen as Anna and Maggie cleaned up. Despite a fifteen year age difference, the two women hit it right off. They laughed as they mused over the shortcomings of their men. Their quick witted banter at dinner toward their men was nearly overwhelming, and had been almost more than the men could stand. By the time dinner was over, they had quickly raced out of the kitchen to their own refuge on the front porch.

"Think I could go for a cold beer. Any of you boys want one?" John asked Billy and Dave.

"Sir, I sure could. That sounds great," Billy answered and Dave nodded.

John returned with three cold beers and a Coke for his son. They opened the cans and enjoyed the first sip in unison.

"Mmm, nothing better than a cold beer on a warm summer

evening. You know what I mean?" With his father now in the hospital getting treatment, Billy felt as if a heavy weight had been lifted off his chest.

Dave nodded as he put out his cigarette in the ashtray and lit up another. Silence filled the porch. The crack of the bat from the ball game down the street caught their attention. All of them gazed out in that direction to where the Meyer boys had a pick-up game with most of the neighborhood kids.

The silence was broken when Andy found his courage to ask Billy the question that had nagged him for some time. "Billy, you ever think about giving the Cubs another shot?"

Billy didn't respond. He just looked out at the boys playing ball.

Andy took a sip of his Coke. "I know you're in the army and all and doing what you want to do. I would think that as close as you came to playing in the bigs…to trade it all in so you could enlist in the army…"

"Andrew." His dad sternly cut him off. His eyes narrowed in warning. "You don't have the right to ask this man a question like that."

"But Dad, I was just wondering why…"

"Not another word from you, Son. You haven't earned the right to ask this man why he decides to do what he does." Clenching his jaw, his dad reprimanded Andy.

"It's okay, John." Billy put his beer down on the floor by his chair and turned to Andy. "It's a good question, and one I think I owe all of you an answer to." Billy nodded, meeting each man's eyes before looking down the street at the kids playing ball.

"I love baseball. As long as I can remember, I always have. For the longest time, I couldn't see doing anything other than playing in the majors. The feel of a Louisville Slugger in my hand as I stared down a pitcher, the rich smell of a well-oiled leather glove as I slapped the ball deep into the center of the web, the happy taste of the dirt in my mouth as I stole third base. Those were things I lived for. They're forever etched in my mind."

Billy turned to John and Dave with a lower tone in his voice. "This sounds kind of silly, but I still have dreams about it. I'm on the mound, staring down a batter with two outs in the bottom of the ninth and a runner on third. Checking the runner one last time and then hitting my wind up. Or sometimes, I dream I'm in the batter's box, getting ready to go to bat. There's an amazing excitement to it all. Then, settling my nerves, I feel the bat in my hands.

"Sometimes it's the last inning. We're down by a run, and I'm getting ready to step up to the plate. I hear nothing. Just the smell of the summer evening, the feel of the soft dirt in the batter's box, the salty taste of sweat, reading how the infield is set, receiving the signals from the coach down the first base line…the anticipation of standing alone with the chips down and everyone counting on me. I wake up wondering if I got a hit—wishing I could drift back to sleep to face that pitcher and finish the game."

Weighed down with the memory of a dream forgone for a higher calling, Billy let out a heavy sigh. "Baseball's a part of who I am, a wonderful part of my past. I reckon it'll always be a part of me and probably a part of my dreams." Billy leaned down toward Andy on the steps and rested his elbows on his knees. "But it's not everything."

At Billy's statement, Andy's shoulders slumped. He had been hanging on his every word, mesmerized by the sound of his voice, the passion in his eyes, and the small gestures he made.

"Baseball's the most wonderful game I've ever played—that I've ever known. But…there's so much more to life than just this game. When you play ball, you play for yourself; you play for your teammates; you play for your team, for your community. Some games you win, and some you lose. You see, winning and losing seasons come and go. If everything works out, maybe somewhere in there is a championship season. But is this all there is to life?"

Billy looked directly at Andy with a fierce intensity in his eyes. "I love baseball, but in the end, it's only a game—a game of many individuals. Nine players who sometimes depend on each other, but who are mostly judged by their individual stats. Nine individuals trying to make a mark for themselves, so they can get to the next level. To make it all the way can be a dirty business, and it often makes for a selfish endeavor. And all for what? So I might be remembered? So I might have a record that someone someday will break? I want more out my life than just serving myself."

Billy took a long drag of his cigarette, put it out in the ashtray, and leaned back in his chair. Gazing out at the kids playing ball down the street, he slowly shook his head. "I love the army. I love what it stands for. I love that I'm serving my country, defending freedom, and there's no question in my mind that right now we're defending freedom. But there's even more to it than that. I yearn for something. For something more."

He let out another sigh and took a sip of his beer. "I want to be on a real team. A team where I affect those around me in a permanent way, in a way that won't be forgotten next week, or the week after, that depends on how many hits I get. I want to affect others in a permanent way that they'll never forget. In a way, they know I love them, that I always loved them, and I'll always love them. Not because I win games for your favorite team or because I sign an autograph. I want to be on a real team and lead them in a terribly difficult struggle—even if in the end there are no apparent winners."

Billy gazed out from the porch and seemed to be in a far off place, but Andy hung on every word. "To lay it all out on the line, to give everything even if it means you lose it all, even if it means you never come home again. To stand up for what I believe, even if in the end I'm standing alone, ruthlessly defending my integrity."

He took another drink of his beer, leaned down closer to Andy, and dropped his voice to a whisper. "It's hard to put into words…but to openly serve others, to bear my heart and love my brothers...to be with other soldiers who are willing to die in order to keep their word—rarely will you feel a love that pure. To truly struggle, to overcome fear, to think when others can't think, to love my brothers and my enemies the same. To tenderly hold my buddy in my arms as he leaves this world. There's a cost…such a horrible, dreadful cost…but if not me, then who? Who will protect them? Who will do it right? Who will accomplish the mission and bring them home?"

Billy sat back in his chair and stared out into the heavy, humid summer evening. The sun had disappeared behind the hickory tree across the street and darkness would soon be settling upon them. For a brief moment, Billy felt embarrassed for opening up and exposing himself. He was surprised at his own emotions. But then he didn't care. These feelings seemed to rise to the surface and needed to come out when he was around men he trusted, and he trusted the Crawford men.

Andy looked up at his dad and his uncle. Both of their eyes were wet with tears, and a deep sadness touched their faces. Silence, immense and heavy, filled the porch for a couple of minutes. They stared out into the darkening evening. June bugs snapped against the screen porch door, locusts chattered their wavering sirens, the first lightning bugs flashed out in the front lawn. The men remained motionless. They sat silent deep in their thoughts.

"You boys sleeping out here?" Maggie asked, interrupting the silence as she peeked out the screen door.

"No honey, just enjoying the evening," John said, shifting in his rocking chair. "That sure was a wonderful dinner tonight."

"Thought you men might want some fresh-cut watermelon—it's really starting to come into season." Maggie carried out a tray full of sliced watermelon and set it down on the porch table.

"Mrs. Crawford, you sure know how to make a dinner taste like no one can. I do believe that was the best I've eaten in five years." Billy took a bite of the watermelon. "And this may be the best watermelon I've ever had, simply perfect."

"Yes Maggie, I don't remember ever having a dinner like we had tonight," Dave added. "It was as if you pulled a little piece of heaven down into your kitchen and served it up for us."

"I don't mind the compliments, but it was my pleasure. Got to take care of my boys." Maggie smiled, glancing at John and Andy. "But to be honest, I wasn't sure what you all thought of it. You're all awfully quiet. Could have heard a pin drop when I saw you boys from behind the screen door. Everything okay?"

John reached for his wife's hand. "We're fine, just enjoying the evening."

"You sure? Seemed kind of heavy out here like I was interrupting a funeral or something." Maggie squeezed John's hand for reassurance, sensing something more between the men.

John diverted his eyes to the boys playing ball down the street. His wife always knew everything. Somehow she knew they were talking about Billy's future, and he didn't know how to answer her.

Andy, unaware of the magnitude of the conversation he had witnessed, answered. "Momma, Billy was telling us all about the army, about honor, and how he would sacrifice everything. About how he loves being with a team of his soldiers…"

"Sacrificing it all for soldiers…" Maggie's face transformed and pinched with anger. "Is that so?"

Andy's words struck a raw nerve with Maggie, and John knew it and tried to recover the direction of the conversation, but it was too late. "Aw darling, we were just talking with Billy about…"

"Don't give me that we were 'just talking' nonsense!" Maggie raised her voice with a sense of desperation in her tone. "There isn't ever any 'just talking' when you're talking 'bout the hurly burly and who did what at Sam Dicken's Hill...about the ultimate sacrifice of this, and honor and integrity of that. The next time I hear somebody at a parade talk about the maximum effort, the last full measure, or some other ludicrous notion that justifies that young Tommy is buried in some wheat field in France or how Jimmy came home in a box from Vietnam…" Maggie pulled away from John and clenched her fists. "It makes me so angry and sad I could just spit. Spit on all the reckless talk. There isn't anything good in it. Nothing. Nothing but grief. It all eventually comes to grief."

Maggie turned to Anna who was standing behind her in the doorway. "You remember that. If you stay in this army business long enough it will all come to grief."

Anna didn't know how to respond. She mumbled something inaudible and nodded as if she understood. But the only thing she understood in this was fear. She froze in the doorway as Maggie steamrolled ahead. Her face was red with deep anguish and tears welled up in her eyes.

Andy sat wide eyed. He had never seen his mother react to his father with such anger. Billy and Dave looked down to the front edge of the porch, not lifting their eyes to Maggie. After a long uncomfortable pause, John spoke. "Maggie, you're overreacting. A man has got…"

"Overreacting? How dare you say such a thing?" Maggie's face turned beet red and anger steamed out of her. "Of all things.

After all these years, after all that we've struggled through. Now, I'm sure Billy has much to be proud of in his service to our country. I'm not questioning that. But in all this highfalutin talk did you tell him about the cost? Did you tell him about the scars?"

Turning to Billy, Maggie narrowed her attention to him. "No, I'm not talking about the physical scars. Not about how some men, like poor Dave, who'll always have to walk with a cane. I'm not talking about the many who are physically crippled for the rest of their lives. I'm talking about something far more insidious. You won't ever see it on a vet and nobody has the guts to talk about it. The scars I'm talking about are inside, and they're very real."

Maggie then shifted her attention to John. Her eyes brimmed with unshed tears. "You may come back from Wong Pong Hill or Chu Puck Knee with all kinds of stories about your exploits in Korea, North Africa or Vietnam, but they don't get at the real truth. The real truth is that war is a horrible and ugly thing."

"Maggie, we were just…" John reached out to Maggie, but she pulled away.

"No, John. You know this. You know this better than anyone. If it doesn't kill you or maim you, it screws up your head so hard that all you can do is drink your beer in the evening and try to remember or make up the truth to help you live with the ugliness of it all. Trying to mend the scars that nobody sees and nobody talks or cares about. Except those who truly love you. Only those who love you, who are with you every day, see the differences and feel the pain."

Maggie was weeping now and pulled out her handkerchief to blow her nose. "The little things, like the fact that you don't smile anymore. The fact that there's never the easy flow of laughter in your life. The fact that there's the loss of innocence…innocence that was stolen away from you. The faraway look in your eyes when you're living it all over again and again, but you can't share it with those closest to you because it's all so ugly. Hell, the funny thing is, you don't even know that the innocence is gone. You just keep keeping on like nothing's changed. But it's gone. And you've changed."

Raising her voice higher, Maggie turned to face Anna, who now had tears in her eyes. "These men are all little boys that lightheartedly go off to war. But it's all so terrible, so horrific, that the little boy dies of fright and is left on that horrible battlefield a world away. And then these men come home and try to pretend they're the same, but they aren't, and they never will be. They call it battle-hardened, but it's a damned excuse for all their anger and hate inside. Their tenderness is gone. The innocence is replaced with an awkward uneasiness. The uneasiness that keeps them up at night, the dullness that this domestic American life brings to them when they're no longer dancing on the edge of the world."

Maggie pointed her finger and John. "You sit out here with your beer and cigarettes and cheap talk about service and soldiers without any thought about the real victims. The wives that have to learn to love a man they no longer really know. The children who lean forward for the words that never come…"

Maggie blew her nose again and now had tears streaming down her cheeks. She pointed to her son and accused her husband. "And to do it in front of him! I see now why it never ends. But I won't let you. I won't let you do it. John, Dave, Billy—I won't let you have your way. You've been changed by the fire, but I won't let you tell the lie to Andy. His heart's still pure. You've all had your chance and made your decision to be touched in the crazy, hell-bent whirlwind of orders and missions that have to be done, but he's mine, and I won't let you turn him with your selfish stories."

Sobbing now, Maggie turned and left the porch through the screen door. The door closed with a loud slam that caused everyone on the porch to jolt up, and then there was silence.

After the longest minute, John spoke. "I'm sorry about the way…"

"No need to apologize," Billy said, stopping John. "If anyone's at fault it's me. I shouldn't have gone on like I did. I'm so sorry. Anything I can do to fix this?"

John had his head down, and he stared at the label on his beer. "It's not your problem, and honestly, this has nothing to do with you. This is something that's been brewing for a while. Actually, it's been there on and off for years, and I need to sort it out. I'm sorry the evening ended like it did." He looked up at Anna and Billy. "Heck, it's only eight o'clock, and it's a Saturday night. I know if I was your age with a pretty girl like Anna, I wouldn't be hanging out with a couple of old geezers. You need to get going and make the most of this fine summer evening."

Billy turned to Anna. "Let's take a stroll down to Main.

Maybe stop by the bowling alley and get a few games in."

Anna, who was still shocked and withdrawn, quietly responded and took Billy by the arm. "John, please thank Maggie for the delicious dinner tonight. I hope we can get together again in the next couple of weeks."

Billy turned to John and reached out his hand. "Please tell Maggie I'm sincerely sorry for opening up the way I did. I meant no harm. I would never do anything to harm Andy. Please tell her I sincerely apologize, and again thank her for the dinner."

"Thanks, now get on out of here and enjoy youth while it's still on your side." John stood up and shook Billy's hand.

Billy and Anna walked down the steps and waived as they turned down Cedar toward Main Street.

"Andy, you get in here and get in the tub. We have early church tomorrow, and you haven't taken a bath in two days," Maggie called from inside the house.

"Go on, Son," John added, tapping Andy on the shoulder.

"Aw, okay, Dad." Andy got up from the step and ran inside.

Now just the two brothers sat alone on the porch. The heaviness of the humid summer evening weighed on them. The siren of the locusts rose to a higher pitch.

"You going to be okay?" Dave asked.

"We'll be fine. It's hard. You know the deal," John answered.

"Yeah, I know. But are you okay?"

"Yeah we're okay. The war—It's always there, somewhere on the edges, and I never know when it's going to reveal itself." John let out a heavy sigh. "It never ends, you know what I mean?"

"Yeah, I know," Dave answered.

VIII

TEN DAYS HAD passed, and Big Joe was still angry. He had thought about brushing it off as if nothing had happened. Even though the embarrassment had been more than he could handle, he had been down before, and he knew this too would pass. Time would heal his wounds and make things right as it always did when bad things happened to him. But now, ten days later, the pain was as real as ever, and it twisted, from pain to hatred, inside of him.

Sitting in his tavern, he felt the hatred building. At first, it was slow, lingering below the surface. But now it flashed like lightning. The heat of his hatred burned at irregular intervals throughout the day. His chest tightened, and a sour taste filled in his mouth. Billy West.

Before all of this, Joe had never really thought much about Billy. A twinge of jealousy would spark when conversations turned to sports, records, and reputation, but talk about high school feats were rare and didn't matter.

Big Joe could shrug off the jealousy. What mattered was the present. Billy was away in the army. As long as he would stay far from Anamosa, he wouldn't be a threat to Joe. 'Out of sight, out of mind' had worked for Joe. But now, Billy was in Joe's town and in his tavern, and the problem was not just Billy's presence. With the altercation, he had become a nightmare for Big Joe. In one instant, Billy had torn away Joe's shroud, exposing who he was for all to see. People in Anamosa knew Joe was a bully, a coward, and a thug. He had heard it before, and he could see it in their eyes, but he had never cared what people thought. They didn't know the truth. While at times he had been known to be a little forceful to get things done, sometimes that was necessary. Most folks didn't understand that.

But with this incident, the truth could be interpreted as weakness—that Big Joe Matsell, at the heart of it all, was a weak coward, hiding behind a confident persona. Big Joe's reputation, his source of strength, was in jeopardy, and he would do what it took to protect it.

Everything had been strangely quiet ever since his run in with Billy. He closed the bar for a few days, and when he opened it back up, the regular stream of locals came as if nothing had happened. Dicky Moss would be in on Thursday evening and wouldn't leave until late Sunday evening. Dicky, Ronnie Wilson, Andy Moore, Sam Larson and a few others kept their normal routines, and Joe believed the incident with Billy had passed.

However, a strange, heavy silence hung in the air, and a dark cloud had settled over the bar. Joe Matsell was worried. He thought about Eddie Gruber and that night on the river bank. Joe did not feel any guilt about Eddie's death. It wasn't personal; it was business. Eddie was a man who had made his choices. He should never have backed Joe Matsell into a corner. That decision had proven fatal.

Joe thought about his other business in Iowa City. That delivery would have set him up and given him a competitive advantage in Anamosa. Hell, it would have given him a competitive advantage in all of Eastern Iowa. Opportunities. Joe believed greatness was born out of how one handled opportunities. With Eddie out of the picture, there were too many risks, and Joe had to let the deal pass. There would be other opportunities in the future. Opportunities that would allow him to take control of all the businesses on Main Street. He would restore his family's business and his family's name.

Joe had to protect the home first. He had been personally threatened in his own home. Credibility and reputation were everything.

As Joe sat at the bar, staring at the pawn on the chessboard, his mind went back to Eddie Gruber. He was gone. Joe had killed a man, and nobody knew it. Joe was surprised at how easy it was to do. Joe looked down at his hands—they had taken a man's life and now seemed alien to him. He didn't feel guilt for his actions, but did feel something altogether different. Maybe it was his paranoia, but something had changed. After Eddie's death, things seemed like they were slipping. The drug deal had fallen through and then all of this with Billy West.

Joe had hoped that after a week he would feel better about the whole ordeal. He had told himself to let it go, reasoning that Billy would go back to the army and that would be the end of it. For the first time in over a week, Joe Matsell was feeling more confident that all of this would pass.

That was until Dicky Moss opened his mouth.

Sitting at the bar, finishing his fifth beer, Dicky let it out. "Saw Anna Jacobs last night at the bowling alley. Damn, she's looking good. Finest woman I've seen in Jones County in a long time."

Ronnie Wilson took a drink from his beer and slammed it down on the bar. "Did you see those tight shorts she had on? And her T-shirt? Wow, you could see everything. Pretty much ruined my bowling game average. I was more focused on her ass than the pins, but it was worth it."

Dicky leaned over from his bar stool toward Ronnie. "Yeah, no shit. She was looking damn fine. Too bad she was there with that piece of shit, Billy West,"

Ronnie put his arm around Dicky. "That Billy West is one lucky son of a bitch. Heard through the grapevine they was getting married…"

Dicky took a long drink from his beer and belched. "One lucky son of a bitch. Hell, he even taught Big Joe here a lesson."

The words stung like the point of a dagger in Joe's chest. As the words were floating from Dicky's mouth, he regretted every syllable. In a flash, Big Joe slung a beer mug past Dicky's head, crashing against the wall on the other side of the bar.

"Get out! Get the fuck out of my bar now! All of you, get out! Now!" Big Joe shouted in anger. His face was red, and his hands trembled as he gripped the bar.

With fear in his eyes, Dicky stammered, "Big Joe, we didn't mean nothing by it. Hell, we all know it was a damn lucky sucker punch. Everybody in town knows that. West is stuck-up, chicken shit trash—we all know that. He ain't one of us. He doesn't really live here. He thinks he's better than us. We all know his pa is trash, and he ain't never going to amount to nothing…not in this town…"

Ronnie slid off his bar stool and tried to find his feet. "Hell, Big Joe, that's why he had to go off and join the goddamn army…he couldn't make it in this town."

"Shut the hell up and get out! Get out! Now!" Big Joe demanded, pointing at the door. "The bar is closed!"

The room emptied. Sally was in the back, doing dishes. She had heard it all but knew better than to come out. In fact, she barely moved. She did not want to make a sound as it might get Joe's attention. Nobody knew Big Joe like she did. This whole thing had been simmering inside him for over a week, and it was best to stay out of his way. She had gotten the back of his hand before and knew if she walked out there right now, she would get it again.

Big Joe had not moved after the boys left. His hands trembling with anger on the edge of the bar, he lowered his chin to his chest and closed his eyes. Billy West. The name pounded in his head, and he could feel it burning in his chest. Big Joe had known anger, but never quite like this. He was dizzy, light-headed, beyond mere anger; more of a new level of awareness, a controlled rage. He was ready to fight and protect what was his.

Big Joe would find his revenge. He would make it all right again. Nobody pushed Big Joe Matsell around in this town. It was time for him to meet force with force.

Big Joe knew only a few truths in his life—truths that had served him well to this very day. Might would make right. It would all be up to him, and he would set things straight. But making things right would not be enough. He was going to cut deep. Deep to the bone. He would bring hurt not just to Billy but to those around him. Billy's pa would pay, and Anna Jacobs would wish she never knew Billy West. And Billy West? Billy would regret the day he had walked into Joe's bar.

Part Two

Joshua

Present

UPON ANDY'S ARRIVAL at the airport in Cedar Rapids, he had rented a car and had stayed the night in a hotel before the final leg of the journey. When he had stepped out of the hotel in the morning, he had felt refreshed and ready to face the day.

Andy turned the rental car off of Highway 151 and onto Highway One at Fairview. Glancing over to the left of the road, he saw the historical marker for the Old Military Road and smiled. A few more miles and he would be home.

Andy enjoyed driving, and the new sedan was what he needed. With the car came control, and being in control felt good. From the instant he'd found out about his father's death, he had been hopping from problem to problem and from one mode of transportation to another. The day before had been nothing short of a whirlwind of turmoil, but today as he gripped the steering wheel, he felt better.

As he followed the winding road the last couple of miles to Anamosa, his mind floated back forty years to the place where he had grown up in the 1960s. For a brief moment, he felt like a boy again. He looked out over the rolling hills and deep woods—they had not changed. Andy wondered if he would always feel this way when he returned to his hometown. There was something utterly magical about it. No matter where he lived or where his life would take him, this would always be his hometown.

Andy guided the car down the long hill into the Wapsipinicon River valley on his final descent into Anamosa. Crossing the bridge over the Wapsi, he stopped the car and got out to get a good look at the river. Looking down from the bridge, nothing had changed. It looked exactly as it had four decades ago when he was a boy. It was as if the river had been suspended in time. Massive trees towered over the dark glassy surface, their reflection vivid in the smooth current. Andy thought they seemed to reach to the sky in victory as if they were a fighter towering over a defeated opponent. Several of the trees hung low, almost parallel to the river. Their branches gently touched the surface of the water as if they were resigned to it—resigned to the inevitable end that time brings to all living things.

A sense of reverence washed over him. The water continued to move with the same mystic force in its current that it had for thousands of years. He looked out at the dark, deep river and could feel it, and a shiver coursed through him. Andy also felt a twinge of fear as the swift current passed under the bridge and poured forward, unaltered by time or change as it continued its southeasterly path to the Mississippi. Then a strange sense of comfort flowed over him. After all these years, the same trees were suspended above the river as if time had not left its scars. The river was alive, and brought life to the land as it always had.

Andy smiled, thinking about his father and his Uncle Dave. His uncle was such a storyteller, and the times they had together on the river were magical. He thought about camping and fishing with his father and the wonderful moments they had shared around campfires and on river banks. He had truly been blessed to be around such incredible men. They had been hardworking men of integrity. Men who could be trusted in moments of crises, who had spoken truth in their words and their actions. They had been men who'd been faithful to their wives and steady and loving to their children. Andy wondered what he would be if not for their influence in his life.

Stepping away from the railing that separated him from the water, Andy got back in his car and continued his drive into town. Passing the Jones County Court House, he read the massive stone monument on the front lawn, "Jones County Remembers All Veterans Who Honorably Served Our Country." Andy's heart warmed at the large, proud words engraved in the stone and thought about Billy, his uncle, and his father.

Looking north beyond the court house, he saw the massive limestone walls of the prison, towering above all the rooftops and dominating the town's landscape. 'The Stone' was still a fully functioning maximum security penitentiary. A generation later and not much had changed. The castle walls, the towers, the bulwarks, and the stone lion statues guarding the entrance were as he remembered them as a boy.

Turning the rental car east onto Main Street, his thoughts and memories were interrupted by what he saw next. The buildings, the store fronts—everything looked tired and empty. His mind flashed back, and he remembered riding his bicycle down Main Street as a boy. Andy smiled as he recalled buying candy at Miller's drug store, closely reviewing all the movie posters on display at Park's Theater, stopping by Gelkie's to get bait for fishing, going into H&J Meats or Bob's Hardware to pick up something for his parents. It had been a magical time to be a boy—so much freedom to roam, to explore, and to ride wherever he wanted.

Andy thought of his own children. So much structure in their lives, so much protection. Everything was so organized. He wondered how all of the elements of control would develop them for the challenges their generation would face. He wished for a brief moment his children could taste the freedom he had as a boy in 1966. And then he wondered if they could handle it.

Andy's thoughts revolved back to the condition of Main Street. It was a skeleton of what it was forty years earlier. He drove by what used to be the Dairywhip restaurant. Once a magical place for meeting girls or getting the best ice cream in town, now it was a dilapidated ad hoc apartment that looked as if it had fallen into complete disrepair. He couldn't believe it was a place of so many fond childhood memories.

Moving further north on Main Street, he came to what once was the main business center of the town. The framework of the buildings was the same, but many were empty on the inside. Andy looked up to the tops of the buildings. The names of the early businessmen, the ones who had built this town, were permanently engraved in the stone. There were still a handful of bars, ironically in the same buildings they were in all those years ago. The names painted on the signs above the doors had changed, but they were still the same old bars. Park's Theater had been closed for years and many of the other stores were empty—those still open were now either an antique shop or a beauty salon. H&J Meats, Becky's Ladies Wear, Strohm's Clothing,

Bario's Shoes, Bob's Hardware…all of them were gone. Just empty buildings remained as a reminder of an earlier time when the community was alive with a vibrant economy—an economy that supported the families in all aspects of their lives.

There were a couple of new businesses that had come in—a winery and a restaurant, a flower shop, and a new bakery and coffee house. A glimmer of hope, Andy thought. He hoped these businesses would bring life back to the community.

Andy remembered an economics class he had in college. Supply and demand. His professor would explain that in business, everything was supply and demand and would spout off that the migration of business from the rural communities to the bigger cities was inevitable. He would go on to explain that it was large retail chains and shopping malls that killed Main Street. Andy knew he was right, but he also knew there was so much more that was lost in the need for better, cheaper, and faster. He looked out at the empty store fronts and knew that in our need for better lives, the heart of the community would dry up and die.

This was not the town he grew up in, and Andy knew it. Sadly, he would never be able to go back.

Andy thought about his father. He thought about his death. Earlier in the morning, Andy had talked to the sheriff on the phone and was asked to stop by his office when he came into town. The sheriff was the person who had found his father, and there were some peculiarities he wanted to discuss. With that in mind, Andy turned onto Ford Street toward the sheriff's office.

ᏕᏓ

Stepping into the sheriff's office, Andy was immediately overwhelmed by the musty smell of old papers and the faint smell of stale cigarettes. It had been ten years since the office transitioned from the typewriter to the computer, but the strange aura of outdated administrative procedures was still alive and well. An aura that included white out, carbon paper, and cabinets overloaded with musty documents.

Looking around the office, Andy was instantly struck by what was perhaps the homeliest woman he had ever seen. Sitting on the other side of the counter at a desk, the older woman with a pen protruding from her mouth, banged away violently at the keyboard. Andy figured her to be in her sixties, but he couldn't exactly tell for sure.

Andy cleared his throat to try to get her attention. It had no effect. He did it again and still was unable to catch her eye. Finally, Andy spoke up to get the woman's attention. "Uh, excuse me, ma'am?" Andy said. The woman glanced up at him and continued typing. "Uh, ma'am, my name's Andy Crawford. I…I ah…I had an appointment with the sheriff today."

The woman stopped typing, clicked a couple of times on the mouse, and then squinted her eyes at the screen. "I ain't tracking an appointment on his schedule," she said, finally lifting her eyes up at Andy with a disbelieving look. She also had a strange squeaky, raspy voice, and Andy figured it was due to years of smoking.

"Well, we talked late last night on the phone, and the sheriff told me to come by in the morning." Andy stepped up to the counter.

"This morning?" Her face was pinched, and for a brief moment, she reminded him of some kind of a sinister rodent.

"Yes, ma'am. He said to come by in the morning." Andy held firmly to the truth.

She raised an eyebrow in disbelief. "Sheriff Barton said that, did he?" The strange woman asked now in an accusatory voice.

"Yes ma'am." Andy rested his hands confidently on the counter.

"Humph," was the only sound she made in an odd grunt, telling Andy he was nothing but an interruption to her work. She promptly got up, walked into the sheriff's office, and shut the door, leaving Andy in the front waiting area alone.

Andy looked over at the homely woman's desk. The name placard on the desk read Marge Wilson. The name seemed familiar to Andy, growing up, but he couldn't quite remember why. Behind the desk on the shelf were pictures of her husband, kids, and from the looks of it, a whole slew of grandkids. Many of them had the same homely features of their grandmother. It seemed strangely funny to Andy. He couldn't imagine anyone making love with her. Her face, her mannerisms, and her squeaky voice were all tolerable, but when combined with her incredibly rude disposition it was too much for him to bear.

Andy sat down in one of the old metal chairs in the waiting area. As he leaned back in the chair, the metal screeched at the joints and echoed throughout the room. The acoustics in the room were amazing, but it completely startled Andy, and he almost fell out of the chair.

Suddenly the sheriff's office door swung open, and the odd

woman reappeared. "Sheriff Barton will be ready to meet with you in about ten minutes," she said as she promptly went back to her desk and resumed banging on the keyboard.

She certainly was peculiar. Not really sociable, just a strange little bird, Andy thought to himself as he looked around the room. Finally his eyes settled on the door to Sheriff Barton's office. Sheriff Barton. Andy thought about his father and the irony of it all. He thought about that summer in 1966, and how things had seemed to turn sideways. He thought about his mother and father. He thought about his uncle. Most of all, he thought about Billy West.

August, 1966

I

THE SMELL OF fresh manure from the stables wafted across the designated parking lots as Billy and Anna walked toward the fairground. Children of farmers from all across Jones County had been working hard for months, getting ready for this event. In their parents' footsteps, kids from Anamosa, Monticello, and smaller farming communities were involved in a myriad of 4-H or Future Farmers of America activities. The stables buzzed with activity as the dairy cattle, horses, goats, poultry, livestock, pigs, sheep, and even rabbits were prepared for their scheduled shows and auctions during the weeklong Great Jones County Fair.

It was early evening, and the agricultural events were winding down. With darkness rolling in, the fair took on a different face. The tractor pull had finished, and the stage adjacent to the track was being set for the night's entertainment. Respected and internationally recognized steel guitar player Peter Drake had just cut a record with Elvis and would be taking the stage in a few hours. The beer tent would be full tonight, and the fair would transition to a strange mix of chaos with kids running here and there between games and rides, drunken folks staggering from the beer tent, lovers strolling amongst the crowds, and all the strangely exotic sights and smells that define a county fair.

Temperatures were still pushing ninety degrees. Billy broke into a sweat walking from the car to the fairgrounds. He saw a lemonade stand in the distance, and without saying a word, he and Anna veered through the crowd in that direction. As they got closer, they picked up the pace; relief was not far away.

Stepping up to the Jaycees' lemonade stand, Billy slapped a dollar down on the counter. "Could I have two large lemonades, please?"

Paying the cashier and taking the two drinks, Billy handed one to Anna. They both took a sip, and wide smiles of relief spread across their faces. "Damn, I'd forgotten how good the Jaycees' fresh squeezed lemonade was. It sure does hit the spot," Billy said as the ice cold lemonade immediately had an effect in cooling him down.

Feeling refreshed and with Anna's arm linked in his, the couple began to weave their way down the rows illuminated by a bright array of games and a myriad of food stands. The smells of cotton candy, fried dough, caramel, French fries, and barbeque pork clouded their senses.

"So, my Anna Angel, what prizes do you want me to win for you tonight?" Billy asked with a cocky grin.

"You sure are confident. Do you think you're lucky enough to really win me a prize? You know, I'm not cheap. It's going to have to be something big, something nice," Anna chided as she rested her head on his shoulder.

"Lucky enough? Luck?" Billy feigned mocked indignation. "I don't believe in luck. Well, maybe a little. Luck favors those who work hard…that train hard…that are persistent…and, of course, are as handsome as me." Billy winked at Anna.

Anna surveyed the game booths with the largest prizes hanging high above the carnies' heads. "Let's see. They've got large stuffed lions over there on the ring toss. I kind of like that purple monkey on the balloon dart throw, and there are red, white, and blue bears on the milk bottle toss. Kind of a patriotic theme, bet that's something you'd want." Anna smiled as she perused the aisle of games.

Turning the corner, Anna stopped in her tracks in front of the basket toss. She gasped and beamed in delight. "Oh, there he is. Exactly what I want, a large pink hippopotamus." She bounced with excitement. "Don't you think he needs a momma like me?" Staring at the prize, Anna smiled at the tacky and somewhat heinous looking hippo. "Bartholomew. His name will be Bartholomew, and he'll be my baby."

"Bartholomew? You want me to win you that grotesque mess of fluff and gaudy pink fur? And you've already named it Bartholomew?" Billy shook his head in disbelief, biting back a smile.

"Him," Anna corrected as she pulled away and crossed her arms in defiance.

"Him?"

"Yes, him. Bartholomew's a boy, my boy." She raised her chin in defense, stifling a giggle. "Yes, he's a little overweight, and he looks like he has been through a few fairs."

"A few fairs? I think they accidently ran over him during the tractor pull this afternoon," Billy argued.

"Yes, he may be a little rough around the edges, but he just needs my love," Anna answered with firm conviction.

"Rough around the edges? He's disfigured." Billy struggled to keep a straight face. "His head is squashed, making his eyes look lopsided and somewhat crossed, and he has a strange, goofy smile…and he has what looks like a bald spot above his right eye. One of his front legs is shorter than the other." Billy pointed at the pathetic hippo. "Look at his rear end. Either his tail's coming off, or he's farting stuffing out of his butt." Billy burst into laughter.

Anna slugged Billy in the arm. "Oh Billy, that's just like you, to see the imperfections in everybody. Bartholomew loves to play. He loves the rough and tumble of life. Sure, his body may be a little askew, but that's his character. He just needs his momma to take care of him."

"And that would be you, Miss Anna Jacobs?" Billy asked, raising an eyebrow.

"That's right, Billy West. Now put your money down. Hurry up and win me my baby." Anna pulled Billy forward to the basket toss game booth.

"Step right up, folks. Come on over and give it a try. Three balls for just a quarter. Come on up here, sir, and win one of these great prizes for your lovely lady." The carnie, with a wide toothless grin, waved to Billy and Anna.

Anna leaned closer to Billy, feeling a twinge of fear. The carnie stood in a heavily stained, once white T-shirt and dirty jeans. With greasy hair and dark blue smudged tattoos down both forearms and on the tops of his hands, he again gestured for them to come over. Anna tensed. With Billy's arm in hers, he pulled her a little closer to his body as they neared the game stand.

"Okay mister, talk me through the objective of the game," Billy said, stepping up to the booth then standing with his hands on his hips.

"Too easy, kind sir. Just got to get all three balls into the basket and any prize is yours. If you get two in, you can pick any of these prizes over here on the right, and if you get one softball in, you get any of these prizes on the left." The carnie pointed out all the prizes.

"Okay, let's get started." Billy slapped a quarter down on the counter.

"Now you're talking." The carnie handed Billy the softballs. "Here you go sir, your three softballs. Just got to get them into the basket."

"Thank you, sir. Now stand back, honey. I need my space." Billy held the balls in his hands, feeling the familiar stitching rub against his fingers. "Watch closely and see Billy West in action." Billy confidently grinned as he postured to throw the first softball.

Gently tossing the ball underhanded, the first ball hit the back of the basket, bounced up, hit the top lip of the edge, and fell to the ground. "Damn! That should've gone in!" Billy shouted in frustration as the carnie picked up the ball from the ground.

"Okay, the hippo may be out, but I can still get you one of the gifts on the right." Billy prepared for the second toss. Again, he gently let the ball go, and it hit dead center of the basket and bounced straight out. "Son of a bitch!" Billy cussed as he failed again. "Okay, let me get this one in. These first three balls were for practice so I could get the hang of it." Gently tossing the third ball, it caught the front lip, rolled down into the basket, and bounced back up and out. "Dagnabbit!" Billy cussed again.

"Okay sir, give me three more balls." Billy slapped another quarter on the counter. Billy quickly put two of the balls on the ground and positioned himself to toss the first ball.

"I love watching Billy West in action." Anna smiled as she lightly patted him on his rear.

Billy stopped and lowered his head to kiss her. "I love you, baby, and I'm going to win you that damned hippo if it costs me twenty bucks." They both smiled and then kissed again.

Billy got in position again to throw his first of three softballs and eyed the target. He tucked his tongue into his cheek. Anna smiled; it was the same look he had when he used to pitch in high school. Stretching as far forward over the counter as possible, Billy released the ball, and it caught the top back end of the basket, but the ball again bounced forward and out.

"Shit!" He cussed as the ball rolled to the ground. Leaning forward again, he tossed the second and met the same result. "Judas Priest!"

The carnie stepped up. "Sir, try tossing it as lightly as you can. Watch me." The carnie, from in front of the counter, tossed a softball, caught the lip, and it gently rolled to the back of the basket.

"Okay, let me give it a shot." Beads of sweat dripped off Billy's forehead as he leaned as far forward as possible and gently released the ball. This time he met a different result. The ball rolled to the back of the basket, hit the softball the carnie previously tossed, and remained in the basket.

"Hot damn!" Billy shouted as he excitedly turned to Anna. "Think I'm getting the hang of it." Billy reached in his pocket for another quarter and slapped it on the counter. "Three more balls, sir."

Turning to Anna, Billy whispered, "Think I've got the hang of this. The only reason that last one stayed in was because the carnie's ball broke down the momentum of my toss, and that's why it didn't bounce out." Billy glanced at the basket and tilted his head to Anna as if he was sharing a secret. "If I can get the first ball in the basket, the other two should be a piece of cake. With enough back spin on the ball to catch the front lower lip of the basket, I've got a chance to win."

Dripping with sweat, Billy wiped his arms and hands off on his shirt. Taking the first ball in his hand, he stepped back up to the counter. Leaning forward, Billy gently tossed the ball upward with his palm down, putting a back spin on the ball. The ball perfectly caught the front edge of the basket, rolled to the bottom where it came to a rest.

"Hell yeah!" shouted Billy.

"Nice toss," the carnie responded with a dejected expression.

"Okay now for the next two balls. Should be a piece of

cake." Billy was confident as he wound up with the second ball. Using the same technique as before, Billy successfully tossed the second into the basket. He turned to Anna, placing a kiss on cheek. "Better get ready to receive your newly adopted son. I'm gonna win Bartholomew with this last softball."

Stepping up with the third ball in hand, Billy concentrated. He visualized himself leaning forward and perfectly tossing the ball into the basket. He postured himself and then let the third ball go just as he had seen himself do it in his mind. The ball caught the front lip, bounced off the other two balls in the basket, and came to a rest inside.

"Hot damn!" Billy exclaimed, clapping his hands over his head as if he had won a championship game. He grabbed Anna in his arms, lifting her off her feet and swung her around in a circle.

"Which prize do you want?" The carnie asked in a reserved lower tone.

"We'll take Bartholomew, the large pink hippo." Billy pointed up above the stand at the obese mass of fluff and fur hanging on the rafter.

Pulling down the hippo, the carnie handed it to Billy, who needed both arms to hold the ugly thing. It was much bigger in his arms than it seemed when it was hanging above their heads.

Billy turned to Anna and shoved the pink mass into her arms. "Here you go, baby. Your son, Bartholomew."

It was almost impossible to see her behind it. All Billy saw were Anna's feet, ankles, and a couple of hands barely reaching around each side of the pink fur.

Billy quickly started walking away. Anna could barely walk and stumbled forward with her prize. Already ten feet in front of her, he looked over his shoulder and chuckled. Anna was quite a sight to see as she struggled with the large pink hippo.

"Okay, baby, maybe I should take Big Bart," Billy said with a mischievous grin.

"Ah, do you think?" Anna smiled as she thrust the hippo back to Billy. "I love him, but I think he may need to go on a diet when we get home. The food at the fair has had its effect on him."

"Good thing I drove Pop's truck tonight. No other way we could've gotten our new child home." Billy pulled the hippo up under his arm and hoisted it on his hip. "I worked up a sweat at the basket toss. How about another lemonade?" he asked as he turned back toward the Jaycees' lemonade stand.

After buying their second round of lemonades, the couple continued their stroll through the maze of games and food stands. Looking out across the fairgrounds, Billy saw the Ferris wheel in the distance.

"What do you think we mosey on over that way and get in line for the Ferris wheel?" Billy asked, nudging Anna.

"That sounds wonderful. I don't think I've been on the Ferris wheel since I was twelve. It's a beautiful evening for a ride." Anna's eyes lit up, and she felt butterflies inside as she leaned closer to Billy.

Billy and Anna slowly worked their way across the fairgrounds. When they reached the Ferris wheel, Billy dropped the hippo to the ground and wrapped his arms around Anna as she rested her head against his chest. They stood in their embrace for several minutes before they boarded the ride.

As they waited in line for the ride it quickly became apparent there was no way in hell Anna, Billy, and Bartholomew were all going to fit on one set of seats. The carnie told them as much in a direct tone that came when someone was given a dose of authority over others.

Anna gasped as she pulled away from Billy. "We can't leave Bartholomew here while we go on the ride. We would be endangering our child. Somebody might steal him."

Billy turned back to the carnie running the ride. "Okay, how 'bout another ticket for our son Bart here?"

"Cost you a quarter for another ride, sport." The carnie chuckled with an air of amazement that they were actually stupid enough to buy a ticket for a stuffed animal.

"Damn, having kids is expensive. I've already spent seventy-five cents on him, and it looks like I'm going to be down even more." Billy handed the carnie a quarter while Anna nose crinkled, and she bit her lip to hold back the smile.

Billy strapped the fat pink fur bag into a seat, then Anna and Billy boarded the gondola immediately behind it. As the ride moved, all Billy could see was a large mound of pink fluff. He surmised it was the head on top of the bag of fur. He could also see the little ears poking out on each side and one of his legs jutting out in an awkward angle to the sky.

Billy and Anna immediately broke out in giggles. "That hippo on the Ferris wheel is one of the silliest things I've ever seen," Billy said, and Anna agreed as they both laughed even more.

Reaching the apex of the ride, the couple looked out over the fairgrounds. They could see everything—the food stands and game booths, rides, the race track, the stage, the beer tent, and the stables.

"Hell of a view up here, ain't it?" Billy said as he wrapped his arm around Anna and pulled her close into him.

"Sure is, honey." Anna smiled, looking deeply into her man's eyes. Leaning forward, she kissed him, and Billy responded in kind. After what seemed like an eternity, Anna sighed with a wide grin on her face.

"I love you, Anna Angel," Billy said with an easy smile.

"Oh Billy, I love you too." Anna snuggled closer to Billy.

Anna and Billy were suspended above the din of the fair. In the distance, Billy and Anna heard Peter Drake playing his hit song on guitar, "Forever." The melody of love and eternity softly floated over the crowds below.

Billy leaned forward and kissed Anna's forehead, and she rested her head on his shoulder. They were silent for a few minutes as the ride continued smoothly moving them up and down over the wheel. Anna could hear his heartbeat, and she was certain he could hear hers. Again, the wheel stopped, and they were suspended at the apex of the circle, gently rocking. They both tilted back in the swinging chair and gazed upon the expanse of stars, spread deep across the summer sky. At that moment, it seemed as if everything had stopped. Time stopped. The world had stopped. It was just the two of them, rocking gently, suspended above time, above worry, above the world.

There were no more yesterdays or tomorrows, just two hearts connected, interwoven together. They were in love. They were one.

Billy took a deep breath and let it out slowly. "You're all I want in this world. You've always been and always will be my only love."

Anna gazed up to Billy. His face was so serious—more intense than she'd ever seen. Yet there was a subtle sadness touching his eyes. Something desperate from the past lingered behind his stare—where the truth always was.

Billy lifted his hand and gently brushed Anna's hair from her face. "I can't see myself living this life without you in it. I don't want to. I don't ever want to have you away from me." Billy ran his fingers through her hair and leaned forward and kissed her softly. "Anna Angel, will you have me? Will you have me at your side? At your side until the stars fall from the sky, and we leave this world? Until it all fades away, will you be with me?" Billy slid his hand down and grasped Anna's hand. "Will you still love me when these bones grow old and the wrinkles come? Will you always love me? Will you still hold my old, feeble, weathered hand when it trembles with age?"

Anna pressed her lips against his. "Oh, yes, Billy, yes…" She wrapped her arms around him, sobbing. Her tears streamed down her cheeks, and they mixed with his as their cheeks pressed against each other in the embrace. "Yes…yes…Billy, I love you. You're my man. You'll always be my man. All I want. All I will ever want. I'll love you always…always." Anna sobbed as Billy held her tight in his arms.

Everything seemed to have stopped in that moment as Billy held her in his arms. They were suspended at the top of the Ferris wheel under the canopy of stars. She finally pulled away and looked up into his eyes and smiled. Not a word was said. The large machine moved again. They were swimming together in each other's eyes, swirling, connected, round and round with the Ferris wheel. They looked out to the heavens, above the buzzing noise and lights of the fairground, to the moon and the stars that shown brilliant that promised forever.

"Always, my Anna Angel. Always," Billy whispered.

Anna snuggled even closer in joyful, silent wonder.

The ride continued for several more minutes.

The Ferris wheel slowed as they went up and over the apex one last time. Finally, they came to a rest with their gondola, stopped at the bottom and their feet mere inches above the ground.

"Going to bring it around one more time so you can get that damned pink thing off my ride." The carnie snarled, breaking the bliss of their moment.

The ride stopped, and Billy stepped over to retrieve the stuffed animal. Folks, in line for the ride behind Anna, snickered when they realized that an entire gondola was taken up by the heinous hippo. But she didn't care. She watched her man with pride, with love, with eternal promise.

With Bartholomew hoisted up under his arm, Billy took Anna's hand, and they ventured back into the labyrinth of rides, games, and food.

"Well my love, what's next?" Billy kissed her cheek.

"Perhaps another ride? Maybe the Tilt-A-Whirl or maybe something a little slower like the carousel?" Billy pointed toward the other rides.

"Those lines look so long. Let's just stroll. Kind of nice to take in all the sights and have you right here at my side." Anna laced her arm in his and rested her head on his shoulder.

The evening was cooling down, and the fair had picked up. People were everywhere. Billy and Anna saw many familiar faces and waved or nodded but didn't stop to talk. They walked hand in hand, confident together, and soaked up the wonder of the evening. They could hear the band in the distance, Peter Drake's steel guitar ringing out above the buzz of the fair.

ꕤ

Up ahead Billy and Anna saw a larger than normal crowd gathered around one of the game booths. A loud cheer rang out from the group as someone obviously won something. Peering over the shoulders of the folks, Billy recognized why they were all gathered around. Two men were hurling their baseballs at the three heavy milk bottles in attempts to knock them down.

Billy heard the men in the group huddled around them. "My money's on Josh. That boy can throw," one of them whispered.

"Okay, I got you. Two bucks on Josh Sanders, but not only does he have to beat the kid from Cascade, he has to knock down all three bottles." The men shook hands on the deal.

Billy stood up on his toes to see over the group of gamblers. "Well I'll be damned," Billy announced and let out a laugh.

"Is that? Is that who I think it is?" Anna was unable to get a clear view.

Billy nodded. In the middle of the group stood his old friend and high school rival, Joshua Sanders. Josh was Billy's age and from the neighboring town, Monticello. They had played against each other in just about every sport imaginable. Both had been pitchers on their baseball teams. Both had been quarterbacks on their football teams. They had run against each other in track, and both had played as forwards on their respective basketball teams. If anyone could give Billy a run for his money in the state of Iowa, it was Joshua Sanders. Ironically, they had grown up eleven miles from each other.

They had routinely faced each other in conference championships and on occasion against each other at state level competitions. In their junior and senior years, the conference, as well as the state, had witnessed one of the best rivalries in recent history. During the regular season, Josh had occasionally beaten Billy, but in the post-season, Billy had always beaten Josh and his team. There had been something about Billy that had made him special. He had found an edge on Josh, and he had figured out a way to win when it had mattered the most.

Billy watched Josh throw at the milk bottles. Seeing his wind up reminded Billy of all those games they had played against each other years ago. His mind drifted back into his memories of Miller's Farm and the summer before his senior year in high school.

The farm was equal distance from both Anamosa and Monticello and Boss Miller hired from both communities. He needed a large pool to choose from because he couldn't usually keep the kids for more than one or two weeks. Bailing hay, walking beans, and laying fence posts was good money, but it was tough work. Most couldn't handle the hours, the heat, and the backbreaking labor, and would seek employment elsewhere.

It was hard work for hard men, and Billy loved it. He would be up at four in the morning, shoveling slop, milking the cows, and then by noon out in the direct, intense heat of the sun bailing hay. Day after day, it required waking up in the darkness to the early coolness of a summer morning, and by noon, he would be soaked with sweat in the midday sun. It was nearly impossible for most, but Billy thrived on the challenge and the sense of accomplishment.

When the sun would drift down on the tassels of corn in the western sky and evening came on, Billy was usually covered with dirt and grime, soaked with sweat, and totally spent in happy exhaustion. Most days, they worked till dinner, ate, and then went back to work, finishing around eight in the evening. The only exceptions were on Sundays when they didn't work (Boss Miller insisted on it being a day of church and rest) and on Fridays and Saturdays when they concluded their work before dinner. This afforded them the opportunity to go out on the weekends, find trouble, and spend some of their hard earned money.

One Friday, a group of boys from Anamosa, responsible for walking beans, was caught out behind the barn, sleeping in the shade. Boss Miller was not happy about it, and consequently everyone had to work until ten o'clock at night to get all the work done and ruined the start of their weekend.

Robby Busman, or "Buzzy" as he was called, was the ring leader of the group from Anamosa caught sleeping. As the entire group was finishing up and walking toward their cars to leave, Billy decided to set things right.

"Hey Buzzy, I want to talk to you and your crew," Billy said,

motioning Buzzy off to the side of the group.

"Ah come on, West, I'm too tired to listen to your rah-rah bullshit. I'm going home," Buzzy fired back at Billy.

"Okay, Buzzy, go home but don't come back. You and your three buddies here cost all of us four hours of work today. I don't want to see your ass here again. Collect your money from Boss and get the hell out of here," Billy ordered.

"Who the hell do you think you are, West? You ain't gonna talk to me like this. Especially after those boys from Monticello been shamming out here all week," Buzzy said, motioning toward the group from Monti.

"Buzzy, I don't know what you're talking about. What I do know is that you sloughed off your work today, and it cost all of us. I don't care where the hell you come from or what team you play on. Out here standards are standards, and I ain't gonna tolerate what you did." Billy stood firm with his hands on his hips.

"Is that so? What you gonna do about, West?" Buzzy squared his shoulders and closed the gap between them, preparing for a fight.

"You don't want to go there with me." Billy stepped forward and towered over Buzzy. "I'm giving you the option to walk away." Billy motioned with his head. "Now go tell Boss that you quit and want to collect your wages."

Buzzy looked up at Billy, saw bold fearlessness in his eyes, and knew he was in trouble. He spit on the ground and took a step backward. "To hell with you. To hell with all of you! Come on boys. Let's get out of here. I don't want to work around some pussy-foot like West."

Buzzy motioned to the other three in his crew. "Besides, I hear Old Man Gelkie is hiring downtown. Come on."

The three boys didn't move. They looked at Buzzy and then at Billy

West.

"Buzzy, you know my pa will whoop my ass if I walk away from this job…especially when he finds out that it was cause I wasn't doing my share," Jimmy Parks said, kicking dirt with his shoe.

The others shook their head in agreement. They were staying.

"Aw, to hell with you, to hell with you all!" Buzzy said as he turned toward the farm house to collect his wages.

"Guess we need a ride home. Can you help us out, Billy?" Jimmy Parks asked as they turned toward the cars.

"Looks like it is true what they say about those Anamosa queers—can't work together as a team, just…" Eddy Jones chimed in.

"Shut your mouth, Jones!" Josh Sanders stepped forward and put his finger in Eddy's chest.

"What? You turning soft to the other side, Sanders?" Jones rebutted.

Sanders turned to one of the boys from Monti. "This ain't about sides. It's about standards. I know you, for one, were out behind the barn sleeping two days ago. Now, not another damned word." Josh clenched his fists and stepped forward to within inches of Eddy Jones.

"Sanders, you ain't got a hair on your balls if you're siding with them Anamosa queers," Jones said as he took a step backward.

"I'll pretend I didn't hear what you just said. I'll give you one chance to get in your car and get the hell out of here. One more word from you, or from any of you, and you'll have to deal with me," Josh said, addressing the group.

The boys from Monti turned slowly and quietly got in their cars then drove away. The boys from Anamosa did the same.

Billy and Joshua stood there alone, looking at each other. Not a word was said. They shook their heads in disbelief and then got in their cars and left.

That event marked the beginning of their friendship. The following days, Billy and Josh started coordinating together to help Boss Miller efficiently run the farm. After about a month, multiple sets of kids had come to work at the farm, found the work too hard, and left. By late July, Josh and Billy were the only original workers left. They worked well together, trusted each other, and led different teams each day.

Boss Miller trusted them too and delegated most of the work to them to coordinate and complete. After a long day of bailing, Boss Miller called the boys back up to the house. Boss handed each of them a beer.

"Boys, been a great summer. Sure couldn't have done everything we did without you two leading the team. Never thought we would get as far as we did. I was running the numbers last night, and I'm so far ahead right now, I'll be out of work by fall. I'm going to have to invent some things to do just so I'll be busy during the winter months." Boss Miller smiled in appreciation for all their hard work.

"Thanks, Boss," Josh replied.

Taking a sip, Billy sighed as he looked out to the sun setting in the west. "Josh, what you got going on this weekend?" Billy asked.

"Nothing really. What are you thinking?"

"Maybe tomorrow, cutting work a little early, getting the girls, grabbing a case of beer, and heading out to Fremont Bridge…that is, if Boss will allow us to cut out early," Billy said, looking up to Boss Miller for approval as he took another sip of his beer.

"I think you boys have earned it. Damn, I ain't been out to Fremont since I was a kid. They still got the rope swing out there?" Boss asked.

"Sure do. Still hanging strong. I think it is one of the best swimming holes in Jones County," Billy answered.

"Going to be close to one hundred degrees tomorrow. I'm in," Josh took a drink of his beer. "We'll try to get out of here by three and link-up there at five."

The following weeks, Billy and Josh continued to run the farm during the week and spent their weekends together. Swimming at Fremont, canoeing down the Maquoketa River, and fishing the Wapsi filled their free time. They never talked about the upcoming year and all the sporting events where they would face each other. They respected and understood each other. The competitions would come, and one would win and one would lose, but they dared not mar the respect they had for each other with what the future would bring.

After graduation from high school, the two young men went their separate ways. Both were offered scholarships to play baseball at the University of Iowa. Billy also had offers to play for the Chicago Cubs' minor league team, but with his aspirations to join the army he turned down all the offers. Josh accepted the scholarship, and after playing several years for the Hawkeyes, he was getting the attention of major league scouts.

Billy smiled as he reflected on that summer out at Miller's Farm. There had been so much ahead of them. So much hope and excitement for what the world would bring. He smiled at what he hadn't known then—how innocent he really had been, how much he had changed, or had he changed? Billy wondered as he watched Josh throw another baseball at the milk bottles. The crowd let out cheers as Josh defeated another opponent and money exchanged between the gamblers.

It had been three years, and now at the fair, they would meet again. Billy suddenly felt uncertain of himself. After three long years, so much had happened. Billy thought he was a different man, or was he? He stood there, looking over the shoulders of men as they bet on who would win. It was so good to see his old friend.

Billy wondered if Josh would feel the same. He wondered if Josh had changed. Would they hit it off as they had several years ago? So much water over the dam. Billy knew he had changed. The war, his injury, and all the wonderful and awful things he had seen and done. Billy tried to push out all those ugly and beautiful things that were still nagging in his memories. They had changed him.

Billy was sure Josh had changed too. A college man. The big man on campus. Success. Big league scouts recruiting him. He was going places, but had their friendship survived? Only one way to find out, Billy thought as he held Anna's hand and maneuvered his way up to the front of the group.

ꕤ

"All right, who's next? Who can beat the young champ here? Step right up. Who can out gun this world class pitcher?" The carnie at the booth announced as Josh beat another competitor and beckoned for another person to come forward to keep the money coming in.

Stepping up behind Josh, Billy said, "Sanders, you ain't got a hair on your balls if you're siding with them Anamosa queers."

Josh smiled from ear to ear in surprise, recognizing Billy's voice, and remembered that night out at Miller's Farm. Turning around he opened his arms and embraced Billy in a full man-hug.

"Holy cow! If it ain't the great Billy West. The Boy Scout is back from saving the world!" Shaking Billy's hand and then embracing him again in another hug, Josh pulled away and looked to Billy's side. "And the stunningly beautiful Anna Jacobs. You guys are still together? What in the heck do you see in this big lug? Don't you know what they say about the boys from Anamosa?" Josh smiled as he looked at both of them. "It's so good to see you. Ah hell, let me get a hug from you too, Anna." Josh dragged Anna into a long embrace and then he let her go. "So damn good to see you guys. I was just talking to Jimmy Forrester the other day about the amazing Billy West, and what had become of you. Best pitcher, best quarterback, hell, the best athlete this county ever produced. That's a compliment coming from a guy like me," Josh smiled as he patted Billy on the shoulder.

"Billy's home on leave. He'll be home for about three more weeks," Anna grabbed Billy's hand and pulled him to her side.

"Still out there slaying the dragons and changing the world. Billy West the Boy Scout. Damn, it's good to see you, Billy," Josh said with genuine affection. "Say, don't know if you've met Charlotte." Josh turned and reached for his girl's hand. "Charlotte Sims. Meet Billy West and Miss Anna Jacobs." Josh introduced his girl to Billy and Anna. "Charlotte, here before you is the only true son of a bitch who has always found a way to take yours truly to the cleaners. This is the one and only, the great Billy West." Josh said as he pulled Charlotte to his side.

"I've heard so much about you." Charlotte smiled, holding out her hand. "And now to meet you in person, at the Great Jones County Fair. This is simply delicious."

Billy took her hand and lightly shook it.

"You'll have to mind his manners, Charlotte. The Boy Scout here has been chasing the woogie-boogie monster around the world to protect us all. It's not often he gets to interact with a sophisticated city girl like yourself." Josh put his arm around Charlotte and pulled her closer.

"What part of Chicago are you from, Charlotte?" Billy asked.

"Well my dear Billy, what makes you think I come from Chicago?" Charlotte asked with her hands on her hips and cocked her head with a little modern-woman attitude.

"Oh, something in your voice. Not quite a Chicago accent, at least not anymore. Must be all the book reading and lectures going on down at the University of Iowa that's pulled the 'city of big shoulders' out of you," Billy speculated, rubbing his chin with his fingers. Billy cleared his throat and started to recite Carl Sandberg's famous poem, Chicago. "Come and show me another city with lifted head singing so proud to be alive and coarse and strong and cunning."

"Billy West, you're full of surprises. I didn't know they taught Sandburg in the Boy Scouts," Charlotte said with a flirtatious tone, tapping Billy on the shoulder.

Anna's eyes dropped and shoulders stiffened. She immediately had a sincere distaste for Charlotte Sims. She was a pretentious college girl who was overwhelmingly full of herself. She didn't even look at Anna or introduce herself but had no problem flirting with Billy—her Billy. Anna thought Billy was handling himself well, but there was a negative current with Miss

Sims that seemed all wrong, especially for Josh. She was not the kind of girl he would date. Had he really changed that much? Anna didn't think so, but something with Charlotte rubbed her the wrong way.

A twinkle formed in Charlotte's eye. "For old times' sake, how about a little competition?"

"Aw honey, no…honey, why do we have to do something like that? I ain't seen Billy in years, and you already want me to compete with him? I was thinking more along the lines of the four of us heading over yonder to the beer tent." Josh motioned toward the beer tent.

"That sounds real good. I could definitely go for a couple of brews," Billy agreed.

Anna was not going to be outdone by this high talking, stuck up, college girl. "Yep, that's what I thought. The great Billy West doesn't have it anymore. What's that you used to say? No guts, no glory? Just a bunch of talking…guess now we know." Anna crossed her arms and turned her nose up at Billy.

Billy studied Anna with a puzzled look on his face as he tried to figure out what the hell she was up to.

"Guess that's what both you boys are, just a bunch of big talkers. Never have seen Josh back down from any challenge." Charlotte put her hands on her hips and stared down her pointing nose at Anna.

Josh and Billy looked at each other in mutual frustration. "I'd really like to go over to the tent and have a few beers." Josh looked at Charlotte, but she stepped away from him.

Rolling his eyes, Josh sighed in resignation. "If we do this, will you stop nagging us and allow us to go to the tent?"

"Best of three pitches, and we'll call it an evening," Billy raised his hands, surrendering to Anna.

"Ladies and gentlemen, step right up. We've got a little competition going on," the carnie announced and then leaned toward the young men. "What are your names?" Billy and Josh responded, and the carnie continued, "A little competition between Josh Sanders and Billy West. Step right up and watch as these two pitchers face off in what promises to be a duel for the ages…"

Whispers escalated to excited talk in the group around the booth as everyone realized Billy West was going to compete against the hometown Monticello favorite, Josh Sanders. Within minutes, the group of people tripled to well over one hundred. Bets were made, and money prepared as the crowd grew with excitement.

"I can't believe we're doing this." Josh shook his head in disappointment.

"When we're done with this little charade, we're going to the beer tent, and I do believe that you'll be driving home tonight," Billy added as he turned to Anna.

Anna smiled. She knew that despite their talk, Billy and Josh took every competition seriously. Even with his injury, Billy would find a way to win. He always did, and he would prove something to the conceited Miss Charlotte Sims. Billy wasn't just a soldier, and he wasn't a washed-up has been. He would prove he still had it, that he was still as good if not better than Josh, and that if he wanted to, he could be pitching in the major leagues right now. Billy was her man, and she was going to protect him and prove they weren't just a couple of country bumpkins.

Grabbing a baseball, Billy rolled his right arm forward, loosening it up. "Do you need a few practice throws to warm up, Billy?" Josh asked.

"Nah, let's get this over with, so we can go drink beers into the evening," Billy responded, rolling the ball in his hands, feeling the stitching under his fingers and the curb against his palm.

Standing about twenty feet back from the stacked milk bottles, Billy and Josh took their positions.

"Best out of three pitches. We have to knock down all the bottles for the strike to count," Josh explained.

"Okay, got it. Want to flip a coin to decide who throws first?" Billy asked.

"Sure." Josh pulled out a quarter. "Heads, I throw first. Tails, you throw first."

"Sounds like a plan. Go ahead and flip it," Billy responded.

Flipping the quarter up and catching it in his right hand, Josh slapped it down on the top of his left hand and announced, "Heads! Looks like I go first."

Grabbing a baseball, Josh rolled his arms in final preparation to throw. In his memory, Billy could see Josh on the pitcher's mound, commanding the field all those years ago. Just as if he was in an actual game, Josh hit his wind-up and hurled the ball at the bottles. Striking them square in the middle, the bottles blasted off the pedestal to the ground.

"Steeeeerike!" The carnie announced just like an umpire at a major league ball game.

It was Billy's turn. Holding the ball in his right hand, he wasted no time, hit his wind-up, and threw the ball right into the middle of the three bottles. All three crashed to the ground. Anna was struck at how natural it was for Billy. As he threw the ball, her memory flashed back to him on the mound in his baseball uniform. It was the same motion, the same perfection. After all he had been through, this was still a large part of Billy.

"Steeeeerike!" The carnie announced again and the crowd went wild.

Silent, both men concentrated and were in the zone. Each stood, preparing their second throws with serious looks on their faces. The crowd around them grew with onlookers.

Both pitchers threw their second ball, and both knocked down the bottles in perfect order. Now grabbing their final baseballs, both men focused on their last toss. Again, both knocked down the milk bottles with perfect accuracy.

"Well, guess that's it," Josh turned to Billy with a smile and shook his hand.

Over two hundred people gathered around them, and many had grown restless if not down-right angry. Money had been passed and deals made. It had to be finished.

"You got to finish what you started!" one of the men hollered.

"Yeah, nobody won. Finish the game!" another yelled.

"Yeah, finish the game!" someone repeated.

The crowd picked up, chanting. "Finish the game! Finish the game! Finish the game! Finish the game!"

The chants grew louder and grabbed the attention of

everyone in the area, including those in the beer tent. More and more people gathered around.

"Well my friend, looks like we need to finish what we started, or else we'll have a riot on our hands." Billy looked around at the increasingly hostile crowd. "I really don't want to get run out of town tonight."

"You know Billy, we could be here all night with the way this game is set up. Let's make it interesting. What do you say we make this regulation length?" Josh asked.

"I'm good with that. The sooner we're done and can get over to the beer tent the better."

Turning from the game booth, the two men paced off sixty feet from the milk bottles to a makeshift pitcher's mound. The crowd grew more restless and louder in the realization that Josh and Billy were going to lengthen the distance. The word about the dual between these two slingers quickly spread, and the crowd neared three hundred. More bets were placed as Josh and Billy double checked the distance and then marked a line that represented the rubber on a pitcher's mound.

Anna and Charlotte looked on, acting as if it was a silly competition, but both secretly yearned with everything they had for their man to win.

With the new distance set, the two pitchers prepared to throw. "Well Billy, should we get this over with?" Josh asked.

"Age before beauty, old pal." Billy grinned.

"Well, at least I got something on you, buddy. You know, with age comes wisdom," Josh responded.

"I'm glad you're learning something from all that book

reading and fraternity bonding at the university." Billy laughed and lightly slugged him in the shoulder.

Both men chuckled as a silence spread over the crowd. Josh started his wind-up. Hurling the baseball, it struck right in the middle of the three milk bottles. Two of the bottles flew off the table and one remained standing on the pedestal. The crowd exploded with applause.

"Well champ, looks like I left one standing. You're going to have to top that," Josh said.

"I sure am thirsty. I'll make sure this throw ends this game," Billy responded, tipping his chin up in confidence.

"Now don't go throwing the game. We got all these on-lookers and got to at least make it look legit. When you miss, at least make it close." Josh looked out over the crowd. "I got a feeling there's more wagered on this game than just our ladies' pride. You do something half-baked now, and we could both get run out of town."

"No worries, buddy. I'll make sure this one counts." Billy glanced at the crowd.

Looking at Anna, Billy smiled and winked. He didn't even look toward the milk bottles as he hit his wind-up. Not taking his eyes off of her, he fired the ball at the intended target, striking the milk bottles square in the middle and sending all three in different directions off of the small pedestal.

Billy never even looked toward the game booth to see if he hit his target. He knew as soon as he released the ball. His smile grew wider, and he winked at Anna again, then turned to shake Josh's hand. The crowd exploded in a deafening applause.

"Well, guess that did it. Now let's get a beer," Billy said to Josh. Although his words were drowned out by the cheers of the people around them, Josh nodded his head in understanding. The two competitors gripped each other's hands for a few more seconds. Both laughed and shook their heads. It was as if they were in high school again.

Releasing their grip, they turned to their ladies. Anna beamed, practically jumping into Billy's arms. Charlotte stood defeated with arms crossed. Josh stepped forward and tried to take her by the arm.

Unsuccessful, he threw up his hands and glanced over at Billy with a look of desperation. "I'm ready for a beer if you are."

Billy kissed Anna in victory and set her down. Then both couples made their way through the large crowd of onlookers. Walking toward the tent, they were finally far enough from the cacophony of cheers that they were able to hear themselves talk.

Charlotte was the first to open her mouth. "Well boys, that was a fine display of sportsmanship. Josh, I don't think I've ever seen you lose at anything." She gave Billy a sideways glance and put her arm around Josh. "My Joshua is so competitive. This has to be eating him up. He hates to lose."

"Charlotte dear, can you stop talking for eight seconds? I want to slip into the beer tent and enjoy some time with a dear friend I haven't seen for years." With Josh's response everyone got quiet. Billy pulled Anna closer to his side, and almost simultaneously, Charlotte pulled away from Josh, dejected.

"All right old buddy, let me buy the first round," Josh said as they found some space at one of the picnic tables under the tent. The tent was loud, hot, and nearly bursting at the seams with people. Four beers in plastic cups were placed in front of the two couples before Josh could order.

"Well that was quick service." Anna nodded impressed.

Looking around the tent, they saw a couple of familiar faces from the game booth raise their beer in appreciation. Josh and Billy nodded to them and raised their beer in a toast to thank them for the kind gesture.

"Guess we could be drinking for free tonight," Billy stated confidently, watching the tent fill up with most of the crowd from the game booth.

"Sure is good to see you, Billy," Josh said with a sincere sense of love in his voice. "What has it been, three years? Think it was that week before you went off to basic training. I double dated with you and Anna out at Prairieburg in the Prairie Moon Ballroom." "We got so hammered that night. I was with Cindy Burnett, remember?" Josh grinned.

"Oh yeah, Windy Cindy. Who can forget?" Billy chuckled.

"Windy Cindy?" Charlotte asked with interest.

"Old Windy Cindy. She farted in my truck the whole way from Monti to Prairieburg. Smelled so bad we had to ride with the windows down the whole trip." Billy crinkled his nose and fanned his hand in front of his face.

Anna slugged Billy in the arm. "You guys are cruel. That's nasty. I can't believe you would say things like that about a girl."

"Anna, it's true. You remember. The smell was so putrid you almost climbed into the back of the truck." Billy leaned toward Josh with a puzzled look on his face. "What ever happened to Windy Cindy?"

"She married Wes Harms. Lives on their farm out north of Monti. Got two kids already, and I think another one on the way," Josh answered, sipping his beer.

"Good for her, making babies. As I recall, she was pretty good at practicing with you." Billy grinned. Anna's eyes widened, and she slugged him in the arm again for his snide comment.

"Yeah, if you drive up 151 toward Cascade and there's a strong wind out of the west, you can usually smell her as you drive past their farm." Josh burst out in laughter.

"You know, we ought to hit Prairieburg while I'm home. What do you think, Josh? Is the place still hopping?" Billy asked.

"Hell yeah! Jessie and the Plainsmen play there almost every weekend. I hear the place still fills up when they play."

"That band is still together? Hard to believe they're still playing."

"Billy, this is Iowa. What else are they going to do? Anyway, heard they got a record deal or something and have been trying to cut an album," Josh said.

"Good for them. I think Prairieburg sounds great. A little music, a little dancing, and a little bit of fun afterward." Billy smiled and winked at Anna.

"I could go for some dancing," Charlotte piped in. "But when we go out, all Josh ever wants to do is go to the bar and drink beer." Charlotte scowled at Josh as he drained his beer in a final gulp.

"Baby, that's what we do in Iowa. That's how we socialize. This ain't Chicago. We don't drink cocktails, attend galas, and talk about the stock market." Josh raised his eyebrows as he mocked Charlotte.

"Well, I think Prairieburg sounds like a grand idea. I haven't gone dancing in years," Anna said as she tried to redirect the conversation.

Another round of beer was placed on the table in front of them.

"Hot damn! Looks like you were right, Billy. We're going to drink for free. I think we should come here again tomorrow night. What do you think? Another competition? Maybe the ring toss or the coin toss? Hell, we could come here all week and drink for free," Josh said.

"I'm up for it, old buddy." Billy put his arm around Josh.

The two raised their fresh beer and toasted each other.

"To my brother, Billy West."

"To my brother, Josh Sanders."

The two men drank the beer in unison and slammed down the cups after they drained them.

"Could be a long night, ladies. I sure am glad you volunteered to drive us home," Billy said with a devilish smile.

Josh shook his head as he got the waitress's attention and ordered another round of beer.

II

ANNA GAZED OUT the window as they sped down Cass Highway toward Prairieburg. She was a little annoyed they were going out with Josh and Charlotte. Josh was a good man, and he made Billy laugh like she had not seen in years. The relationship with Josh was good for Billy; he needed it. Just this week, she had come to realize that Josh brought a stronger, sharper edge to Billy that she couldn't provide.

Maybe she was jealous of Josh. He could touch a chord with Billy that she didn't know was there. It wasn't negative; it made Billy a better man. It was a brotherhood she didn't quite understand. Billy had grown up an only child. He was competitive and excelled. He had been popular, but his discipline had separated him from his peers, and he never had any close friends. Despite those around him, the accolades, the attention, and the success growing up, he had been very much alone.

Anna thought back to a couple nights ago at the county fair. After too many hours in the beer tent, she had driven Billy home. Although inebriated, he'd been happy. During the drive home, he had talked about Josh, about their lasting friendship, and how good it was to see him again. He had mused about Charlotte and how annoying she was. Anna had remembered a part of their conversation just before he dozed off.

"He's my iron," Billy mumbled as he looked to Anna with his eyes half open.

"What?" she asked, not sure she understood what he meant.

"You're my best friend, Anna Angel. You're the love of my life, my companion for life. You're a part of me, my better half, and you always will be…" Billy rambled. "But he's my iron." Billy's tone was confident. "A man needs iron."

"Your iron?" Anna repeated, questioning Billy. She wondered if this was the beer talking or if they were having a meaningful conversation.

"Yep. You know what the Good Book says, iron sharpens iron. Josh does that for me." Anna looked at Billy. Even in the darkness, she knew his eyes were closed. He was drifting in and out of the alcohol induced sleep.

"Oh, okay, honey. Why don't you close your eyes now and get some rest." She comforted Billy though she knew he was already well on his way to being sound asleep. He leaned into her side. Within seconds his breathing got heavy, and she knew he was out.

Now, driving toward Prairieburg, she realized that was it. Although he had said it in his drunkenness and would never admit it sober, Billy needed Josh in different way than he needed her. She leaned over and kissed his cheek. Billy smiled, keeping his eyes forward on the road. He pulled Anna close to his side. She leaned into him, resting her head on his shoulder, and smiled.

However, Anna was annoyed and not because of Charlotte Sims—although she freely offered plenty of reasons. It was because she had to share her Billy with someone else. She was angry at herself for her jealousy.

Her anger slipped away as she nestled into Billy. She looked out across the fields as the sun merged on the tassels of corn. An orange-red pinkness stretched across the horizon. With the sun setting across Iowa, the sky was absolutely breathtaking.

Sadness stirred in Anna's chest. The summer moved too fast. So many questions were still unanswered. Their future loomed like a dark cloud ahead of them. Marriage, the army, Vietnam…it all scared her. She closed her eyes and leaned tighter against Billy. Anna didn't want to count the days before he would leave again, but she did. The pain it would bring was too hard to think about. She wanted to slow everything down, to stop time, to have her Billy all to herself. Time was slipping away, and here they were, going to the Prairie Moon Ballroom of all places.

She wasn't jealous of Charlotte. She wasn't even jealous of Josh. She just didn't want to share Billy with anyone else. She wanted to bottle them both up together, away from time, and away from the world.

But she would give in to Billy like everyone else did. No one could tell Billy no, not because of fear but because of love. Billy had a way about him that no one else had. He was selfless, and it made you want to please him. She knew this better than anyone. It was his gift. Somehow he was always able to make anyone want to be the best version of themselves for him. It was no surprise to her that he was already a sergeant in the army, decorated for valor in combat, and that he was being groomed to be an officer. The army had figured it out too, and they would make the most of it.

She felt a current of anger course in her veins. The damn army. They were taking Billy from her again. She closed her eyes tighter to try to stop the negative thoughts from coming. She had her Billy now, and she trusted him; she trusted his love. He loved her. Nothing could touch that or ever take that away. That would be enough.

"Do you think Josh will actually be able to pull Charlotte out to Prairieburg?" Billy smiled a cynical grin.

"Not sure if she'll find a dry martini anywhere in Jones County." Anna's tone was sarcastic as her eyes fluttered up to meet Billy.

"I just don't get it." Anna sat upright in her seat. "Their relationship is all wrong. Like you, Josh is a straight shooter. What does he see in her?"

Billy gave Anna a sideways glance, and a grin began to curve at the corners of his mouth. "I can think of a couple things."

Anna slugged Billy's arm. "Is that all we are to men? A place to put that thing? I really don't know how you all walk around with that little thing getting in the way all the time." Billy's smile widened with his eyes on the road, not saying a word.

Anna's voice became serious. "He has to see through her façade and know, at the heart of it all, she's a selfish person."

"You're right, Anna darling. I suspect his fling with her is probably temporary and won't last." Billy glanced at Anna and then turned his eyes back to the road. "You know, not everyone finds the love of their life their first time around. In fact, I'll bet most never do," Billy added as his tone became solemn. Billy pulled Anna close to his side again. "But I did. And I'm never going to let you go, Anna Angel."

She looked up at him. He had a serious, confident look in

his eyes as he steered the truck on the winding road toward their destination. That would be enough. Billy's love would be all she would ever need in this world.

"Holy-moly!" Billy broke the moment and exclaimed as they approached Prairieburg. "Look at all the cars. This place is packed!" Billy surveyed the lot adjacent to the ballroom. "The lot's already full, and it ain't even nine o'clock yet. Looks like folks are already parking in the hayfield on the backside."

Parking the truck, both Billy and Anna stepped out and walked across the field toward the dancehall. Their pace picked up as they heard the rumble of the band inside playing.

Anna stopped and pulled Billy close. "Kiss me, Billy West. Kiss me like you love me." She smiled, and Billy's lips touched hers. "Let's stop all this. Let's run away. Me and you. Away from Josh and Charlotte and Iowa and the army. Run away with me, darling," she said as she held Billy's hands and looked deep into his eyes.

"Oh Anna, what am I going to do with you, baby?" he asked, tapping his forehead against hers.

Anna pulled away from him and looked up at the stars beginning to shine overhead. "Look at them, Billy. Just look at the stars coming out tonight. Aren't they beautiful?"

Billy glanced at Anna. Her face was full of magic. He could picture her as a little girl with that excited look. This was probably how she looked when opening presents on Christmas morning. She was grown up now, grown into a beautiful woman, his woman.

Billy pulled Anna close, wrapping his arms around her

tightly and looked up into the darkening sky. "Look over there. I see Cassiopeia, and there's the Big Dipper. And over there, that's Orion. Do you see it, honey?"

Anna nodded her head as she rested in his embrace. She really didn't see them, but it didn't matter. She was with Billy and wondered if there was anything he couldn't do?

"Pick one out for us. Pick one out for us, my love. Find our star. Find one we can always turn to and remember this moment, remember our love…"

"Oh Anna, you know that…" Billy started to say something, but then he looked down into Anna's eyes. They were full of tears again, stopping him mid-sentence. She was sincere. He thought for a moment, looked back up, and scanned the heavens.

"Okay, Anna Angel. I've got it. I've got our star. Now let me show you," he said.

Anna smiled, looking up into Billy's eyes and then up into the stars. "Now, do you see the Big Dipper, over there?" Billy pointed at it in the sky. "Do you see the long handle and the kind of square cup at the end?" He followed the lines of the constellation with his fingers, and Anna nodded her head when she recognized it.

"Now hold your hand up and put your fingers on the edge of the cup. Like me, see how I'm doing this?" Billy showed her, his arm extended out and his hand up toward the sky. Anna nodded and mimicked him.

"Now, go five hand lengths to the right of where your hand is, and you'll find a star standing alone. Do you see it?" Billy asked. It was a dim star, but Anna did see it. She nodded again.

"That's our star, my love," Billy announced proudly.

"It is? It is kind of dim. Don't you think? I mean, it's not quite as bright as many of the others." Anna had an air of disappointment in her voice.

"Anna Angel, that's our star," Billy whispered softly. "It's the North Star, our North Star." He looked down at her and smiled. "The world will keep spinning and spinning, but it'll always be there. Changes will come, and at times, the sky will be full of confusing patterns that keep moving, that won't make any sense, but this one, our star, will always be there. Right there where it is right now. Holding strong, unmovable, it'll always be there for us. Our truth. Before the break of day in the early morning and in the deepest and darkest of nights, it'll always be there for us. It's our true north. Our love. Always there, always guiding us, no matter what this world brings."

She pulled Billy close. "Oh Billy…Billy, I love you…I'll always love you," Anna declared as they embraced again. They held each other for what seemed to be an eternity under the blanket of stars spreading out overhead.

Finally they pulled away from each other. "Always, Anna Angel. Always," Billy said as they both looked up into the stars in silent wonder.

ꕤ

Billy and Anna had not been to Prairieburg since he had left for the army. Opening the door, they were greeted by blaring music and the stench of stale beer, sweat, and heat mixed in a whirl of several hundred people tightly packed in and dancing.

They immediately realized that nothing had changed.

"Do you think we'll find Josh?" Anna shouted into Billy's ear, trying to be heard over the pounding music.

"We'll find him. I bet he's already here," Billy shouted back, and Anna nodded.

Hand in hand, Billy pulled Anna as he pushed his way through the sea of people, moving toward a corner at the edge of the main bar. There, they could get a better perspective of the dance floor and view of all the groups of people.

"That's a little better. Now we can at least see across the room," Billy said as put his arm around Anna and pulled her close.

Jessie and the Plainsmen were on the stage at the other end of the dance floor. Billy remembered them the last time he was there several years ago. They looked different. He remembered them to be kind of a clean-cut band that played a lot of country music with some rockabilly mixed in from time to time. He always thought they reminded him of the Beach Boys. Now their hair was longer, fuller, and a few members had facial hair. They looked like a grungy version of the Beatles. Their music had changed too, with an edge to it he had not remembered. All the members were the same, but they had changed.

Billy was startled when he felt a hand on his shoulder. "Hey Boy Scout!" Billy heard Josh shout in his ear from behind.

"Well, I'll be damned. I didn't know if you would make it. I know it is only eleven miles, but did you need a map to get here?" Billy smiled as he shook Josh's hand.

"Charlotte, I'm not sure you know what you're getting yourself into. Them boys from Monticello…well they're…how should I say this? 'Special'." Billy grinned as he lightly shook Charlotte's hand. "They have a tendency to get lost. I don't think they could find their way to the bathroom if they didn't carry very simple instructions with pictures on what to do." Billy broke into a chuckle.

"Don't listen to him, Charlotte-honey. Billy's just jealous. Them Anamosa boys are as lost as a bastard on Father's Day. In fact, most of them are all bastards lost on Father's Day." Josh laughed.

"And it's not that they don't know who their family is. Fact is, they're all family, related in some way or another—everyone eventually marries a cousin. They just have a hard time keeping a grip on who their daddy is," Josh chided Billy.

"Do you boys ever stop? Don't you ever get tired of putting each other down?" Anna implored.

"What, honey? I'm just stating the truth. I want Charlotte to have all the facts, so as a sophisticated city woman, she can make an educated decision as to who she associates with," Billy replied.

"Anna, I just want you to know what you're getting yourself into. You come from a well-respected farming family. Well educated, hardworking, with good values not inbred like this townie here." Josh motioned to Billy. "In the event you and Billy here should ever decide to marry, and God forbid have children, I want you to know there are a few peculiarities with his family tree. In fact, I'm not sure I would call it a tree at all. It's more like a large tangled up ball of weeds." Josh smirked.

"Okay boys, you can go on like this all night, but I'd like

something cool and refreshing from the bar." Charlotte took Anna's arm and led her toward the bar.

"I'll have a gin and tonic. What would you like, Anna?" Charlotte asked as they stepped up to the bar.

"That sounds good. Thanks, Charlotte."

"Four beers!" Billy shouted over their shoulders to the bartender.

"Four beers?" Anna repeated. "Charlotte and I already ordered our beverages, no thanks to your manners."

"I know," Billy responded as he draped his arm over her shoulder. "Four beers. Two for me and two for Joshua. If we're going to tear up the dance floor tonight, I've got to hydrate for it."

"You boys and your beer." Charlotte shook her head in disappointment.

"I know it, honey." Josh cut in. "I tried to introduce young, knuckle-dragging Billy to something a little more sophisticated, but he wouldn't hear of it." Josh laughed as he put his arm around Billy. "Guess with all your worldly traveling, you haven't learned too much about the world."

Billy answered in simple terms. "Real men drink beer."

The band finished the song and left the stage. Jessie stayed behind. Picking up an acoustic guitar, he announced to the crowd he wanted to sing one more song before their break. "This song, written by Paul McCartney and John Lennon, is called 'And I Love Her.'"

"I love this song, Billy. Please dance with me. It's a slow song. Please dance with me." Anna grabbed Billy by the hand, pulling him out to the dance floor.

Jessie began to play as Billy swept Anna into his arms on the dance floor. He looked deep into Anna's eyes as they slowly moved together.

As the tender words and soft melody filled the room, Anna felt herself drifting away. Away from the ballroom, away from this world, away from what the future might bring. None of it mattered. Right now there was just Billy, and that would be enough. Not a word was needed to be said. The words to the song did it all for them. It was just the music, and their eyes fixed together; their eyes said it all.

Tears formed in Anna's eyes. She loved her Billy, and she could see in his eyes that he loved her.

Jessie continued the song, repeating the final verse several times. At the conclusion, they held each other. The crowd applauded for Jessie as he finished and exited the stage, but Billy and Anna continued to hold each other for a few more seconds.

It was magic. It was a moment that made the evening. Anna knew it. The doubts she had on the drive earlier, the fear for their future, the pain of Billy leaving, it was all worth it now. Here on this dance floor, they were suspended in time. This moment made it all worth it.

Charlotte's shrill voice interrupted the moment. "It's too hot and smoky in here. We thought we would step out and get some air."

Still holding Anna close, Billy caught Josh's eyes and knew they were headed out to Josh's car to do more than just get some air. "We're going to share a few more dances. Maybe we'll catch up with you in a bit," Billy responded, swaying with Anna in his arms.

"No rush, brother. We'll find you. Enjoy the evening," Josh responded as he grabbed Charlotte's hand and pulled her toward the door.

Billy pulled back slightly from Anna. "Guess they don't want to be interrupted. Wonder what they would be doing that they don't want us to come out and find them?"

Anna swatted Billy on his shoulder.

Billy smiled. "Maybe we should go out get some air?"

"Billy West, I know what's on your mind. You have a one track mind…"

"Yes…yes, Anna Jacobs. Yes I do, but it didn't seem to bother you last night." Billy's smile widened.

"You hush…hush that mouth of yours…" Anna smiled and swatted him on the shoulder again.

With a smile, Billy pulled Anna tight, and they continued to sway out on the floor. "I love you, Anna Angel…I do love you."

Anna rested her head to his chest. She could feel the deep thump of his heart. She smiled; this was all she would ever need.

ꕥ

From across the smoky ballroom, Big Joe Matsell sat out of view. With Sally by his side in the shadows of the corner, he drank from his bottle of whiskey—something he'd been doing all day long. Joe's eyes held a steady gaze out on the dance floor as he watched Billy and Anna. The wheels turned in his head. Sally saw the trouble coming, but she was helpless to stop it from creeping in.

Sally dared not challenge Joe when he drank this heavily, especially with Dicky and Ronnie at the table with them. It would be a recipe for disaster. She had seen him like this many times before. The best that could happen would be them getting in an ugly argument that would result in him hitting her. They would more than likely fight over the keys so she could drive him home safely. Sally dreaded what the evening would bring, and she wondered if he would ever change. Sally swallowed hard and closed her eyes as sadness flashed across her face. Yes, Sally knew how the evening would end.

Big Joe had been drinking consistently for almost a week ever since the night when Dicky opened his mouth about Billy West. Sally leaned closer to Joe at the table. There was trouble in the air, and she would likely have to sacrifice herself to keep it from getting too messy.

"Joe, could I have sip of your whiskey?" Sally asked, hoping to separate the bottle from him, if only for a while.

"Nice try, Sal. Think this here bottle is a little hard for your choosing." Big Joe kept his eyes on the loving couple swaying to the croons of the band and rejected Sally, knowing what her motive was. Instead, anger took deeper root inside of him. "Loyalty is a damned funny thing." The comment was directed at Sally. Once again, she was meddling in his affairs. She would pay for that comment later. But not now, not there. At that moment, his anger was directed at settling the score with Billy West. "Yes boys, it's a damned funny thing."

Ronnie and Dicky exchanged looks and then looked over at

Big Joe. There was an uncomfortable pause. They weren't sure what he was talking about but figured it must be about them. Dicky was afraid of Big Joe, afraid he was still angry about his comments about Billy West earlier that week.

"We gonna cut the cards tonight?" Dicky tried to lighten the mood with the hopes of a game of poker even though he couldn't afford to gamble. For the last two nights, they had sat at the table, playing poker with Big Joe. Dicky was down $800, and Ronnie was down over $600. Neither had the money and neither liked owing Big Joe anything.

"Ain't you had enough punishment for one week? Besides, I doubt you even have the money you owe me," Big Joe said, his eyes glued on Billy and Anna.

The anger jolted like electricity in his veins. Joe had planned to face Billy again and was ready, but he had not expected the anger to course through his body so intensely. As Joe watched Billy on the dance floor, happy and unaffected by his actions, his hands trembled, and he slid them off the table to his sides. He could barely control himself. Tonight he would set things straight. Tonight he would make Billy pay.

"Sally, why don't you mosey over to the bar, get us boys a round of beers, and get yourself something to your liking. Can't have a pretty girl like you sipping from a bottle with the boys," Joe mocked, tossing a ten dollar bill toward Sally and waving for her to leave.

Taking the money, she stood up from the table and walked toward the bar, looking over her shoulder a couple of times. Joe was planning something, and it was going to be bad. She had been watching this build all week. A negative vibe had been growing stronger and stronger, and tonight it was at its breaking point.

Sally was Joe's girl. She had tried all week to ease his pain, giving herself to him on multiple occasions. But he wouldn't have anything to do with her. He knew she understood him better than anyone and was trying to make it all better, but his pride wouldn't let anything happen. She was not what he had wanted. It had nothing to do with her. It had everything to do with setting things right, and, she was in the way.

"How would you boys like to make back the money you lost at the table?" Big Joe asked, turning to Dicky and Ronnie. He wasn't asking a question. They didn't have a choice. They did not have the money and saying no to Big Joe was impossible.

"What you got in mind, Joe?" Ronnie asked, wishing he had never sat down at the poker table with Big Joe.

"I got a mind to teach young Billy West a lesson. That son of a bitch needs to learn you don't mess around with Big Joe Matsell. You meddle in my affairs, and you're going to pay." Big Joe glanced at Ronnie and Dicky and then back out toward the dance floor.

Again, Ronnie and Dicky did not know if he was talking about Billy West or about them. Dicky spoke up, "We got your back, Big Joe. Just tell us what you got in mind."

"Well the way I figure it, we need to separate Anna from Billy. I don't want no girl mixed up in my dealings with West," Big Joe said, baiting the two boys. "I'll take care of Billy. All I need the two of you to do is distract Anna Jacobs."

"Ah heck, Big Joe, that's easy enough. I'll cut in and show her some of my moves out on the dance floor. That ought to keep her occupied for twenty or thirty minutes," Ronnie said, hoping Big Joe would agree.

"Not sure that'll do, Ronnie. Gonna need something a little more permanent than you mixing it up with her on the floor. Besides, you both each owe me over $600. Gonna have to be something a little more…something more permanent."

Permanent. He said it. The word hung heavily in the air.

Dicky's stomach turned with a sick feeling. He was being pulled into something dark, down to a level he never thought possible. How had it come to this? He always liked to have fun, hanging out with the guys. He hadn't done much since high school, but he had held down a few jobs here and there, enough to pay his tab at the bar. He was lazy, and he knew it, but he was no criminal. Things were slipping. Down. Deep into an ugly level of darkness. He should never have sat down at the poker table with Joe Matsell. Now he was in trouble, trapped in a corner with no way out.

His throat felt tight. His voice squeaked as he answered Big Joe. "I think we can probably offer her a few drinks at the bar. Maybe loosen her up a little bit and get her separated from Billy." Dicky glanced at Ronnie. He could see in Ronnie's eyes that he was scared, too.

"Dicky, why don't you pull your car up around the back?" Joe laid the words out like cards on the table. "I reckon she'll probably make a move for the ladies room after their dance. There's a back door down the hallway from the restrooms. Try to get your car as close to the door as you can." Dicky and Ronnie sat in disbelief, unable to respond. "When she comes out of the restroom…" Joe paused, his eyes dark and hard to see in the shadows of the old ballroom. "I want you to take care of it."

"But, Big…" Dicky tried to respond.

"Take care of it!" Big Joe shouted, cutting off Dicky in mid-sentence. "Goddamnit, you punk-ass, weak bastards, I ain't nobody's fool! You think you're gonna walk away from the poker table, owing me money? You think you can get away with it? That you can pull one over on Big Joe? Everyone pays. You hear me? Everyone pays!" Big Joe shouted across the table, and Ronnie and Dicky both simultaneously slumped in their chairs.

Ronnie and Dicky were stuck. He had them both against the wall, and they were sliding down into Joe Matsell's darkness.

Joe leaned across the table, staring them down with his beady eyes. "You get her in your car and meet me out at Johnson's Bridge on Chicken House Road. You got it? I'll be there in about two hours. If I'm late, don't leave. I don't care if you're there all night. Don't leave until I arrive. You got it?"

Neither Ronnie nor Dicky spoke a word. Ronnie opened his mouth, but nothing came out. They both slowly nodded.

"I'll take care of Billy. You man up with your end of the bargain," Joe said in an exasperated tone.

At that very moment, Joe watched when the music ended. For some reason, Billy West turned from Anna and was weaving through the mass of people toward the bar. Simultaneously Anna moved toward the restrooms…and the back door.

"Okay, they're moving. They're moving. Now go. Go!" Joe

shouted as he pounded his fist down on the table.

Ronnie and Dicky quickly sprung to their feet and moved out of the shadow of the corner and onto the dance floor. "Two hours. I'll meet you at Johnson's Bridge," Big Joe reminded them one more time as they stepped out with their orders.

Big Joe watched for a few moments. Billy stood in a long line at the bar; that was good. He would be there a while, waiting for Anna. At some point, Billy would realize she was not coming back and would look for her. That would be when Billy would be vulnerable. That was when Joe would make his move.

ঙ্গ

"You suppose we'll see Josh and Charlotte again tonight?" Anna asked Billy as Jessie was finishing his song up on the stage.

"That there is a darn good question. I think they'll be back. Charlotte seems to be the prudish type. I don't think she'll let him go too far out in the back seat of his Chevy." Billy smiled.

"Jessie is sounding good tonight. I think he and the band have gotten better," Anna responded, ignoring his comment about Charlotte. "I wouldn't mind a few more rounds out here on the dance floor."

"Let's head on over to the bar, have a couple more drinks, and then we'll wear out this here dance floor," Billy agreed, leading Anna toward the bar.

"Okay, honey, but first, I'd like to pay a visit to the ladies room to freshen up," Anna said as she pulled away from Billy.

"Looks like there's a pretty long line at the bar. I'll wait for you right down there at the end." Billy pointed toward the corner of the bar.

Billy stepped forward and reached for Anna. "Now don't you go standing me up, Anna Angel. I'm likely to find me another dance partner if you're away too long," he said with a cocky, confident smile.

Billy pulled Anna into his arms. "What am I ever going to do with you?"

Anna fell into his arms and looked up into his eyes. She shrugged her shoulders, unable to respond.

He looked deep into her eyes and smiled. "Marry me, Anna Jacobs. Marry me and make me whole, make my life complete. That would be a start." Billy said it in a tone that seemed he was lightly mocking her, but she knew he was serious.

Anna's stomach dropped, and her heart skipped a beat or two. Her knees weakened. For a second, she thought her legs would give out, and she would faint. She took a deep breath, glanced away from Billy, and then recovered. "You wait for me here. If you're here at the bar when I get back from the ladies room, maybe we can discuss the future. That is, unless I find you on the dance floor with one of them highfalutin Monticello girls."

"I'll be right here, waiting for you." Billy loosened his grip on her.

Anna stepped back, slowly dragging her hands down his arms, keeping her eyes on him. Then, she turned and walked toward the ladies restroom.

ꙮ

"We really gonna go through with this?" Dicky asked Ronnie as they moved down the back hallway, out of Big Joe's sight.

"Can't say as we got much of a choice. Big Joe's got us hamstrung. Damn, I wish I'd never sat down at the poker table with him," Ronnie said, crossing his arms.

"You still got that flask of gin?" Dicky asked, needing something to settle his nerves. This felt wrong. He would need some liquid courage to be able to follow through.

Ronnie reached inside his jacket pocket where he kept the flask. "Take a couple hits, but leave some for me." Ronnie handed the flask to Dicky.

Dicky took a long draw from the flask. The gin burned going down. The heat ripped at his throat. He shuddered for a moment. Then the warmth overcame his jitters, and his nerves settled.

"Thanks Ronnie. Exactly what I needed." Dicky tried to smile as he handed the flask back to Ronnie. Ronnie tipped his head back and tilted the flask upward, taking a full drink. "I'm gonna go out and pull the car closer to the building. You wait here. If Anna comes out, you're going to have to get her attention and hold her up."

Ronnie shook his head and took another long pull from the flask. He handed it back to Dicky and motioned for him to take another drink. "I'll think of something. You hurry up and get your car up here."

Dicky took one last deep drink from the flask and handed it back to Ronnie. "I'll be back in a few minutes. Make sure you keep her here." Dicky turned away toward the door.

"I got it," Ronnie responded. As the gin worked its magic, he felt more confident about what they had to do. "This might actually work out fine," he thought to himself. "Just get Anna's attention, stall, and somehow convince her to go for a ride. That might work. We'll have to do all of this without gathering any attention." He took another long drink from the flask and looked out the back door. Dicky was already on the far side of the back lot, moving toward his car. So many cars out there. He wouldn't be able to get as close as they wanted. That would be a problem.

Ronnie heard the laughter of ladies, coming from behind the door leading to the restroom. He glanced out the back door and saw Dicky slowly maneuvering his car in the lot. He was taking too long. Dicky drove like an old man, Ronnie thought, wishing he had brought his car.

He wished he had not been talked into all of this by Big Joe. Damn pride. Ronnie should never have sat down at the poker table. He tried to block the negative thoughts in his mind. Can't think about that now. Put it behind. What's done, is done. There's only right now. That's all that matters. Right now.

Ronnie was growing anxious. He heard another wave of laughter, coming from the ladies restroom. His nerves were getting the best of him. His hand trembled as he reached back into his jacket pocket for the flask and took another long drink. The gin warmed him, settling his nerves.

The door to the restroom opened. Five girls from Monticello exited. He knew several of their faces, but he didn't know them well. Ronnie looked out the door again. Dicky was about forty feet from the exit, leaning against the front of his car. Ronnie caught his attention, and Dicky gave him a thumbs up motion.

What an idiot, Ronnie thought. How did I ever get mixed up with Dicky Moss? It didn't matter now. What was done was done. Ronnie took another long drink from his flask and propped his hand against the wall to steady himself. He suddenly heard movement from behind. Startled, Ronnie turned, and standing in front of him was Anna Jacobs.

Ronnie's chest tightened up. A short gasp of air escaped from his throat. He took a deep breath and calmed himself. It was his turn now to act. He would prove Big Joe wrong. He would earn Joe's respect. He would show him he was a dependable man who got things done.

Ronnie opened his mouth, unaware of exactly what was going to come out. "Ah…um…Anna, Anna Jacobs."

Anna looked up at Ronnie, a little startled at his strange presence in the hallway. Anna knew Ronnie. He was several years older than her in high school, but they had been in a few activities together. She remembered him to be a nice boy that was kind of quiet growing up. He had always liked to have fun but tended to be a follower. She remembered toward the end of school he had mixed in with a rough crowd, and there had been some trouble that followed him. Something had happened, but she couldn't remember what it was. Billy had even mentioned once that Ronnie was a good kid who just didn't have a moral compass. He had no clear direction, and depending who he followed, he would one day probably end up on the wrong side of the law.

"Anna, Anna Jacobs?" Ronnie spoke up louder, saying the words again, and gaining some confidence in his voice. "Suppose you're looking for Billy. He was here looking for you. Asked if I'd seen ya. I told him I hadn't, but if I was to run into you, I'd send you his way," Ronnie lied.

"Oh," Anna replied, a little confused that Billy had come looking for her. "Billy's here? Where? Where is he?" She questioned, looking around for him.

"Well, he was here. He asked about you, and then he slipped out the back. Said something about getting a little fresh air in the lot," Ronnie continued his lie.

"Huh. What am I gonna do with that Billy West. That boy is always out wandering." Anna felt uncomfortable and tried to smile as she looked out the back door.

"He was here, maybe five minutes ago. Probably just out there, not too far in the lot." Ronnie pointed out the back door, hoping she would leave the building. He had to get her away from people, alone, where no one would see her getting into their car—especially if he had to use other methods of coercion.

The car was still a good forty feet from the building and getting her there was going to be a problem. "Billy went out that way." Ronnie pointed toward Dicky's car.

"Huh." Anna flinched. "That's weird." Something was not right. Anna sensed it. She looked out across the lot with a confused expression and then walked in that direction. "I'm going to walk around the side of the building and come back in through the front entrance. If you see Billy again, tell him I'll be waiting at the bar." Anna started walking away. Ronnie let her get a few feet ahead and then followed. He felt a shot of confidence—she had fallen for it. Once she got over to Dicky, he would make his move.

Sitting in the driver's seat, Dicky saw them coming. He was a ball of nerves, wondering what would happen next. Anna walked right toward him with Ronnie about ten feet behind her. Dicky's hand trembled as he turned the key and started the car.

Anna held up her hand to shield her eyes from the bright lights from the car, blinding her. A wave of fear overcame her. This was all wrong.

Before she could think or act, she felt arms, wrapping around her from behind, pushing her forward, and squeezing her so tight she could barely breathe.

"What the…what are you…what are you doing?" Anna was bewildered. She couldn't believe this was happening to her. Then, a strange shot of anger and a deep wave of fear burst inside of her. She let out a shrill scream. "Get the hell…get away from me…let go of me!" She fought back against him, thrashing her head and scratching with her nails.

Ronnie was surprised at her strength. She was putting up a heck of a fight, kicking and screaming. It was not going to be easy getting her into the car. "Dicky, get your ass out here and give me a hand!" Ronnie shouted as he shoved Anna against the car.

Dicky sprung out from the driver's side and ran around to assist. "Open the goddamn door. She's fighting like a tomcat!" Ronnie yelled.

Dicky opened the car door, and both men grabbed her.

"Get your hands off me! What…what are you doing?" Anna shrieked in her high pitch and let out another scream.

Dicky and Ronnie managed to wrestle her to the ground where the struggle continued. Anna kicked and dug her heals into the gravel lot. "Get away from me! Get your filthy hands off me!"

Dicky had her legs now, and Ronnie wrapped his arms around her shoulders. They lifted her, and in one move, they crammed her into the backseat of the car.

Ronnie turned and slammed the door. He was filled with a quick shot of relief and wiped his brow. They had done it. He would prove Joe Matsell wrong.

As he dusted the dirt off his shirt, Ronnie heard a dull thud and looked to see Dicky face down in the gravel lot.

"What the f…" Before he could finish, he was struck in the side of his shoulder with a force that sent him hurdling to the ground. Deep pain shot in his arm, and his fingers trembled with a cool, strange tingle. Ronnie saw someone with a baseball bat standing over him. He could not make the figure out in the shadows from the headlights.

"Get up, you son of a bitch!" the man shouted in a fierce tone.

Ronnie didn't recognize the voice. He felt the first wave of pain as he got to his knees and tried to find his feet. His left arm was not working right. He cradled it in his other arm. Getting to his feet, he looked down and saw Dicky face down in the gravel. He was out cold. "You bastard! Do you know who you're dealing with? You're going to pay for this." Ronnie spit at him in deep anger.

His head buzzed, and the pain came on. The headlights silhouetted the man. Ronnie couldn't make out who it was, but he realized the man held a baseball bat in his right hand

The second blow was much harder. This time to his right side. Ronnie knees buckled, and his body fell face down onto the ground. He felt himself sinking, fading in and out of consciousness. It took all the strength he had to let out a deep moan.

He heard the crashing sound of the bat as it smashed against the car. He could not see, but could hear the sound of glass and metal as the intruder destroyed the car. Then he heard the door open and voices.

"Get away from me! Get away…" Anna screamed at the man with the bat. She was delirious with fear.

Anna's screams would be the last thing Ronnie Wilson remembered from that night. The pain overtook him and everything shut down. He sank into the earth and then everything sped up in his mind. His eyes were closed, but he could see stars whirling faster and faster around him. Down, down, spinning down away from the pain to unconsciousness. He was out.

"Anna, Anna, it's me. It's okay. It's just me." She heard the man's voice, but she couldn't place it.

"Billy? Billy, are you there?" She asked as hope replaced the fear in her voice.

"No Anna, not Billy. Billy's not here. It's Josh, Josh

Sanders," he replied.

"Jshh…Josh…Josh? Where? Where's Billy?"

Josh detected in her voice a strange emptiness. He wondered if she was coherent. "Anna, it's Josh, Josh Sanders. We're at the ballroom in Prairieburg. I came here with Charlotte and you and Billy. Remember?"

"Where's Billy? I want Billy…I want my Billy!" Anna grew belligerent, and she was definitely not herself right now.

Josh knew fear could do funny things to people and could shut down reason. Anna was irrational. Hopefully he could get through to her. He had no idea how she ended up in this car. Where was Billy? Why was she being assaulted behind the dancehall? If Billy wasn't out here, then there had to be more of them, and they would be there soon. He had to get Anna away, out of the car, and someplace safe.

Charlotte finally arrived. She and Josh had been sitting on the hood of his car across the lot when they had heard Anna screaming. He had instinctively grabbed his Louisville Slugger from his trunk and had run a dead sprint toward her voice.

"Who are…what? What the hell happened? Josh?" Charlotte questioned as she surveyed the situation and saw two men lying face down beside the battered car.

"Charlotte, I need your help. We've got to get Anna out of the car. She's not right. She ain't responding to me," Josh said.

"What… Josh… What happened?" Charlotte asked. "Where's Billy?"

"I don't know. And that's what's bothering me. I don't know where he is. He should be here," Josh answered. "Now go around to the other side and open the door. We've got to hurry. I got a feeling there will be more of them coming soon. We got to get her out of here and find someplace safe," Josh said as he scanned the lot for sanctuary.

ഌ

"I'll take another beer, please," Billy shouted over the din of the band now playing up on the stage. He had already finished the first two while waiting for Anna and figured he better have fresh drinks for her when she returned.

"Where the hell is she?" Billy said openly to himself. With the band back on the stage, the entire ballroom began to move. He gazed toward the dance floor. Cigarette smoke clouded the air, and there was a strange motion to it all. It was like a loud, thumping dragon, posturing for battle. Strange. Very strange. He shook his head and tried to look for her in the shadows.

"What is taking Anna so long?" he asked himself. This was not like her. He sensed deep inside something wasn't right. His instincts were taking over, and he knew something was definitely wrong.

He stepped away from the bar and quickly darted into the crowd of people.

"Hey buddy, where you going? You got to pay for these beers," the bartender shouted toward Billy. But Billy didn't hear him and was already deep into the mass of people dancing on the dance floor.

It was hard to see. "Got to get someplace clear," Billy said to himself as he moved toward the back hallway. Maybe she met some friends in the restroom. Billy knew it didn't make sense, and that's what worried him. Not this long. She wouldn't leave him for this long.

Joe Matsell watched and waited for Billy to leave the bar. He knew that Billy would, and now it was Joe's time to set things right. Joe could feel the old anger coming again. Just like Eddie Gruber, Billy was going to pay tonight.

"Joe, take me dancing…the band's playing one of our favorite songs. Take me dancing." Sally tugged at Joe's arm, but he didn't hear her. He was focused on Billy, and he was moving.

Joe quickly jumped up from his chair and started toward the dance floor.

"Joe? Joe? Honey baby, where are you going?" Sally questioned and reached to pull him back.

But he didn't even look back at her. Sally sat at the table dejected and wondered what he was up to. Sally could see the anger boiling inside of him. She feared for how it would all come spewing out tonight. She sat helpless, unable to stop him or to save him from his troubled mind.

Sally wished she could fly away. Fly away from the pain of her love for this man, away from the ugliness of his bar, away from the booze, away from the town that was slowly draining the life out of her. But she lacked the courage. Deep inside, she was a coward. She would never leave, and in the end, this life with Joe would take its toll. Like all the others who came in contact with Joe, she too would pay. With a desperate sadness in her eyes, she watched Joe wander into the crowded dance floor until eventually he disappeared.

Joe had his whiskey and he took a long drink from the almost-empty bottle. Billy stood about twenty feet ahead of him. Joe didn't want to get too close but needed to get Billy alone to make his move.

Billy finally cleared the large group of people and was in the hallway out of Joe's sight.

Big Joe continued to follow. He exited the crowd and slowly peeked around the corner down the hallway. Billy had his back to Joe and was looking out the back door.

Billy peered out across the dark lot. After a few seconds, his eyes to adjusted. There were cars parked five deep all the way across the lot to the tree line. The wind had picked up, and it smelled like a thunderstorm was brewing. For a brief moment, he thought he heard somebody talking, but the wind shifted direction, and he couldn't make it out.

The hallway was empty. Billy still had his back to Big Joe. Now was the time to act. Now. Now. Now. The words pounded in Joe's brain. Now! Go now! Make him pay! Now! Now…

Everything slowed down. Big Joe would not remember how quickly he closed in on Billy. It was as if in one step, he literally flew in the air, across the entire hallway. Gripping the whiskey bottle tight in his right hand, he glided down the hall. He cocked the bottle back over his head, and then in one complete motion, he released the bottle forward like a hammer, pounding it down on the back of Billy's head.

All of his anger, all of the pain and humiliation that had been building for so long, released as the bottle in his hand met its intended target with a dull thump. A short gasp and groan came from Billy. Then he fell forward. His legs buckled, and his face smashed into the door. He crumpled to his knees and curled into a smaller ball in the corner by the back door.

Billy lay motionless and silent.

Big Joe stood above him with the whiskey bottle still in his hand. Adrenalin pulsed in his veins. His heart pounded like a drum. He was dizzy with euphoria. He had done it. He told himself he would make Billy pay, and he followed through. He would regain his honor and reputation.

Looking down on Billy, Joe thought Billy looked pitiful. This was the great Billy West. Big Joe was disgusted by him. He could not believe that this lump in the corner had challenged his manhood. Joe still tasted his anger for him. His mouth was dry, but he brought himself to spit, spattering Billy's back with saliva. This would teach the great Billy West and everyone not to challenge Big Joe Matsell. Ever.

Standing over Billy, Big Joe felt as if he was suspended by time and space. The energy left his body. All of a sudden, a wave of exhaustion passed through him. His eyes fell on Billy's limp body. Joe wondered if Billy was breathing. Was he dead? Joe noticed the small trickle of blood down the back of Billy's neck, and he wondered if he had killed him.

"Fuck you," Joe said to motionless body. He didn't care. Billy had it coming. He always had it coming. And now he paid.

Big Joe heard some girls laughing. Somebody was coming. He had to get out of there. "Fuck you," he said again. "You had it coming." Joe spit on Billy again. He hated everything about Billy. He would always hate Billy.

Joe took one last look at Billy, smiled at what he had done, and slipped out the backdoor.

ꕤ

Josh and Charlotte held up Anna on each side and guided her toward their car. She was weeping openly. "Where's Billy? Where's my Billy?" Where…?"

"Anna, it's Charlotte and Josh. Charlotte and Josh, from Monticello. Remember? We were at the fair together, and now we're at Prairieburg," Josh tried to explain.

Anna looked at him with confusion in her eyes then she looked at Charlotte. "Is Billy here?"

"Yes, he's someplace around here. We met at the bar earlier. He was with you, remember?"

Anna was confused. She looked at Charlotte and tried to recognize her face. Suddenly pieces came together. "You're that highfalutin, stuck-up city-girl from Chicago. Billy says you think you're too good for all of us. He wonders what Josh sees in you." Anna blurted out to Charlotte as she tried to fill in all the pieces of their evening at Prairieburg.

Josh cleared his throat and tried to suppress a chuckle. "Anna, you came here with Billy. You were out on the dance floor with him. Jessie and the Plainsmen were up on stage. Charlotte and I stepped out to get some air. Do you remember now?" Anna looked at Josh and then nodded as everything started coming back to her.

"We were going to dance some more. I went to the ladies room, and Billy went to the bar. That's it! He's at the bar, waiting for me." Anna was excited now and took a step away from the car toward the ballroom.

"Whoa, Anna, just hold on a second. Something's going on here. After those two boys tried to jump you, I'd feel just a tad bit more comfortable if you stayed out here in the car with Charlotte. Besides, ain't nobody going to be able take on a tough city-girl like Charlotte." Josh smiled and glanced at Charlotte. She was not overly amused at his comment or of Billy's perception of her.

"I'll find Billy. You two hold tight out here. I'll be back in a little while," Josh assured the two ladies then moved toward the front of the building.

A few seconds later, Josh entered the ballroom through the front door. The rumble of the band was overwhelming. The dance floor was jam packed, and the place was in full swing now. He made his way to the bar where he hoped to find Billy.

"I'm looking for Billy West, you seen him?" Josh tried to shout over the band to a couple sitting at the bar. They shook their heads, and Josh asked a few more people. None of them had seen him.

Josh caught the bartender's attention. "I'm looking for a guy. About my height. Name's Billy West. Has he been here?"

A look of anger crossed the bartender's face. "Yeah, he was here. Left without paying his tab. Are you going to pay it for him?"

Josh reached in his pocket, pulled out a dollar, and threw it on the bar. "How long ago?"

Reaching for the dollar, the bartender responded, "About

an hour ago. He had a couple of beers, ordered a couple more, and then just stormed out of here. Looked like he was waiting for someone."

"Was anyone with him?" Josh asked. The pieces were coming together. He had to figure out who was trying to hurt Billy.

"Nah, like I said, he was alone. If I remember, he was making his way toward the restrooms in the back hallway." As the bartender responded to the questions, Josh had turned from the bar and was walking through the mass of people toward the back of the building.

ꕥ

"Do you think he's really that drunk?" Mary Branston asked Janie Parker as they stood over what looked to be a passed out man in the hallway.

"Hey mister, time to wake up. Time to wake up now." Mary giggled, lightly nudging him with her foot.

"I think he's three sheets to the wind," Janie concluded. "Looks like he started early and never stopped. I'm sure he'll have one heck of a hangover in the morning."

Mary nodded. "I don't know. Seems kind of weird he just passed out here in the corner of the hallway. Maybe we should go get Buzzy and Fred to help get him up."

"Come on buddy, time to get up now. Sleepy time's over," Janie said, reaching down to tap him. She tapped him again, but he didn't move. Then she shook him vigorously. "Come on sleepy head. It's time to get…" She stopped midsentence and jumped back startled.

"He…He's bleeding…th...there's blood all over his head and under his neck," Janie said with fear in her voice. She leaned down again, and lightly nudged him. "Mister. Mister, are you okay?" Janie heard a slight moan from him. She tapped him harder and repeated the words again a little louder.

Billy slowly moved his hands up to his head and let out a deep groan.

"Are…are you okay?" Janie leaned over him, speaking in a soft voice. She heard him mumble something.

"Kill them. Kill those mother fuckers…shoot…shoot them…" he mumbled incoherently.

"Sir, are you okay? Can I help you?" Janie was cut off.

"LT…LT…Jimmy, LT is down. Get…get them…" he shouted and thrashed his arms. "No! Jimmy, No! Shoot them, Shoot them now! Now!" He moved to his knees.

Mary and Janie jumped back, startled at his responses. They saw his face for the first time. It was filled with anguish and fury, the look of a rabid monster, lost and distant…a face transformed into some dark and sinister place. They'd never seen anything like it in their lives, and it scared them to their core.

"Die, you mother fuckers! Die, you…" In one quick move, he was on his feet and pouncing forward. Billy grabbed both of the girls in his arms and slammed them into the wall.

"Billy, Billy! Whoa, Billy," At that moment, Josh entered the hallway and saw Billy attack the two young ladies. Josh instantly wrapped his arms around Billy.

"You fuckers are going to die! Jimmy…don't… Jimmy…the

LT…they will pay."

"Whoa. Whoa, pal," Josh said, pulling Billy off the girls.

"Billy, its Josh, Josh Sanders. Come on, buddy. It's Josh." Josh separated him from the girls and braced him up against the wall. He saw the blood down the side of his head and neck.

"Billy, it's Josh. Joshua. Remember, buddy? Josh? We're at Prairieburg? With the girls, remember?" Josh held Billy up against the wall and looked into his eyes. Tears streamed down Billy's face. Josh had never seen this sadness in his eyes or this pain.

"Buddy, its Josh. You…you okay?" Josh saw a flash come over Billy's face as if a light came on in his mind.

"Josh…Josh…Joshua?" Billy mumbled, bringing his hands up to his head.

"Oh God, my head…my head…oh, it hurts…what…what happened?" Billy asked as he was coming to.

Janie chimed in. "Your friend here is off his rocker." She and Mary were both shaken up.

"He was going to kill us. I don't know what the heck got into him, but he ain't right," Mary added.

"I think he may have broken my wrist," Janie said, holding her hand forward and rubbing her wrist.

Josh looked at her wrist. "Move it like this." He motioned. "Now push against my hand. Squeeze my hand now. Where are you feeling the pain?"

She looked down at her wrist. "Well, it feels a little sore here," Janie explained, pointing to the top side of her wrist.

"Do you feel sharp pains as you move it?" Josh asked.

"Well, no," she responded in a disappointed tone.

"It ain't broke, but it does look like you may have sprained it when you fell against the wall. I suggest you go to the bar and see if you can get a bag of ice. That ought to keep the swelling down," Josh recommended.

Janie smiled now. She was taking a liking to Josh, and Mary knew it. "We're going to go get the law." Mary jumped into the conversation. "He attacked us like a monster. He needs to be locked up."

"Well buddy, seems somebody jumped you." Josh rolled his eyes and ignored the girls as he turned back to Billy.

Mary was frustrated that Josh was ignoring her. "We're going to get Buzzy and Fred. They'll take care of this, and if they don't, we'll get the law. You boys wait here." Mary pulled Janie by the hand, and the girls walked toward the ballroom.

There was a flash of panic on Billy's face. "Anna! Where's Anna?"

"She's fine, buddy. She's out in the car with Charlotte." Still braced against the wall by Josh, Billy tried to pull away. "Hold it right there, buddy. She's fine. Charlotte's got her." Josh held him in place. "Somebody jumped you tonight, somebody with something to prove. I think this was planned. Now what the hell have you gotten yourself into, Billy?"

Billy shook his head. A dull pounding pulse beat behind his temples. The band in the ballroom opened up with another song, and the thump of the drums shot like sharp nails to the back of his head. Billy closed his eyes and grimaced.

"Got to be Joe Matsell," Billy responded. "Figured he would be coming back around. Just didn't see this one coming."

Billy shook his head in frustration. "I should've seen it coming." Billy looked Joshua in the face with a new realization of what happened. "He planned it out. He was tracking me, waiting for us to be separated. Josh, you sure Anna's okay?"

Josh smiled. "Yeah, nothing that me and my Louisville Slugger couldn't take care of."

Josh put his arm around Billy and pulled him close to his side. "Come on, partner. Let's go find our girls and get out of here. We don't need no rub with the law tonight," Josh said, mocking the two girls who just left.

Billy turned to Joshua and looked him in the eye. "Thanks, Josh. You saved my ass. I mean it, buddy. Thanks."

Tears welled in Billy's eyes, and he leaned into Josh as he guided him toward the backdoor. "I got your back, brother. I'll always have your back."

ꙮ

"Get up!" Joe growled, standing over Ronnie Wilson. Ronnie and Dicky crawled on their knees to the side of the car and pulled themselves to their feet. "I gave you one simple task. One thing. With a girl, a goddamn girl, and you fucked that up." Joe was disgusted. "What the hell am I going to do with you boys? What's it going to take for me to turn you into men?" Joe shouted as he leaned forward into Dicky's face.

"He…he had…he had a bat…" Dicky stammered.

"Don't give me that weak-ass bullshit! He had a bat. There were two of you and one of him, and you couldn't take him? This is bullshit." Joe spit on the ground.

"We didn't see…we didn't see him coming," Dicky tried to explain.

"Shut the hell up! I don't want to hear any damn excuses. Who was he? Did you get a look at his face?" Joe asked.

Both Dicky and Ronnie looked down to the ground silently.

"You don't even know who did this to you? You boys are real pieces of work, you know that? Give you a simple job to do, and you fuck it up. Pure and simple." Joe was on a rant now. "You know? When I gave you this job, I knew you wouldn't get it done. That you would fail. You know why? Because you're both losers. That's right, flat out losers. You'll always be losers. Just look at yourself. All beat up, full of excuses." Joe spit again and shook his head. "Pathetic." Joe looked down at them with his hands on his hips.

The boys leaned against the car. "Neither of my arms are working right," Ronnie groaned. "Think they're both broke."

"Broke? Broke? That's what you get when you can't get a job done. Broke? I'll give you broke. How about all the money you still owe me? This here tonight don't cover it. Not even close," Joe shouted at them again. "Looks like I'll have to take care of this business myself." Joe was furious with them.

"My whole right arm is numb." Dicky turned to Ronnie. "Something ain't right with it. And my collarbone, it ain't right…I…I think…I think it's poking out of the skin." Dicky grimaced as he lightly touched his right collarbone with his left hand. He felt something strangely jagged and sharp protruding from his skin.

"Well, don't that just cut it? I got a couple of girls here that skinned their knees and need some bandages. You are really something." Joe Matsell was disgusted with Ronnie and Dicky.

Joe turned and saw what looked to be a police car turning into the back lot. He figured Sheriff Barton must have gotten a call about them.

"Looks like we got visitors tonight. Not a damn word about any of this. You got that? If I hear a whisper that I was involved with this, you'll both pay, and I'm not talking about money," Joe threatened.

Light-headed, Dicky slowly swayed back and forth. He thought he might pass out at any moment. Ronnie leaned against the car and couldn't move. They were silent to Joe's threats.

"Pathetic. You boys are pathetic." Joe spit on the ground, looked both men up and down, turned, and walked toward the tree line on the other side of the lot.

"J…Joe…what? What you want us to do?" Ronnie asked as Joe walked away.

"Not a word, girls. Not a goddamn word," Joe responded as he disappeared into the shadows.

III

"TUCK YOUR SHIRT in, Andrew," John Crawford said to his son as the family walked up the steps of United Methodist Church.

"Did you even make an attempt at combing your hair this morning?" Now Maggie took note of their disheveled son. "Looks like you rolled out of bed, threw some clothes on, and got in the car with us for church. I'm not even going to ask if you brushed your teeth."

Andy patted down the bushy mop on his head and shrugged his shoulders at his mother's comments. He honestly couldn't remember if he had combed his hair, and he was pretty sure he hadn't brushed his teeth. He could still taste the potato chips he snuck into his bed the night before. He had managed to get dressed in the right clothes. After all, his mother had set them out on his chair before bed. As for the rest, he knew he had meant to, but whether he had or not, well, he wasn't sure.

"I think I did," Andy responded, tucking his shirt in.

"You think you did? What in Sam Hill does that mean? You either…"

"Good morning, folks," Pastor Jones said, interrupting Maggie and probably saving Andy from further correction.

Maggie's face lit up as she greeted Pastor Jones, and then in a split second, flashed to exasperation as she turned back and glared at Andy.

"Morning, Pastor," John greeted solemnly. John Crawford was a man of few words, and Sunday mornings did little to change this.

The Crawfords moved down the aisle past the first four rows of pews and then sat down on the right. This was close, but not too close to the front. It also wasn't all the way in the back either. It was the exact same place they sat every Sunday

Andy mused. It was like this every Sunday. His mom and dad would correct him on his appearance just as they entered the church. Pastor Jones would meet them at the door with the same greeting, and they would sit in the exact same spot. In fact, everyone in the church sat in the exact same place. Nothing ever changed. Andy thought it was kind of like school where everyone had their own assigned seating. He wondered if someone sat in "your" seat, if it would throw the whole world off its axis. One thing was for certain, everyone in the church found comfort in their routines, right down to the pew they sat in.

Andy remembered last year when Old Man Gelkie had brought his whole extended family from eight surrounding counties. He couldn't believe it. His eyes had nearly popped out when he'd counted nearly thirty members of the Gelkie clan pouring into the pews and had watched in amazement as they subsequently disrupted the morning of a number of routine-loving church goers.

Andy remembered the look on his dad's face when he saw the great mass of Gelkies that had invaded the church and had occupied their pew. Andy knew the look well because it was usually the one he got right before he got a whooping. That day they had ended up sitting clear in the back on the left side. It was like they had landed on Mars. Not just completely unfamiliar territory, it had been an entirely new world—one occupied by strange and somewhat hideous creatures. They had sat behind Beatrice Hampton and her sisters, Agnes and Claire. All three had their hair pulled up at least fifteen inches above their head. Andy's mom had compared their big bouffant hairstyles to some kind of a strange and massive prehistoric bird nest. The big hair, towering above their three heads at awkward angles, had made it nearly impossible to see up to the altar.

Change was never good. And in this case, they had the bopsy-beehive sisters in front of them, which in turn, had put a damper on the entire morning. In fact, the situation would cause the rest of the day to twist into a horrible tailspin. It had put his dad in a bad mood, and that was never a good thing. When they got home from church that day, he had decided Andy would clean out the entire shed. It had been hard work, and Andy had cursed Old Man Gelkie throughout the entire affair.

Andy had learned that Sunday morning church routine was good. He knew it was best to do what you were told, go through the motions, and get it over with. If all went well, he would be free for the rest of the day to do what he wanted. The whole service never lasted much longer than an hour—a couple of songs, some prayers, a sermon, tithes and offerings, and that was about it. Maybe they would have cookies and lemonade after the service. As long as his mom and dad didn't get wrapped up in a conversation with somebody, he would be home by ten-thirty or ten-forty-five tops.

Andy remembered the previous year when he spent the night with Jimmy Landers. Jimmy was Catholic, and the morning after the sleepover he went to church with him and his family. Andy never did figure it all out. The pastor had spoken in Latin and Andy wasn't sure if anyone had understood him. He knew he hadn't, but when he had asked Jimmy, he realized he hadn't either. Andy thought it seemed like there was a lot of jibber jab and too much standing and kneeling going on—unfortunately it went on and on. By the time the service was over, Andy had been worn out. Lesson learned: don't go to a sleepover at Jimmy's house on a Saturday night.

Andy preferred the Methodist church. He could sit and zone out. The only time they stood was for a few songs and for some reading in the Bible. All in all, it was pretty simple, just the way he liked it.

"When we get home," Andy's mom said, "I want you to change out of your church clothes. We're going to the picnic, and I don't want you messing these up." Maggie straightened her son's collar.

Andy nodded. In all the commotion that morning, he had forgotten about the picnic. Now he was excited. Uncle Dave would be there, and Andy was pretty sure Billy would be there, too. As long as they made it through church unscathed, he was going to have a great day.

"Good morning folks and welcome to the United Methodist Church." Pastor Jones started the service, and Andy smiled, hopeful that in sixty minutes it would be over.

"Please rise as we sing today's opening hymn, 'How Great

Thou Art.'"

Andy didn't mind the singing part of church. Most of the time he didn't sing. He just moved his mouth to the words. It was easy to do because nobody could hear themselves sing over the ruckus of Ginny Ford and Laura Lee Meyer—two of the elder members of the congregation who used Sunday morning as their own personal audition for the opera.

These women always sat in the front row with their families. Each of them seemed to be up front so they could command the stage. Each wailed over the other, jockeying for control of the song, stretching the notes out a little longer, a little louder and drowning out the entire congregation. They usually started slow, but as the song went on, their volume would increase. By the third verse, both ladies forcefully belted out notes at a maddening pitch. Usually by the end, they were up a couple of steps on the altar, facing the congregation. Often times, they added personal touches to the hymns with their own interpretations that included hand gestures and movement. One morning Andy had thought one was going to tackle the other right off the altar when they hit a crescendo of "Joyful, Joyful, We Adore Thee."

This morning was no different. As the congregation completed the last stanza of "How Great Thou Art", Andy didn't think the song would ever end. Both ladies stood up front, red faced, stretching the final notes far beyond the congregation, far beyond what June Miller played on the organ, far beyond what the author of the song ever intended.

Finally, Pastor Jones came to the rescue and interrupted the two virtuosos. "Today's Old Testament reading comes from the

Book of Psalms, chapter one, verses one through four. And the New Testament reading comes from the Book of John, chapter fifteen, verses nine through seventeen. Beatrice, could you please come forward and read the scripture?"

Beatrice's large beehive swayed above her head as she stepped up to the podium. Opening her King James Bible, she read, "Blessed is the man that walketh not in the counsel of the ungodly, nor standeth in the way of sinners, nor sitteth in the seat of the scornful."

She paused for a moment and looked up and pinched her lips, as if to make a point with certain members of the congregation, and then continued, "But his delight is in the law of the Lord; and in his law doth he meditate day and night. And he shall be like a tree planted by the rivers of water, that bringeth forth his fruit in his season; his leaf also shall not wither; and whatsoever he doeth shall prosper."

Beatrice glanced up again and then resumed with what Andy thought to be a very long passage. He wondered if she would ever be done and slouched down between his parents to get comfortable for the long haul.

"Therefore the ungodly shall not stand in the judgment, nor sinners in the congregation of the righteous. For the Lord knoweth the way of the righteous: but the way of the ungodly shall perish."

Beatrice looked down on the congregation from the pulpit, smiling briefly. She seemed proud of her command of the Scripture, maybe even of her command over the church.

Pastor Jones stepped up to the podium and put his hand on

her shoulder. He nodded to her, relieving her of command. Beatrice dipped her chin, smiling humbly and stepped down.

Pastor announced, "All rise for the reading of God's word."

In unison, everyone in the church stood up. Clearing his throat, he looked out at the congregation, "The second reading today comes from the Book of John, chapter fifteen, verses nine through thirteen."

Looking down at his King James Bible, Pastor Jones began to read. "As the Father hath loved me, so have I loved you…"

Andy's mind wandered as it usually did at church. He smiled as he thought about the picnic with Billy West. He couldn't wait to spend time with Billy and his Uncle Dave at the park. He was so excited for what the rest of the day held. He wished time would go faster and that church would be over. Andy looked up at Pastor Jones. The pastor's mouth moved and Andy could hear his words but he had no idea what Pastor was saying.

"…This is my commandment, that ye love one another, as I have loved you. Greater love hath no man than this, that a man lay down his life for his friends." As he finished reading, Pastor raised his eyes to the congregation. "May God add his blessing to his word."

At that prompting, everyone in the congregation responded with a united "Amen".

Lifting his hand, Pastor Jones motioned. "Please, everyone, take your seats."

Like every Sunday, Andy was completely lost. All those "haths" and "ye's" and "doeths" made following too hard for him, and he wondered who in the world talked like that. Nobody he knew in Anamosa did. If he ever talked like that at school or when hanging out with his friends, he would be the laughing stock of the town, and they would probably beat the crap out of him. No way could he get away with it. Only folks like Beatrice Hampton and Pastor Jones could pull it off, looking so pious with their serious words and proper clothes.

With the scripture read, Andy entered the phase of the church service when folks dosed off. Pastor Jones had a dry, monotone delivery that would put every baby and most adults to sleep like a soft lullaby. Unfortunately, his message was often lost in the drowsy conditions he created. Across the aisle, Old Man Gelkie already had that glazed-over look in his eyes and would probably be out soon.

Andy could almost time it by his watch. In eight minutes, most men in the church would be sound asleep, their heads bobbing and weaving to the tempo of the sermon. Depending where one sat in the pews, they might catch the snoring rhythm from Sheriff Jim Barton and Old Man Gelkie. These two men sat on opposite ends of the congregation, one on the front left, the other on the back right. But they were like dueling banjoes, tossing notes back in forth in a vicious tennis match of snores.

Judge Swanson regularly sat in the middle of the church with his wife and three daughters. He was one of the few men that never slept during church. Andy figured it was probably because he was caught in the crossfire between Gelkie and Barton—a dangerous place that would keep anyone awake.

Pastor Jones started the sermon. "Two amazing passages of scripture today. The first is an incredible start to the Book of

Psalms about obedience—about obedience to God, about the decisions we make in our lives and the fruits or consequences of these decisions. The second, in one of the last great scenes of the Gospels, Jesus foretold his own death on the cross. He knew he was going to give up his life. It had to have been heavy on his heart, but what was he talking about? What were his parting words to his disciples?" A quiet pause flowed over the congregation as Pastor Jones asked his first question, glancing around the room. "He's talking about love. He's talking about loving each other."

Pastor Jones' expression was resolute. "Obedience is simply love in action. The passage from the Old Testament is a beautiful depiction of the power of faith and obedience. Yet the passage from the New Testament is so much more refined. Perfected, if you will, and gives us all a glimpse of the true nature of God."

Pastor Jones looked over the congregation. "I'm often amazed at the nature of God. Back in the beginning in the Garden of Eden, everything was perfect. Then with Adam and Eve's disobedience, sin entered the world and separated us from God and his perfection. All along, God knew this would happen, yet he created them anyway."

Pausing again for a moment, he looked out at all the families. "God knew that he would have to sacrifice his son on a cross to cleanse us of our sin. He knew he would have to sacrifice his own son on an altar so we could all be free."

Scanning across the room, he caught the eyes of a number of mothers and fathers. "He willingly gave his son, so we could be free. The parents in this room may have some insight as to how horrible this would be. To see your own son, dying on a cross in horrific, unbelievable pain, crying out for his father… And his father did what? God, for an instant, turned away from his son because he had taken on all the evils of this world, all of our sin. He left him there, hanging in excruciating pain, alone as his life slipped away, and for what reason?" Pastor Jones raised his voice. "For what reason, I ask?"

Pastor Jones slammed his hand on the podium, changing the rhythm of his message. "For love. Exactly what Jesus was talking about. He did it all for love. Exactly what is in the Psalms. This is a strange mystery to us. I don't think any of us understand how much God loves us. We know he loves us so much that he gives us free choice. He gives us the choice to accept or deny him."

Pastor Jones stretched his arms wide. "I'm not sure we, as humans, will fully understand the depth and mysteries of his love until we're standing before him on our judgment day. I think maybe then we'll gain a better understanding of what love really is. Yes, we catch glimpses of it here and there in our daily lives. A mother holds her newborn baby for the first time. A young man drops to a knee and asks a woman to marry him. A man and woman, who have been married for over sixty years, hold their old, trembling hands and smile with a joyful confidence in their eyes that they would do it all again."

Pastor Jones' expression turned soft and he smiled. "I believe God reminds us of his love in his creation, the beauty and wonders of this world. We see it every evening in the setting sun, in the call of a loon, in the majestic blanket of stars covering the night. He shows us his perfect nature in nature.

"I love the picture of the tree by the stream that the psalmist paints for us. Don't you? Here in Eastern Iowa, it's easy to relate to. If you walk down to the banks of the Wapsi, you'll see magnificent, ancient trees towering overhead. Some straight up, some slanted at angles over the river, some fallen to their side are a remnant of what they once were.

Pastor Jones lifted up his Bible over his head. "The psalmist writes of a river that brings life to the trees and the leaves never wither. I think about the mystery of this river in the Bible, and then I think about the Wapsi—the Wapsipinicon, with its depth, its beauty, and the mystery of what lingers beneath the surface as it moves. The river with its currents, its force, its life. Can you imagine a river that brings life but never dies?"

The congregation sat silent. Unlike previous sermons, Pastor Jones captured the attention of everyone in the room. Even Jim Barton and Old Man Gelkie were awake.

"From a historical perspective in Eastern Iowa, we can relate to this notion. Anamosa was settled over a hundred years ago where the Buffalo meets the Wapsi. Ironically, the first settlement who planted the seeds for our community is now marked by Riverside Cemetery. But it was at this junction of the rivers that brought life to the land.

"The community grew over time with more businesses, a main street, the railroad, a dam, and then a prison. Later came more schools, a library, more churches, and a hospital. A community full of life, of drama, of generations striving to make this region a little better for the next."

Pastor Jones smiled and glanced back up at the congregation. "And it all started with the river. It's still flowing, still strong, still at the core of what brought life to our community.

"Here is the true mystery of it all." Pastor Jones stopped again, taking a long pause. "That river is flowing inside all of us. All of us have the power to love. To bring life and dreams and joy and hope to those around us. By accepting Jesus, the Holy Spirit flows within us, guiding us toward righteousness. All of us have the freedom to choose."

He paused for a few seconds and then he asked, "Are we going to live through love or through fear? Life flowing through our veins like a never-ending river? Or fear and eventual death, in a dry desert, where everything withers and dies? Your hope, joy, love, and peace are all here," Pastor Jones said, lifting his Bible over his head.

Andy glanced around the room, astounded. For the first time he could ever remember, the congregation was listening. Not just listening, but captured by his message. They hung on every word, wanting him to continue.

Pastor Jones gazed out into the congregation. "Today on this beautiful summer Sunday morning, I end this sermon with a question for your eternity. Love or fear? The choice is yours."

The room was silent. Everyone sat motionless.

Pastor Jones cleared his throat. "Would the ushers please come forward to accept the offering?"

Looking back to the corner of the congregation, Pastor asked, "Beatrice, can you please come forward to lead us with the first and last stanzas of 'Amazing Grace'?"

The plate was passed and money collected, followed by a rousing rendition of "Amazing Grace." Andy thought there might be a wrestling match with Beatrice up on pulpit and Ginny Ford and Laura Lee Meyer vying for the lead role. By the end of the song, all three of them had tried to outdo the other with their longer and louder notes, shrills, and theatrics. Pastor Jones cut them off with a short and quick benediction, and the church service was over.

ꕥ

John led his family down into the basement of the church for refreshments. If there was a favorite part of church for Andy, this was it. There was usually a solid assortment of chocolate chip cookies, seven layer bars, and his favorite, scotcheroos. The snacks were brought in by several of the ladies each week—each of them trying to gain the pastor's favor by outdoing the other with their baking.

As John poured a cup of coffee, he heard Sheriff Jim Barton from across the room. He was surrounded by all three Hampton sisters, Ginny Ford, and Laura Lee Meyer.

"Yep, had a late one last night. Had to head out to Prairieburg. Seems there was quite a ruckus out there," Sheriff Barton said to his audience of curious gossipers as he sipped his coffee. "Seems Billy West made quite a mess out there."

At the recognition of Billy's name, John Crawford's ears perked up.

The ladies nodded, hanging on Jim's words. The large bird's

nest, beehive hairstyles swayed in unison. Sherriff Barton popped a cookie in his mouth before he continued with his version of the facts. "That boy is always finding trouble. Seems wherever he goes, he makes a mess. Seems he put quite a whooping on some folks out there. Ronnie Wilson is in the hospital with both arms busted. Dicky Moss is in the hospital, too. His right arm is broke, and his collarbone is, too. Only it was a compound fracture. Bone was sticking clear through the skin."

The women's heads all popped back at the same time when they heard this statement, followed by a deep gasp from all of them. "Ewwwoooo."

"Are the boys going to be okay?" Claire Hampton asked.

"Yeah, they'll be fine. Doc Thompson says it looks like somebody took to them with a baseball bat." Sheriff Barton pressed his lips tightly and shook his head, adding more drama to his story. Again the ladies heads bounced back at the report. "Billy West sure made a mess of them. But Doc assures me that they'll be out of the hospital later today or tomorrow tops."

Sheriff Barton's eyes lit up. "This ain't the first time I've had problems with old Billy West. Seems that boy thinks he can come back here from the army and do whatever he pleases. Already investigating him for tearing up Gus' Tavern a couple weeks ago."

Ginny Ford nodded. "I think I heard about that."

Jim grabbed two more cookies off the plate while telling his account of the events. "Only this time I got me some eyewitnesses. The boys don't remember too much. Whoever it was, they say he had a bat, but it was hard to see in the darkness.

It seems he just jumped them out of nowhere."

"Oh the poor boys, who would do such a thing?" Claire Hampton asked, patting her lips with a napkin.

John Crawford moved closer and closer to the group of ladies surrounding Sheriff Barton and tried to hear what happened.

"I got me a material witness this time. Sally Mayfield says she saw it all. Billy was dead drunk and exploded into a rage when these boys asked Anna Jacobs to dance."

"Humph, that Billy West…dead drunk…sounds like his pa if you ask me. The apple don't fall far from the tree in that family," Agnes Hampton said, and the other ladies nodded in bopsy-beehive unison.

"And Anna Jacobs. Don't that girl have a lick of sense? I know her momma raised her better than that. I saw her a few weeks ago at Buddy's Café. She was all over him," Ginny Ford added as she pressed her lips tightly together in disapproval.

Sheriff Barton nodded. "Sally says she seen him in a rage after the boys asked Anna to dance. He followed them boys out of the ballroom and then out into the parking lot. Supposedly he went and got his bat, and that was when the assault happened." The Sheriff paused for effect and even stopped chewing and slurping. "I've seen my share of fights out in the parking lot at Prairieburg, but I can't remember one this violent."

"Apple don't fall too far from the tree, if you ask me," Agnes Hampton said again, shaking her head.

"Seems he also smashed up their car pretty good. The lights was busted out and the windshield, too," Sheriff Barton added as he popped two more cookies in his mouth.

"That Billy West made quite a mess of things this time," Ginny Ford concluded, and the ladies agreed.

"But that ain't all." Sheriff Barton tried to continue talking but was struggling now with his priorities. He was thoroughly enjoying the attention from the ladies, but he was also eyeing a chocolate brownie on the platter.

He paused from his story for a moment and stuffed the brownie in his mouth. The dark brown goop seeped out the sides of his mouth with a drop of something black on his chin. John Crawford was close enough that he could see the chocolate brownie chunks and grit stuck in Barton's teeth. Taking a long drink from his coffee cup, the Sheriff cleared his throat. "That ain't all he done. There's more."

"More?" the ladies all responded in curious unison, their mouths agape and hands clasped against their bosoms.

Jim Barton stopped again to maximize the effect. He searched the eyes of each lady in his audience and dropped his voice a notch. "Seems he also assaulted a couple of girls."

"Assault?" The ladies gasped in unison.

"Got one, maybe two girls from Monti that claim he attacked them, too. Still checking their statements cause there seems to be some inconsistencies, but it sounds like Billy West tried to have his way with them."

All of the women's heads swayed back in unison, and it was an act of God that they didn't fall to the ground. They were uniformly stunned with the potential of the juicy gossip.

"Bad things seem to happen when Billy West is around,"

Sheriff Barton concluded.

"Apple don't fall far from the tree in that family," Agnes repeated again, and all were in agreement.

Taking a bite from another brownie, Sheriff Barton stated with authority, "I suppose once I get all the statements from all the parties involved I'll be seeking a warrant for his arrest."

The words stung at John Crawford's senses. He had been quietly listening as long as he could and now spoke up. "Jim, I'm not buying it."

There was an uncomfortable pause in the room. Maggie had watched her husband as he listened to Sheriff Barton use the story to bask in the attention of these women. She knew John often said Sheriff Barton was not a man that could be trusted. He was like a ship without a rudder, willing to do anything to gain anyone's respect.

Maggie watched as her husband inched closer to the sheriff. She could see in his posture that he was going to challenge the sheriff. She could see it happening, right there at church, and she wouldn't be able to stop him. His pride to do right would make it impossible for him to not challenge the sheriff.

"First of all, it's not in his nature." John let the words hang out there for the group to absorb. No one responded. John looked into their eyes and several of the ladies looked down to the floor. He saw fear and even guilt. They had been quick to judge, and now John Crawford was judging them, rightfully.

John clenched his jaw, straightened up, and spoke with authority. "You mean to tell me that after two boys asked Anna Jacobs to dance, that Billy West went after them in the parking lot with a baseball bat?"

The protective circle of ladies around Sheriff Barton opened up to allow John into the discussion.

"Yep, from the looks of it." Sheriff Barton proudly defended his story.

"From the looks of it? From the looks of it, you say?" John mimicked the sheriff. "From the looks of it, you're getting played on this one. From the looks of it, you're going to end up looking like the other end of the horse," John mocked him.

"Now hold it right there, John…" Sheriff Barton tried to respond, but he still had a large brownie in his mouth, and it got caught in his throat. He coughed, took a drink of his coffee, and was going to continue when John spoke again.

"No, you hold it." John's chest rose and eyes bore into the sheriff's. "Who did you say your primary witness was?"

"Sally Mayfield," the sheriff responded confidently.

"Right, Sally Mayfield. Now let me see…as I recall, Sally works at Gus' Tavern. As I recall, I've seen her hanging around with Joe Matsell for some time. In fact, I think we would all agree that they've been together for years."

The ladies now nodded, agreeing with John.

"Well, I—" Sheriff Barton tried to respond, but John put his hand up to stop Barton mid-sentence.

"I think we would all agree there's no love lost between Joe Matsell and Billy West. And, in light of recent events at Gus' Tavern, there might be some kind of motive for Joe or even Sally to pin this on Billy."

"Well, I'm still investigating. Like I said, I still got some statements to collect and such…" Sheriff Barton started to say.

"Still investigating? I just heard you announce to these ladies, in front of God and everybody, that you were ready to arrest Billy West on several counts of assault!" John raised his voice and stepped closer to Sheriff Barton.

"Well, I am, but…"

"But before you do, I know you're going to ask yourself a few logical questions. To start with, how did Sally see Billy follow the boy out into the lot, grab a baseball bat, and attack them if she was inside the ballroom?"

The ladies in the circle, gasped in unison, suddenly struck by the fact that Sheriff Barton's story had some holes in it. They looked among themselves, acknowledging that he might not have any proof of what really happened out at Prairieburg.

Sheriff Barton sensed he was losing credibility with the ladies. "Now you just wait one minute, mister." Sheriff Barton squared his shoulders.

"No, you wait and listen." John jabbed his finger in the middle of the Sheriff's chest. Maggie could see the intense look in her husband's eyes and where this was going. She knew this was not going to end well. "Barton, first of all, if you had a damn bit of sense you'd know Sally is Joe's girl, and her story doesn't add up."

"Well, yeah, but—" Barton tried to respond and again was cut off by John Crawford.

"Yeah, but? Don't that seem a bit peculiar?" John stood firm with his hands on his hips.

"Well it might be, but—" the sheriff tried to answer

defensively.

"So, you would agree the first report is usually wrong, and there might be more to the story?"

"Well, yeah, everyone in my line of work knows that." Sheriff Barton was not going to let John Crawford speak over him again and raised his voice. "And I'll be conducting my investigation. Once I get all the facts, I'll make my decision." Sheriff Barton wiped the chocolate off his mouth and tried to regain some authority amongst the group of ladies.

"Well, I hope you've got your eyes wide open on this one because right now, you're not seeing the whole picture." John's eyes were intense as he scanned the group of ladies standing around Barton.

"I've got a solid set of witnesses." Sheriff Barton raised his voice to reassure his audience he was in control.

"And before you go out pressing charges and locking people up, you make damn sure to get all your facts straight. You don't want to be the one that ends up being played the fool in all of this." John's face was turning red as he challenged, and many of the women leaned uncomfortably away from the Sheriff.

Jim Barton knew he was losing ground to John. "Now don't you go telling me how to do my job. I've been the sheriff in this here county for over three years…"

"And for three years, you haven't done a damn thing to ensure the safety of the citizens of this town." John's face was pinched with anger as he pointed his finger into the sheriff's chest.

The room was heating up at this point, and most of the

congregation gathered around the two men as they sparred. Andy stood at his mother's side, amazed at his father's fearlessness in his confrontation with authority.

"John Crawford, don't you go raising your voice at me. I'm the law in this here town, and it would be in your best interest if…"

John stepped forward and was inches from the Sheriff's face. "Barton, I'll raise my voice if I damn well please! I'm a citizen of this here town. Last time I checked, you work for me. And the next time you…"

Maggie stepped in between the two men and broke into the conversation. "The next time you're up on the north side of town, please stop by the house? The cherries have really come on this summer, and I've already got a mess of jars filled with cherry jelly for you to have."

Maggie graciously smiled at Sheriff Barton as she tried to diffuse the confrontation. She had her arm hooked around her husband's and was pulling him out of the circle of women.

"Well thank you, Maggie. Don't mind if I do. That's mighty nice of you to offer," Sheriff Barton responded, relieved she broke up the quarrel and the tight spot he was in.

"Just come by anytime this next week, and I'll have some ready for you." Maggie smiled flatly, dragging her husband toward the steps leading out of the church basement. John grinned, knowing he had gone too far with Barton. Maggie had saved him from real trouble. Such a fine woman. She was always saving him from his stupid pride.

As the Crawford family reached the top of the stairs, they

were met by Pastor Jones. "Thank you for coming today. Hope you folks will be able to get out and enjoy this beautiful day."

"Thanks, Pastor. Great sermon. I always enjoy hearing you share the Word." Maggie smiled pleasantly.

"Thanks, Maggie. Have a great day, and I hope to see you here next Sunday." Pastor shook hers and John's hands before they exited the church.

Not another word was said from that moment on as the Crawfords got into their car and drove across town. Andy felt the heavy silence weighing down on them. He had never seen his father get angry like that or seen him stand up against somebody. Andy always knew his dad was strong, but this may have been the first time he caught a glimpse of his father's strength.

From the backseat, he saw his mom's hand resting in his dad's hand. She was always there for him—always at his side, always there to support him, to love him, to take care of him. Andy smiled. He never thought his mom was cool, but she was. She was in her own beautiful way. Andy was proud to be called a Crawford boy.

Andy smiled again. He was looking forward to the picnic that afternoon. Uncle Dave would be there and so would Billy West.

"I can't wait to see Billy at the picnic today." Andy broke the silence in the car.

"Me too, Son. Me too," his dad responded.

IV

JOHN, DAVE, JOSH, Billy, and Andy all stood in a circle around the grill, gazing into the coals as they turned from black to an ashy gray. The men had been quiet up until this point. Each had a drink in their hand and appeared to be deep in thought.

"Nothing better than standing around a grill with a cold beer." Dave held up his beer and toasted Billy and John.

"Pure joy. Something about building a fire to cook your own food. Makes a man feel like a man." Billy smiled and took a sip of his beer.

After a few more minutes of silence, John turned to Billy and asked the question. "So, quite a night out at Prairieburg, eh?"

"What? What'd you hear?" A flash of concern washed over Billy's face.

"Well, it's got half the town talking this morning," John replied, taking a long draw from his beer.

"Half the town?" Both Billy and Josh responded simultaneously.

"Well, maybe not half, but if Sheriff Barton has his way, it will be."

"Sheriff Barton is involved?" Billy's mouth hung open, and his eyes widened in surprise.

"Seems he is." John poked the charcoal to see if it was ready. "I had quite a discussion with him this morning at church."

"You should've seen it!" Andy jumped into the discussion. "I thought Dad was going to knock his block off right there in the church."

John glanced at his son with eyes that told him to stay out of the conversation. Andy, disappointed, dropped his shoulders and obeyed in silence.

"I've heard one version of the story. Now, are you going to add some truth to all of this?" John asked, looking Billy in the eye.

"What? What'd you hear?" Billy never wanted any trouble with the sheriff, and his tone was uneasy.

"Well, from the sounds of it, Ronnie Wilson and Dicky Moss got into quite a scrape. In fact, both of them are still in the hospital with multiple broken bones."

A large grin formed on Josh's face. "Let me start by saying that those boys were up to no good, and I only did what had to be done." John was taken aback at Josh's admission. He had not heard his name mentioned in any of this. "They grabbed Anna and pulled her out into their car."

"Anna?" John was even more surprised now. Clearly, Sheriff Barton had only gotten one side of the story.

"God knows what would've happened if I hadn't been out in the lot with Charlotte at the time," Josh said, motioning back toward the park pavilion where Charlotte, Anna, Dave's friend Nancy, and Maggie were preparing lunch.

"I heard a woman scream. Didn't know it was Anna at the time, but in a way, I knew it was her." Josh had a puzzled look, and he paused for a moment. "I have to say, I don't think Charlotte has ever seen me move that fast." Josh smiled. "And I'll add that she wasn't too happy about it. In a flash, I had my Louisville Slugger in my hand and sprinted across the parking lot."

The men stood silent and let Josh tell his story without interruption. "So, I see these two guys shoving Anna into the backseat of a car. She's screaming wildly, and from the looks of it, she was fighting like a tomcat. Quite honestly, I can't explain what happened next. My instincts took over. I was in complete control, taking well aimed and deliberate swings at the two men. It all happened at once, and the next thing I knew, those two boys were both face down in the dirt. I stepped over them, and immediately coaxed Anna out of the car." Josh paused as he gazed into the hot red coals.

"Let me tell you, it took some doing. She's better today, but last night, I don't think she knew where she was. Strange what fear will do to a person." Josh glanced up at Billy, who was lost in his own thoughts as he too stared into the coals.

John didn't say a word. He let Josh fill in the holes of the version he had heard earlier in the morning from Jim Barton.

"I should've never let her out of my sight." Billy's tone was grim. "I should've known. Just didn't see it coming. I mean, I figured Joe Matsell would come back for me at some point for what I did to him, but I never saw this…" Billy's voice tapered off.

"Billy, you can't…you can't control everything." John tried to console him.

Billy looked up at John, his face red and full of anguish. "Not Anna…she…she had nothing to do with any of this. I can't believe…I mean, I don't even want to think about what could've happened if Josh hadn't been there for me."

"Did you see Joe?" John asked.

"No…" Billy shook his head. "No, I didn't, but I suspect he was the one that jumped me."

"What? You? You got attacked, too?" John asked, again surprised by the new information.

"Yeah. I was looking out the back door of the ballroom for Anna, and then the next thing I know Josh is holding me against the wall." Billy said as he put his arm around Josh.

"You should've seen him. Screaming like a madman. About the LT being down and killing all of them. Pure rage. I ain't never seen anything like it. He was about to take it out on a couple of girls from Monti. Not sure what he would've done if I hadn't been there." Josh patted Billy on the back.

Dave and John glanced at each other knowingly, but didn't say a word.

"It wasn't quite as dramatic as Josh tells it." Billy tried to downplay Josh's description.

"You don't even know, Billy. You didn't even know where you were. It took at least five minutes for me to get through to you. You didn't even recognize me. Thought you were going to come after me too."

John sensed Billy was uncomfortable and broke into the conversation. "So, how are you and Anna doing today?"

"My head feels like a freight train tore through it," Billy said, rubbing the back of his head. "I think we're going to lay low today. And Anna? She seems fine now, almost like it never happened. Kind of strange really. But I think she's going to be okay. I still don't know what I would've done without Josh here." Billy toasted Josh and took another drink of his beer.

"And no one ever saw Joe Matsell?" John asked again.

"Not directly. Well, really, we're not quite sure," Josh answered. "When I went back to find Billy in the ballroom, Anna stayed with Charlotte out in my car. It was dark and all, but Charlotte thought she saw a large man talking to the two boys that had the run in with me and Mr. Louisville Slugger. She doesn't know Joe Matsell, and it was dark, so she couldn't tell for sure."

"I see." John thought through Jim Barton's version of the incident and Sally Mayfield's role in it all.

"Hearing Sheriff Barton this morning, there's a good chance there may be charges pressed," John warned.

"Charges?" Billy and Josh responded in unison.

"Says he's got a material witness who saw it all. Sally Mayfield says Billy here followed Ronnie and Dicky out of the ballroom after they pestered Anna for a dance."

"What? That's chicken shit! Absolute chicken shit! That never happened. We never saw them in the ballroom." Billy stepped back and raised his hands in frustration.

"Billy, don't shoot the messenger…at least not yet. I'm giving you the version coming from Sally Mayfield. Never heard Josh's name in any of this. According to the sheriff, Sally says she saw Billy here attack the two boys with a baseball bat out in the lot. Says he beat them badly and then took it out on their car too."

"What? If I ever heard a bunch of no good, low down, chicken shit…" Billy's frustration turned to anger, but John raised his voice and spoke over him.

"It gets better, Billy. Seems that in your rage you went after two girls from Monti back in the ballroom. I don't know if that part of the story came from Sally or from these other girls, but that's what Sheriff Barton is going on right now."

"Joe Matsell is behind all of this. That no good, back stabbing, dirty son of…" Billy squeezed his fists.

"Easy, Billy. There's a little bit of truth to this…" Josh reached out and put his hand on Billy's shoulder to calm him down.

"What? This is absolute horse…"

"I ain't saying that it ain't. But the part about them two girls from Monti. There's some truth there. You may not know it. Hell, from what I seen in your eyes, I'm not sure you even remember it. But I'll be damned if you wouldn't have done something terrible to them. I saw it in your eyes. Something in you I ain't never seen. Billy, I'm not ashamed to say this, but what I saw in you…it was ugly. There was a darkness there. Something I ain't seen before. It scared me," Josh said.

"Don't be giving me all this. You don't know. There ain't nothing." Billy struggled to find the words. "There ain't nothing to worry about."

"I just want, I just want you to get…" Josh replied.

"To get me another beer, too," Dave broke into the

conversation. "In fact, why don't you pull the cooler over here to the grill, more efficient that way." Dave pointed over at the cooler under the pavilion.

Billy smiled and turned from the men standing around the grill and began his walk over to the pavilion.

"Billy, while you're over there, get the burgers from Maggie. Looks like the coals are ready," Dave called out as he adjusted the grill over the coals.

Billy returned with the cooler and a dejected expression on his face. "Looks like I've got some details I need to work out with that fat ass Barton."

John could see the wheels turning in Billy's mind. "Patience, Billy. I would let it work itself out. I got a feeling old Sheriff Barton is going to see that things aren't quite what they seem in all this. Let him come to you. Quite honestly, I'll be surprised if he ever does. Jim Barton isn't a finisher. He talks a big game, but he lacks the persistence to find closure. My gut says that like most things, he'll quickly become overwhelmed with other issues that seem more pressing than this."

John took a sip of his beer. "Now that doesn't mean you don't need to get your ducks in a row. He may come to you directly this week. I doubt he will, but it is possible. Based on everything I've heard from the two of you and from Barton this morning, I think Miss Charlotte over there is probably your ace in the hole. I'm sure with some coaching, she'll realize that Joe Matsell was out there in the lot last night and is the ringleader in all of this." John looked directly at Billy. "Quite honestly, that's what you need to be thinking about. Joe Matsell is your problem.

There's a darkness in him, and I'm not sure how far he'll go with all of this."

Billy had already thought about these things, but it was good to hear them from someone he trusted. He considered stopping by to see Judge Swanson, but he didn't want to bother the good judge about a scrap he got in at a dancehall. And besides, the Judge had mentioned he was going to be in Washington this week for business. Billy would wait on Sheriff Barton. Let him make the next move. But Big Joe… Big Joe was another problem altogether. Billy would need to get ahead of him and stay at least one step ahead of his next move.

ꙮ

"Those burgers smell incredible," Josh said as the burgers sizzled on the grill.

"You should see what Maggie and the ladies have over on the table. Saw them lift the lid of a large pan of fried chicken. Not sure I've ever smelled chicken quite like that, so good I can just taste it." Billy licked his lips.

"Andy, run on over there to your ma and get me a platter to put the burgers on," John told his son.

"Ah, Pa, do I have to?" Andy asked, although he knew the answer.

"You go on and do as you're told. Go get the platter from you mother." Andy's shoulder slumped as he obediently walked over to the pavilion.

The men looked over at the ladies setting the tables when John turned to Dave. "Brother, you going to tell me about this girl you picked up off the street?"

"Yeah, I was meaning to tell you that I been…" Dave was interrupted by his brother.

"How much you paying her anyway? Does she charge by the hour or by your personal desires?" John smiled as he lightly slugged his brother in the arm.

The men laughed as John gave his older brother the business about the new girl in his life. John was very happy for his brother. Dave hadn't dated anyone in years, and John and Maggie wondered if Dave would ever find anyone. Not that this would be "the one," but, it was good to see a woman in Dave's life. And to think that he and Maggie didn't even know about her until this morning.

Maggie had been scheming for years to set Dave up with women. She went as far as to have them over for dinner, conspicuously on the same night Dave was there. Dave understood John and Maggie were trying to do what they thought was best for him, but in the end, he grew frustrated with their meddling. In fact, he had a few words last year with John that put an end to the surprise female guests at the Crawford's dinner table.

"So Maggie and I are getting ready for church this morning when I get this call from Mr. Casanova here. He's explaining that he won't be going to our church today. Something about meeting with a friend over at the Catholic Church this morning," John explained to Josh and Billy.

Dave broke into a smile. "Well I was meaning to tell you that…"

"You didn't even tell us that your friend was a woman." John interrupted him again.

"Well you know that I don't like to..." Dave tried to respond.

"Don't like to date women? Yeah, I think most the folks in Jones County know this." John chuckled.

"Come to find out after all these years that you do have affection for the opposite sex. Now I know it's just that you're very particular about them."

"Now brother..." Dave tried again.

"Now brother, from the looks of it, you only go after the beautiful ones. So I guess we Crawfords have something in common after all." John smiled as he put his arm around his brother, sincerely happy for the new relationship in his life.

Dave glanced over at the pavilion where the ladies were preparing lunch. The grin on his face widened as he thought about the amazing woman who had entered his life.

Dave had met Nancy three weeks earlier at Buddy's Café. Nancy, Mabel Lewis' second cousin from Waco, Texas, was visiting over the summer and working part time at the café. Dave had been having breakfast alone that morning, and he had not expected this relationship to enter his life. In fact, he guarded himself against it. But with Nancy it had come so easily—the words that flowed between them, the shine in her eyes, the easy smiles they shared.

With other women, relationships had always been hard. Nothing was ever easy. The uncomfortable pauses in conversations, the worry of a future together, and the wonder if this could be the person he would spend the rest of his life with. For Dave, love was not just difficult, it had become almost impossible. Dave had all but given up on love. He often looked to his brother and Maggie in jealous wonder that they had found each other. He didn't believe the right man and woman could find each other in this world and live a lifetime of devotion together in love.

He had not expected to find love on that Saturday morning, but there it was. Within moments after Mabel made their introduction, he and Nancy felt something incredibly special between them. Something that could not be denied. Something that should not be denied. Something easy, lovely, and right. At forty-three, he had all but given up on love, but love had not given up on him. With Nancy, Dave started to believe that love was possible in this world.

During the last three weeks, the couple had long conversations, long drives across the countryside, and late evening walks. Dave even took her fishing. Nancy filled his heart with a warmth he had never known, and his thoughts were constantly preoccupied with spending time with her.

Even though Nancy was eight years younger, the gap in their age did not negatively affect their relationship. It strengthened it. Their age differences complemented their love. It made each of them better individuals. This new found love was like nothing he had ever known. It filled the cracks in his life. For the first time since before WWII, he felt whole.

Dave had come to realize both of them had their scars. He carried the visible crippling of one of his legs and the secrets he dared not to share from the war. Her scars were from a different kind of war.

Straight out of high school Nancy had married a controlling and incredibly brutal man, bent on making her life a living hell. Not long after their marriage, it had become clear she would not be able to bear children. From that point on, he had abused her for eight long and tortuous years. At first he had played games with her mind, evolving into torment and a mental state of imprisonment. Then it had gotten worse as her husband drank more and more, and the abuse became physical. He would often come home late, dead drunk, and would force himself on her. The first few times, she had fought him off, but he would beat her for it. Eventually, she would give into it. Feeling nothing, numbness had taken over her body as her husband had his way with her.

Years of abuse and torment had ruined her. For some time, she had felt a sharp hatred for him that she never knew she had in her. But toward the end, she had stopped caring and had been unable to feel anything but darkness—a death crept into her veins, and she had wanted it all to end.

Then one day, he had left her for a woman down in Austin. She had known about the other women. The fact he was leaving her for someone else didn't faze her. He had left her before and would come back. She had thought he would be back within a few months, and she had waited with dread for his eventual return. But he never returned. Instead of her husband coming back to her home, it had been the sheriff. She had come to find out that he had been with the woman of a very jealous and violent husband, who had found them together at a hotel and had ended it all with his twelve gauge shotgun—killing them first and then taking his own life.

As the sheriff explained what had happened, Nancy was overwhelmed with grief, anger, and disbelief that he was actually gone. She could not believe the nightmare was actually over. She never thought it would end in her life. For weeks after the funeral, she had wondered if she might have been dreaming and that she would wake up to find him passed out on the couch after a long night of drinking. Years passed and eventually all she felt was emptiness. He had taken a part of her away. Up until this summer, Nancy had wondered if she would ever be whole again.

Her husband was gone, but Nancy struggled every day in Texas to escape the nightmare he had made her life. This past spring, her cousin Mabel had asked her to come and spend the summer with her. Nancy knew something had to change. She had never left Texas and had thought she never would. Then she found life after Texas and a world where she might find hope and…love.

Dave beamed as he looked over at Nancy with the other ladies. He didn't care about her past. It made her the woman she was today and that was all that mattered. He wondered how she had come into his life. They both had their scars, and in just a few short weeks, they had found a love that could heal them. He smiled at the wonder of it all.

"What can I say, John. She just…" Dave tried to explain to his brother when he was interrupted by the voice he longed for.

"Dave, it's about time to eat. Can you come over here and

give a hand with cutting the watermelon?" With the sound of Nancy's sweet voice, Dave smiled again. It just seemed so right. John said something in a sarcastic tone, but Dave didn't hear him. He walked over to the pavilion, took the knife from Nancy, and cut the watermelon.

ᢀᢁ

"That is some damn fine fried chicken," Josh declared, rubbing his stomach.

The men nodded. They were too busy eating to make a comment. It was a spectacular day in late July. Ice cold beer, amazing food, and great friends.

"Now you boys slow down. There's plenty to go around. And don't forget to leave some room for the watermelon Nancy brought. Oh, and there are two of my homemade cherry pies," Maggie pointed to her desserts at the end of the table.

"Homemade cherry pie?" Josh asked. "I don't know if I'll be able to make room for…"

Maggie raised her voice over Josh. "You had better find room for it. You know I made it with fresh cherries from the trees in our backyard, and the crust is my grandmother's very own recipe from scratch."

Nancy leaned over and placed a hand on Maggie's. "I swear, Maggie, you do know how to feed the men in your life. Homemade cherry pie, fried chicken, burgers, baked beans, deviled eggs, and the potato salad is simply wonderful. I hope you'll share your recipe."

"You should try some corn on the cob. It is amazing,"

Anna said, handing the platter to Nancy.

"What do you think, Dave? Can it get any better than this?" John asked, looking up from his plate and across to the picnic table to his brother. But his question was not about the food or the picnic. There was more depth in his tone. Dave knew it, too. It was about this new found love in his life. He knew his brother was sincerely happy for him.

"You know, Johnny, I didn't think it could be this good," Dave said, reaching for another chicken breast. He glanced over at Nancy, and they both caught each other in a smile.

Josh and Billy joined in with a conversation about baseball and the Chicago Cubs. But Dave didn't hear them. He was lost in his thoughts of Nancy. When he caught her in a smile, he realized how beautiful she was. She was plain but in a beautiful sort of way. She had a natural beauty that didn't need to try hard, it just was. However, when they had first met, he had detected a sad dullness in her eyes, and something was lacking—a plainness covering up her truth. As their relationship grew, he had come to understand her past and watched that sadness melt away.

The first time they had kissed, Dave felt an electricity jolt through his body like nothing he had ever known. It was as if he had been asleep for years and was suddenly awakened to a world of fresh beauty and color. Since then, they had kissed a number of times, but they were moving slow. He was not ready to reveal his scars. His crippled leg was battered and ugly. He had always worn pants. Even today as the temperature would reach the mid-nineties, Dave wore his pants.

He had come to understand that she had scars too, much

deeper, and she too wanted to go slow. Other than her husband, she had never been with another man and was not ready to open herself up to Dave. Time. Let it grow. Dave would wait and enjoy what they had. He would enjoy their love as it blossomed over the summer.

Charlotte reached across his plate for the salt and pepper and broke Dave's trance. She then cut in on the conversation. "I've never been here to the Wapsipinicon Park. It's absolutely stunning. How long has the park been here?"

Dave took a sip of his iced tea. "I think it opened in the early 1920s. It was one of the first parks in the state of Iowa. As I understand, the inmates from the prison did much of the work to develop it. Clearing the road, building pavilions, even setting up the golf course," Dave answered with a trace of annoyance in his tone.

"Well I must say, they did a fine job. There certainly is a fascinating beauty to it. The high bluffs and cliffs, the deep woods, the Wapsipinicon River cutting through. It's the perfect setting for a park," Charlotte added as she took a bite of her corn on the cob.

"You're right. This is a special place in Iowa, and it's always attracted the local residents. For centuries, it was likely occupied by Indians, maybe as far back as 10,000 years before Christ. The Algonquians and the Sioux were some of the first that we know of. The Sauk and Fox, decedents of the Algonquians, were here when settlers arrived, and there have been some indicators that Indians were here long before that." Dave's face was radiant as he spoke like an enthusiastic history teacher giving a class.

Anna interjected to pull the conversation away from Charlotte. “I’ve always thought there was something special about the dolomite cliffs throughout the park. A mysterious ancient beauty coupled with formidable strength. They probably provided shelter for the residents here.”

“Yeah, the clean limestone cliffs, the deep ravines, and the hidden caves probably provided a safe home for Indians through the ages.” Dave nodded.

“Uncle Dave, tell them about the skeletons in Horse Thief Cave.” Andy’s eyes lit up as he asked excitedly.

“Skeletons?” Nancy and Charlotte responded in unison.

“As I understand back in the early 1920s, Horse Thief Cave was excavated and nine ancient skeletons were dug up. Some think it may have been a burial ground long ago,” Dave added with an animated expression.

“Wow, an actual burial ground? Sounds kind of spooky.” Charlotte shuddered at the thought.

“Did they really use the cave for stolen horses?” Nancy asked, leaning on her elbow, completely enthralled by Dave’s story.

“I don’t know. Over the years, there have been legends that it was, and that the cave went all the way to Cedar Rapids. Which doesn’t seem possible.” Dave took a drink of his iced tea.

“I’ve been in that cave a dozen times. Never have seen any skeletons or ghosts if you’re worried about it. Mostly empty beer cans and cigarette butts.” Billy laughed sarcastically.

“Other than the caves and cliffs, what else is there to see?” Nancy encouraged Dave to go on with his history lesson.

"Several swimming holes. Not in the river though. Current here tends to be too fast for swimming, too dangerous. When folks come here to swim, they go over to Dutch Creek. The two most popular places are the upside down bridge and Indian Dam," Dave said as he raised two fingers.

"Can we go swimming today, Pa? Can we go to Indian Dam?" Andy asked excitedly as he tugged at his father's arm.

"Not unless you're going skinny dipping. You didn't bring a swimsuit, and your ma will have your hide if you go swimming in those clothes," John replied as he took a bite out of a chicken leg.

"Aw Pa, can we just…" Andy tried to push his parents but was cut off mid-sentence.

"I tell you what, Andy. If your ma and pa don't mind, after lunch I'll take you down to the upside down bridge, and you can wade through the water there," Uncle Dave chimed in.

"That sounds great. A walk would be nice after this large meal," Nancy said as she smiled to Dave.

"He best not fall down in the water, Dave, or you'll be doing the laundry when we get home," Maggie warned.

"No worries, Maggie, we can take care of him. I wouldn't mind going for a walk myself," John said as he took a sip of iced tea.

"I was thinking about a hike up to the top of the cliffs. Maybe all the way up to Pinicon Ridge. What do you think, Billy? You in?" Josh asked, turning to Billy.

"It's been a few years since I've been up there. But if I remember, it has an amazing view of the entire river valley," Billy replied as an excited expression flashed across his face.

"Of course, I'm not sure if a Boy Scout like yourself will want to go up to a place where warriors have been known to make some silly decisions." Josh smiled as he jabbed at Billy.

"You boys can hike the cliffs all you like. I'm going to the upside down bridge to cool down," Charlotte said wiping perspiration off her forehead with her napkin.

"Sounds like a plan. You girls go ahead to Dutch Creek. I'm going to take this college boy on a real hike up the cliffs," Billy said in a cocky tone.

Anna suddenly had a dejected expression on her face. She was hurt by the way the afternoon was unfolding. Charlotte and Josh had wedged themselves in, and she would be not be able to be alone with Billy during the picnic.

Billy sensed her dismay. "It'll just be a short hike. Josh here probably won't be able to make it to the top. We shouldn't be gone any longer than an hour. Anyway, it's a mile walk down to the upside down bridge. You go ahead with them, and after the hike, I'll bring the truck, and we can all come back together."

Anna glanced away. There was a pause in the conversation, and Billy realized he had hurt Anna with the plans for the afternoon. It frustrated him too, and he instantly wished he could rewind the last two minutes and fix it. He knew that more than anything, Anna craved time with him.

Nancy seemed to have sensed it, too. Although she didn't know Anna well, Nancy suspected Anna wanted Billy to desire time with her. As a woman, she knew she wanted to be desired and not to be another obligation. Nancy chimed into the conversation. "So much history to this area. I find it fascinating.

Where did the name Anamosa come from?" she asked, turning to Dave.

"That's a darn good question. Like most good questions, it has a good answer with a story behind it." Dave took a sip of his tea. "Dates all the way back to the early 1830s and the Black Hawk War." He smiled and started in with another history lesson.

"You may recall this was a time in history when the settlers were slowly creeping their way across what is now the Midwest. Well, the Indians in this area, namely the Sauk and Fox, weren't too excited about losing their land and their way of life." Dave looked around the table and had everyone's attention.

"One of the Sauk and Fox leaders, Black Hawk, decided to go to war against the United States. Well, it didn't fare well for him or his people. After a year of fighting, they were pretty much decimated by the army."

"What about Anamosa? How does this fit in?" Andy asked excitedly. He loved Uncle Dave's stories.

"Well toward the end of their war, the Sauk and Fox Tribe got pinned down on the banks of the Mississippi River. Not just the warriors, but the women and children too. It became what the history books call the Battle of Bad Axe."

Dave's tone turned somber. "There was no place for them to go. Many were killed on the banks of the Mississippi. Many more tried to swim across the river and drowned in the process. Hundreds died in the massacre. Now Andy, you asked about Anamosa and how she fits into this story?"

Dave glanced up at Andy to ensure he had his attention.

"Legend has it she was one of just a few survivors of that battle on the Mississippi. She was a baby at the time of the massacre, and it's said her mother strapped her to her back and swam all the way across the river. Her ma's actions saved Anamosa and herself from certain death." Everyone at the picnic table hung on Dave's words as he told the story.

"Now the history books will tell you that this was the glorious Battle of Bad Axe where Black Hawk and his people were defeated. In truth, it was anything but glorious. But at least, one baby girl survived, and it's from her that our town got our name." There was a moment of silence as everyone stopped eating and looked at Dave in deep thought.

Nancy smiled. Dave surprised her at every turn. At first glance, he seemed hard and weathered by life's storms. Crippled and leaning on his cane, he hobbled into her life weeks ago on that Saturday morning. Initially she didn't see it, but below the surface was real love like none she had known in Texas. Of all places she might find it, she never thought it would be in Iowa. She smiled again. This life never ceased to surprise her. She had found an honest man, one she never knew could exist in her life. She had all but given up on it, but here he was. All man, all heart, bringing her pure joy and hope for a new future.

As Nancy listened to Dave's story, she was enthralled. She could feel his courage, his strength, and his love. Nancy found it interesting that at the picnic table she was probably the only one who saw it in him. She smiled again and thought of their first kiss—Dave's lips so soft on hers, his heavy, hard, thick, weathered hands caressing hers. She was amazed at his strength and how it transformed and delivered a soft, gentle, and sure touch.

Charlotte rudely broke the silence, and Nancy's sweet memory, as she derived a connection of the story to current events. "Did you see the report on television last night? There was a lot of footage about us bombing civilians and killing hundreds of innocent people in Vietnam."

No one was quite sure how to respond. Then finally, Billy broke in with an agitated tone. "Charlotte, as the saying goes, believe half of what you see and none of what you hear."

"All I'm saying is it's kind of interesting how history repeats its…"

Billy's voice became cold. "What you're seeing on television isn't the truth. It's just somebody's version of it that they want you to hear."

"I was just saying it's kind of an interesting similarity between…" Charlotte tried to defend herself.

"And I'm telling you, what you're seeing on TV isn't necessarily the truth. In Vietnam, there are always at least two sides to every story and most of the time many more. It's pretty hard for reporters to tell the truth when most of them aren't even there. Very few are actually out there where it all happens. Most are back at some hotel or in a bar getting bits of information from drunk soldiers who may not have been there themselves," Billy rebuked her.

There was an uncomfortable pause at the table, and Dave tried to steer the conversation back toward his story. "What I find fascinating about Anamosa is what she must've seen in her life. All the changes. Can you imagine it? Being pulled across the Mississippi during the Black Hawk War in a hail of bullets, and then to later see all your land taken from you in the Black Hawk Purchase. Witnessing the spread of white settlers as they slowly took their land away from them, field by field, river by river.

"This community started with just a few folks right up the river. Andy and I were up there, fishing just a few weeks ago at what they originally called Buffalo Forks. But more and more settlers kept coming, taking the land for their own. They tied it all together with their own roads and fences. And of course, the Old Military Road was developed and cut through the heart of their land from Dubuque, a major trade town on the Mississippi, to Iowa City which was the state capital at the time. Heck, you can see the old steel bridge from here, where the road crossed over the river. It was built back in 1887, but it's still standing strong as a symbol of Anamosa's emergence as a community in the last century."

John reached for the pitcher of iced tea and joined the discussion. "It is hard to imagine what it must have been like, to see the town of Anamosa transformed from a wooded area along the river to what it is today. Many of the early buildings are still here—Shaw's Block, Niles and Watters Bank, the Reformatory. Even the old bridge on the river, and she probably saw it all."

Everyone at the table became silent as if they were deep in thought.

"It's time for dessert. Who'd like a slice of my homemade cherry pie?" Maggie interjected, lightening the mood.

"I'll have a slice, honey," John answered as he lifted his

plate to Maggie.

"I will too, Maggie. I love your homemade cherry pie," Dave added as he grabbed his plate.

"How about you boys? You going to have some dessert?" Maggie asked, looking directly at Billy.

"Yeah, that's probably what I need right now. Some of your homemade cherry pie," Billy answered in a dejected tone, still incensed by Charlotte's comments about the war.

ƦƧ

"Just look at them over there. Smoking their cigarettes and telling their stories. Posturing, always posturing," Maggie said as the women looked at the men throwing horseshoes. Meanwhile, they cleaned up after the meal.

"They seem to have all the fun and relax after dinner, and we get stuck with the dirty work of cleaning up," Anna responded, picking up several paper plates and throwing them in the trashcan.

"Separation is not always a bad thing. They got their time together, and we got ours. Horseshoes or cleaning up after dinner? I'll take the latter." Maggie smiled.

Nancy nodded, clearing off the table. "Sometimes you got to let men be men, and women be women."

"What in the heck does that mean?" Charlotte asked, reaching for another piece of pie.

"It means exactly what it says. I remember what my mother used to tell me. They're the head of the household and need to feel that way. But we ladies, we're the heart, and we have certain abilities and can gently guide them any way we want," Maggie said with a satisfied grin, and all the ladies burst into laughter.

"I've heard that before," Anna chimed in. "My momma says you can't control a man's eyes and Lord knows we can't control what they say. But she says we got to help them. We got to help them to help themselves. We got to help them keep their heart pure. Help them feed their heart with the right things."

"Like cherry pie." Nancy smiled, lifting an empty pie pan. Once again, the ladies let out another burst of laughter.

"This really is good for Billy, being with John and Dave. Don't you think, Anna?" Maggie asked in a more serious tone.

"I…I don't know…I guess…I mean…he really does enjoy spending time with them," Anna answered. "But this summer is just going so fast. I can feel it slipping through my fingers, getting away from me. I can't believe that in ten days, Billy's convalescent leave will be over. He'll be heading back to Fort Benning and leaving me again."

"Trust me, Anna, I've been there. I know what you're going through," Maggie said as she reached out and grasped Anna's hand.

"What I'm going through?" Anna questioned.

"It was a different war and a different time. John was enlisted. We were just married and living in Hawaii. He was gone a lot, training and such. We didn't see it coming…Korea, I mean. But there it was. One day, we were planning on him getting out and moving back here to Iowa, and the next thing we knew, he was boarding a boat for Korea. It happened quickly, but I remember it all and the intense pain of him leaving. We dreaded the time as it slipped by. Then he left, and I was alone. But it wasn't the separation that was so bad. It was the lead-up to it. I know the dread you're feeling."

Anna looked at her, slightly nodding.

"I remember the horrible pain that filled my heart, so much so I thought it would burst. Such a heavy fear, I dared not to give it words. And then…and then he was gone." The women all looked at Maggie.

"But that wasn't really the worst of it. For me, the worst of it was after he came home. The worst was the scars that come later. Not really the noticeable ones like with Dave but the ones beneath the surface. They're real, and they take much, much longer to heal. I wonder if they'll ever heal, or if they'll just be a new normal in our lives." Maggie looked up at Anna. Her eyes were wet with tears. "You know what I'm talking about. You've seen it. The ugly guilt and shame. None of them are the same after they've been touched by fire. They come back, but they're different. The smile is gone from their eyes…"

Anna turned away and wiped a tear from her cheek, unable to respond to Maggie's words.

"Anna, the truth is, Billy needs you. He'll never admit it. Men never do. Their silly pride won't let them. But if they didn't have us in their lives every day, lifting them up, they'd wither and die. They'd kill themselves off with their pity and their shame. Disgusted for the things they've done. They might do it slow, turn heavy to the bottle, or they might speed it up, end it quickly with some pills or something else. Trying to deal with the ugly black seeds in their hearts—the horrible weeds. Nothing seems to keep them from growing."

The ladies sat silently. None of them had seen this side of Maggie before.

"Except love. I'm telling you that without you, he's lost." Maggie paused. She let the words settle in the pavilion. The ladies heard the clink of the horseshoes and the distant laughter of the men and turned their eyes out toward them.

"Maybe it's us. Maybe there's something in women like me and you that are attracted to men who are driven to do those things. Maybe it's our curse that we would love a man who will climb mountains, a man who will not dare to take the easy route. The kind of man that will take on life's challenges with integrity and courage."

Maggie stopped and then continued in a more serious tone. "We know real joy comes through the struggle of doing right. There are far worse things in this world. It could be much worse. A woman could love a man who never stood for anything."

Nancy turned away. Maggie had struck a deep chord. Nancy held a handkerchief to her eyes, crying. Anna and Maggie went to her and wrapped their arms around her.

"Aw, honey, I'm sorry. Sometimes I let my emotions get the best of my mouth. I'm sorry," Maggie said, hugging Nancy.

"Just look at us. We're quite a pair, aren't we?" Anna said to Nancy, smiling as tears rolled down her cheeks too.

The ladies all laughed and wiped the tears from their eyes.

"He's getting out, you know," Anna murmured.

"What? What do you mean?" Maggie's eyes lifted with a questioning expression.

"Billy. Billy's getting out," Anna reaffirmed more confidently. "He's only got four months left before he can get out of the army. He's going back to Benning to complete his recovery, and then he's getting out of all of this for good." Anna smiled and looked out at Billy tossing a horseshoe. "He's talking about coming back here, going to school, maybe even playing ball again."

"Well that's a breath of fresh air, honey," Maggie smiled.

"Yeah, and I think being around Josh has helped. He's gotten a better view of what he could be doing with his life. I think he's excited about it. He's ready to come home so we can start a family." Anna's eyes lit up, and a warm blush touched her cheeks as she smiled. "Oh, did I forget to mention? We got engaged!" Anna blurted out excitedly to the ladies.

"Well, I'll be…" Maggie stepped forward to hug Anna.

Nancy jumped up as she and Maggie surrounded Anna, excited about the prospect of their marriage.

"Did he get you a ring?" Charlotte asked as she ate her pie, barely glancing up at them.

"Well, no, not exactly. But he will. Says he has one already picked out down in Columbus, Georgia. He said he was going to propose down there when I visit in a couple of months, but it slipped out over the last few days."

"So, when's the wedding?" Charlotte questioned as she took another bite, unimpressed.

"Well, we're looking at next spring. Billy will be getting home from the army in December. He's going to apply for school at Iowa for the following year." Anna's face was animated with joy.

Maggie smiled, excited for them. "Well, I'll be, Anna Jacobs and Billy West going to tie the knot… wait a second, you aren't pregnant, are you?" Maggie turned serious with her question.

"Oh gosh, no. It was just, well…we just knew. We've been talking about it for days and then last night, we were dancing out at Prairieburg and it kind of came out. It wasn't formal or anything, just serious talk, but then this morning, Billy came by to pick me up for the picnic. When I came down from my room to meet him at the door, he was already in the middle of the living room, waiting for me on one knee. Did it right in front of my parents." Anna giggled. "Thought Momma was going to faint in her excitement and that Daddy was going to shoot him."

"Well, I'll be, Billy and Anna getting married. If that isn't the best news I've heard since I don't know when," Maggie proudly announced.

"Well, you can't say a word. Billy asked that I keep it under wraps. He wants to do it all proper with a ring and such."

"Aw, poppycock! You know women are horrible with secrets. Especially something as tasty as this," Maggie said in a dejected tone.

"I know. That's what I told him. How does he expect me to keep this all a secret?" Anna smiled.

"Doesn't matter, really. Secret or no secret, Anna and Billy are getting married. I'm so happy for you, for the both of you," Maggie said, hugging Anna again. "This is shaping up to be the best picnic I've been at in years. All of this is wonderful. Simply wonderful."

The ladies all smiled simultaneously. They heard the metallic clank of a horseshoe as it hit the peg. The men let out a cheer. The ladies smiled and watched their men out in the sun with their horseshoes and beer. Posturing, always posturing.

ꕥ

As Billy reached the top of the ridge, his head was pounding. He was still recovering from the night before at Prairieburg. Sweat ran down the side of his face. The afternoon had gotten hotter as the day wore on. His heart was beating fast, and his head was throbbing all the way from the back to his temples. Billy closed his eyes. For a brief moment, he was reminded of a patrol near Dak To—the heat, the pounding in his head. The memories were never out of reach.

Walking toward the edge of the ridge, the river valley opened up below them. Billy almost felt like he was in a trance, floating above the trees and the clouds. His legs were numb. He was angry. He had gotten out of shape since his injuries.

"So here we are, Pinicon Ridge. We made it," Josh announced. Sensing Billy was struggling, he patted him on the shoulder as they stepped to the edge of the cliff and looked down on the river.

"Careful buddy, you know that at least one great warrior has lost his footing up here on this ridge. We don't need another one." Josh chuckled as he referenced the legendary suicidal death of Pinicon.

Billy didn't respond as he glanced over the edge, trying to slow down his breathing.

"Look at them down there. Dave and John are still playing horseshoes. They're so competitive. It looks like the ladies have joined them. They sure do look small from way up here," Josh said, turning to Billy.

"Hmm? Yeah," Billy responded. He heard Josh, but he wasn't listening. His mind was somewhere else. Seeing the men and the ladies down below made him feel like an outsider. He could not get used to this world of picnics, barbeques, and horseshoes. Talk of babies, and movies, and ballgames made him feel like a stranger in his own hometown. He wondered if anyone on this side of the world had any idea what was happening in Vietnam.

Vietnam had changed him and had given him a deeper sense of what life was really about. Life was really about keeping your word, about trust, about doing your duty, about loyalty—even if it meant giving up this world and everything in it. Over there, a man's honor was everything. Here at home, he wasn't sure if it even mattered.

Josh could tell Billy was deep in thought, distant, and separated from him. "You going to tell me?"

"What?" Billy answered surprised, looking over his shoulder at Josh.

"You going to tell me now?" Josh asked again.

"Tell you what?" Billy answered with another question, not wanting to play this game with Josh.

"You know, Billy. The truth." Josh looked out over the cliff at the valley below.

"Truth?" Billy chuckled to himself, unsure if Josh would

understand it.

"Yeah, the truth about last night."

"I'm pretty sure it was Joe who cracked me over the head last night. And from the way I'm feeling right now, it was probably a large whiskey bottle," Billy answered in a dismissive tone.

"That's not what I'm talking about, and you know it," Josh responded, frustrated, as he reached down and picked up a stone.

"No, I don't know what you're talking about, Josh," Billy replied evasively.

"Last night when I pulled you off them girls from Monti, you weren't you—the Billy I know. I don't know who that was, but it was someone else—somebody I've never seen before," Josh explained as he chucked the stone off the cliff.

"Josh, now don't be..."

"No, Billy, there's something going on. And I'll be as honest as I've ever been with you. It scared the hell out of me. You were going to kill those girls. I saw it in your eyes. You weren't you at all. If it weren't me that showed up, I don't know who could have stopped you." Josh stood up to Billy with his hands on his hips. "Hollering something about the LT, cussing up a storm. Billy, I think you need help. I want to..."

"Stay out of it. I'll be fine. I'll be..."

"Aw, bullshit, Billy! You're not fine. There's something going on inside you, and I really care about you. I know you're going to fight me on getting help. Hell, you probably fight Anna about it, too. But at least, give me some truth, so I can help." Josh reached forward to put his arm around Billy, but he pulled away.

"Truth? You want truth?" Billy mumbled with his head down as he kicked at a rock on the ground.

"Yeah Billy, I want…"

"Truth? What is truth?" Billy reached down and picked up a rock and stepped forward to within in inches of Josh with his jaw clenched and anger in his eyes.

"I just want you to tell…"

"You want to know the truth? What if I was to tell you that I ain't sure I know what truth is anymore? What if I was to tell you that to face the truth scares the living hell out me? Truth…" Billy shook his head and tossed the rock over the side of the cliff, watching it fall below. "I don't think I can face the truth anymore." Billy looked out over the ridge. "And no one would believe me anyway. It's too much to ever understand. We don't have the imagination for it, at least not here. Not here on a beautiful, sunny, summer afternoon in Anamosa, Iowa. There's just too much, too much to take in."

Billy squatted down and started to dig at a stone imbedded in the ground. "I'm not good enough and neither are my words to give it justice. Just for me to speak about it, disgraces me and dishonors those that gave their lives so I would live."

Billy cleared his throat and looked up at Josh. "My feeble attempt to speak the truth won't give them the honor they've earned. These words cheapen it. No, the truth is too damn hard. And I'm not worthy of it."

"Billy." Josh placed his arm on Billy's shoulder in a brotherly way, trying to connect, to comfort, to understand. "I saw it in you last night, and I want to help. I see your pain. You need help. Let me try to help you."

Billy's head pounded. He sat down on a large boulder in the shade of an oak and gazed out over the river valley. He felt tired and defeated. Picking up a stick, he tapped it on the ground between his feet. Josh sat down next to him and put his arm around his shoulder.

Billy held the stick up. As he peeled off the bark, he spoke. "I remember the first one. We were flying in a Huey at night over the Central Highlands. I spent a lot of time with the LT or the Old Man, serving as their RTO in those early days. They liked me as their radio operator because I was stronger than the rest. I carried two radios and could still hump twice as fast as the other soldiers. Anyway, we were coming back from a recon that night, bouncing above the canopy of the trees, it was dark.

"I looked toward the cockpit when I heard this tink-tink-tink metallic noise." Billy paused for a moment. The images flashed before his eyes. "At the same time, I felt a wet spray on the side of my cheek. We banked hard to the right. The pilot announced we were taking on some small-arms fire, and he was going to maneuver out of it."

Billy picked at the notches on the stick with his hands. "The strong, warm smell of iron filled the cockpit. I tasted it in my mouth. I couldn't figure out why my face was wet, and I dug around for my L-shaped flashlight. Turning it on, I looked over to my left and there was our RTO, Sal Marzielli. Only he wasn't Sal no more. His head was blown clean off. And where it once was, spurts of blood shot out of the cavity of his neck and sprayed all over the entire cockpit."

Billy dropped the stick in his lap. "It was then that I realized his blood had sprayed all over my face." Billy reached up and touched his face and then looked down at his hands. "My hands were covered with his blood. They were warm and thick. Then I shined my light down the side of my leg, and there was gray chunks splattered all down my left arm and leg. It was his brains, or what was left of them. They were splattered all over the walls inside of the aircraft.

"The flight went on for another thirty minutes or so. I really don't remember. It seemed to go on forever. The CO caught some shrapnel in his hand, but he was okay. He was on the radio the whole time, talking to the pilot like nothing was even wrong. I tried to cover Sal with my poncho, but there was a warm mist in the helicopter from his blood. I was breathing it in. I tasted it in my mouth, I felt it in my lungs. I couldn't escape from it." Billy explained as if he was in a trance.

"That was the first one. The first time I saw somebody killed. We had only been in country a few weeks and really hadn't been on any patrols yet or seen any action. But that was when I knew this was for real. People were dying, and I could be killed, too. Sal was right next to me. Before we took off, he was happy and going on about his girl back home. In a split second, he was gone. Just inches away from me." Billy stopped for a moment.

"I finally climbed out of the helicopter, trembling—trembling with fear like a little girl—and fell to my knees. I vomited. My body heaved and tensed as I openly cried." Billy looked over at Josh with red-rimmed eyes.

"I was ashamed of myself. After that, the fear was always there. Fear was a viral current, coursing through my veins. Nobody really ever talked about it, but it was there for everyone. Always there, stronger some times than others. You had to learn how to control it and keep it from getting the best of you. That first time it got me good, and I vowed I wouldn't let it happen again. But it did. It happened to everyone. Eventually fear got to everyone. Everybody has their limits." Billy's expression was serious, and Josh wasn't sure how to respond.

Grabbing the stick on his lap, Billy dug into the dirt at his feet. "That was the first, but there would be more. Eventually, death became another member of our squad. Every day, he was there with us, ready to lend his helping hand—whether we wanted it or not. You came to expect it. Some days you welcomed it. You wanted him to take care of your horribly, mangled friend quickly, or if need be, to take care of you. And you hoped it wouldn't be in a terrible, painful way, but that he would bring you peace. Peace far away from the ugliness of the world."

Billy's eyes remained focused on the ground where he carved grooves into the dirt with the stick. "When he would come to visit us, we could smell him, ugly and putrid. He filled our nostrils with a terrible thick, sour acid that would make anyone gag if we let it. After a while, we surrendered to him, and he became a part of us. Each new day was its own little miracle, and that gave us a reason to go on."

Josh listened as Billy told his story. "After that first one in the helicopter, I didn't think it could get much worse. But it did.

It got much, much worse."

Billy looked up from his stick and gazed out over the valley. "The whole battalion was deep in the Ia Drang Valley on what we called a search and destroy mission. We were going there to look for a scrap with the enemy, to punch him in the nose and kick him in the ass. That's what the LT told us." Billy sneered and his voice dropped. "And we found him. Oh Lord, we did we find him. The enemy was there, deep in that valley, ready and waiting for us to come."

Looking down at the stick in his hands, Billy nodded almost in disbelief. "LT was right in front of me. We were getting overrun. These weren't no VC. They was North Vietnamese regulars. And Lord they could fight. Damn good fighters. They kept coming on and on. We'd shoot them down, and more kept coming in waves, crashing down on us until finally we were overrun.

"We couldn't shoot them fast enough. I was on the radio next to LT, and he decided it was time to attack. I looked at him like he was crazy. Attack? We were surrounded. That's when he jumped out from behind the huge ant hill we had been hiding behind and was preparing to shoot his M16 when he was hit by three bullets. The first two struck him in the chest simultaneously, and he dropped to his knees right in front of me. Then the third bullet hit, taking the top of his head clean off.

"I had shouted, 'NO,' at the top of my lungs when he had gotten up. An instant later, my mouth was filled with a sharp fragment of bone from his skull and a soft warm chunk of his brain. His blood splattered all over my body. I spit and cursed. A piece of shrapnel from his steel pot tore through my left arm.

"Everything went sideways after that. The fear that held me tight to the ground was all of a sudden gone. I vaguely remember the strange sense of rising above the ground and looking down on myself. There were NVAs everywhere. I shot four of them in seconds and then jumped into a hole on the left flank of our platoon. The M60 had been knocked back into the hole. Manny and Stimpson were both in the hole, but they were dead.

"I grabbed the M60 and rested it on a dead NVA on the top edge of the hole. I started firing, firing at everything that moved. There were so many targets. It was like fish in a barrel. I mowed them down. Hatred flowed in my veins. I never knew I could hate so much. My sweat and bullets were laced with it, like venom seething out of me. The gun had become a part of me, a part of my very being, and I was spewing bullets with a deep, sinister hatred.

"On and on they came, and I kept going with an unquenchable, intense anger. It was so messy. There was nothing noble about it. Their gruesome corpses and clumps of mangled flesh and bone littered the ground around me. And the blood. Oh God, the blood. The earth became something altogether different. It was as if a deep, brownish-red heavy blanket covered everything.

"They pulled back and then attacked again, but I kept shooting them down. Wave after wave they kept coming…oh, the ugly and horrible destruction of human beings. I didn't know how long it could go on. I found myself in complete awe of their bravery. Their courage was incredible. At some point, I got lost in their struggle and yelled at them, cheering for them. Telling them to stop. Hoping they would stop. That they would stop the madness. That we could agree to stop this horrible dirty affair." As Billy looked at Josh, his eyes were wet with tears.

"I reloaded several times, but they kept coming on. The ground was covered with so many of their dead that you couldn't see it anymore. It seemed to go on and on. Somebody jumped into my hole, and I was ready to kill him, too, but it was Johnson with more ammo. He fed the gun, and I kept shooting. I shot so much that the tube was glowing deep red. And just when I thought it was about to shatter from the heat, they stopped. I heard whistles in the tree line and then an eerie silence. A complete stillness. So quiet, you would've never known just moments before that hell had been there with us, scorching the earth.

"I looked at my trembling hands. They didn't seem to be a part of my body. They were alien to me. I looked at the carnage done by my hands. These hands." Billy stopped and held his hands out to Josh as if he was pleading with him.

Josh's eyes were wide with sorrow. Unable to respond, he leaned away from Billy.

Billy looked down at his hands and clenched them into a fist. "Night came on in the Ia Drang, and they came back with it. But we fought hard and held the ground. I didn't know if that night would ever end. I didn't think I would see the sun again. But I did, and that next morning, we held the ground.

"There were more days like this. After a while, they overlapped in a blur. More death. More killing. We were completely numb to it. It became a part of our day. It's what we did. We surrendered any notion that we would make it out alive or that we would ever come home. That kind of hope was a dangerous thing. Those of us that did the ugly things—the ones that needed to be done—gave up on hope all together. It was a worthless notion that got in the way of the business we were there to do," Billy said in a matter of fact tone.

"Truth? You want the truth? Truth is... it's a horrible and ugly business, and I did it. And I must've done it well because here I am. But I won't paint some picture with happy colors. It isn't true. I find it silly how people, often politicians, talk about honor and sacrifice, about the last full measure, about the altar of freedom, and all that. It isn't true. It isn't at all what it's about.

"It's about doing what you got to do for your brother. It's about not letting him down. It's about being there for him. I guess it all comes back to love."

Billy looked up at Josh. Josh had tears streaming down his cheeks. "Truth? See, I told you. Nobody would believe it if I really told them. We don't have the imagination for it. Hell, I was there, and I'm not sure I believe much of it anymore. Guess that's what happens. We tuck it away because we can't deal with it. We can't explain it. And then down the road, it bears its head again. But this time, it isn't quite as ugly. The ugly parts, we keep hidden deep in the backrooms and the closets of our mind." Billy looked up at Josh. "Do you want me to keep on?"

Unable to respond with words, Josh slowly nodded, indicating he did.

"I could tell many stories that no one would ever believe.

Like I said, I don't even know what to believe anymore. The visions in my head, the memories get cloudy with time, and then the faces…I can't remember their faces anymore. Stimpson, and Manny, Johnson and Sal, Washington and Ruffolo...they still come to me in my dreams, but their faces are just one face. Just one face with a look that questions me. Questions us all. Asking why, why they were the ones that gave everything. Why we're here, and they're gone. Why any of this had to happen…"

"But," Josh said, interrupting Billy. "You had to do what you had to do. You didn't have options. You were doing your duty." With his arm around Billy, Josh leaned closer to try to comfort him.

"My duty? Duty? What the hell is duty? Slaughtering women and children? Is that my duty?" Billy snapped back.

Josh pulled away, stunned. Unsure of how to respond, he reached down and picked up a stone and studied it in his hands.

"Dave had to tell that damn story about Anamosa as if there's something so romantic about it all. We had our own Battle of the Bad Axe over there. God, the children. We butchered the children, and there wasn't any reason for it. Oh hell, it was ugly. Will I ever be forgiven for what I've done?" Billy asked, his face pinched with sorrow, his eyes wet with tears.

"Billy, you were just doing—" Josh tried to respond, but was cut off by Billy.

"After the LT was gone, we didn't get a platoon leader for a while, and Sergeant First Class Lancaster stepped up and took care of us all. My God, he was good. There was a man that could lead. Korean War Vet, platoon sergeant in Vietnam—he always knew what needed to be done. He was from the old school and as hard as woodpecker lips. Some of the boys griped about it, but he covered our asses, and we loved him for it. No matter how bad it got, he was always there to take care of us. Even when the new LT came on board and none of us trusted him, it didn't matter because we knew Lannie was there, and he would get us through.

"But things started to slip. We were slipping sideways. Then we were falling, falling sideways down, down, upside down, and around. We were slipping and couldn't stop the dark drift of things as they crept in under our skin. Everything was upside down, and there was no truth anymore. Nothing to tell us where our true north was."

"Billy, you don't need to tell…" Josh reached out and tried to stop him, but Billy pulled away.

"'Zulu, bravo, tree, six, four, two, niner, tree, niner, one.' The LT looked at me, and then he said it again only this time even louder. 'Zulu, bravo, tree, six, four, two, niner, tree, niner, one,'" Billy said as he firmly gripped the stick and pushed it into the dirt.

"We were on patrol one day. Moving through some elephant grass, about three hundred yards south of some village that wasn't on our map and nobody had ever heard of before. We had been through the village earlier in the day, searched it, and moved on. Just farmers and their families. Some men and women. Lots of children. No contraband or intel. It seemed pretty clean.

"Anyway on the way back to the pickup zone, we were

going to skirt the village to play it safe on our way out. Just a short walk—a beautiful sunny stroll. But the LT wanted to make time and go back through the village. We should've never gone back through that damn village, and everybody knew it.

"That's why we hated the LT. It wasn't his personality. We just didn't trust him. Not because he took risks either. We all took risks—that was part of the game. It was because he was a gambler. He took unnecessary risks with too many unknowns. I'm not sure if he thought he was lucky, or if he was lazy, or maybe just plain stupid. Probably a combination of all three. He did things we didn't need to do. We all knew that in Vietnam you couldn't gamble. The cards were always stacked against us, and in the end, we would lose. Never should've come back the way we came. That was basic, and everyone knew it. Why didn't any of us say anything?" Billy paused, and Josh saw sadness and guilt in Billy's eyes.

"There was a heavy tension overshadowing the platoon when the LT made the call. You could see it in everyone's eyes. It felt wrong. Nobody was going say anything until finally Lannie confronted him and tried to talk him out of it. The LT wouldn't have any of it. Maybe if we all spoke up he might've changed his mind. I wish I would've said something. Damn West Pointer with an ego as big as Texas. He was stuck in his own visions of grandeur. He wouldn't listen to Lannie or any of us. It was his way or the highway." Billy shook his head with disgust as he tapped the stick on the ground.

"So we went through the village. Everything was tense and eerily quiet. It felt wrong. So wrong. We got through and were about three hundred yards south in the elephant grass. I started feeling an air of relief. Everything was going to be okay. Maybe we got lucky. We had gone back through the village and nothing had come from it. We would be at the PZ within the hour."

Billy looked out over the ridge with a sincere look of sadness on his face. Josh didn't interrupt.

"All of a sudden I heard this loud 'swap, swap, swap' wet sound, like you were hitting a wet hanging rug with your baseball bat. I turned to my right. Sergeant First Class Lancaster, who had been standing right beside me, was down. Lannie was down.

"I immediately ripped out bandages and tried to treat him. Three rounds to the chest. He was laying on his back, eyes wide open, looking up to the sky. His arms trembled. Me and the LT ripped open his uniform to find the bullet holes. God, there was blood everywhere.

"He mumbled something, and then he cried out, crying out his wife's name. 'Mary, Mary, Mare…I love you Mare…I'm so…I'm so sorry…Mary.'

"He trailed off while we applied pressure to his chest, trying to stop the bleeding. Oh God, it was everywhere. Lannie…"

Billy cleared his throat. "We didn't know where the shots came from. Somebody thought they saw movement in the tree line and opened up with the sixty on it. The people in the village scurried around to get some cover from our fires. Like so many times before, nobody knew where the enemy was."

A look of deep sadness formed on Billy's face. "It was then that the new LT looked at me and said those words, 'Grid, zulu, bravo, tree, six, four, two, niner, tree, niner, one. Do you hear me, West? Zulu, bravo, tree, six, four, two, niner, tree, niner, one, adjust fire. Large bunker complex in the tree line. HE in effect,' he ordered. I stopped and looked at him.

"Now do it, goddamnit, do it! He shouted at me. I was stunned. I just looked at him. He wanted me to destroy the entire village.

"I glanced down at Lannie. He was a mess, looking up to the sky with that damn questioning expression on his face. He wasn't talking any more. Just looking up…his life slowly draining from his body.

"The LT kept shouting at me, 'Do it, West! I told you to do it, and that's an order!'" Billy stopped talking. He looked out in the distance, somewhere far away. "I finally complied and called in the artillery mission. The first adjust rounds impacting just beyond the village, and the LT's adjustments. 'Direction 350, Drop 100, fire for effect!'

"After that, I mimicked the LT into the radio handset. I wasn't thinking anymore. Just relaying whatever he wanted. I looked down at Sergeant First Class Lancaster. The blood was everywhere, and he had that questioning look frozen on his face. He was gone.

"The artillery barrage hit at that moment square in the middle of the village. The first volley was thirty-six high explosive rounds. Oh God, the ground shook and rattled underneath us.

"And the LT came back again, 'Repeat! Goddamnit, West, repeat!'

"I did as I was told and again mimicked the LT into the handset. And again the barrage rolled over us and onto the village. Trees, rocks, and pieces of their huts blew up into the air and rained down around us as we hugged the ground.

"'Repeat!' The LT barked again. And I thought, oh God, really? How long could this go on? Again? 'Repeat, West. Fire that goddamn artillery again!' he barked at me.

"I looked at him and shook my head. I wasn't going to do it. I couldn't do it anymore. There wasn't any need for it. I looked down. Lannie was dead. I looked up at the LT. His eyes were wild and lost. I mumbled the words, 'No LT,' and he went crazy.

"He pulled out his .45 and pointed it into my face and shouted, 'West, I told you to fire it, and that's an order. Now fire it!'

"I couldn't believe what was happening. He had completely lost it. I gave the order again into the handset, and again the high explosive rounds screeched overhead and detonated in the village. I lifted my head up in the grass to see the village, and there was nothing left of it. The remnants of a few of the huts were on fire, but it was now a large pile of trees, assorted debris, and churned up earth.

"'Willie Pete, repeat!' The LT gave a new order. He ordered me to fire white phosphorous on the village. I couldn't believe everything that was happening. 'Willie Pete, repeat!' The LT shouted louder, once again waving his gun in my face.

"I wasn't going to do it. I'd done enough. I started crying and curled up on the ground, turning my back to the LT. I sobbed and shouted out, 'You're going to have to kill me, LT. I'm not going to do it no more. I ain't no murderer.' The LT grabbed the handset out of my hands, and spit on me, 'West, you're a fucking pussy.' He called in the white phosphorous."

Unable to look up at Josh, Billy's eyes were focused on the ground where he continued to dig into the dirt with his stick. "I can still remember the explosions, and the heat coming from the village. And the smell. Oh God, the smell. He repeated the mission again, burning everything to the ground. We waited about half hour and called in a medevac to get Sergeant Lancaster evacuated. And then we walked into what was once a village.

"Oh God, we butchered them. We butchered them all," Billy said, tears rolling down his cheeks.

"But Billy, Billy you didn't…" Josh tried to console him, but Billy yanked himself away.

"I remember the first one I saw. There was a clump of flesh that was once a little girl. Her clothes were burnt off. But there was enough left of her to know it was a girl. Her head and legs were gone. There were pieces of them everywhere. I stood there, looking down. I was on someone's hand. And in front of me was part of a jawbone, teeth still attached, and what looked to be part of a ribcage that was on fire. The carnage of it all…there were pieces of them in the trees, scattered across the burning piles of the village. They were everywhere. Just clumps of butchered flesh.

"And the smell. Oh God, the smell of burning flesh. The white phosphorus. I'll never forget the smell of it all." Billy wiped the tears from his eyes and looked up at Josh.

"Billy, you did what you were told. You didn't have a choice. You were following orders," Josh tried to explain.

"And then I heard a baby crying." Billy paused and took in a deep breath. "It was coming from my left, over on the west side of the village. My body reacted, and I ran toward the crying sound. I remember having this burst of hope in my heart that maybe someone had survived what we had done. I found it hard to believe, but maybe someone had lived.

"Then I saw him. I really don't know if the baby was a boy or a girl. He was so badly burnt, you really couldn't tell. His legs were on fire, and his body was swollen and black up to his belly. But he was still alive. Screaming. Oh God, the screaming. I quickly took off my shirt and tried to smother his legs. But he was so hot, so hot that my shirt quickly lit on fire, too. And he wouldn't stop screaming. Oh I wanted him to stop screaming.

"At that point, I panicked; I didn't know what to do next. I felt so helpless. I drew up my M-16 on him. I tried to put pressure on the trigger, but my finger couldn't squeeze hard enough. I cried out loud along with the baby. I had to stop his pain. I had to save him from it, but I wasn't no murderer.

"How had I been pulled into this place? To the point where I was willing to murder a child? Oh, God, it was horrible. Everything I knew to be right turned against me. What had I become? And then I heard the exploding sound of a gun firing. Startled, I jumped to the side. On my left stood the LT with his .45 drawn out and pointing down at the now silent and lifeless baby. He said to me, 'You ain't no soldier. I'd heard the Old Man talk about you in the Ia Drang, but you ain't nothing, nothing but talk.' He walked away, and I dropped to my knees, head in my hands, sobbing. Sobbing over the baby, over all the ugliness, over all the loss."

"But Billy, you were…you were just…" Josh tried to put his arm around his friend, but Billy pushed him away.

"I still hear that baby crying. At night, I wake up, soaking wet in my sweat, and I hear that baby crying. Sometimes he's in the other room, and I run in and turn on the lights, but he's not there. Sometimes I hear him outside, and I run out into the night, out into the front yard, but he's too far off in the distance, down the street, or the next block over. I still hear him. No matter how far I run, I just can't reach him."

Sitting on the rock with his head in his hands, Billy sobbed. "Will he ever forgive me? Will he ever stop crying?"

Josh didn't know what to say. He was overwhelmed with a respect and deep sadness for his friend. All this time home and he had never asked. He had never noticed. He had been going on and on about college, baseball, and Charlotte. And here was his friend, permanently injured and in pain, and he didn't see it.

Josh was ashamed of who he was, of what he was doing with his life, of how he hadn't even thought about where Billy had been and what he had done. And somewhere deep inside, Josh envied Billy. Billy had done and seen things he, himself, could never do. Billy had walked through the fire and come safely home to tell the tale. He had lived more in the past two years than Josh would in his lifetime.

But more than anything, Josh wanted to make Billy better. He stood up, reached down, and grabbed Billy's hand and pulled him to his feet. Giving him a hug, he held him tight in his arms. "I'm sorry, Billy. I'm so sorry for everything...but I want to thank you. Thank you for everything you've done for me. For all of us…"

Billy pushed away from Josh and wiped the tears from his eyes and his face. "You know I told her I was done. I told Anna I was done with it all. That I wouldn't go back. That I'd get out."

"I'm sure she would…" Josh tried to respond.

"I told her I would put all this behind me and come back to Iowa. But I don't know if that's really the truth. Truth. I don't know what truth is inside me anymore." Billy shook his head as he reached down and picked up the stick.

"But you could just…" Josh tried to support him but was cut off again.

Holding up the stick Billy closely studied it. "I wake up in the night and see their faces, all as one face. They come back to me with the question. The question of who's going to lead them? Who will take care of the boys that are out there doing this dirty work? Who will bring them home? My heart's broken and bruised for all the terrible unspeakable things I've done. Truth. I wish it was in me. I wish I knew what it was.

"Anna's my life, and I could put all this behind me, and she could be my true north. She could keep me safe. I could stay here and make the safe play."

Josh looked at him, unable to respond, and Billy tapped the stick against his leg. "But if I can lead them out, if I could bring them home, maybe then I could find forgiveness for all the things I've done. Maybe I could come home. Maybe then I could find some sense of honor in all of this."

Josh didn't know what to say anymore. He stood with Billy

at the edge of Pinicon Ridge and looked out over the river valley. He couldn't see anyone at the picnic site down below. Wiping the tears from his eyes, he tried to smile. "Looks like everyone left to go swimming at the upside down bridge."

Billy didn't acknowledge Josh's comment. Instead, he looked out toward the horizon. "Look, Josh." Billy pointed. "You can see the Old Military Road and the old steel bridge that arches over the river."

"Huh? Yeah, I guess you can. That's a good distance off." Josh was unsure how to respond as he looked out over the river valley.

"The Old Military Road. I wonder if it'll ever end." Billy's voice was distant and tapered off.

The two of them stood there, silent for over five minutes. Billy tossed the stick over the ridge and watched it bounce off the stone cliffs below. Finally he turned to Josh. "I've never told anyone what I told you here today. For a while, I didn't know all that was inside of me. It kept pouring out…it kept coming out of me." Billy tried to explain.

"Maybe it needed to," Josh responded, putting his hand on Billy's shoulder.

"Yeah, I suppose you're right," Billy said, and then he turned directly to Josh.

"You're not going tell anyone about this. You got that, Josh? No one."

"Yeah, I got it."

"No, I mean it. No one. Not a word. Especially to Anna. You give me your word. You give me your word on this right now." Billy put his finger in Josh's chest.

"You got it, Billy, not a word. I won't say a word." Josh tried to reassure him.

"Josh, I mean it. Give me your word. Now say it," Billy demanded.

"Okay, you got it. You have my word. I won't tell anyone about anything that was said up here," Josh promised.

Billy didn't say anything more. He turned and looked out over the valley.

Josh eventually broke the silence. "The Old Military Road. I can see it twisting from the bridge up through the hills."

Billy didn't respond to his comment. He stood, lost in a trance—his mind somewhere in the jungles of Vietnam. After several minutes, he let out a deep sigh and turned to Josh. "Come on, we got to get going. It's time to go."

Billy backed away from the edge and started the long trail down Pinicon Ridge.

V

JOE GOT OFF of Sally and moved to the side of the bed where he put on his pants. The room was cold and dark. Even in mid-summer, a musty cold darkness loomed over the bedroom that even the sunlight could not touch. Joe didn't look up to acknowledge her. He used to hold out and would wait for her to finish, but that was a long time ago. It was purely mechanical for him now and only when he wanted it.

Sally's emotions were barren and ragged. She was beyond used up, empty, and fully aware that their love was a shadowed reflection of what it once was. Sex with Joe left her feeling dirty and degraded, and she needed to get to the bathroom to clean up.

She slipped out of bed, naked, and stumbled toward the bathroom in the darkness. Joe ignored her as she moved past him and into the bathroom.

Nothing was said.

Sally went through the motions, hoping for hope, or just for something to change for the better. From the bathroom, she heard Joe rummaging around in the bedroom and then the familiar clank of bottles. She glanced up at the clock on the bathroom wall. It was only ten thirty in the morning. Every day, he seemed to start a little earlier.

Over the past few weeks, Sally had watched everything spin

out of control, spiraling outward, outside of her grasp. She couldn't stop the darkness from creeping inside of her. It had started slow, but now was heavy and thick, the darkness smothered her. A shock of panic shot through her body, and she gripped the sink. She was falling faster and faster and didn't know how to find her feet. Sally reached up and opened the shades. The morning sunlight burst in, exposing her in the dingy bathroom.

She looked up into the mirror. "My God, Sally Mayfield. What have you become?" she asked herself. For a split second, Sally could see her mother and her grandmother forming together in one face, her face, but she was much more tired and sad. Her eyes were dark with shadows and deep wrinkles. She felt heavy and too old for her age. Sally splashed water on her face and hoped it would make a difference. Looking back up at the mirror, nothing had changed.

Getting dressed, she heard an unfamiliar, metallic sound. She walked out of the bathroom and leaned against the doorframe. Joe sat on the bed, oblivious to her presence and lost in his task.

Sally's mouth fell open, unable to utter any words. Then they finally came out. "Joe… honey…is that…is that a…is that a shotgun?" she asked, moving slowly toward him.

"Don't you pay it no mind, Sally," Joe grunted, his eyes focused on the gun in his hands.

Her feet were like lead, and she stood paralyzed. She couldn't come to grips with how far they had declined. Now deep into the darkness they were falling.

"But Joe, what do you…what are you going to do…"

"I said, don't you pay it no mind!" Joe repeated, this time louder with a frustrated, angry tone. "Now be on your way!"

"But Joe, I've got…" Sally tried to reason with him, shying back against the wall.

"I said, be on your way! I told you last night I needed you to open the bar this morning." Joe's voice grew more agitated.

"But Joe, don't you want…" Sally stood at a crossroad. Did she move forward toward him or back away? Would her feet even let her?

"I got business to tend to today, and I need you to run the bar. Now get going!" Joe pointed his finger toward the door.

She looked at him with a deep sadness, remembering who they had been and wondering what they had become. Joe took a long pull from his bottle of whiskey and stroked the stock of the gun in his hands. She couldn't see his eyes; they were black from the shadows. For the first time in her life, she was afraid—afraid of Joe and the monster he was becoming. Fear cut through whatever love she had left for him.

In her mind, she heard a voice. "Get out. Get out of this dark place. Get out of here. Get out while you still can." But she couldn't, no matter how much the voice pleaded.

She shook off those thoughts and tried to change the subject to something positive. "Dicky Moss should be getting out of the hospital today. I thought I might bake some cookies and…"

"Don't you pay him no mind. Dicky and I got some business to tend to. Now you git. Git going. I need the bar open by noon for the lunch crowd. And don't forget, you need to git over to see Sheriff Barton today and make sure he's got your statement from Prairieburg," Joe said in a firm voice. His hand wrapped tightly around the shotgun. With a menacing voice, he added, "Don't screw this up! Now git, git going!"

Joe pointed at the door but never looked up. His eyes were fixed downward, fixed on the gun in his hands.

ꕥ

"I hear they're going to tear down old Shaw's Block." Billy glanced over at Anna as they drove past it on Main Street.

"That so," Anna responded, reaching for Billy's hand.

"Heard from John Crawford they're tearing it down next year. Going to build some kind of a department store," Billy said as he gently squeezed Anna's hand.

"A department store?" Anna paused, tilting her head to the side and rubbing her chin. "Guess that seems practical, something the town could use."

"Practical?" Billy's head snapped back. "I find it kind of sad." His voice dropped just a bit as he looked on to the row of buildings. "Old Shaw's Block getting torn down. Probably the only landmark, other than his mansion, that stands as a testament to what he did for this town."

Anna started to smile but didn't say a word. Billy was about to start another one of his speeches about honor, change, love, or the injustice in this world. She would let him go on and then reel him in, back to the here and now.

Billy slapped his hands on the steering wheel and raised his voice. "Not only was he a famous Civil War colonel, he was a visionary for economic development and civic responsibility."

"I didn't know he was in the Civil War." Anna glanced away to hide her downcast eyes from Billy. The Civil War always saddened her. Such a horribly violent affair. So much loss, it almost tore the country apart. Even now, several generations later, the country was still tending to the scars from it all.

"He commanded Iowa's 14th Regiment and probably saved Grant's Army at Shiloh. His actions at what they called the Hornet's Nest are legendary." Billy's tone was serious, and his eyes were solemn as he glanced at Anna.

Anna had heard of Shiloh but not about Shaw at the Hornet's Nest. The Civil War seemed so long ago. She knew the men who had fought in it and lived were the same ones who had come back to towns like this one, hoping for a better future.

Billy maintained a steady gaze on the road. "Of course he was captured there and spent months in Confederate prisons. Eventually, he was released and managed to lead troops at Grant's siege of Vicksburg and a handful of other battles in the West."

Anna looked at Billy with adoration and smiled. Her eyes lit up; she loved to hear him tell stories. She marveled at how he seemed to know everything about anything.

"He was originally from Maine, from a wealthy family that settled our country and defended it at every chapter of our history. He was the grandson of one of George Washington's finest officers in the Revolutionary War. Not only that, he was also the cousin of Colonel Robert Gould Shaw, the famous commander of the 54th." Billy took a deep breath and sighed. He glanced over at Anna and waited for her to respond, which she did.

She looked at Billy a little puzzled. "The 54th? What was so famous about the 54th?"

Billy smiled. "It was one of the first black regiments in the war and made famous for their sacrifice at Fort Wagner. They were a fighting black regiment, which was uncommon at the time, and tragically they were almost wiped out in a frontal assault on the fort."

Billy looked off into the distance, lost in the story and the harsh realities of war. Anna moved in closer to him and stretched up to kiss his cheek.

Billy glanced down at Anna. "Anyway, before the Civil War, William Shaw enlisted and fought in the Mexican War at Buena Vista."

"Buena Vista?" Anna asked, looking up at him and memorizing the angles of his face.

"The last major victory against Mexico," Billy replied, keeping his eyes forward on the road. "Shaw led an amazing life. After the Mexican War, he took multiple trips west to California, during the Gold Rush, and he made a small fortune."

"Billy, you're a walking encyclopedia. I don't know how you know so much about everything. Well, almost everything." Anna smiled sheepishly.

"Almost everything? What are you talking about?" Billy firmly gripped the steering wheel, a little dejected by her comment.

"You don't know anything about women." Anna let the words fill the air, and there was an uncomfortable pause.

Finally, a guilty smirk formed on Billy's face. "You're right about that, Anna Angel. Absolutely right. I don't know much about women, but I'm not sure any man does."

Anna snickered and squeezed Billy's hand. "You're doing fine, my love. I'll keep you. At least for a while, until I find someone better."

"Someone better?" Billy playfully pulled his hand away and gripped the steering wheel.

"Oh baby, don't get defensive. So sensitive. I didn't know you had this in you. Please continue with your story about Shaw. I want to hear more." Anna actually did want to hear more, so she put her head on Billy's shoulder, ready to listen.

"Where was I? Oh yeah, California. I remember. Anyway, before I was distracted." He gave her a sideways glance and grinned. "I was saying, Colonel Shaw went on to make his fortune in California and then came back. He was instrumental in the beginning stages of this town."

Billy's eyes became pensive as he tried to remember everything. "He was the first mayor of the town, and then left Anamosa to fight as a commander in the Civil War. When he returned, he became a business leader for the community. He built most of the buildings on Main Street, the first churches, and one of the first schools over on Strawberry Hill. Most importantly, he worked hard to ensure that Anamosa was at the crossroads of multiple railroads. This really put the town on the map and accelerated its growth. No question, this town probably wouldn't be what it is today had it not been for him." Billy cleared his throat. "I can't believe they're going to tear down this building. Heck, it served as the first courthouse for the entire county."

Anna looked up at Billy; his expression was grim as he spoke. "Men of honor. What would this world be without them?" He let the words settle in the truck. "Pa, says there's one, maybe two, out of one hundred that make all the difference, who advance us all. That change the world. That lead." Billy tapped on the steering wheel as he pondered history. "I look at our Main Street and see a faint reflection of what this town once really was. Of what it could be. It's a more tired version of someone else's hopes and dreams. There was so much potential back then, and now? Now I wonder. I wonder where all this is going."

"Oh Billy, you're a hopeless romantic," Anna said, lifting her head from his shoulder and kissing him on the cheek.

"Few ever come along that actually break the mold and advance us as a society. When they do, rarely do we take notice. Think how much better we would be if we took their lessons in life and started with them as a foundation. Each generation better than the next. But we don't. We muddle through it in our ignorance and hope and pray for the best only to find ourselves making the same mistakes in the same patterns."

Billy turned up Ford Street toward the sheriff's office. "Take Shaw, for example. He was a hero of the war in Mexico, of the Civil War, and the first mayor of this town. He came from a family of abolitionists, who believed in the equality of all people and put their beliefs into action. Heck, he was even an acquaintance of Frederick Douglass, one of the greatest civil rights leaders in our nation's history."

"Oh Billy, you expect too much from people. You're not being fair. Life's hard as it is." Anna cleared her throat and smiled as she looked up lovingly at Billy. "We all have our gifts, but some are endowed to rise above it all and make a difference in this world. But not everyone will move mountains. Not everyone is like you, Billy. You push. You push so hard…" Anna tried to connect with Billy, but he stopped her with his words.

"This isn't about me, darling. You know that. I see this world and wonder if anything is sacred. Great people go before us and try to make the world a little better for future generations. They struggle, they dream, they accomplish great things, and then they die. Are we better off for what they've done? Does anyone remember? Is anyone willing to step forward and take their torch to light a better future?" Billy's eyes were worrisome, and his tone was genuine. "I fear for our future. I wonder what this town—what our nation—is becoming. If we aren't progressing, we're dying. Things seem different in this generation. It feels like we're slipping backward."

"Billy, you can't mean that. We're about to put a man on the moon. We're reaching for the stars." Anna reached up and touched Billy's chin and kissed him softly on the cheek.

Billy kept his eyes on the road. "I don't mean technology or science or any of that. I mean character. Our nation will be judged by the character of our leaders. They'll determine our future."

Anna leaned forward and rested her head on Billy's chest.

She nestled closer to him and felt the beating of his heart. Billy was legitimately concerned. She knew he could be hardheaded, but he was probably right. He was always right. He was one of those leaders he spoke about. She believed he was one of the rare, select breed that would push the envelope and would lead the rest, making this world a better place. He knew it too, and she saw no reason to remind him of the obvious. But she also knew the world wasn't ready for Billy. He would challenge others to go beyond what was thought possible and achieve greatness, and he would be disappointed with the many who couldn't meet his standards. She worried he would be rewarded with a lifetime of disappointment and struggle.

Billy sighed and put his arm around Anna, pulling her close to him. "Heck, in fifty years, Main Street may not even exist. Definitely not like we know it today. Today it is inhabited with new generations of people with their own dreams. Moving, following their hearts, changing; but are they ever really changing? Are we any better human beings than they were one hundred years ago? Today we have Becky's Ladies Wear, and Strohm's, Bario's Shoes, H&J Meats, and…"

"Don't forget the Park's Theater." Anna looked up and kissed Billy on the cheek again and then laid her head on his shoulder.

"And the Park's Theater." Billy kissed the top of Anna's head. "That cultural mecca, known for its great movies, fresh popcorn, and passionate necking." Billy ran his fingers along Anna's arm and down toward her breasts.

Anna slugged Billy on the chest. He reached for her hand,

squeezing her even closer to him, and with an announcer's voice, he sang the praises of the theater. "The Park's Theater is now open. Great movies, great sex, all at one low price."

Anna slugged Billy again. "Samuel William West, you are simply incorrigible! Whatever am I going to do with you?"

"Take me to the movies and do whatever your imagination lets you." Billy smiled and leaned his head down to kiss her

"No, no, no. Billy West, no," Anna said, her lips hovering over his before pushing him away. "Keep your eyes on the road. Besides, we have a busy day today. Lots to do…but who knows, if you play your cards right, maybe we'll find some alone time later."

Billy stretched forward and pulled her back into him. "But we're alone right now, and we could drive out to the park…"

"Now Billy West, stay focused." She pushed away from him and giggled. She was, after all, mature and responsible. Billy was the dreamer, but she was the practical one, keeping his feet on the ground.

"We have a lot to do today. First of all we need to get over to the Sheriff's office and set things straight from the other night at Prairieburg. Then we'll probably want to grab some lunch." Anna surrendered and rested her head on his shoulder, and he brought his arm around her in a possessive hold. "And we told Josh and Charlotte we would meet them out at Fremont later this afternoon." It was a bright and beautiful summer morning and Anna knew that they had a lot to get done.

Billy smiled. Anna was so organized. It was one of the many characteristics that complemented their relationship. He rested his head on hers. "Where would I be without you, Anna?"

"You know, I often wonder that myself," Anna snickered, mocking him.

"Probably at the Park's Theater." Billy laughed as he pulled in front of the sheriff's office and turned off the ignition.

ℬℭ

When Billy opened the door for Anna, they were greeted by the sound of a typewriter, stale cigarette smoke, and the strong smell of dusty paper and ink.

Stepping up to the counter, Billy cleared his throat, but failed to get Margie Pitts' attention as she puffed away on the cigarette and pounded the keys on the typewriter. "Excuse me, Margie. Is Sheriff Barton available?"

Not looking up from her work and with the cigarette dangling from her lips, she responded in a high-pitched nasal squeak, "He's out of the office, but I'll take a message if you'd like."

"Will he be back anytime this morning? I have information that…"

Still not looking up from the typewriter, Margie stopped him right there. "He's up in Monticello today," she said, tapping her cigarette on the ashtray while keeping her eyes glued to the sheet in front of her. "And he's probably stopping by Prairieburg, and then he should be back in town later this afternoon."

Her voice grated on Billy's nerves, but he had to get this sorted out. "I have some things I need to talk to him about. It's probably about what he's investigating right now."

That got Margie's attention. At last, she looked up with dissatisfaction and pointed toward the tray on the counter. "There are the forms. You can make a written statement if you'd like."

Billy turned to face Anna with his lips pressed tightly together and then raised his hands in frustration. He exhaled and regained his composure so he could impress on Margie the urgency of the matter. "Well I'd really like to talk to him in person. There's been a big misunderstanding with all of this. I can clear things up if I talked to him for a few minutes. Are you sure he won't be in town any earlier?" Billy leaned forward and rested his hands on the counter.

Margie ignored his comments about the misunderstanding and resumed her typing. "He's out. As far as I know, he won't be back until late this afternoon. I'd be more than happy to leave him a message for you, if you'd like."

"That would be great. Please tell him I'd like to come in tomorrow, if possible, and meet with him about the incident in Prairieburg last weekend. I think he'll know what I'm talking about," Billy said, pushing away from the counter.

Margie glanced up at Billy and Anna with the cigarette hanging out of her mouth. "Tell you what. If you could write that down on the ledger up there on the counter, I'll make sure he gets your message."

"Sure thing," Billy said, picking up the pen to write a note on the ledger.

"Please tell the Sheriff we know he's busy and truly

appreciate his support in this matter." Anna put her hand on Billy's back and leaned forward in support as he was writing. Margie didn't look up from the typewriter and acted as if Anna didn't exist.

Finishing his note, Billy left it on the counter. "Thank you for your assistance. I look forward to meeting with the Sheriff in the next day or two."

"No problem. Thanks for coming in." Margie brushed them out the door without looking up.

As Anna exited the building with Billy, she reached for his hand. "Margie Pitts is one strange little biscuit."

Billy stopped, pulled her close, and pressed her against the wall. "Old Squirrel-Face?" Billy asked, leaning into her with a grin.

"Squirrel-Face? You call Margie, Squirrel-Face? Where in Sam Hill did that come from?" Anna giggled and nudged him in the side.

Billy pulled out a cigarette and lit it up. He was tense and needed to set things straight with this incident at Prairieburg.

"Come on, honey, you've never heard her called that?" He took a deep puff, calming his frayed nerves before blowing out the smoke away from Anna. "That's been her nickname for years. I never call her that name. I find it hateful and mean, but just about everybody else in town does."

Anna placed her hands on his waist. "You're making that up. Nobody calls her that."

"Next time we see somebody, anybody, I'll ask them what her nickname is. I'll bet a dollar you hear the name Squirrel-

Face." Billy smiled, bringing the cigarette to his lips for another puff.

"Now why in the world would she earn such a name?"

"Really, baby? You have to ask?" Billy asked in a shocked manner as he pulled her body tight against his.

Anna smiled and nodded. She was not accustomed to this type of name calling and teasing, but in this instance, it seemed to fit.

"Well to start with" –Billy tapped her on the nose, smiling— "have you heard her voice? Sounds like four squirrels in a barrel fighting over an acorn."

Anna's smile grew. She pushed away and slugged him on the arm.

Billy grimaced in mock pain and chuckled. "Second, what do you notice about her teeth? I mean you did notice they are a bit peculiar."

"Well, she is a little buck-toothed." Anna glanced away sheepishly. Billy had made a very good point.

"A little buck-toothed?" Billy exhaled the smoke and shook his head with a grin from ear to ear. "She's damn near a saber-toothed beaver. She could gnaw through an oak tree like butter." Billy chuckled but tried to maintain his composure. "And her eyes, would you say that her eyes bulge out from here face?"

"Well yes, a little. I mean they do seem to be a little…different." Anna blushed.

"Different? She's got the eyes of damned sea bass, and they tend to look in different directions simultaneously, like some strange pre-historic lizard."

Billy pulled Anna's hips to his, and she wrapped her arms around his neck. "She has been called Squirrel-Face for years, but you've never heard it from me. It's just downright mean, but I suppose folks could call her a hell of a lot worse. Anna, you heard her squeak like a squirrel in there today. Did you see her in there hunched over her typewriter, cigarette dangling from between here bucked-teeth."

"Well, I refuse to be hateful and call somebody such a degrading name," Anna said, pulling away and crossing her arms in front of her body.

Billy finished his cigarette and flicked it to the ground. "I'm with you, honey, but next time we go in the office, take a close look at her. She's got the lips and eyes of a large-mouth bass and makes the sound of a rabid squirrel."

Anna fought off the smile forming on her face. Billy was right, but she refused to respond. Instead, she just looked at him, unable to hold back her love.

Billy put his hands around her waist. "Okay baby, but we got a bet. Next person we see, you're going to owe me a dollar," Billy said, winking.

Anna ignored his bet and glanced over his shoulder at the door to the Sheriff's office with a hint of concern in her eyes. "I just thought that when we were in there, she was acting a bit peculiar."

"You got that right, baby. Just flat out weird." Billy pulled out another cigarette and put it in his mouth.

"Even kind of creepy." Anna agreed, nodding.

"Do you think Barton will get my note?" Billy asked,

lighting his cigarette and taking Anna by the hand.

"From Margie Pitts?" Anna asked, squeezing his hand as she tried to shake that unsettled feeling she got from Margie. "Probably not. We better come back again after lunch."

Billy agreed as he opened up the door, and Anna got into the truck.

ꕤ

"He's leaving the Sheriff's office. He's leaving!" Dicky said in a nervous high-pitched voice. "Don't follow him too close. You're following him too close." Dicky squirmed in the passenger seat, trying to duck down. Joe didn't respond. "You're following him too close. He's going to know we're tracking him."

"Shut the hell up, Dicky. If you think you can do better, than why don't you?" Joe said, gripping the steering wheel with white knuckles. "Oh that's right, 'cause you got the shit kicked out of you by little Anna Jacobs."

"It weren't Anna. There was somebody else…" Dicky started to defend himself.

Joe stopped Dicky before he could give another lame excuse. "Beat up by a girl. By a goddamn girl!" Joe paused, shaking his head in disappointment. "Pathetic. You're just pathetic. I don't know why I let you get wrapped up in anything I do."

"You know, I just want to…"

Joe wasn't listening to anything Dicky had to say. "Can't even drive a damn car. You got that silly-ass cast from your hand to your shoulder, holding your arm straight out from your body.

You truly are a sorry excuse for a man," Joe said in a hateful, demeaning tone and spit out the open driver's side window.

Dicky didn't say another word. He winced in pain instead. His left arm was broken and so was his collarbone. He had gotten out of the hospital a few hours ago, and the painkillers were wearing off. He pulled out his bottle of pills from his pocket and attempted to open it with one hand.

"What did you and Ronnie tell Sheriff Barton when he visited you at the hospital?" Joe asked.

"We told him exactly what you told us to. Billy West's going to take the rap for all of this," Dicky responded, struggling with the pill bottle.

Joe was satisfied with Dicky's answer. Things were falling together the way he wanted. Joe looked over at Dicky and watched with a bit of amusement. He refused to help with the bottle and then said, "Well, you can't drive, but at least you can shoot."

"Shoot?" Dicky stopped fighting with the pill bottle. Once again, he felt that dreadful sinking sensation. The word "quicksand" popped into his mind. Quicksand. He was in quicksand. He couldn't get out. The more he struggled, the deeper he sank into the ugly thickness of it. He was in trouble, but he had no idea just how fast he was sinking. A twinge of fear jolted him. He was afraid—afraid of what he was getting himself deeper into. Quicksand. The words were on his lips. Even if he said them, he knew he couldn't get out.

"I got deer slugs and some double ought buck shot. I wanted to get some triple ought but they was out. I figure double will do." Joe pointed over his shoulder with his thumb toward the backseat.

Dicky tried to think of something more positive. He could not believe what he was about to do. Something positive, anything positive. His mind raced. His thoughts turned to his ma and pa. His family would be so disappointed in him. The only thing positive he could think of was that at least he didn't have to face his pa at the hospital. Dicky had had a huge argument with him weeks ago about going to college. He ended up getting kicked out of the house. He had not talked to his pa since. He definitely didn't want to see him now.

Dicky was lucky that Joe had been there to pick him up at the hospital after he had gotten released. Maybe that was a good thing. He always thought Joe was deceiving and a big bully. That was just his way. He couldn't be trusted, but Dicky hoped he could stay above it all. Maybe Joe had some goodness in him after all. When things got bad, Joe was there, and true to form, he had been there for Dicky today. Had Joe not gone to the hospital, Dicky would have had to call his pa to pick him up. He would have gotten a whooping right there in the hospital waiting room.

Dicky smiled and tried to convince himself that everything was going to work out fine. With Joe's help, he could lay low for a while and figure things out. Maybe a month of rest would give him time to heal—time he needed before he faced his family again. Time. It kept ticking, but he couldn't seem to find any traction. He had seen a number of his peers get jobs or even go to college. Time. It was the constant reminder that he had not gone anywhere with his life or amounted to much.

Dicky didn't know what he wanted to do, but he was pretty sure college was not in his future. It wasn't for him. His pa pushed him toward college, but Dicky didn't understand why. The harder his pa pushed, the more Dicky pushed back. They never got anywhere.

"Try to think positive," Dicky mumbled to himself. "Something positive. You're in control. Stay in control. Joe isn't going through with all of this. He's just going to teach them a lesson. Put a little fear in them. Fear wasn't a bad thing. What did Pastor say? The source of wisdom? Something like that. All those confirmation classes as a kid and this was what I had to show for it?" A slow smile crept across Dicky's face. Church. He never understood it. It seemed so final like folks were giving up on life. Giving up on pulling more from this world. Giving up on pushing the limits on everything. To Dicky, that wasn't living. It was going through the motions every Sunday.

This was living. He was afraid, but he was living. His fear mixed with the excitement of the moment. He was with Joe. Together, they were going to let Billy West know who was boss in this town and set things right. Stay with Joe, and it was all going to turn out okay.

Dicky glanced over at Joe. He felt a twinge of fear coupled with a sharp painful stab in his side, deep inside. Joe was a manipulator and a liar. Full of lies, that's what his pa used to tell him. Dicky didn't want to think about his pa. The one thing he couldn't stand was disappointing him. Dicky could not bear to see the sad look of disappointment in his pa's eyes. He knew there was nothing worse. Nothing.

But Dicky knew his pa was right, he always was. Joe Matsell was a master at taking advantage of people. He had seen him in action down at Gus' Tavern for years. Joe had the keen ability to sense a person's weakness then back them into a corner. He would take advantage of them and exploit the weakness as he needed. Joe could pull people in and get them to do things—things they ought not to do. Give them only one option that played into his hands, options that indebted them to him.

Dicky thought back to the day when Billy walked into the tavern. Dicky smiled again. That was how all this started. Butch West had been working at the bar for drinks. They all knew Joe had been taking advantage of him and that probably wasn't right, but it just was, and nobody seemed to mind. Butch West had what he needed, and Joe had been content with his work. Sweep the bar, clean the tables, do the dishes. It was good work for a man down on his luck, and Butch West had been getting free drinks to boot. A square deal if Dicky had ever seen one.

Everybody had been good with it. At least nobody had paid it no mind. Well, nobody except for Sally. When Joe would be out, she would cook Butch eggs, toast, and coffee, and then they would talk. Dicky remembered them in the backroom, and he could hear them jabbering away. Sally would plead with him to leave Anamosa before it killed him. She had suggested maybe trying to get some help, getting into a hospital to get cleaned up.

That didn't surprise Dicky. Sally was the soft side of Joe, always trying to help those in need, bringing stray cats and dogs into the bar. Heck, he remembered the day she had brought in a bird that had hit her windshield. She had kept it in a cage for a month and had tried to bring it back to health. Dicky smiled and wondered, whatever happened to that damn bird?

Sally was such a sweet girl. He never understood how she ever got mixed up with Joe. Somehow they complemented one another. Other than Sally, nobody had seemed to mind Butch West working at the bar. Well, except for Billy. Billy had been the only one that Dicky ever saw that couldn't be manipulated. He couldn't be bent to Joe's ways.

Everything had changed that day when Billy West walked into the tavern. Joe never saw it coming. Dicky didn't think anyone had. Billy West, all cock-strong and big talking, had walked into Joe's bar and called him out on it. Why did he have to do that? If he had let well enough alone, things would never have gotten so muddled up. Why did Billy West have to be that way? Nobody had ever called Joe out on anything. Then to see Joe get dropped by Billy. In one fell swoop, Joe's reputation was crushed. So many witnesses. It had changed everything.

Dicky glanced at Joe. Joe couldn't go back now, too much damage for him. He had been backed into a corner by Billy and would have to do something. Up the ante as Joe said. Dicky was disappointed in himself. He should have never sat down at the poker table. Owing Joe Matsell money, Dicky knew Joe was manipulating him, too. Dicky took a deep breath and calmed his nerves. He could handle this. He was okay with it as long as it didn't go too far.

Dicky awkwardly shifted, trying to position himself to look into the backseat. The cast made quick movement next to impossible. On the seat laid a shotgun case. And the dreadful feeling was back. Quicksand. Joe was pushing Dicky deeper and deeper into the darkness.

Looking forward, Dicky was getting nervous, beads of sweat dripped down his face. They were only two cars behind Billy's truck as they drove west down Main Street. Too close. They were following too close. After several blocks, the truck turned left into the Dairywhip parking lot.

"Yep, picked up two boxes of ammo. I figured that ought to be enough," Joe said out loud. He had that crazy sound to his voice. Dicky wasn't sure if Joe was talking to him or to himself.

"To be enough? Enough for what?" Dicky wondered. He didn't want to know and was too afraid to ask.

"Well, looks like young Billy West and your archrival Anna Jacobs are stopping for lunch." Joe mocked Dicky with a sneer.

Dicky wasn't listening. He was thinking about the gun and the dreadful sense of how fast he was sinking. Quicksand. Finally he asked Joe a question. "Where'd you get the gun?"

Joe ignored Dicky's question and kept on talking about Billy and Anna. "We'll just drive down the street here and get in a position where we can see the parking lot in case they leave."

Joe didn't answer about the gun because Dicky didn't need to know. He just needed to be able to use it when the time came. It was all part of Joe's plan. So far, things had not gone well for Joe. Prairieburg should not have fallen apart like it did. He had relied on others too much. Trust. Can't trust anyone, especially in this town, Joe thought to himself.

Eddie Gruber was evidence of this fact. Joe thought about

Eddie. He had gotten himself in over his head. Eddie should never have tried to back Joe into a corner. Joe smiled. Nobody was going to control Joe Matsell. Not Dicky or Sally, not Billy West, and definitely not Eddie Gruber. He had tried, and he had paid the price.

Joe had given Dicky and Ronnie too much credit. Prairieburg. They had screwed it sideways. He would have to do better this time. Joe felt confident now. His new plan would set things right. In fact, this would be even better. The debacle at Prairieburg gave him his motives. Dicky Moss was central to all of this. Dicky didn't even know what was going on, but he would deliver Joe his facts and motives. It would take some convincing and handholding to guide Dicky, but in the end, it would work. He would push Dicky into a corner where he had no other option but to follow through.

Parking in the lot across the street from the Dairywhip, Joe smiled again. He was going to remove Billy from the picture entirely and would walk away clean as a whistle. Just like Eddie Gruber, Billy would pay and nobody would suspect Joe Matsell was even involved. It was all about facts and motives. Joe was feeling proud. He had positioned himself so well that when Billy West was dead, Joe would be the last one that idiot sheriff would ever consider.

He even had Margie Pitts, Barton's own secretary, working on the inside. Squirrel-Face was a regular at the bar, usually when Sally was off her shift. Joe had known for years that Margie had a crush on him, and he would use her like all the others. Except being with Margie was a chore. She was so damn homely, and her high-pitched, shrilling voice was so grating he'd want to put cotton in his ears whenever she talked. It took everything in him to get past her flaws and further their relationship. Joe smiled—the sacrifices he had made were ridiculous.

Margie had become a valuable asset to have. She worked at the Sheriff's office for over a year and had access to all the paperwork. Joe had started flirting with her after the first incident with West. He figured she might be someone who would come in handy. In light of Prairieburg and how everything had evolved, she had become invaluable.

Even though he was with Sally, he had always had other relationships on the side, sometimes two or even three at a time. Margie Pitts was just another in a long line of broken relationships that would run its course. Joe would get what he needed and be done with her. Actually, the sex with the Squirrel was not bad. She was a little kinkier than most women he had been with, surprisingly active and strong. She even did things he never would have imagined. He played along and pleased her the way she wanted. With the information she was giving him, it was all worth it.

Margie was very organized and kept Joe informed of Sheriff Barton's schedule. He knew where Barton was almost every minute of the day, and this gave him an edge. He had free reign over Anamosa to do as he pleased. Joe had even convinced Margie that keeping him informed was like helping Barton. After all, if Barton was out of town and a problem arose, Joe would be there for her, for the town, to help out.

Joe had also completely convinced Margie that Billy West

was the source of many of the recent problems in the community. Joe knew he had her turned when she had told him that Billy was a no-good dreamer, who stirred folks up and put ideas in their heads that only resulted in chaos and loss.

What the town needed was control. Joe knew it, Sheriff Barton knew it, and Margie Pitts believed it, too. Control. Billy West stood for everything against this notion. His pa was a good example of how a good thing—take drinking, for example—could go bad. Butch West was a drunk, a menace to the town, and probably needed to be locked up. He had Margie convinced that Billy, from the same seed, was a direct threat to the livelihood and safety of the community.

Joe's efforts were paying off. She was prioritizing all the documentation for the Prairieburg investigation. Through Margie, Sheriff Barton seemed certain West assaulted Dicky, Ronnie, as well as the two girls from Monti. She had also processed the sworn statements about Billy's attack at the bar several weeks earlier. Joe had Margie bending Sheriff Barton into his plans. She fully supported Joe and believed the faster they arrested West, the better it would be for everyone in this town.

There was one more thing. Joe had her convinced that Billy had affected his business at the bar. Billy was a menace to the patrons in the bar. He had assaulted Joe with a crazy sucker punch and now many of his regulars were afraid to come to the tavern. Joe's sales were down, and he was under a lot of stress. He had told Margie he loved her, but he couldn't leave Sally until the problem with Billy was resolved and his business situation improved. Sally was too important of an employee at the bar.

Firing and replacing her during this period would disrupt everything, but he reassured Margie that once the situation had improved, the two of them would be together.

"What you need the deer slugs for?" Dicky asked, breaking Joe's train of thought, but Joe didn't answer.

"I got a good view of the Dairywhip from right here. Can you see okay?" Joe asked, but he didn't care if Dicky could see or not. Dicky nodded, even though he could hardly move to get a good view of anything. With his cast, he could barely turn his head to see up the street.

Everything was working out as planned. Barton was up in Monticello today, questioning the girls about the assault at Prairieburg. He wouldn't be back for hours. Today was the day he would make everything right. Joe hated Billy West. He hated everything Billy stood for. He hated how easy things came for Billy and how easy success was for him. But more than anything, Joe hated the fact he couldn't turn Billy. Joe had known a few like him. Men who were hard-headed, stuck in their values, stubborn, and stupid. They could not be swayed through fear. If anything, fear made their resolve that much stronger. No. He would have to resort to a more permanent alternate measure. With Sheriff Barton out of town for the day, everything was set, and Billy would pay for his ignorance.

Joe had stolen the shotgun, the ammo, and a handgun the previous day from Ronnie Wilson's parents' house. They wouldn't notice them gone. Only Ronnie would know they were missing, but he would be in the hospital for another three or four days—plenty of time for action, plenty of time to make things right.

Ronnie and Dicky had shared a hospital room for several days and presumably had planned their revenge. This motive, along with Sally's statement about Billy attacking Ronnie and Dicky, added up. Joe would add statements that Dicky had been very upset and had been drinking heavily at the tavern, talking crazy—talking about murder. With Ronnie's actual guns, Dicky would finish their plan. In the end, Sheriff Barton would arrest Dicky for the murder of Billy West.

As for Joe, he would have his alibi. At the time of the murder, Joe would be with Margie Pitts, Sheriff Barton's own secretary, having sex with her in his car. That had become their routine. He would pick her up around four in the afternoon, and they would drive past Larsons' Farm and park in the field. He would convince her in his own way of the actual time they were together.

Joe's plan was coming together nicely. This was all about facts and motives, and Joe was convinced he had enough to pull it off. It would be easy, even for Sheriff Barton, to draw the line from West's death to Ronnie and Dicky.

"You know, Dicky, I was thinking. In your condition, you may want to lay low for a while," Joe said.

There was a long silence in the car and finally Dicky responded, "What? What are you thinking?" Dicky was surprised Joe would take a genuine interest in him.

"Well, I was thinking that in your condition and all, you should probably lay low for a while. I mean, I couldn't imagine what your pa will say when he sees you like this," Joe said in a concerned tone.

"I…I know. I ain't figured that part out yet. I wasn't even sure where I was going to sleep tonight." Dicky chuckled at himself. He had hoped Joe would have a solution.

"I was thinking…I mean, if you want, I could let you work at the bar for a few weeks. Get back on your feet. I can't pay you much. But I do have a cot upstairs where Butch West was living. It ain't much. There's a toilet and a sink, but it might be what you need right now."

"Joe, that would…that would be great…that…really? Really, you would take care of me like that?" Dicky asked, stunned by Joe's kindness.

"Now I said I can't pay much. Just a place for you to rest up, get healed, get better. But I figured you would need it. Especially with your pa…" Joe tapped his fingers along the steering wheel. Yes, his plan was coming together perfectly. Today everything would be made right.

"I'll take it. That would be great. Just great," Dicky exclaimed. He instantly felt better about Joe. Joe was going to take care of him. Dicky glanced out the passenger window and felt a knot of guilt in his stomach for thinking ill of Joe. What did his pa know anyway? Joe had his faults, but who didn't? He was like everyone, doing what he needed to get by.

"Did you take your painkillers?" Joe asked in a concerned tone, and glanced over at Dicky.

"I…I couldn't get the damn bottle open. This cast makes it darn near impossible to do anything." Dicky held up the bottle in his free hand.

"Give it here. I'll open it for you." Joe took the bottle from Dicky's hand and opened it. He gave him a once over before handing Dicky a pill. "Now take this. I can't have you whining all day today. We got work to do."

Dicky took the pill, and almost immediately felt better about everything. Things were going to work out. He and Joe might even have a little fun in the process. Scare that snot-nosed punk Billy West. Scare him straight. Dicky looked past Joe further down the street. Something caught his attention. Squinting his eyes, he said, "Damn. I'll be damned. If it ain't old Sheriff Barton pulling into the Dairywhip."

Joe's head snapped quickly to the left and he shouted, "What? Who? Sheriff Barton? Barton? Where? Well I'll be damned. That son of a bitch is supposed to be in Monti today." Joe's face turned a bright red as pounded his fist on the steering wheel. Looking at Dicky, he shouted, "He's supposed to be in Monti right now! She told me…" Joe stopped mid-sentence and composed himself. "What the hell is he doing in Anamosa?"

Dicky couldn't answer. He didn't know what to say and feared Joe would get angrier at him.

"Sheriff Barton isn't supposed to be here. He's always meddling in my business. I'm getting tired of this damn fool. We can't have this. We can't have this at all."

Dicky looked at Joe. His eyes were dark and fierce. It scared Dicky. He shuddered and wondered if he had just seen someone who was truly evil.

ꕥ

"Um, we'll take two tenderloins, two baskets of fries, and a couple of Cokes," Billy ordered from the sign above the window.

"That'll be a buck and a quarter," said the young high school girl, working behind the window.

"Crime in Italy! One twenty-five for lunch! Tenderloins used to only be twenty cents and same with fries. Now they're both up to a quarter? What do you think I'm made of, darling?" Billy asked, turning to Anna. He had a false look of anger, pinching his brows together and pursing his lips that he quickly transformed to a smile. Anna swatted him on the arm and failed miserably to hold back her own smile.

The Dairywhip was very busy, even for a Saturday. It was good to see. This had always been a special little restaurant for them and most kids growing up in Anamosa. It was the "hang out" for teenagers and many a first love was born at these tables. The food wasn't bad either. In fact, it was excellent. They had great tenderloins and burgers, but they were probably best known for their soft serve ice cream cones.

Billy looked up at the prices. "They have the best ice cream cones in Jones County. It doesn't look like they jacked the prices up on them—at least not yet, anyway."

He winked at Anna, and they both turned to find a table. They didn't have much of a choice with only a couple left, one way back in the corner and one up front by the counter.

"Let's sit back there. It'll be quieter in the corner," Anna said, pointing as they walked toward the vacant table.

Sitting down, Anna immediately turned to Billy. "I hope we're able catch up with Sheriff Barton today. He's up in Monti and Prairieburg…that concerns me. We need to talk to him and give him our side of the story." She laid her hand over his. She was worried and Billy could see it in her eyes.

Trying to lighten up the mood, Billy said, "Don't you worry about a thing, darling. Give me fifteen minutes with Old Jim Barton, and everything will be taken care of."

"What are you going to tell him?" Anna squeezed his hand.

"Well for starters, Joe Matsell's role," Billy said in a confident tone, taking a sip of his Coke.

"His role?" Anna questioned, tilting her head to the side.

"Absolutely. Any person with a bit of sense will see that Joe's had a hand in all of this. I can't prove it, but I know he was at Prairieburg. The fact that Sally Mayfield is lying to the Sheriff about what happened proves it. Matsell is behind all of this. Once the Sheriff gets our statements and one from Josh, everything will be settled. There's no way Judge Swanson will see this any other way." Billy caressed Anna's hand, wanting more than anything to assure her, and maybe himself as well. "I'm not going to let this get to me. I can't let it. We got one week left together, and I'm not going to let the likes of Joe Matsell have any effect on it."

One week.

The words stung.

Anna's eyes filled with tears, and she looked away from Billy. Tomorrow would be the fifth day of August. She still wasn't ready for July to end. It was going too fast. Summer would soon be over, and all of its promises were starting to break. Anna was angry at herself for believing them. August would bring Billy's departure, and then the fall and then the cold winter. August. She didn't want to think about it.

"Anna Angel, what's wrong? What'd I say?" Billy asked even though he knew the answer. He reached up and gently ran his hand over her cheek and through her hair. Time was quickly slipping away from them. He felt it, too. They were facing their last week together. Soon it would be a couple of days, and finally it would be their last day. They both knew it. The pain of their separation was real and pierced both of them.

One week.

She dreaded those words. Anna felt a sick stabbing emptiness needling inside her chest again. The same pain she had at the bus station several years ago when Billy left her for the army. Would this pain ever end? Would the hurt ever stop?

One week.

Billy knew his words had cut deep. His own heart ached, and a lump formed in his throat. Sitting across the table, he took both her hands in his. Tears suddenly rolled down her cheeks. She looked away, trying to hide her sadness. He knew it was real. He had to say something. He was wired to solve problems. He had to make this right. He loved her so much and couldn't stand to see her this way. Of all the horrible and ugly things he had seen and done in the past, at this point, none of it compared to the pain Anna's sorrowful eyes seared on his heart. Her tears cut through him. He would move mountains to bring a smile to her face, to give her the joy her love deserved.

"Anna Angel." Billy softly wiped the tears from her cheeks. "Anna, my darling, just four months. In four months, I'll be done." His words promised her forever, but she knew something in his eyes was lacking.

He leaned forward as he brought her hand up to his lips and lovingly kissed them. "I'll be out of the army, and all of this will be behind us. I'm done with it all, and I'll be back. I'll find some work, or maybe I'll try college. Heck, if Josh can do it, you know I can. And we'll be married." Billy smiled tenderly, hoping to reassure her, to give her something to hold, to set a permanent cornerstone for their future.

With these words, Anna flashed her eyes at Billy and tried to wipe her tears away. She couldn't say anything. The tears kept rolling down her cheeks. Married. She desperately wanted to believe him. Married. It seemed like a dream. He had proposed, but it seemed too good to be true. She didn't have a ring, nothing to show for his words. Yet she had no reason not to believe him. Since she had known him, he had been a man of his word. If he said it, it would happen.

But something was different with Billy. Something she couldn't describe. Something she couldn't touch. He wouldn't let her. It was far too deep, too deep for her love. She desperately wanted to believe him when he said they'd get married, but deep down inside, she felt she was holding him back. He probably would marry her. But would he truly be happy? She couldn't see Billy settling. Even though he loved her and always would, she wondered if this future life would be enough for him. Would she be enough for him?

Anna cupped Billy's face with her hands. She steadily held his cheeks as she gazed deeply into his eyes. She wanted to find truth. It was there, and she knew it. She held him for what seemed an eternity. In his eyes, she saw sorrow, determination, and destiny, then suddenly an electric jolt of fear shot through her.

Anna shuddered as she dropped her hands to the table and turned her face away from him. A profound and sorrowful pain overtook her as she answered the question. Despite his promises, she didn't think she would be enough for him.

Billy wanted so much. He wanted the world. He had too many dreams. Anna couldn't picture him settling in Iowa. College, baseball, even the army, he was bigger than all of those things. This world would probably never be enough for him. The truth stabbed her; she would be holding him back. He would never say it, at least not with words, but his eyes would betray him. Married. She wanted to believe him, but she couldn't. The future was too uncertain.

Billy stretched his hands across the table and grasped Anna's. "Anna Angel, in four months…just four months, I'll be back. I'll be out of the army, and we'll be together. We'll be home and can get on with the rest of our lives together."

No words would come to Anna so she nodded. She wanted to believe him with all her heart. She wanted to believe everything he had promised.

Billy leaned across the table and kissed her forehead. Then he moved his lips down and kissed each of her cheeks, brushing the tears away.

Feeling his soft lips, she tried to smile. She wanted to believe it all. She loved him for everything he was; his strength, his integrity, his courage and even his restless heart. This restlessness was the spark that made him so special. It was a side of him most never saw. He was so persistent. This spark was the source of his drive. It drove him to go on and on, further and better than anyone. It made him ask hard questions, to listen, to seek, to explore, to discover, and to learn. It was this spark she feared she would smother in him.

Anna's eyes drifted toward the windows, the parking lot, and the street beyond. She mindlessly watched the cars pass by, and her imagination wandered as she wondered about their occupants. She wondered about their dreams. She wondered what they worried about, and what occupied their minds. She secretly wished she could live another life…an easier one. She felt Billy's hand caress hers, and a sense of guilt washed over her. Gazing out at the lot, Anna was suddenly distracted in her thoughts by a car she recognized.

Billy was in tune to her every action and immediately noticed a change in her demeanor. "What, what is it?"

"Looks like we won't have to spend the day waiting for the Sheriff to show up at his office." Anna tried to smile and was surprised with a new sense of hope.

"What? I thought he was..." Billy turned around and saw Sheriff Barton enter the restaurant. Billy's eyes followed Barton as he sat down at a table with a glass of soda and immediately buried his head in a newspaper. "Well, I'll be damned. That makes things easy. Sometimes it's better to be lucky than good." Billy smiled, relieved to see Sheriff Barton in their presence.

Billy immediately stood up and moved toward the front of

the restaurant where Sheriff Barton was sitting when Anna reached out and grabbed his hand. "Hold it, Billy. Let the man eat his lunch. Besides, we haven't even gotten ours yet."

Billy sat back down. He looked back over his shoulder at the Sheriff. "Guess Margie Pitts doesn't know everything going on in this town." Billy felt a sense of relief at his change in luck. He turned to Anna, and they both tried to smile.

ꙮ

Billy stepped up to Sheriff Barton's table and nearly stood at attention with broad shoulders arched back. From his experience with protocol in the army, he was wired to respect authority. Billy waited for Sheriff Barton to lift his eyes from his newspaper.

Barton took a bite of his cheeseburger and wiped the grease from his lips with his sleeve. "What can I do for you, boy?"

"Uh, Sheriff? Sheriff Barton, sir, do you have a second?" Billy cleared his throat as he stepped closer and towered over the table where the Sheriff was finishing his lunch. Billy felt awkward. Sheriff Barton's appearance did little to command respect.

Billy was uncomfortable when Jim Barton sucked out the last few drops of soda from his glass—there was a loud, high-pitched slurping sound that could be heard across the restaurant.

Barton looked up from his newspaper, his lips still wrapped around the straw. Billy looked down on him. He was much heavier than Billy remembered. His head was balding, and his face was fleshy. Fans blasted on his table from multiple directions, and the room was relatively comfortable, but Sheriff

Barton had a sheet of perspiration forming above his upper lip and on his forehead. His gut protruded over his belt with multiple bulges filled his uniform and pulled it tight across his torso.

As a professional soldier, Billy's eyes studied Barton's uniform and general appearance. He was disgraceful—there was enough pressure on the buttons of his shirt that if one popped off it could shoot across the room. Billy suppressed his smile. He was embarrassed for Barton and for the town. Billy wondered how this was the best man the town could find.

Billy thought the sheriff was a sad excuse for a man. Seeing him in his uniform, Billy wondered what old Sergeant Lancaster would say about him. He would call him out on his appearance and on his pathetic condition that was for sure. Lannie wouldn't let it go, and he would be right. Old Lannie. It was a shame to even mention him and Barton in the same sentence. Lannie was every bit of the leader that Jim Barton would never be. *Oh Lannie, why did we have to go back through that damn village?* Billy suppressed it all. He had to make this work with this sad excuse of a man if he was going to clear himself of this mess with Prairieburg. He had absolutely no respect for Jim Barton, but he couldn't let it show.

"Sheriff Barton, I stopped by your office this morning to give you a statement about the incident out at Prairieburg." Billy stood firm, his posture exuding confidence.

The sheriff cleared his throat and wiped the catsup and mustard from the corners of his mouth. Billy noticed a mustard stain on the front of his shirt and tried to subdue his disgust.

"Is that so?" Barton answered, sucking in his stomach.

"Yes, sir. I've heard quite a few rumors lately, most of which aren't true. If you have the time later this afternoon, I'd like to meet and give you my side of the story." Billy's tone was decisive and steady.

Barton looked up at Billy and was startled by his commanding presence. He had never seen Billy West up close and in person -only pictures in the newspaper and at a distance on the football field—but this was an entirely different experience. Sheriff Barton was surprised at how tall and muscular Billy was. He must have been at least six two, but looking up at him from the table, he could easily be six five. Towering over the Sheriff with his muscular frame, Jim Barton knew, in an instant, that the stories about Billy were true—his feats in sports and all of his records, his heroism in the army, and even his altercation with Joe Matsell. At first, Jim Barton had a hard time imagining anyone getting the best of Big Joe, but seeing Billy now in front of him, he had no question it probably had happened as he had heard.

Something else struck Jim Barton in this initial encounter with Billy. He knew instantly that Billy was a better man than he was, not just physically, but intellectually and morally. Barton knew to his core he was in the presence of greatness. This was hard for him to come to grips with. Barton had a hard time believing this was the son of Butch West. Barton was in the presence of a force far greater than he had ever been around. Billy had a special aura and commanding dominance. Billy instantly made him want to be a better man and he immediately felt shame for himself.

Barton couldn't imagine what he looked like next to West. But in an instant, the shame disappeared and was replaced with a flash of anger and then jealousy. A new thought entered Barton's mind. *Who the hell does Billy West think he is? Walking in here, trying to tell me what he's going to do. This is my town, and ain't nobody going to tell Jim Barton how to run his town.* Barton tried to suppress his anger, but it wouldn't go away entirely, and the jealousy would probably never leave him.

Keeping a straight face, Barton looked up at Billy and then down at his watch. "Actually, I do. I think I've got maybe an hour open this afternoon."

Barton surprised himself with that statement. He couldn't believe he agreed to spend time with Billy West. He was angry at himself. Why did he concede to him so quickly? It was Billy West's presence. West was so positive and overpowering. Barton was struck by something that made him want to be a better person and made him want to serve Billy. A jealous flash of anger suddenly pulsed again in Barton's veins.

Barton was embarrassed by the way he felt and tried to cover his tracks. "But not much more. A lot going on right now in this town. Maybe you could give me some information that would shed some light on all of this? I tell you what. You get in your car and follow me over to my office, and we can get some statements." Barton overcompensated for his feelings with the forceful response.

In this initial engagement, Billy sensed some resentment from the sheriff. He had heard that Barton was a stubborn, hard-headed man. Billy had expected him to be more difficult. Instead, he was surprised Barton was making the time for him and Anna to meet today.

"Let me pay my tab, and we'll head over to the office." Barton tossed his napkin on his plate with a sneer, indicating to Billy he was a disruption to his lunch.

As the sheriff stood up from his table, his protruding gut knocked his soda glass over on the table. The ice from the glass poured out over his plate and onto the floor. Barton flushed with embarrassment. Billy tried to brush it off and reached out his hand to shake Sheriff Barton's. Jim Barton looked down at Billy's hand but wouldn't move. It was an awkward moment.

Barton refused to shake his hand and uncomfortably reached back into his back pocket and pulled out his wallet. "I'll pay my bill and be ready in just a minute."

"Okay, I'll get Anna. We'll wait for you in the parking lot," Billy said, a little disturbed at Barton's unwillingness to shake his hand.

The sheriff turned to pay, and Billy motioned to Anna with a wave that it was time to leave. She stepped forward, and Billy took her hand as they walked out of the restaurant.

"So, you're actually going to get some time to meet with the sheriff and set things straight?" Anna asked as they walked toward Billy's truck.

"I hope so. I sure hope so." Billy put his arm around Anna with an air of uncertainty in his voice.

ജ

"They're leaving! They're leaving! Dicky pounded on the

dashboard with his free hand as Billy West turned his truck out of the Dairywhip parking lot back onto Main Street. "I don't like this. It looks like the Sheriff is following them. They're turning back on Main Street toward the Sheriff's office," Dicky ran his hand through his hair with a worried, excited motion as the Sheriff quickly followed them out of the lot. "I don't like this at all. He's going with Sheriff…"

Dicky was abruptly cut off by Big Joe. "Shut up, Dicky! We don't know if they're together or where they're going. Hell, we don't know anything yet. Besides, we got plenty of time," Joe responded with a dejected tone. In reality, he knew they didn't have a lot of time. Today was the day. He had it all planned. That fat ass Barton was meddling in his affairs and screwing everything up.

"You're following too close. You're too close again!" Dicky was shaking nervously.

"Will you just relax? Damn you're wired tight, Moss," Big Joe complained as Dicky once again grated Joe's nerves.

Joe was three cars behind Barton and West as they drove east up Main Street. At Ford Street, both the Sheriff and Billy turned south. Joe realized Dicky was right. They were going back to the sheriff's office together. Joe didn't turn to follow them, instead he drove a couple of blocks down Main and then turned around.

"Well I'll be damned, Dicky. You might be right. They just might be stopping in at the Sheriff's Office." Joe was trying to keep the situation positive, but he knew this would put a wrinkle in his plan for the day. At the intersection of Ford and Main

Street, Joe's concerns were validated. He saw Billy, Anna, and Jim Barton open the front door of the sheriff's office and walk in.

"Looks like we'll just have to go to plan B," Joe announced in a positive tone. Dicky nodded and smiled although he had no idea what plan B was. Joe was purposely keeping the atmosphere in the car light, but inside he was seething.

As Joe continued driving down Main Street, he struggled to control his anger as he sorted through his next move in his mind. He thought about the game of chess, a game he played regularly with the patrons at his bar. He had become damn good over the past few years. In fact, no one had ever beaten him. He was often referred to as the "Chess Master" at the bar. He had a few solid challengers, but nobody could keep up with him when they got into a game. He became their master just like when they sat down at the poker table. There were two things he was damn good at, chess and gambling. They were his gifts, and he used them.

Joe reasoned the situation was very much like a chess piece, and he started to self-talk in his mind. *Stay flexible. A plan is nothing, but planning and preparation are everything. Always be ready, always anticipate…anticipation, that's the key. Know your next move and the next move after that, and the next, and the next, and be ready for change. Change is a part of any strategy. Got to use your pieces according to their capability—got to use them and even sacrifice them when necessary. Nothing ever goes exactly according to plan. No plan survives the initial moves. Survival of the fittest. Sometimes the weak have to be sacrificed. The fittest is the one that reacts to change the quickest.*

Joe was confident that he would prevail. His reputation, his very survival, was at stake. It was all on the chess board—he could see it so clearly. Joe would do whatever was necessary to win. He had to fight fire with fire.

Dicky cut into Joe's train of thought. "Sure wouldn't mind stopping and getting something to eat. Haven't eaten anything since breakfast at the hospital. And that weren't much of a breakfast. Dry toast and…"

Joe ignored Dicky's drivel about food and focused his thoughts on the changing situation with his own self-talk. *In chess, nothing goes according to plan. Got to anticipate. Anticipate the change. Sometimes there will be challenges that are really opportunities, and sometimes opportunities aren't worth the challenge. That damned Billy West. Got to fight fire with fire. This change is an opportunity. This latest wrinkle in my plan isn't ideal, but it certainly isn't a fatal blow. It gives me more time. Time, always swimming in time. A little more time…and I'll use it. This plan all comes back to facts and motives. Time. A little more time to firm up the facts and motives.*

Joe interrupted his own train of thought and turned to Dicky. "Hey, we got a little time to kill. Why don't we head back to the bar, get a bite to eat, and get you moved in? Maybe have a beer or two in the process?"

"That sounds like a grand idea. I could eat just about anything right now. That food at the hospital was absolutely…" Dicky answered, but Joe was no longer listening.

Joe continued with his thoughts. *Got to get Dicky drunk. But not too drunk, he still has to be able to move. Just drunk enough that I'll be able to bend him into the tool I need.*

Time. This extra time was an opportunity, and Joe Matsell would make the most of it. Capitalize on the element of surprise and focus strength on his opponent's weakness at the right time and place. Billy would eventually have to return home, and when he did, Joe would be ready for him.

ꙮ

When Sheriff Barton entered the office, he was smothered by a cloud of smoke from Margie's cigarettes. It irritated his breathing, and he cleared his throat. He had asked Margie to consider smoking outside the office during her breaks, but she hadn't followed his guidance. He had not been direct, but her disobedience really got under his skin. The problem Barton struggled with was that he didn't have the courage to confront her about it. And he didn't want to lose her. She was a hard worker and very good at paying attention to details when it came to administrative tasks, something that was not his strong suit.

Jim knew there was something about Margie he didn't trust. She was very efficient and got all of her tasks done, but it always seemed like she was doing something else, doing more than he never saw. This, coupled with her disobedience, made him worry. He pushed the thoughts out of his mind. Good workers were hard to come by, and he convinced himself to tolerate her weaknesses.

"I didn't think you were going to be back in town until later this afternoon." Margie's voice wavered as she blurted out. She stood up anxiously as the Sheriff unexpectedly walked in with Anna and Billy behind him.

Margie had an uncomfortably surprised air in her high-pitched, screechy voice and immediately pulled out another cigarette and lit it up.

Anna sensed Margie's nervous edge. A smile started to form as she thought about her nickname, Squirrel-Face. It was a horrible, degrading name, but Billy was right. It fit her perfectly. Anna sensed something else from Margie that wasn't there this morning. Something in her tone indicated she was worried, possibly even fearful. Anna thought it was a bit odd, but she reasoned that Margie Pitts was a bit odd.

Barton waved away the haze of smoke. "I got a call earlier this morning and had to go out to Bert Wilson's farm. He said somebody was out there prowling around last night. He never saw nothing. But his dogs were barking like crazy as if somebody was there and was a threat to his home." Sheriff Barton rubbed his irritated eyes.

"That Bert Wilson is as crazy as a loon. That whole family is crazy." Margie tapped her cigarette in her ashtray.

"You're probably right, Margie. But old Bert says somebody was prowling around out there. He thinks they might've stolen a couple of his son's guns. But he can't say for sure. He can't exactly remember the last time he saw them." Jim Barton covered his mouth as he choked and coughed on the smoke. "It did seem a bit peculiar. I don't know if I've ever gotten a call from Bert. Heck. I think this was the first time I've ever been out to his place. Bert and his family are a private lot, and he ain't one to call if there ain't a problem."

"Private is putting it kindly. They're just flat out weird." Margie stood up to pour Sheriff Barton a cup of coffee.

Barton took the cup from Margie and sipped. "I didn't

make it out to Monti today. But that's life in Anamosa. There's always something. Pretty hard to plan out an entire day when you're serving at the will of the people."

Jim Barton pulled out his notepad and scratched his head. "There's always something that's going to change your day. But you know how it is, sometimes you just got to go with the flow. Anyway, stopped in at the Dairywhip for lunch and bumped into Billy West and Miss Anna Jacobs. So I thought I'd make the most of the limited time I have and get their side of the story." Barton took another sip of his coffee and wrote something in his notepad.

Anna hoped she and Billy would set things straight with Blowhard Barton and be done with this dark cloud hanging over their heads. She would do whatever it took to protect her Billy. She was ready to give Barton more information than he bargained for. Anna wasn't afraid of him, and she knew she could do it in a way that was quite convincing.

Anna felt Margie's beady eyes on her as Margie made a full vertical assessment of her. Anna sensed an uncomfortable tension between her and Margie. It was a tension only women picked up on. They were always judging each other, always sizing each other up, and reaffirming their own self-worth. It was a constant comparison that seemed to go on continuously in women's lives that men were not dialed in on.

But to Anna, this was more than affirmation; this was hostility. Margie's tone had more than an edge to it. She seemed to be surprised when the sheriff walked in—it was as if she had been caught red-handed. Anna couldn't quite put her finger on it.

She thought Billy probably hadn't noticed, and she was certain Sheriff Barton didn't have a clue that Margie was up to something.

Anna was not going to be intimidated by the Squirrel. She looked Margie square in the eye and spoke with confidence. "Did you pass our message to Sheriff Barton?"

Putting down her cigarette, Margie pretended she hadn't heard the question. She feigned a cough and began organizing some paperwork into folders.

"Billy and Anna were here today? Has anybody else been in?" Sheriff Barton asked Margie with a puzzled expression.

"Pretty quiet. Except for Sally Mayfield. She was in about an hour ago. She wrote out a long statement about everything that happened at Prairieburg." Margie stood up and handed Sally's statement to Sheriff Barton. "You just missed her."

The Sheriff glanced at the document, and then his eyes turned back up to Margie. "Could you brew up a fresh pot of coffee? Had one of those huge cheeseburgers over at the Dairywhip, and I need to get a little caffeine in me if I'm going to make it through the afternoon."

Running his thumb under his belt to loosen it, Barton turned to Billy and Anna. "Guess we better get started. Which one of you would like to go first?"

"I'll go first." Anna leaned forward and kissed Billy on the cheek. She knew she could influence Sheriff Barton and that he would not be able to intimidate her. He tried to talk big around other women, but her daddy always said he was nothing but a big blowhard. She had heard her daddy say on more than one occasion, "There ain't nothing that comes out of Barton's mouth but bullshit and brown hot air that smells like bullshit."

Anna's daddy had had some dealings with Barton in the past when someone had stolen some of his farm equipment. They had stolen some of his tools right out of his barn. Barton came out, talked a big game about how he had a good hunch on who it was and that he would likely make an arrest and get the tools back. But nothing ever happened. Barton never did anything and nothing much ever came of it. Anna remembered that her daddy was convinced the sheriff was a weak and lazy man.

Billy put his hand on Anna's arm. "Honey, why don't you wait out here and let me go in with the sheriff."

Anna took his hand in hers. "I'd like to go first. Why don't you wait out here? Have a cup a coffee and take some time to catch up with Margie." Before he could refuse her, Anna smiled, walking past a dumbfounded Billy and into the Sheriff's office.

Margie's mouth dropped open, gawking at Anna as she took control of the situation. Margie's cigarette dangled from the corner of her mouth as ashes fell on her typewriter. She quickly mumbled something and lowered her head. Margie immediately added a fresh piece of paper, rolled it into the typewriter, and began pounding violently on the keys.

Billy was uncomfortable when he was not in control. He had not expected Anna to meet with Sheriff Barton first. He wanted to settle it all himself and felt uneasy with her alone in Barton's office.

Billy glanced at Margie banging away on her typewriter and wondered why anyone would be so deliberately unpleasant. He was confident she would not be one for friendly conversation and looked around the office for something to do to pass his time. Billy picked up a newspaper and took a seat in a chair, feeling edgy about everything. He didn't like that Anna was in there alone with Barton, but when the sheriff's office door clicked as it locked in place, helplessness washed over him. He trusted her, but he didn't trust Barton. Billy reasoned away his worry. Anna was a big girl; she could take care of herself. She had a strong side which probably came from her pa. Nobody would push her around, not even Jim Barton.

ꕥ

"Miss Jacobs, I've got a witness saying she saw Billy West storm out of the Prairieburg Ballroom and chase after Ronnie Wilson and Dicky Moss. Seems he was on the dance floor with you and some words were passed between Billy, Ronnie, and Dicky that had set him off. I've come to understand Billy acquired a baseball bat and proceeded to incur serious bodily injury on both of them with a violent attack." Sheriff Barton started his questioning with this statement. Anna sensed he was trying to talk down to her with his condescending tone. Barton was trying to intimidate her with his power and presence, but she would rise above it.

"Sheriff Barton, that's just a bunch of nonsense. Everybody in Anamosa knows that Billy had nothing to do with those two boys getting beat up. And everybody knows Joe Matsell was behind all of this." Sitting in her chair, Anna confidently leaned across Barton's desk.

Sheriff Barton's eyebrows rose and a look of surprise formed across his face. He had not expected her to come back at him so strongly. Strong like her daddy. He didn't like Sam Jacobs, but he respected him. He was a strong, principled man, and he could see where she got it from.

Anna cleared her throat. "I'm going to tell you what really happened, and you're going to want to record everything I say. It's the truth and will clear up this whole mess." Anna stood up and pointed her finger at Barton. "I want to start by telling you, that you, of all people, should be ashamed of yourself. I can't believe you've allowed yourself to be manipulated by people in this community. I'm disappointed I have to come in here, listen to all these lies, and spend what precious time I have with Billy so I can set the record straight."

Anna took a deep breath and leaned forward with her hands on his desk to maintain control. "I'm disappointed, and you should be too, that there are people in this community that have been so quick to judge Billy for something they have no clue about. And I'm disappointed in you. You, of all people, should be above such rhetoric, but you can't seem to keep yourself from making rash assumptions and openly talking about it. You've compromised your integrity and been quick to judge. You're the only person who can protect Billy. You, of all people, have been tainted by the darkness that lingers in this town."

The words stung Jim Barton's ears. He could feel his face turning red. Nobody talked to Sheriff Jim Barton this way. Nobody. Especially not this young lady. "Miss Jacobs, you can't…"

Anna could feel the anger burning inside her chest as the strength of her convictions pulsed in her veins. She sat down in her chair to regain control and then raised her voice to cut him off. "First of all, Billy had nothing to do with any of this. It's true that Billy and I were out on the dance floor, dancing. But Ronnie and Dicky never approached us. In fact, Billy never had any contact with them the entire night."

Sheriff Barton's eyes rose even higher, and the wrinkles on his forehead coiled up into fat little rolls. Everything she said was a complete contradiction to Sally Mayfield's statement.

"Billy and I danced, and then I went to the ladies' room. Billy waited for me by the bar, but I never returned." Tears filled up her eyes as she remembered that horrible night, and her voice cracked when she said these words. "When I came out of the restroom, Ronnie was waiting for me. He told me Billy was in the back parking lot, looking for me."

Anna could feel her emotions building inside and she tried to maintain her composure. "For a second, I thought it was strange. Why would Billy be outside? But he guided me out the back door. I wish I never would have gone outside. I should have gone back to the dance floor. I was confused when I stepped out the back door. Something wasn't right. It felt wrong. Everything outside was very dark. But I kept walking. Ronnie followed me." Anna's words slowed. Tears welled in her eyes and then she whispered, "Why didn't I run? I should've run."

The tears poured out of Anna, and her body trembled as she fought to control them. She was ashamed of herself. She hadn't talked about this with anyone and was surprised at how painful it was to revisit. She sobbed like a child. She'd started off strong but now cried uncontrollably. She was angry at herself and started to self-talk. *Get a grip. Got to get a grip. Got to protect Billy. Get control of your emotions. Got to set things right.*

Sheriff Barton, unsure what to do, handed her a tissue and hoped she'd just stop. Anna blew her nose, wiped the tears from her eyes, and regained her composure. She had to go on and get it all out. "That was when Ronnie grabbed me from behind. I felt his arms wrap around me. I couldn't believe what was happening. He was strong. I tried to fight back—clawing and screaming—but he kept pushing me forward. Pushing me…"

Anna paused to wipe the tears from her eyes. "It all seems like a blur now. He was pushing me toward the car. Dicky Moss was there, too. Ronnie tried to shove me into the backseat. But I fought. Yes, I fought hard, kicking and screaming at them. Dicky grabbed my legs and dragged me into the car when..." Anna took a deep breath. Her lip quivered, and she worried that her tears would return. "That was when he showed up."

Anna blew her nose and gathered her strength. "I heard a large thump and then another and another. Someone else was there and I wasn't sure who he was. Words were exchanged between them, but I don't remember what they were. Then there was the crash of something slamming into the car. He was smashing the car, too. I was afraid. I thought he was coming after me and that I was next. I was hysterical." Anna touched the side of her head. "I felt dizzy from the fear, and I thought I might faint. I might've lost consciousness for a moment or two. I don't remember. But then he talked to me, and I knew I'd be all right."

Anna looked up at Sheriff Barton, her eyes puffy and red. "He saved my life."

"Who? Billy? Billy did this?" Barton asked.

"No. It wasn't Billy. It was…" Anna looked away, unwilling go on.

"Tell me. Tell me who it was." Barton leaned forward, urging her to reveal the identity.

"I can't tell you. I told him I wouldn't. But he will. He'll be coming to talk to you when he's ready—probably in the next couple of days."

Barton didn't want to believe Anna's story, but he knew it was probably true. Unfortunately, it created more problems for him. It wasn't enough, and it contradicted what Sally had said. Sally Mayfield's story tied everything up for him neatly and solved the problem. Now there was more to this. There was always more to a story when he was dealing with people. Nothing was ever easy.

Barton rubbed his forehead. "Why couldn't anything be easy?" he muttered to himself. He was worried. He would be getting pressure to arrest somebody. He had two young men badly beaten, and something had to be done.

Nothing was ever clean. It was possible that Ronnie and Dicky were the culprits, and they were severely beaten to save Anna. A vision of pretty little Anna Jacobs flashed in his mind—she was sitting on the stand, crying. He knew it wouldn't go well for Dicky and Ronnie. "I need to know who attacked Ronnie and Dicky. You need to tell me so I can settle this matter."

"I'm not going to tell you. Like I said, he'll come forward

and give you his statements in the next couple of days," Anna said in a confident tone.

"Miss Jacobs, without his testimony, your statement doesn't mean much in a court of law." Barton was lying, but he thought it might work.

"I'm sorry, Sheriff. I can tell you Billy didn't rescue me from those boys, but I can't tell you who did."

Sheriff Barton rubbed the back of his neck. He could feel it warming up, and he knew his face was turning red.

Anna could see he was growing frustrated with her. "Billy came looking for me because I never showed up at the bar. He went over to the ladies room, but I was already gone. He was attacked, too."

"By the same man with the bat?" Sheriff Barton asked surprised. He didn't know Billy had been attacked, too.

"No. No, it was someone else. Billy was looking out the back door when somebody hit him over the head from behind. Knocked him out cold. When he came to, there were a couple of girls from Monti, standing over him."

"Are you sure? Are you sure it was someone else? Who was it? Who hit him?" Barton asked. He was suspicious of her for not giving up the name of the assailant.

"I can't say for sure, and I don't think Billy can either. He was knocked out cold. Thinks that whoever it was probably used a bottle."

Barton didn't want to believe her. He wanted it to be clean. He rubbed his eyes again. Nothing was ever easy. He wondered why people did what they did. He had all but given up hope for what human beings would do. And yet, he was still surprised at the depths they would fall. He was more frustrated now than when he started work this morning. That was not a good thing. Barton knew there was a lot more to this, and he didn't know if he had the energy to sort through it all.

All he had up to this point was Sally's statement, and that wasn't enough. He needed more information from Ronnie and Dicky. He would also need Sally, Ronnie and Dicky to give very convincing testimonies in court to have a shot at convicting Billy.

"Do you have anything else to say?"

"No, not at this time. Do you need me to write out a sworn statement?" Anna wiped her eyes with her tissue.

"No, I think I've heard enough." Sheriff Barton scribbled something down on his notepad. "This is all I need for now. I'll contact you if I need more information."

Anna thought his response was strange. She got a sick feeling Barton was covering something up. She wondered if her statement had been a waste of time. She was still worried about Billy. But she had told the truth, and she knew the truth was all she could give. She hoped it would be enough.

"It won't be a problem. I can write one out while you're talking to Billy." Anna leaned forward.

"Don't you worry about it, Miss Jacobs. You've given me enough." Barton stood up from his desk and opened the door for her to leave.

ꕥ

Billy had gotten a cup of coffee from Margie and was sitting back in a chair, reading the newspaper. She feverishly typed away behind the counter. Billy could see the top of her head and the smoke rising up from her cigarette. About every minute or so, she would pause and then continue typing. He leaned back a little more in the chair, and it let out a loud, creaking screech-like chirp. Billy was surprised at the noise and how it echoed in the room. He shifted his weight, and the chair made the sound again. Billy smiled. The sound reverberated off the walls and filled the room. It kind of reminded him of a cricket with a bit more of a cackle to it. Then a large grin spread across his face. It sounded exactly like a squirrel.

He looked over at Margie again. She was pounding away on the typewriter. He watched and waited for her to pause so she could hear him. Billy waited, waited, and then she stopped, and he quickly shifted in the chair.

CCHKKKCKKKCKKK. CHHKCKCKCKCCCCKKCHKKKK. Two loud screeching chirps filled the room.

Billy saw Margie's head move, but she didn't stop typing. He was sure she must have heard it. He waited again. He watched her head moving as her hands pounded the typewriter in a rhythm. Billy tried to predict when she would stop. He adjusted his weight and was poised, ready to let out another noise.

The typing stopped, and Billy shifted his left cheek in the chair. *CHKKCKKKCKK. CHHKCKCKCKCKCHKCKCKKCHKK. CCHKCHKKKCHKKKCHKK. CHKKCHCKKKCHK. CHKCCK CHCKKKCK.*

Billy anticipated her pause beautifully. An animated conversation between two excited squirrels echoed throughout the room.

Margie's head lifted up, and Billy thought he heard her grunt something. She commenced her rhythmic typing, and Billy positioned his weight in the chair for another squirrel conversation.

She paused, and again Billy nailed it perfectly as he shifted his left cheek on the chair. This time he was able to draw out the screeching chirps.

CCHKKKCKKKCKKK. CHKKKCKCKCKCHKCKCKCHKK. CCHKCHKKKCHCKKKCHKK. CHKKKCHCKKCHK.CHKCKK. CHCKKKCCK. CCHKCHKKKCHCKKKCHKKK.

"What the…did you hear that?" Margie's head popped up from behind the counter.

Billy buried his face in the newspaper and acted as if nothing had happened. "Huh? What? What did you say?"

"Did you hear that? Did you hear that sound?" Margie asked again, searching the room. "Did you hear that noise?"

"I wasn't paying much attention. What? What did it sound like?" Billy asked innocently, flipping to the newspaper to the next page.

"It sounded like… It sounded like a squ…" Margie stopped herself and asked, "You didn't hear it?"

Billy kept his face down in the paper. He knew if he looked up at Squirrel-Face he would burst out in laughter. "No, I didn't hear it. Do you hear it now?"

"No. It stopped," she replied, appearing confused.

"Huh. Whatever it was, must be gone now." Billy kept his face down to hide his smile.

Margie's head dropped back down, and she started to feverishly type. This time with a new, more pronounced vengeance, pounding away at a new rhythm. Billy could tell she was angry. He tried to predict when she would stop, but it was too difficult. She paused and then continued, paused and continued, and Billy waited for her to go back to her original rhythm. Billy remained silent for a few minutes. He could tell she was relaxing again. He knew she had started to reason it away. If it was a squirrel in the office then it must have gone back out the same way that it had come.

Ten minutes passed. Margie was back in her rhythm, and Billy adjusted his weight again, he was poised for another adjustment. Just as she stopped typing, Billy shifted his left cheek once more.

CCHKCHKKCHCKKKCHKKK. CHKKKCHCKKKKKCHK. CHKKKCKKKCKKK. CHKCHKCKCKKKKCHKKKCKKKCKKK. CHCKKKCHKKK. CHKKKCHCKKCHK.

"What the hell was that?" Marge shouted as she stood up from her typewriter in a cloud of cigarette smoke. "What the hell's in this room?" she shouted at Billy, looking around.

"What? What are you talking about?" Billy tried not to look up at Squirrel-Face.

"You didn't hear that?" She asked in an exasperated tone.

"Hear what?" Billy still maintained his innocence.

"That sound again. I think it's coming from inside of this room. Something is in here." Margie lowered her voice to a whisper.

"What do you think it is?" Billy asked from behind his

paper.

"I don't know. I think…" There was an element of terror in her voice. She paused for a moment, looked to her left and then her right, and then whispered, "I think…there might be squirrels in here."

"Oh that sound? I guess I did hear that. From over here, I wasn't sure what it was. You might be right. Come to think of it, it did kind of sound like there were a couple squirrels in the room." Billy briefly looked up from his newspaper, trying in vain to suppress his smile.

"They're in here, all right." Margie turned and grabbed a broom. "And we're going to find them."

"We?" Billy's head popped up from his paper, still trying to control his expression.

"Now get on up here and put yourself to work. First we're going to move this shelving. I think they might be hiding behind here." Margie motioned with her hand to have Billy come forward.

Billy got up and moved in behind the counter and shifted the book shelf. He was still trying to suppress his smile when the sheriff's office door swung open and Anna and Jim Barton stepped out.

"What in the hell are you doing?" Sheriff Barton asked in disbelief.

Billy slid the shelf from the wall while Margie stood poised with the broom over her head, ready to take a swing at anything that crawled out.

"Sheriff, I think we've got squirrels in the office. Billy here is helping me catch them," Margie answered in Billy's defense.

Anna looked up at Billy, and he lowered his head behind the shelf to hide his sheepish grin.

"Nope, don't see any behind here. Maybe they got into the ventilation system." Billy looked up at the ceiling to divert his eyes from Anna.

"I ain't got time today to be hunting no damn squirrels. West, come on in here so we can talk." Exasperated, Sheriff Barton gestured for Billy to enter into his office.

"Margie, why don't you look behind the other shelves over there, and if you don't find nothing, clean out the utility closet. That closet ain't been touched for years, and God only knows what could be hiding in there." Sheriff Barton rolled his eyes and entered his office.

ஐ

"I got at least three witnesses saying you assaulted Ronnie Wilson and Dicky Moss." Sheriff Barton smirked at Billy as he leaned back in the leather chair at his desk. Sheriff Barton felt powerful as he looked down on Billy in a smaller chair.

"Sheriff, what you got is three people lying about something I had nothing to do with. The real question is, who's behind all of this?" Billy clenched his jaw in frustration as he leaned forward.

"I've got about twenty minutes before my next engagement. Why don't you give me your side of the story so I can take it into consideration?" Barton nonchalantly rolled his wrist and looked at his watch.

"There isn't much to say. I was out on the dance floor with Anna when we decided to take a break. She went to the ladies' room, and I sat at the bar and waited for her to return. After a good fifteen minutes and she hadn't come back, I went looking for her. The last thing I remember was being in the back hallway by the restrooms. I vaguely recall peering out the back door, and that was when it all happened."

"What happened?" Barton asked as he studied Billy's reaction.

"Well, I can't say for sure, but I know something did happen because I still got this swelling on my head about the size of a grapefruit." Billy felt the back of his head with his hand. Billy leaned closer in his chair and put his hands on the sheriff's desk. "Somebody clocked me from behind. I think they probably hit me with a bottle, but I can't say for sure. After he hit me, I was out. Then when I came to, one of my friends helped me up. It was a lot like getting a concussion out on the football field; I really had no idea where I was."

Billy's story matched Anna's so Barton changed his line of questioning. "How much did you have to drink that night?"

"To drink? Oh, I don't know. It was still pretty early in the evening. No more than three beers and that was in the span of at least two hours. I wasn't drunk; I can tell you that." Billy slapped his hand down on the desk, frustrated in the direction the discussion was going. "Sheriff, I had nothing to do with what happened to Dicky and Ronnie. You got to believe that. The question I have is why they're all lying about it?" Billy lowered his eyes as he reached up and rubbed his chin. Clearing his throat,

Billy lifted his eyes to meet Barton's. "You got Sally Mayfield, Dicky Moss and Ronnie Wilson all singing the same song. Sally's Joe Matsell's girl and Moss and Wilson practically live down at his bar…"

The Sheriff raised his voice and clenched his fists on the desk. "I don't give a damn about Joe Matsell. What I got is two busted up boys and some pretty credible witnesses telling me you did it. Why should I believe your story and not theirs?"

"Because I didn't do it," Bill exploded as he gripped the desk with both of his hands.

"Well, somebody beat the hell out of them with a baseball bat. Why don't you tell me who did?" Barton lowered his voice as he glanced up at the clock on the wall.

"I wasn't there when it happened, but I know who it was." Billy took a deep breath and regained his control. "He'll come forward and give you his account in the next couple of days."

Sheriff Barton crossed his arms over his chest and leaned back in his chair. "Oh yeah, the mystery man. Your friend Miss Jacobs mentioned him, too. The real assailant is someone nobody has even mentioned in this incident. How convenient." Barton's faced flushed red as he stood up at his desk and pointed down at Billy. "I got folks breathing down my neck to get to the bottom of this. I ain't got time to wait. And you say that he's going to reveal himself in the next couple of days? Now how in the hell do you know that?"

"Well, for one, he told me he would. And also because he's like me. He's an honest man." Billy stood up across from Barton and squared his shoulders. His eyes were sharp and serious, his expression intense.

Sheriff Barton's face was still beet red, and he sighed as he leaned over his desk and wrote down a few words in his notebook. He glanced up at Billy briefly but was unable to look him in the eye.

VI

ANNA DUG HER feet into the soft sand and leaned back into the cool and refreshing water that whirled around her body. Tilting her head back, she looked up into the sky and watched a couple of soft white clouds float high above. Anna smiled. This was the first time she was able to relax all day. She thought about her exchange with Sheriff Barton earlier. She was surprised at her own strength, and her smile widened. The water lifted her up in the stream, and she floated weightless like the clouds overhead.

For the first time in a week, she felt confident again. She had protected her Billy and done everything she could for him. She wasn't sure if Barton was convinced about the truth, but she did her part. With Josh's testimony, Billy would be cleared of all of this.

Anna's hair freely swirled in the water as she lay back on the surface. The stress drained out of her into the stream. She was at peace.

"Come on, Charlotte. Get in!" Josh shouted to Charlotte who stood on the massive dolomite boulder towering over the river bank.

Startled from her relaxed state, Anna stood upright in the water. "The water's absolutely wonderful once you get in."

Charlotte shouted back, "I thought we were going out for a nice dinner when we finished swimming. I don't want to get my hair wet."

"I would hardly call the Stone City a nice dinner," Billy said under his breath to Josh.

"Hey pal, I had to bribe her to get her to come. Quite honestly, I'm surprised we've gotten her this far." Josh smiled sheepishly.

Josh, Billy, and Anna stood side by side about thirty feet from the bank in the middle of Buffalo Creek. The clean, clear water, just over three feet deep, flowed around them. Billy looked back up at the massive boulder Charlotte stood on. She had a tight grip on the rope swing that dangled from the tree branch high above her head. Holding the rope she tried to balance herself on the edge of the rock.

"Come on, Charlotte. Try out the rope swing. It's to die for," Billy shouted.

"It's really a lot of fun, baby. You can do it." Josh lifted his hands from the water and beckoned her to swing off the rock.

Charlotte looked over the edge of the boulder. She was about twelve feet above the surface of the water, but in her mind, she was at least thirty. The rope shook in her trembling hand. "I…I think I'm just going to lay out up here in the sun."

"Oh hon, come on. You don't know what you're missing." Josh splashed his hands on the water and called up to her.

"No. No. It's nice up here. I'm going to lay out up here," Charlotte said more confidently.

Josh turned to Billy and grinned. "She's scared to hell."

"Scared? That rope's safe," Billy said.

"Well, it ain't exactly the rope she's afraid of. I told her about the turtles, snakes, carp, and crawdaddies that live in Buffalo Creek." Josh chuckled.

"Well, they ain't nothing. They don't mean no harm to anyone." Billy leaned back into the water.

"I know that, you know that, and Anna knows that, but Charlotte, she doesn't know that. She's afraid she's going to get bitten or even eaten by something in the creek."

"Now where would she get an idea like that?" Anna's eyes were suspicious, and her tone was accusatory.

"Well probably because I also told her about the 'Great Woolly Pike' that lives out here under the rock." Josh lowered his voice and chuckled.

Billy joined him with a grin and added in a more serious tone. "Ahh, Old Woolly. Yep, I've seen him out here at Fremont a few times myself. Sometimes over yonder under the bridge. Sometimes he lurks under the rock, waiting…waiting for some young, frightened girl, preferably from Chicago, to enter his waters."

Anna slugged Billy. "You're absolutely horrible. The both of you, just horrible. She's sitting up there on the rock all alone, scared stiff of some crazy story about a silly fish."

Billy ignored Anna and turned to Josh. "What would you say, Josh? Old Woolly is probably about five or maybe even six feet in length."

"Yeah, I reckon Old Woolly is somewhere around six feet long by this time. Heck, last time I remember seeing him was way back in the summer of '62 when we would come out here after working at Boss Miller's farm." Josh smirked as he dove forward in the current and let it carry him back to Anna and Billy.

"Okay, you've got my curiosity. Not that I believe you, but why do you call him Old Woolly?" Anna asked.

"That there is a damn good question, Anna Darling, and it's a mighty peculiar story. You see, Old Woolly don't shine like your normal northern pike. He's darker and his scales are dull looking—like they're covered with some moss-like dark cloth. They say that's what happens to a northern after fifty, sixty, or even a hundred years." Billy sank low in the water, knowing Anna was going to splash him.

"I can't believe you would…" Anna jumped forward onto Billy to dunk him under the water.

Josh swam to Billy's rescue and pulled her off him. Tossing her into the water, Josh laughed as she emerged. "Come on Anna, you've heard the legend." Josh's eyes widened. "He's ancient. And when you see him, he's dark and has what looks like a thick, grey-green wool coat, covering him. He don't look like a normal northern, not at all."

"Except for his mouth." Billy smiled, pinching Anna from behind. "He's got the biggest teeth I've ever seen on a northern or on any fish. What would you say, Josh, you think his teeth are over an inch long?"

"Inch and a half." Josh raised his hand and illustrated the length with his thumb and his forefinger.

"Inch and a half, and I've seen him use them, too. Remember that time he bit into Jenny Lawson out here?" Billy tried to keep a straight face.

"I do. Dang near cut her leg right off. Hey, wasn't her

family from Chicago?" Josh asked as he and Billy nodded.

"You boys are full of it. Absolutely full of it." Anna slugged Billy in the arm again.

"Hey, why do you keep hitting me? I never told Charlotte about Old Woolly. It was Josh's doing." Billy rubbed his arm in jest.

"You boys are all the same. Horrible. Horrible and hopeless." Anna turned away from them and swam toward the rock.

"Hey, where are you going?" Billy shouted at her.

"I'm going to lay out for a while on the rock with Charlotte. It'll be nice to have a conversation with a mature adult," Anna said as she reached the boulder and began her climb to the top.

"Women. What are we ever going to do with them?" Billy said to Josh with a grin.

Josh smiled. "I'm sure you boys from Anamosa don't have a clue, but coming from Monticello, I can think of a couple of things."

They both laughed. It was a beautiful afternoon at Fremont Bridge. To Billy, this was one of the best swimming holes in Jones County. The Buffalo was clear and clean, and the weather was perfect. The river bottom was smooth, wavy sand, and free of debris. The water was three to four feet deep in most places. The only deep area was adjacent to the rock, where it was a good ten feet deep. The rope swing, which had been there for as long as Billy could remember, was still in great condition. Over the years, it had been used by most boys in Jones County.

Billy looked up at the old iron bridge spanning the stream.

A tractor crossed over it, and the wood planks slapped against the iron frame as it moved across. The farmer waved down at the boys, and they waved back. Built in the 1870s, the bridge was still holding strong.

Billy smiled to himself as he thought about the history of Fremont Bridge. The bridge originally spanned the Maquoketa River on the Old Military Road north of Monticello. As the region grew, the Military Road was replaced with a newer, faster highway, and the bridge was moved to this quiet corner of Jones County. Change. Always change. The bridge was once a vital part of one of the original main roads in the state. Billy suddenly felt a sense of sadness, for now the bridge's only use was by a small group of farmers traveling to and from their fields and for kids coming out here to swim.

Change. Billy's mind drifted to the future. He thought about Anna and the army and wondered if he could change, too.

Billy looked over at Josh and felt another wave of remorse. This would probably be their last day together. He would leave for Benning in a few days, and Josh had to work as a counselor at a church camp for the next three weeks. Summer would soon turn to fall, and their time was slipping away. A sharp pain stabbed his stomach as he thought about it. He had to make the most of the moments he had now. Nothing could be wasted. He had a couple of things he still had to do that included Josh.

"What do you say we walk up the stream a ways and float down?" Billy asked Josh as he pointed up the river.

Billy and Josh looked up stream. The sunlight shimmered on the surface of the water. It was so inviting. "Let's do it." Josh smiled.

Billy and Josh turned and trudged upstream. Josh could feel time slipping away from them, too. He didn't want to go to church camp again this summer. He had gone to the camp every summer since he was a boy, and in the last couple of years, he had been invited back as a counselor. He would rather spend the summer with Charlotte, having fun, but his mom insisted on it. She seemed to know it was what he needed. Other than his time with Billy and Charlotte, he spent most of his waking hours with his father at his mother's bedside, and it was wearing him down.

Like Billy, Josh was an only child. He had always been there for his parents just as they had been there for him. He did not want to leave them now. He especially didn't want to go to a place where he had to teach children about the goodness of God. He was angry—angry at God for what was happening to his mother. He would feel like such a hypocrite as a leader at the camp. But he would go because she had asked.

"I need your help, Josh," Billy said in a somber tone that broke Josh's train of thought.

"I know you need my help. You need all kinds of help." Josh chuckled.

"No, I'm serious. I need your help with a couple of things," Billy said again in the same serious tone.

"I told you I'd go see Barton tomorrow morning. I'll wait there all day, come hell or high water. He's going to get the truth from me." Josh waded through the water.

"Thanks. I know you haven't been able to get over to see him with everything going on at home, and I really appreciate it."

Josh looked up at the sun. Tears were burning in his eyes. It had been a tough week in the Sanders' home. His mother had been diagnosed with cancer over a year ago, and it was now taking its toll and ravaging her body. This was another common bond he and Billy shared. Billy lost his mom to cancer years ago, and now Josh was facing the same possibility. They never talked about it, but they both knew it was something they understood. Josh tried to push the vision of his sick mother, lying in her bed and crying out in pain, out of his mind. It was too much to think about.

"I'm not afraid of Barton or anyone. Besides, I didn't do nothing no honest man wouldn't do." Josh glanced at Billy with a confident and determined expression.

"Thanks, Josh." Billy put his arm around him.

"You got it. You know I've got your back." Josh wrapped his arm around Billy and pulled him closer as they continued their walk upstream against the current.

"You going to get some help?" Josh asked in a direct tone.

"What do you mean?" Billy asked.

"You know exactly what I mean." Josh looked Billy in the eyes and waited for him to respond. After a long uncomfortable pause Josh continued, "The other day up on Pinicon Ridge… You got the ugliness of that war all bottled up, still going on inside you."

"It ain't nothing. Nothing I can't handle. I got it. I don't need no help from no one. There ain't nothing anyone can do anyway. It just is." Billy's face was full of anger as he pivoted away from Josh and dove forward into the stream. Coming up from the water, he turned toward the bank and refused to look at Josh.

Josh grabbed Billy's arm and firmly pulled him back. "Billy, I see what it's doing to you. It's toxic, and you can't let it eat you up inside. There has got to be somebody that can help you."

"I know, I know. When I get back to Benning, I'll look into seeing if there's some kind of support available," Billy said, but he knew he wouldn't do it. He had seen others go to see the quack doctor about issues they were having, and they were immediately cast out from their team.

Josh didn't believe him but hoped he would seek out help. "I'm worried about you, buddy. You've done things most people never even dream of, and it can change you."

"I'll be fine." Billy raised his voice and cut off Josh. Billy laid his hand on Josh's shoulder and spoke in a lighter tone. "Besides, I got you, I got Anna, and I always got a little whiskey to get me through. What else is there?" Billy smiled at Josh.

"I know, buddy. I just worry for you."

"Well don't. I'm fine. It'll all work itself out. I'll be okay. All right?" Billy's smile quickly faded. He wished he hadn't said anything to Josh about the war.

"All right," Josh answered.

"Now let's float down stream." Billy quickly submerged himself in the stream, and Josh dove in after him, gliding in the water to his side.

"Hey, looks like Anna is talking Charlotte into swinging off the rock on the swing," Billy said to Josh as they floated down toward them.

"I've got an idea." Josh's face lit up with a mischievous grin. He quickly swam over to the bank and grabbed a long stick and pulled it out into the water.

"That stick is at least eight feet long. What the hell are you thinking?" Billy's face lit up, too.

"Just watch," Josh said as he pushed at something under the water. Billy thought it looked like he was taking off his cutoff jeans. A second later, he saw that he was right as Josh's cutoffs floated up to the surface of the water.

"What in the hell are you doing?" Billy asked, laughing.

"Give me your cutoffs," Josh demanded.

"What?" Billy thought Josh had gone crazy.

"Give me your shorts. But do it slowly. Don't let the girls know you're taking them off. Stay below the water."

Billy took off his shorts and handed them to Josh. The cool water ran over him, and it felt great. He had forgotten how liberating skinny-dipping was.

"What in the hell are you doing now?" Billy asked.

"Just watch." Josh tied both pairs off the cutoffs to the end of the stick.

Billy started to get the picture. "You're horrible, Josh. Absolutely horrible, and I like it."

"Once we get down by the rock, I think old Woolly Pike will be making his grand appearance," Josh said proudly.

"Charlotte's going to freak out when she sees this," Billy responded with excitement.

"Precisely, my dear friend, precisely." Josh agreed as they floated down the creek and closed in on Charlotte and Anna who were still up on the rock.

"Come on, Charlotte. You can do it!" Billy shouted up at Charlotte and Anna.

"Do a cannon ball, baby!" Josh added.

"Stop your chattering down there. You're going to break her concentration," Anna yelled back.

"Watch this," Josh whispered to Billy. He stretched the stick out under water and then started to tilt it upward to the surface. Just in front of the large rock, they watched as the shorts surfaced and then disappeared as Josh pulled them back down. Both boys smiled and tried not to laugh.

"They didn't see it. Do it again. Do it again!" Billy nudged Josh with his elbow.

"You boys watch out. I think Charlotte's going to do it," Anna said from the boulder.

Charlotte gripped the rope tight in her hands and peered over the edge of the rock one more time. The height made her dizzy with fear, but her pride wouldn't let her back down now. She had watched the boys swing off it earlier, and even Anna had done it a few times. Charlotte had been intimidated and even jealous of Anna since the first time they had met weeks ago at the fair. She had noticed how Josh looked at her and how well they had gotten along. It wasn't lust or even love. It was respect. These were eyes Josh never had for her. She would not let them show her up this time. She would do it.

Now looking down over the edge of the rock, she tried not to tremble with fear. She was just about ready to step back and swing forward on the rope when something caught the corner of her eye. Something large was surfacing in the water below, just a few feet from Billy and Josh. A jolt of terror shot through her body as she recognized the monster coming up from the depths. She screamed frantically and could barely get the words out.

"Wwww…Wooooool…Woolly…it's…it's Woolly! It's the Woolly Pike! Josh, the Woolly Pike!" Charlotte screamed out at the top of her lungs in a shrieking pitch. She pointed down at the water and was jumping up and down in a fearful and silly dance. "Woolly Pike! Woolly Pike! It's the Woolly Pike!"

Anna stepped up beside her and looked down on the boys below. They both had sheepish grins and were smiling up at Anna and Charlotte. "You dirty, rotten bastards!" Anna shouted and then jumped off the rock, landing almost right on top of them.

Coming up from the water, she splashed both of the boys. "You're both horrible, just horrible!"

Anna yanked the stick from Josh's hands and immediately lifted it out of the water, then swung it violently at the pranksters.

Charlotte realized it was a dirty trick. She could feel her anger beginning to boil. Once again, she had been taken advantage of. Her rage immediately overwhelmed any fear she had. She stepped back with the rope in her hand, ran forward and then jumped over the edge, swinging in a high arc above the water. It was exhilarating, but she was so angry at Josh that she wouldn't let herself enjoy it. As the rope reached the end of the pendulum arc and started to swing back toward the rock, she let go and fell for what seemed like an eternity. Entering the water, she found herself several feet below the surface and immediately shot upward. Euphoric, she realized she was safe. She had done it. She proved she could do anything Anna could do.

"You mean to tell me there's no such thing as the Woolly Pike?" Charlotte swam toward Josh and shouted angrily.

"I'm afraid not, Charlotte." Anna dropped the stick and reached out for Charlotte's hand and pulled her to toward them in the shallow water. "Once again, these boys have proven why we have to treat them like they're twelve year olds."

"Josh, grab the stick. I need my shorts so I can show these ladies how a real man jumps off the rock." Billy pointed as the stick floated downstream.

Josh swam with the current, and grabbed the long stick, pulling it up toward them. Josh tugged and got a sick feeling in the pit of his stomach. The stick was lighter than it had been. When he lifted the end of the stick out, he realized his nightmare had come true.

"Where in the hell are my shorts?" Billy asked fearfully.

"Oh no," Josh replied in an ominous tone. Both Josh and Billy gazed down at the end of the stick, and there was a long pause. No words would come. They stared at the stick in a confused state of disbelief.

Josh finally broke the silence. "They must have come off the stick when Anna grabbed it."

"Oh shit." Billy was now in deep, deep trouble.

The girls burst out in laughter as both boys simultaneously jumped up out of the water, bare-ass naked and ran down stream in the shallow water in search of their shorts.

"Look at them run!" Anna laughed.

"Wow, impressive tan lines!" Charlotte added, giggling at the stark contrast between their bright white rear ends and the rest of their bodies.

"You know, I thought Billy said that boys from Monti were challenged with their size, but now we know that boys from both towns are equally endowed." Anna joined in on the banter.

"And from the looks of it, there's not much there." Charlotte laughed.

Stark naked, Billy and Josh dashed downstream frantically searching for their shorts.

It was one of the most comical things Anna had seen in a long time. She laughed so hard her sides ached.

"You know Charlotte, it couldn't have happened to a more deserving set of guys," Anna said, turning to Charlotte.

"I hope they can find their shorts before we leave." Charlotte shrugged. "Guess that would make it difficult for them to join us for dinner."

"They're taking us to dinner. Pants or no pants. They'll have to figure it out. And besides, the sign at the restaurant says 'no shoes, no shirt, no service'. It doesn't say anything about no shorts." Anna laughed.

Charlotte stood with her hands on her hips. "It serves them right for what they did."

"They had it coming. They really had it coming." Anna chuckled as she stood by Charlotte in the water, watching their men run naked further and further down the bank in search of their shorts. "Yep, Charlotte, it serves them right. What comes around, goes around." Both ladies laughed as the boys disappeared around the bend.

ꕥ

Billy waved down their waitress. “Bonnie, another round of pitchers, please.”

“You boys better slow down. You’re not going to make it to dinner at the rate you’re going,” Anna said, eyeing both of them with an air of disapproval.

“Bonnie, could you add two shots of tequila to that round please?” Josh added.

“Shots? You’re not doing shots, are you?” Charlotte asked, not enthused about how heavily the boys were drinking.

“No. These shots ain’t for us. They’re for you. We need to loosen you ladies up a little. That’s how you like them up in Monti, right Josh?” Billy patted Josh on the back.

“Monticello, Anamosa, don’t matter where they come from. We all like our ladies loose. Besides, this is our last evening to party together. We’re going to make the most of it, and we may need some loose ladies.” Josh raised his beer to toast the girls.

Ignoring their comments, Charlotte turned away from Josh and leaned closer to Anna. “This really is a quaint little restaurant. I’ve never been to Stone City before.”

“It is special place. Like most buildings in this town, it was built with limestone from the quarry at the turn of the century.” Anna moved away from Billy and closer to Charlotte.

“It has a charming atmosphere. The stone fireplaces, the old pictures, the candles and lighting, and the old oak bar. There’s even a stage—do they have live music here often?” Charlotte asked.

"About every weekend. Mainly locals, but some folk musicians travel from Iowa City, even a few from Chicago and Minneapolis." Anna pointed at photographs of musicians behind the bar.

"I'll bet these old walls can tell some interesting stories." Charlotte looked out across the room.

"Before it was the restaurant it is today, it served as an apartment, a post office, and a store." Anna paused for a moment as they both looked around at all the pictures on the walls. "Billy knows his history, and he says that back in the 1800s when stone masonry and the quarries were in their heyday, this little town was a bustling community. This building was the only outlet to provide services to all of the workers. For a short time, it was basically the center of the community."

"What happened?" Charlotte asked.

"According to Billy" –Anna shot Billy a sideways glance to let him that she did, in fact, listen to his stories— "by the turn of the century, cement was cheaper to make and became much more popular, and the demand for the stone quickly diminished. As I understand, it didn't take long before the quarries went out of business. We have a few stone buildings like this one, but they're all that's left in this little community that once provided stone for many of the major structures in Iowa." Anna looked round the room, seeing it through Billy's eyes and amazed at how special it was. "If you get a chance, drive into Anamosa and see the prison. With its stone lions and high castle walls, it's a cross between something from the *Wizard of Oz* and Disneyland…only a little more austere."

"That's what I've heard. In fact, I took a course at Iowa on turn of the century architecture, and our professor referred to it. I think he called it something like the 'white palace of the West.' He did recommend all of his students see this Midwestern marvel." Charlotte looked around as well before straightening her napkin on her lap. Anna got the feeling Charlotte was trying to prove her intelligence.

"Well, you should. It would be worth the drive into Anamosa," Anna said, not letting Charlotte get to her, and continued with her history about Stone City. "This little town had a brief resurgence in activity in the 1930s when an artist colony was formed here by famous American painter, Grant Wood. He's probably best known for his paintings *The American Gothic* and the one that showcases this building, *Stone City*."

"I didn't know this building is part of a famous painting?" Charlotte suddenly felt a sense of awe of the historic landmark.

Anna took a sip of her water. "It's right in the middle of the picture, nestled in a bend along the Wapsipinicon River."

"Does it have any kind of symbolic meaning? Charlotte asked with an intrigued expression.

"I'm really not much of an art expert, but I know Billy can tell you just about all you want to know about Grant Wood's paintings." Anna reached over to Billy to get his attention. "Billy, tell Charlotte about Grant Wood's painting, *Stone City*."

Billy's eyes lit up, and he took a long drink from his beer and slammed the mug down on the table then replied with a crooked smile, "I'll tell you whatever you want to know."

"Charlotte was asking about the symbolism of the painting." Anna squeezed Billy's hand, hoping he would have an answer.

"Well, Miss Chicago…" Billy lowered his chin and belched. "The painting was done during the Depression and represents transitions in life. It's an image of a business that has gone under, and the community that was left behind."

Billy took another long drink of his beer and leaned across the table closer to Charlotte. "It represents loss, and those who are forever changed by it. A stone quarry that has gone bankrupt—a surreal picture of a beautiful land torn by men and vacated. An image of change and the scars left by the change."

Billy settled back in his chair and grinned. Draining his beer, he reached for his shot of tequila and proudly asked, "Since I won't be driving home tonight, do you want to know about his painting *Death on Ridge Road*?"

Charlotte shook her head. She was repulsed by Billy's manners but mildly impressed at his knowledge on art. She found it all romantic and had more questions for Anna when her thoughts were interrupted by Billy's abrupt toast.

"To our beautiful ladies!" Billy raised his shot glass.

"To our beautiful ladies!" Josh echoed and both of the men downed their tequila.

Charlotte turned to Anna. "I think we're both in for a long night of babysitting."

Anna nodded. "I need to go to the ladies room. Would you like to join me?"

Charlotte agreed, and the ladies stood up from the table.

"Hey where are you going?" Josh asked. "We're just getting

started."

"We'll be back in a little while. We're going to the ladies room, and then I thought I'd show Charlotte around," Anna said, placing her hands on Billy's shoulders

"Okay, just stay together. I didn't bring my Louisville Slugger with me tonight," Josh responded with a laugh.

Josh's words stung Anna, reminding her of the horrible night at Prairieburg. But she let it slide since both Josh and Billy were well on their way to a happy state of inebriation. "I think we are going to be the ones saving you from trouble tonight." Anna forced a smile as she turned away and reached for Charlotte's arm, and they walked toward the restrooms.

Josh poured beer into their two empty glasses. This was the best he had felt all week. He had spent most of the week at the hospital with his mother. *Damned cancer,* he thought to himself. It was evil. Over the past year, he had watched as the disease ravaged his mom's body. It was ruthless, a monster taking everything from her and not giving anything back. Just eighteen months ago, she was a beautiful, vibrant woman. Now she was almost impossible to recognize.

Josh and his father were doing everything possible to give her peace. Peace. He didn't want to think about it—there was only one way for her to truly be at peace. He wasn't ready to accept that. He loved her too much to even let the thought enter into his mind. He pushed it away and looked over at Billy, who for some reason had a deep, heavy look of sadness on his face.

This would be their last night together. Tonight they would overdo things, drink too much, whatever it took to distract them.

He looked at Billy, knowing he was feeling the same thing. Josh smiled. Billy was the best friend he had ever had. He was surprised he could love another man like this, like a brother.

"What is it with these women? Can't live with them. Can't live without them." Josh tried to lift both of their spirits, but Billy didn't respond. Instead he looked into his glass of beer and seemed deep in thought. "Hey partner, another toast. Lift up your glass with me. To the best damn athlete this county has ever seen…to Billy West!" Josh toasted at the top of his lungs, and the crowded restaurant went silent for a moment. Folks turned to look at Josh and then continued with what they were doing.

"Well, that didn't work out too well," Josh said, a little embarrassed for the scene he had made. "Aw, screw them. They're just jealous. They know who you are, and they know I'm right." Josh looked around the room. "They're all caught up in their own day to day lives. Ain't got no respect for the past. Just stumbling along, making it up as they go, and one day they'll wake up and wonder how their own lives got so bad."

Josh was livened up with the tequila coursing through his veins, but Billy sat quietly. "Hey partner, cheer up. This is our last night together before you go back to Benning for a while. Let's give these folks something to talk about. Let's tear this town up."

Billy still didn't say anything. He was deep in his thoughts as if he was searching for words but couldn't find them. A deep sadness seemed to wash over Billy. Josh could feel it coming out of him, and he knew why. Damn war. Billy had been in the thick of it and had come out changed. Billy's eyes were downcast and heavy. Josh had recognized that look the first time he saw Billy weeks ago at the fair. Billy had changed. All those things he had done. The scars were there. The spark Josh remembered was replaced with a dull emptiness.

Josh tried to cheer him up. "When I go back to school next month, I'm going to talk to coach about you coming onto the team next spring. We always need more pitching, and God knows how you'll crush the ball at the plate. I wouldn't be surprised if you were offered a scholarship after the spring semester."

Finally Billy broke his own silence. "Josh, thanks for letting me open up to you about all those things…"

Maybe it was the tequila or maybe it was just what was truly in his heart. Josh didn't know for sure, but he could see that Billy was emotional and cut him off to make it easy. "It ain't no problem, buddy. You got to let it out. It all seems so toxic. I never knew about all that. What you've done, and the pain, and the scars that you bear. I'm grateful you trusted me."

"You know, Josh, that's my problem. I think about Lannie, Sal, Bobby, Manny, the squad…they're always with me. I know it's wrong, but they're a part of me, and I can't stop comparing them to the people I meet every day. Nobody measures up to them." Billy's eyes shot up to Josh and then back to his glass. "It ain't fair to folks for me to make the comparisons. That's probably why I don't have many friends. I have trouble liking other people. It scares me because I might like them too much. It don't matter because most don't rate up with the boys. Damn loyalty has its costs."

Billy stopped and looked around the crowded room. He

hated crowds. All these people, fleshy and thick, were crowding in on him, in his space. He couldn't trust them. The noise, the movement. He had to have his back to the wall in crowded places. He couldn't let anyone get behind him, out of his view, even in a restaurant. It made him want to crawl out of his skin.

Billy put his beer on the table and gazed into the glass. "The boys…to talk about them at all…to give words to their names and their actions. No words can truly give them the honor they deserve. And then to talk about them to anyone who doesn't measure, well, it's not right at all. Most people haven't earned the right to hear about them. It dishonors them and cheapens what they've done. What they did for their country, for all of us. It hurts to even mention their names to someone who they wouldn't respect—someone they wouldn't approve of. There aren't too many men in this world like them. It's a tough mark to reach. That's why, other than Anna and you, I don't have any close friends. There's nobody to really talk to. There's nobody else that measures up."

Josh was moved by Billy's words. He hadn't expected it, but he felt exactly the same way about Billy and was relieved to hear him say it. Billy's words choked him up, and he was surprised by his own emotion. Josh had never had a friend closer than Billy and would probably never have another. At that very moment, he knew it. Tears welled in his eyes. He looked down at his lap and nodded, acknowledging what Billy was saying.

"Josh, there's something I need to ask you. I tried earlier, but I couldn't find the words or the courage. I'm running out of time and need to ask you now." Billy's eyes remained focused on the beer on the table.

Josh tried to look up at Billy, but it was too hard. His vision was blurry with tears. He leaned forward with his arms on the table and kept his head turned downward, his eyes focused on his hands.

Billy's tone was steady and distant. "If something were to happen…if something happens to me…" There was a long pause as Billy struggled to get the words to come out. "If something happens to me, I need you…I need you to look out for Anna…I need you to look out for Anna for me…can you do that? Will you do that for me?"

Billy tilted his head down lower. He couldn't look up either. It was too hard. The words were hard enough and weighed him down. "Loyalty is a painful part of love that has its costs. I need you to look out for Anna for me. I need your word that you'll do this for me."

Josh lifted his eyes from the table. He quickly glanced at Billy and then diverted his gaze out across the restaurant. "Billy, nothing's going to happen to…"

Billy grabbed Josh's hand and looked up directly into his eyes. "Just shut up and listen to me. Damn it, listen to me."

Billy squeezed Josh's hand to the point it hurt him. "Anna's the only woman I've ever loved and will ever love. I've always loved her. That's why this is so important to me. I'm not asking you to love her like I do. I just want somebody, somebody I trust, to look after her. I love her too much to let her go. I ain't asking a lot, just for you to look after her. As my friend, can you do that for me? Will you do that for me?" Billy asked, not releasing his firm grip.

Looking into Billy's eyes, the words wouldn't come to Josh, but he nodded that he would.

Billy's eyes were intense. Josh felt them, penetrating into his heart. "She's a young and beautiful, kind-hearted woman. She deserves all the best…all the best this world has to offer. Josh, I mean it. All the best it has to offer, joy and peace…and love. If something were to…"

Billy took a sip of his beer and cleared his throat. The emotions swelled inside of him and made it hard for the words to come out. "If…If I…if I wasn't around…I…I want…I want her to find love…I want her to find love again. I don't want her going through this life alone. I don't want her to live with regrets or with pain. I want her to move on. Anna's strong, but I don't think she's strong enough. She'll need someone to help her through it all. It could destroy her, and she'll need help…will you do this for me? Other than my pa, you're the only man in this world I truly respect and trust. Will you look after her for me?"

"Billy, stop talking like this…" Josh tried to turn him away from this talk, but Billy wouldn't let him.

"Damn it Josh, I ain't got time! I ain't got time to argue about this. I got this feeling. Something inside gnawing at me. I don't know what it is, but there's trouble brewing. I need you, Josh…promise me you'll do this…promise me…" Billy's voice tapered off as his eyes dropped down to the beer on the table.

Josh was choked up, and he could not lift his head up to look at Billy. Tears ran down his cheeks. No words would come out. He thought about Billy's comment, 'loyalty has its costs', and he wondered what the future would bring. But Josh would do it. He loved Billy. Their relationship had always been more than just about sports and girls. It was deeper. He knew love could leave its scars, but Billy was more of a brother to him than he would ever know. Josh nodded. He would keep his promise.

VII

"SOMEBODY'S COMING." DICKY pointed at a pair of headlights, piercing the night at the end of the street. "They're coming this way!" Dicky watched as the lights got bigger, and the vehicle slowly moved down the street toward where they had been waiting. "I think it's him. I think it's him!" Dicky repeated as he bounced in the seat, unable to control his emotions.

"Looks like he's pulling into the driveway." Joe looked down at his watch. "It's about time."

Dicky and Joe watched as Billy's truck pulled into the driveway in front of his pa's house. It was past midnight. Joe shook his head. They had been waiting in the darkness for over three hours, and he had wondered if West would ever show up.

"There's somebody with him," Dicky said.

In the darkness, they could see two figures getting out of the truck. Both Dicky and Joe listened closely for their voices. They heard the metallic sound of the car doors slamming shut.

The first voice was loud and slurred. "Josh is my brother. I love that guy. I just, I just…I love him like a brother."

"That sounds like West. I think he's…I think he's drunk." Dicky grinned.

Both Joe and Dicky looked at each other and nodded, then leaned forward and listened for the other voice. Silence. The thickness of the night filled their ears with a black heavy noise. It was suddenly broken by the crashing of something hollow and metallic.

Dicky's wide eyes shot over to Joe. "One of them must have stumbled over the trash can."

And then they heard the second voice. "Come on sweetheart. Let's get you up. Let's get you inside and to bed."

"That's a woman's voice. Must be Anna Jacobs." Dicky concluded.

Dicky and Joe watched as the two figures moved in the darkness. They heard the front door open and slam shut. In a few seconds, a light turned on, dimly lighting the front room of the house.

"Give me the gun." Joe's voice was cold and lifeless.

Dicky struggled to retrieve the shotgun. He wasn't in much pain now. The pain had subsided since his release from the hospital earlier in the morning. Partly because of the painkillers he had taken, and partly because of the alcohol. He and Joe had started drinking in the afternoon and had been going steady ever since. He just had a hard time moving with the large cast on his arm.

"Here. I loaded triple ought, and it's ready to go." Dicky handed Joe the twelve gauge shotgun. Joe traded Dicky the bottle of whiskey in exchange for the gun. Dicky noticed Joe was wearing leather gloves and started to feel more confident. He was reminded how Joe thought of everything and always had his bases covered.

Dicky took a long draw from the bottle. The whiskey settled his nerves, and he felt good. In a few minutes, they would be done with this, and Dicky would be free. Free from Joe Matsell. Free from gambling. Free from Ronnie and the rest of the boys.

Dicky's mind drifted. He thought about leaving town, finding good work, or maybe even going to college. His parents would be proud.

Dicky smiled to himself. Just a few more minutes, and they would be done. As they drank throughout the afternoon, he and Joe did a lot of talking about Billy West and about people who thought they could come in and try to take over the town. Joe explained he wanted to scare him a bit, not do any real harm. He wanted to let Billy know that no outsiders were going to push the locals around. West wasn't a local, not anymore. When he had left town for a so-called better life in the army, he had stopped being one of them. No outsider was going to tell them how to run their town. They were going to scare him a little—just a little, and that would be enough.

Joe turned and pointed the shotgun out the driver's side window. He had the barrel aimed center on the large picture window on the front of the house. Other than a dim light on the other side of the curtains, the house was dark. Joe would wait for another light to come on, and then he would take his shot.

"What are they doing? Can you see anything? What's going on?" Dicky raised his voice. He was getting impatient.

"Shut the hell up," Joe whispered.

Silence filled the car. A few minutes passed. Dicky took another long drink from the bottle. Joe began to wonder if his plan would work and started to think through other options. Suddenly a light went on in the front room of the house. Joe could see shadows in the window, but with the curtain drawn, he couldn't differentiate who it was. Then very clearly, he saw the silhouettes of two people embracing.

"Billy West, time for you to pay," Joe said under his breath as he squeezed the trigger.

The explosion from the gun was deafening. Dicky jumped and dropped the liquor onto his lap, dousing himself with half the bottle of whiskey. The smell of gunpowder and alcohol filled the car.

Joe smiled. He felt confident he got them. The front window of the house disintegrated from the blast of the shotgun. He thought he saw them drop as the spray of pellets peppered the window. The light was still on, but he couldn't see any movement. Nothing.

A dog barked down the street. After a couple of minutes, Joe saw the porch light come on at a house up the street. He knew the police would be arriving in a matter of time.

"Time for you to finish what you started." Joe pushed the shotgun into Dicky's lap.

"What? What I started?" Dicky was surprised. He hadn't expected this.

"What you started. If you and Ronnie hadn't screwed everything up at Prarieburg, we wouldn't be here tonight." Joe put his finger on Dicky's chest and pushed so hard the pain radiated inside his cast and throughout his body.

"But I thought…I thought we was just going to scare him a little and…" Dicky winced in pain as he tried to pull away from Joe.

"We ain't got time to talk. Now take the gun and get in there and finish this thing." Joe grabbed the shotgun on Dicky's lap and forcefully pushed it into him, slamming Dicky against the passenger door.

The pain in Dicky's arm and collarbone shot through him, leaving him stunned. He didn't know what to do. He took another drink of whiskey and tried to somehow ignore what was happening. Dicky felt a thick, heavy stillness in the night. The dog barking in the distance was drowned out by the pounding of his heart drumming in his chest, faster and faster. Fear. He tried to take one last swig from the bottle to suppress the fear.

"I can barely move with this cast. How do you expect me to carry a gun?" Dicky asked, trying to find an exit to the situation.

"You need to git in there and finish this thing. Besides, you can't drive. If somebody comes, we got to be ready to leave. I'll be right here with the car ready to go."

"But I thought we was just going to scare…" Dicky reverted to his initial argument and again tried to reason with Joe.

"The time for talk is over. Now git in there and do it! Do it now!" Joe growled.

"But I, I… I can't. I can't kill." Dicky trembled. The words came out of his mouth and felt foreign to him.

"Damn it, Dicky. We ain't got any time! Now git in there and finish this thing!" Joe pulled out a revolver from below his car seat and pointed it in Dicky's face.

Dicky was in disbelief. He couldn't believe what was happening. All he could see was the barrel of a pistol staring down on him. *Was this really happening?* Dicky wondered as he became paralyzed with fear.

"Git out and do it, Dicky! Or as God is my witness, I will put a bullet between your eyes and take care of it all myself. Now do it!" Joe's voice was emotionless and cold.

Dicky was out of options. He struggled to exit the car. He stood up and looked at West's house across the street and felt his body walking toward it. He held the gun in his right hand and rested the barrel on his cast. It was heavy, but he could balance it without too much pain.

He didn't want to do this. Everything in him said to turn around or to run. But Joe would be there, waiting for him with that gun. Dicky wondered how he ever got himself into this mess. He wondered what his pa would say. He felt sorry for himself and started to cry. Tears were streaming down his cheeks as he walked toward the house. He tried to think. How had it all come to this? Everything seemed so foreign to him—even his own body. He didn't feel like himself. It was all so strange.

"Got to get control. Get control of yourself," Dicky said to himself as he walked up the driveway to the house. "Get control. You can do this. Probably won't have to do nothing. What is done is done. Joe already took care of it all." *Positive thoughts, stay positive.* He tried to convince himself nothing was left to be done. He reached up and grasped the door knob to open the door. Before he turned the knob, he put his ear to the door. He thought he heard movement inside.

ꕥ

"Come on, baby. Come on over and help me get my shorts

off." Billy teetered side to side with a crooked smile.

"You're incorrigible. Just incorrigible. We're going to get you to bed. I think you and Josh had a little too much fun tonight." Anna put her arm around his waist to help him steady himself.

"Too much fun? The fun's just getting started, baby. Let's go on back into the bedroom, and I'll show you some fun." Billy pointed to the bedroom door and leaned down to kiss Anna's neck.

"Oh darling, whatever am I going to do with you?" Anna said in a motherly tone as she guided him across the living room.

"Well I can think of a couple of…" Billy's response was drowned out by the explosion of glass across the living room.

Billy instantaneously reacted and tackled Anna to the floor.

"What the hell!" Billy shouted as the adrenalin pulsed into his veins. He instantly sobered-up. He found himself on top off Anna on the floor and covered with glass. "Anna! Anna Angel! My Anna…are you, are you okay? Anna baby, talk to me." Her eyes were closed, and she didn't seem to be conscious. "Anna! Anna! Open your eyes! Can you hear me? Open your eyes!" Billy shook her and suddenly her eyes opened. "Anna Angel…my Anna…are you…are you okay?"

"I…I…what happened?" she questioned with a confused look in her eyes.

"Feel around your body. Feel for wet spots and check your hands to see if they're red." Billy quickly checked himself. If either of them were injured, the pain would come later. Right now, they were running on adrenaline. The best way to determine if they were hurt was to use multiple senses—to look and to feel.

"I think…I think…I'm all right." Anna said, sitting up.

Billy looked around the room and quickly realized what had happened. "Matsell!" Billy said under his breath. This was Matsell, raising the stakes and getting even.

"What happened? Billy? Who would do this?" Anna started to cry.

Billy held his finger up to his lips. "Shh. They may still be out there."

A look of terror filled Anna's eyes as she looked around the room. She slowly became conscious of what had happened. Fear shot through her body—she knew they might be coming for them.

"Come on. Follow me." Billy crawled toward his pa's back bedroom.

ಬಲ

Dicky turned the door knob and entered the house. He was in the kitchen. It reminded him of his own home except the colors were different, and it was a little smaller. But it was definitely the same style. "Focus, Dicky Moss. Got to focus," Dicky whispered as he tried to think about what he was doing.

He entered into the living room. Glass was everywhere. He was simultaneously hopeful and fearful of what he might find. If Billy and Anna were on the floor, it would probably be horrific. He tried to prepare his mind for what he would see. He had never seen a dead body before and could only imagine what gunshot wounds would look like. It would be ugly, but at least he could leave and not have to kill somebody.

He scanned the room. Nothing. "Where the hell were they?" Dicky asked himself, and a new wave of fear jolted through his body. They were there, somewhere in the house, hiding, or worse, waiting for him. Now he would have to find them.

Dicky tried to listen. He could hear the dog barking down the street. The house was quiet. As he walked across the living room, the pieces of glass under his feet cracked and popped. He switched off the safety, pointed the shotgun out to his front, and walked toward the bedroom at the back of the house.

ꕤ

"Somebody's in the house!" Anna whispered as she heard the kitchen door open.

"Shh." Billy motioned for silence with his finger to his lips. He had Anna crouched down, hidden behind the bed.

Anna watched with stunned amazement. Billy moved deliberately, yet incredibly efficiently as he pulled out his pa's shotgun from the closet and loaded it with shells. He had a cold, sad look on his face—not fear, just a matter of fact expression that was almost void of any emotion. He was in a mode she had never seen in him. He motioned for her to get as low to the ground as possible.

Anna heard the footsteps in the living room and the glass crack on the floor. It sounded like whoever it was, was coming toward the back bedroom. She lay down on the floor. From under the bed she peered through the crack at the bottom of the door. Even though the door was closed, she could see the shadow of someone in the light at the base of the door. There was somebody there. Coming to get them. She trembled with fear and suddenly felt a warm, wet liquid on her leg. She smelled her urine but didn't care. She had never been so afraid. She couldn't control herself. She wanted to scream but couldn't get anything out. Her throat felt tight. She didn't know if she could even breathe.

She looked up at Billy. The light from under the door shone up on his face—he looked so calm, like this was normal. Not even a hint of fear in his eyes. It confused her. How could he be calm in all of this? He had the gun resting in his hands in front of him on the bed. She felt a strange sense of pride and fear. She never really knew the man she loved. For a brief moment, she marveled at him, and it scared her as he crouched down and was in a position ready for whatever came through that door.

Suddenly they both heard the doorknob start to turn.

Billy broke the silence and stated in a loud and direct voice, "I'm giving you one warning. If you come in through that door, I have a shotgun, and I will use it."

The figure on the other side of the door paused. Everything seemed to stop and hang suspended in the room. The door slowly opened and light exploded into the bedroom. Anna saw the barrel of the intruder's shotgun silhouetted in the light. Her chest tightened up, and she couldn't breathe. Billy immediately recognized the threat. Calmly and without hesitation, he squeezed the trigger. This action was seconded by the incredible explosion of his shotgun. Anna's body jerked in fear. She had never heard anything so loud. She smelled the gun and saw smoke from it hanging in the light.

Anna looked up at Billy. He remained in the same position he had been in just moments before, crouched down with the gun pointed toward the door, ready to fire. Billy had no expression on his face, just a cold, calm look in his eyes. He looked down at her behind the bed and motioned for her not to move. She heard movement in the living room and tried to understand what had just happened.

ℬℭ

Barton got the call just past midnight. He was still in the office, sorting through the statements from witnesses of the assault in Prairieburg. Sally Mayfield, Dicky Moss, Ronnie Wilson, Anna Jacobs, Billy West. None of it added up. He knew something was going on, but he couldn't prove it. Joe Matsell might be involved in this, but right now with what he had, Billy West was his primary suspect.

When he stopped at Judy Chambers' home to investigate her call, he realized more pieces were quickly adding to the puzzle. She explained she had heard one gunshot, and then right before he had arrived, she had heard a second one. Both shots came from down the street around Butch West's house. She said that after the second gunshot, she had heard a car start up and drive off at what sounded like a high rate of speed. She was surprised the sheriff hadn't seen the car. It had left moments before he arrived.

Sheriff Barton looked down the street. He reached for his flashlight, patting his pocket. He had left his flashlight on his desk back at the station. He was angry at himself, but he had no time for anger. He regained control and reasoned he wouldn't need it. Sheriff Barton saw the truck in front of the West residence and hurried off in that direction.

ꙮ

Dicky adjusted the gun in his hands. He looked down at the door knob. He was going to have a difficult time opening it. He balanced the gun on his cast, kept his good hand on the trigger, and used his crippled hand to turn the knob. At that moment, he heard Billy's voice, telling him he also had a gun.

Dicky panicked. He trembled with fear and didn't know what to do. He fumbled with the knob and had been ready to open the door when Billy called out from the room. The problem was he couldn't turn the knob back with his bad hand. He meant to turn and leave, but he was caught half way in the motion to open the door and couldn't stop. All he could do was finish turning the knob and try to swivel away from the door. However with both the shotgun and his cast, this would be a difficult maneuver.

He never heard the blast from the shotgun. One minute, he was standing behind the door, and the next minute, he was spun around and on his knees. He was dizzy and confused. His ears rang with a sharp white buzz, and he struggled to get to his feet. His shotgun was no longer in his hands, but he didn't care. The living room revolved around him. He choked as he tried to breathe. Dicky stumbled to the kitchen, slipped on the floor, and then pulled himself up with his good arm.

Dicky saw his reflection in a mirror behind the sink and didn't recognize who or what he saw. Blood splattered down his chest and on his shoulders. He had never seen so much blood. It revolted him, and he gagged as though he was going to vomit. He then looked up into what was left of his face. Initially, it was funny like something he would see in a cartoon, and he wanted to laugh. But that feeling quickly turned to fear as he realized that what he was looking at was someone real.

Staring back at Dicky was a heinous mess of shredded flesh that used to be someone's face. It reminded him of the meat that got processed at the butcher shop down at H&J's. This thought was replaced with a sheer, raw panic. He was looking at himself. His face. His ruined face. He couldn't believe the grotesque monster that he had become. His jaw and entire mouth were ripped away in a mangled lump of bloody matter, dangling down on his shoulder. One of his eyes was missing, and his nose was somewhere in the churned flesh that once was his face.

Dicky thought he heard a car start up and drive away. Matsell. Matsell had left him behind. Matsell. All of this for Matsell. He had been fooled. This whole time, everything, it was all Matsell. And now he was gone.

Dicky had to get out. He had to get help. It was late at night. Was it past midnight? He couldn't remember. He staggered out the kitchen door into the darkness. Falling to his knees in the grass, Dicky fumbled with the cast holding his arm out from his body.

Goddamn cast. This damn, no good cast, Dicky cursed to himself as he attempted to get to his feet.

He couldn't believe what had happened. He wanted to cry—cry out to the world at what he had become. He never had any luck, never caught a break in his life. In these few weeks, it had all added up to the ruined man he had become.

Dicky stammered out behind the house. Again, he wanted to cry but couldn't. His mangled body had betrayed him of any emotion. It was over. His life. All of it. What would his parents say? What would they think? He was such a disappointment to them. A failure. Nothing ever came easy for him. Nothing. He couldn't think about his pa. He imagined his pa's eyes and their disappointment for him. He couldn't…

"Halt! Halt! Stop right there, and drop your gun!"

Dicky heard someone shout at him in the dark shadows behind the house. He turned and tried to tell the stranger who he was and that he needed help, but nothing came out. His mouth was not working anymore. He couldn't talk. He couldn't communicate. He was light-headed and dizzy, too much blood was gone out of him.

Dicky looked up at the sky, and the stars spun into a blur above him. He was slipping away and everything moved in circles. He had to get help, but he knew it was probably too late as he wobbled forward toward the voice.

"I said drop it! Drop the gun now! Drop it!" the voice called out again.

He thinks I have a gun. Panic raced through Dicky's mind, it wasn't a gun. It was his cast. It was his damn cast. He didn't have a gun anymore.

Everything spiraled for Dicky as he muddled toward the man in the shadows. The figure was so dark, too dark to see. He was having a harder and harder time moving. Quicksand. So thick and dark and deep. He needed help. Couldn't this man see that he needed help?

ꕥ

"I said stop and drop the gun. Drop it, or I'll shoot! Don't come any closer, or I'll have to shoot!" Sheriff Barton ordered Dicky not to come any closer. "This is the Sheriff. Stop and drop the gun!" Barton's voice wavered with fear.

Barton stood with his revolver out in front of him in his trembling hand. He tried to keep it pointed at the dark figure coming at him. Sheriff Barton had never fired his gun at anyone and was not sure if he could do it now. His hands shook, and he gripped the Smith and Wesson revolver with all the strength he had. He didn't want to shoot this man, and he pleaded with himself in his own mind. *Am I really going to have to shoot someone? Please don't shoot. Don't shoot this man. You can't kill a human being. Why won't he listen to me? Why won't he drop his gun? Too close now. It's me or him. Me or him.*

"Stop! I said stop, or I'll shoot!" Sheriff Barton shouted with terror in his voice. "Please stop. Please, please stop."

Those were the last words Dicky Moss would ever hear.

VIII

"AND HE SHOT Dicky Moss?" John asked Dave as he threw another log on the campfire.

"That's what I heard. Emptied his revolver, all six rounds. Three in the chest and three in the head," Dave answered.

"Six rounds." John paused as he thought about it. "There can't be much left of him."

Both knew what a man could do with a gun when he was afraid. Six rounds would only take a few seconds, and he probably wouldn't even know he had fired them. Both men also knew what six rounds would do to the target.

Dave, John, and Andy sat silently, staring into the hot glowing coals of the campfire. The night was alive around them. The crickets' rhythmic chirping, the crack and pop of the fire, a light breeze in the trees above, and the river softly flowing by just a few feet from their camp site—the night air caressed them as they remained silent in their thoughts.

Andy leaned back and looked up at the ocean of stars that became deeper and deeper as he gazed into them. He thought about the events of the past couple weeks, about Billy West and what some people thought about him. Andy wondered about leading others and how difficult it must be. He recalled his friend Jimmy Ray and all the things he had said about Billy when he first got home on leave. Jimmy was wrong. So wrong. Andy had heard his father say Billy was a good man, committed to what he believed. Andy thought about how Billy West faced adversity. He didn't let it define him but stood firm on principle and integrity. Andy pondered giving up major league baseball to enlist in the army even though it still didn’t make sense to him. He wondered if someday it would.

Uncle Dave nudged Andy with a wink. "You look like you're a million miles away."

"Nah," answered Andy, feeling a surge of pride that his uncle was curious about what he might be thinking. "Just thinking of Billy West."

"Ah, I see." Dave stirred the coals in the fire with a stick.

Andy leaned forward next to his uncle and looked into the fire. "Yeah, Jimmy Ray was all wrong about Billy West. I'm not sure I can trust what he says." The fire cracked and popped as sparks floated over their heads. Andy was mesmerized. "When I grow up, I want to be like Billy West."

"Oh, is that right?" Dave smirked with a nod.

"Yup. I want to marry a pretty girl like Anna Jacobs and change the world." Andy smiled as he leaned back dreamily and peered up at the stars above.

Andy’s mind drifted. He thought about spending time with his uncle and his dad, and how much he treasured this. He thought about the wonders of camping. He loved camping, everything about it—the fire, the food, fishing, the sounds of the night, the talks with his dad and his uncle, and even the long pauses and silence.

They tried to get out at least once every summer, and they

usually came to the same spot—a private area at the base of the large stone cliffs overlooking the Wapsi, just on the other side of the river from the park. It had become an event that Andy looked forward to. It made him feel alive. He learned more about honor and manhood sitting by a campfire with his father and uncle than he ever would in a classroom.

"Well, it's all a crying shame. I feel horrible for Jim Moss and his family, just terrible. I can't imagine what they must be going through right now. I just can't imagine it." Dave shook his head.

"I feel bad for Barton, too. To have all this on his conscience. It's got to be tearing him up," John said.

"Yeah, I'm sure it is." Dave gazed into the campfire. He tapped his stick on a log in the fire and looked up. "I ran into Josh Sanders down at H&Js earlier this afternoon. He had been waiting around all morning to meet with the Sheriff about the scuffle out at Prairieburg. He said he told Barton everything and that the sheriff didn't seem to care. Said the sheriff looked like living hell. White as a ghost and gaunt, like he lost thirty pounds and aged twenty years overnight."

John lit a cigarette. "Killing a man…it changes you." John inhaled deeply and blew out the smoke. "Changes you forever."

"Josh said the sheriff's office was crawling with folks from the state police this morning. None of this is going to be good for Barton." Dave pulled out his cigarettes.

"Yeah. But in the end, nothing will come from it." John took another puff.

"Well, at least they can't pin it on Billy this time. No

question it was self-defense. And anyway, if they were going to press charges, they'd have to charge Barton, too. And we all know that isn't going to happen." Dave lit a match and held it up to the cigarette in his mouth as he inhaled to get it started.

John said, "Not with his uncle's involvement. We all know Earl Barton is a close personal friend of the governor. I'm sure he's already spinning this. Josh mentioned he saw him at the sheriff's office, too."

Changing the direction of the conversation, Dave asked, "How are Billy and Anna doing?"

"I think as well as can be expected. Josh told me they had been at the sheriff's office all night. He said Billy's holding strong—just tired. Been a hell of summer for him. I'm sure he'll be ready to go back to Benning this week."

"Getting out of this town, away from all this riffraff, will probably be a break for him," Dave agreed.

"Josh said that Anna's still pretty shook up. Can't imagine what she must've gone through. Heard that Dicky shot out the front window and then came in to kill them both. Hard to imagine he would do that. Never knew he had it in him. All of this is hard to imagine. Just don't seem real, that it could happen here in Anamosa." John took a long drag of his cigarette, and then he asked, "What was Dicky doing out there after midnight anyway?"

"Damn good question. And even better, who was with him?" Rubbing his chin, Dave added, "Word at the diner this morning was that someone else was there with him and drove off moments before Barton arrived."

"Just a damn shame. Jim Moss is a good man and to see his family go through all of this…just a shame…a damn shame," John replied as he stared into the fiery coals.

"What is our world coming to?" Dave asked, not expecting an answer. "The youth today, they're different than we were growing up. I see on the news that crime is going up. Almost ten times higher than it was in the 1950s. There just don't seem to be any respect for authority, for what this country is about."

John finished his cigarette and flicked it into the fire. "There definitely don't seem to be any respect for our veterans and what we're asking them to do over in Vietnam. The cruelty of war that most people, to include our politicians, have no clue about. The ugly unmentioned things soldiers do in the defense of our nation…and the freedoms most Americans take for granted and most other countries only dream about. I see huge riots out in California, soldiers getting spit on in the airports when they return home. It's disgraceful."

"They know not what they do. They have no idea what that means to somebody who has fought for this country. This will leave scars for all of us. I wonder what the consequences of our nation's actions will be." Dave's eyes lowered to a steady trance focused on the fire.

John lit another cigarette. "I look at these spoiled college kids out in California rioting against our country for what's happening in Vietnam. Picketing for freedom and peace in this world. And then, I look at the nineteen year old kid, wading through a rice paddy with a little girl in his arms, taking her to safety. That nineteen year old in Vietnam ain't never stepped onto a campus, but he's done more in one day to advance the cause for freedom than those college students will do in their lifetime."

"But that's California..." Dave tried to reply but was cut off by his brother.

"I know it's the West, and you see the same thing on campuses in the East. These are the extremes of America. We'll know we're in serious trouble if we see this same rebellion on the campuses here in Iowa. I fear the consequences of our actions. I fear for our future. What's this nation becoming?" John stopped for a moment and let the question hang over the campfire.

Dave didn't answer. He seemed to be hypnotized as he looked into fiery embers. Andy listened to the night breathe around them, the crackling of the fire and a barred owl calling out from across the river.

John broke the silence. "We're at a fork in the road. Or maybe we're already beyond it. It feels like things are starting to slip away from what made us so strong over the years. I look at the laws being passed, the language on television, the words in our press. There seems to be a complete disdain for any type of authority. It already feels like we're starting to decline from what we were after the last world war." John took a long draw of his cigarette. "Maybe I'm paranoid, but it feels like things are shaking at the foundation, and we're becoming something significantly less than what we were ten years ago. I wonder what we're becoming. What we'll be in ten, twenty, or fifty years from now?"

Dave reached for another log and threw it on the fire. He glanced up at his brother with a serious expression. "It all depends on the character of our leaders, of the men and women our nation produces. The strength of our families, our schools, our neighborhoods, and the values they produce…they will directly affect the character of our future leaders and the future of our country."

John picked up a stick and poked at the fire. "Well it scares the hell out of me. It feels like the lines between what's right and wrong are becoming relative and blurred. Where do our leaders find their truth? Their compass for a clear vision of what's right and the courage to act on what they believe?"

The questions floated above them over the light from the fire. There were no good answers. There was a negative tension that lingered as the men gazed deeply into the campfire. The sounds of the night wrapped around them like a blanket. Andy thought about their words and didn't understand. He wondered what it would all be like when he grew older. He wondered what the world would be for him twenty years from now. Twenty years was such a long time—it seemed so foreign to him. He could not imagine that far in the future and being an adult.

Dave realized the downward direction the conversation had taken and attempted to lighten the mood. "You know, this area along the river used to be Shaw's land. He used to own everything from his mansion to these cliffs along the north side of the river." There was a glint of mischief in his eyes.

Neither John nor Andy replied and Dave asked, "You've heard of Colonel Shaw, haven't you, Andy?"

"The colonel that was in the Civil War?" Andy answered his uncle with a question, hoping he would tell another one of his great stories.

"Right, the Civil War colonel. Are you familiar with what he done?"

"Well, I know he fought for the Union. I think at Shiloh, but I really don't know what else he did," Andy admitted with a slight shrug of the shoulders.

"He fought at Shiloh, all right. That's where he was captured. But I'll bet you never heard the whole story. The real story about what happened. The story you won't find in no history books." Dave smiled with a lively look on his face.

"No, I just know that…" Andy yawned and tried to finish his sentence, but his uncle leaned close to him and spoke.

"He was wounded at Shiloh. In his final charge into what they call the Hornet's Nest. It was there that his hand was cut off by a confederate officer wielding a sword. Moments later, he and one of his aides were captured." Dave started into his story with a low steady tone in his voice.

The light from the fire glowed on Dave's face. "Well, on the hand he lost was the wedding ring his dear Helen had given him just before he left for the war. He gave her a locket with his picture to wear around her neck, and she gave him the ring. This was a part of their promise that no matter what happened, he would return to her.

"Colonel Shaw was madly in love with Helen. He had said no matter what happened in the war, he would always be true to her. He believed losing that ring was a terrible omen for things to come.

"Shaw was a peculiar and superstitious man. They say that

sometimes losing a limb will change a person. Well, it may have affected Shaw. That night after the battle, he pleaded with his captors to allow him to return to the Hornet's Nest to find his ring. They did not want to lose such a high ranking prisoner, but out of honor, they allowed his aide to go out and search for the ring. His aide crawled back onto the battlefield that same night to find the hand."

Dave looked around the fire to see if Andy and John were listening. Content that they were, he continued in a serious whisper. "Well, he found the hand, but it was so swollen that he couldn't get the ring off of it, so he brought the hand back to Shaw in an ammo pouch."

Andy pinched his face with a look of disgust. "Aw, that's creepy!"

"As the war continued, Shaw was sent off to prison, and he took that pouch with him. One night while sleeping on his cot, he was awakened by someone tapping him on his shoulder. He reached up, only to feel a cold hand moving along his neck. He thought for a moment he was dreaming, and then he was astonished that it was really his own dead, cold hand, alive and moving!" Dave's eyes widened as he shouted this line. The fire flickered in the night, and Andy felt a twinge of fear as he looked at his uncle—an eerie glow illuminated his uncle's face.

"The hand was alive?" Andy asked nervously.

"Dave, I'm going to grab a beer. Do you want one?" John broke into the story as he got up from their circle around the fire.

Dave nodded, and then he continued his story in the same whispering tone, "It was alive. But not always. For some reason, it only came to life at certain moments. This ability seemed to be tied closely to Shaw's own heart. At different times, he could will it to do things for him, but at other times, it seemed rebellious and wouldn't move at all. Despite this, it became Shaw's secret companion. In fact, it helped him escape from prison."

Andy's eyes widened, and his mouth fell open. He sat still, clinging to every word his uncle spoke.

"One dark night, the hand crawled out of the cell and strangled the jailer. It returned to Shaw with the keys to the cell. Shaw escaped, and after weeks of movement behind enemy lines, he rejoined the Union and continued to fight in a number of major battles." Uncle Dave's eyes danced with excitement.

"Most of his peers thought he was a bit peculiar. Wherever he went, he always carried that old ammo pouch with him. But it wasn't until after the war that things got really strange."

"What did he do with the hand?" Andy asked, becoming more anxious with the story.

"Well, he returned to Anamosa and settled with his wife and two kids up in the mansion just a ways north of here. But that was when things turned for the worse for him. The hand that had been so useful during the war now had no role in Shaw's life. Yes, it still had his wedding ring, but he had his Helen and that was all that mattered to Shaw.

"One night, Shaw woke up and saw the cold hand next to him in bed, lightly caressing his wife's neck. It chilled him to his core and filled him with terror. It was as if the hand was jealous and was warning him that it would kill her if it had to. It would kill her to regain his complete loyalty."

Andy's eyes were wide with a new wave of fear, and Dave slowly stirred the coals in the fire. "Shaw was distraught with paranoia. He thought about destroying it, but he couldn't gather the courage to do it. His hand had become his companion, during the war, and saved him from the horrific Confederate prison camps. It was a part of who he was, and he couldn't let go of it. Eventually, he locked the hand up in his ammo pouch, inside a trunk, deep in the basement of the mansion.

"Everything seemed fine for a while, and Shaw's worry subsided. That was until one night in late summer. One terrible night. In fact, I think it was about this time of the year when it all happened.

"One evening, that same aide, who had saved the hand for him years before back at Shiloh, was passing through Anamosa. He stopped to spend the evening with his old colonel. That very night, Shaw woke up from his sleep to the sound of a gunshot. He ran out of his bedroom and into the guest room where his friend was sleeping. His friend was in bed, dead from a gunshot wound. Shaw turned and ran back to his bedroom for his wife, and she was still lying in bed. He reached down to wake her, and when he touched her, she was cold. She was dead, too. Her neck was deeply bruised by a strong hand—she had been strangled to death.

"Terror filled Shaw's body, and he ran down to the basement with a large knife ready to destroy the hand. When he got there, he expected to find the trunk open, but he was surprised to find it was still locked. When he opened it, deep in the bottom he found the hand still in the pouch. He felt a strange sense of relief that it wasn't the hand that had killed his wife and his friend. But then he noticed, resting in the palm of the hand, the locket he had given to his wife before the war. The same locket she had on when they went to bed that evening.

"Shaw was full of rage, and he took the hand and rode his horse out here to the river, to these cliffs. From up there, he tossed the hand off the cliff and into the river." Dave stopped and pointed up at the cliffs above the camp site.

"What happened to the hand?" Andy's face was animated with a mixed combination of anxiety and exhilaration.

"No one really knows. We don't think Shaw ever saw it again. One thing we know for sure, he was never charged with the murder of his wife. His old aide—the one who recovered the hand at Shiloh and who was shot in cold blood—took the fall for everything. They made it look like the aide killed the wife, and Shaw, in his rage, shot him.

"Although he went on to build much of this town and was by all rights a founding father of this community, most folks never really knew him. They say Colonel Shaw always had a strange air about him. Only a few people could say they were his friend, and that was mostly his family. Some say he spent the rest of his life, dealing with his guilt from the war, the death of his wife, and the loss of his hand. All around, it was a sad affair."

Dave knew he had Andy's attention and broke into a whisper, "Funny thing, though." Dave leaned closer and looked around. "Over the years, folks have drowned in the waters off these cliffs. The strange thing…the thing that's really odd, is that all of them, every single one, had the same bruise mark of a handprint on their throat."

At that moment, Andy felt a hand on the backside of his neck, sliding around to the front. He jumped up and screamed wildly. In the moonlight behind him was his dad with a mischievous grin. Both Dave and John burst out in laughter, and Andy didn't know if he wanted to laugh or to cry. The whole event scared the hell out of him.

"That wasn't funny! That wasn't funny at all! You're both terrible! Just terrible!" Andy wiped a tear from his cheek and pushed his dad away, angry at him, angry at both of them for playing him with this story.

Realizing he had scared his son and hurt his feelings, John tried to rescue his son's pride. "You know, Andy, I think your Uncle Dave told me a similar story when I was about your age. As a matter of fact, I think I was a year or two older. I couldn't sleep in my own bed for weeks. Our ma and pa got tired of me ending up on the floor in their bedroom every night, and when they found out why…well, I think your uncle still has scars from the lick'n Pa gave him."

"You can say that again. He blistered my hind end with that leather belt he had. Guess I never learned my lesson cause here I am telling you a similar story," Dave replied apologetically.

"Come on, Andy. Let's string up a couple of these poles for some midnight fishing. I got a feeling there are a few catfish out there waiting for us," John said as he picked up a fishing pole.

"Maybe we'll catch some catfish, or who knows, maybe we'll catch Colonel Shaw's hand." Andy laughed nervously.

Dave and John joined the laughter, and all three walked

down to the bank of the river.

IX

SALLY WAS WORRIED about Joe. She had not seen him eat for two days, and he wasn't sleeping at night. She looked across the kitchen table at him. He looked terrible as he sat reading the newspaper. Dicky Moss' death had been all over the news for the past three days, and Sally watched as Joe became more and more engaged with the story. She knew Dicky had been his friend, and he felt personally responsible for what had happened.

According to Joe, he may have been the last person to see Dicky alive. He had told Sally that Dicky had stayed late at the bar that night. In fact, he had stayed until the bar closed and had been the last to leave. Before Dicky left, he had been ranting and raving about Billy West and how he had taken a cheap shot at him with a baseball bat at Prairieburg. Dicky had said he and Ronnie were going to get even and settle the score.

Joe had explained to Sally that he had needed the shotgun the other day because of Dicky. Joe had been afraid Dicky might do something crazy, and Joe needed to protect himself at the bar—especially after being attacked by Billy West. People were changing in Anamosa. They were doing things they shouldn't do. Crime was going up, and he was certain it was only a matter of time before he would have to do the responsible thing and do whatever was necessary to defend her, his patrons, and the bar.

On the night of the shooting, Dicky had scared Joe with all

his talk about getting even. Joe claimed he had tried to talk Dicky into staying the night in the room above the bar. Joe had even gone upstairs and gotten all of Dicky's belongings situated and the bed ready, but when he had come back down, Dicky was gone.

That was when he had noticed the shotgun he had hidden behind the bar was missing. Joe had claimed being scared, and he had even gone out looking for Dicky. He had driven all over town that night trying to find him. He had even gone over to Billy West's house to see if he might be there, but Dicky had been nowhere to be found.

As a last resort, Joe had gone to Sheriff Barton's office to report the missing gun and his concern about Dicky. When he had arrived at the sheriff's office, it was all locked up and closed. Unfortunately, he had been too late.

Joe's explanations had made sense to Sally, and she wanted to believe him. She did believe him. She had to believe him. She couldn't imagine Joe being involved with this tragedy. It was too hard to imagine. Joe was strong. He was tough and could be hard on others when necessary. But she always saw him as a survivor, a leader—he had qualities she admired. But he was not a murderer. He couldn't be a murderer. Not Joe, not her Joe Matsell.

She had always wanted to believe that he loved her, but over the summer, the relationship had grown cold, and she didn't know anymore. She had wanted to leave him but didn't know how. But Dicky's death had changed things between them. Joe was now vulnerable, and he leaned on her. She had never seen him like this. In a strange way, it attracted her to him. For once, she thought he actually needed her and might even love her.

She had been aware of some of the other women in Joe's life, but she turned a blind eye to the things she didn't want to accept. She believed that if she pretended long enough they didn't exist, then they didn't. As long as she denied those ugly truths and kept them far away, she would never feel betrayed.

She knew some of these women but was certain he did not go to them for real love. When he was hurting, he always came back to her, and that was all that mattered. Even last night after they made love, he was sensitive to her needs and had been gentler than he had ever been. She could not remember him this way. He seemed to have changed. Afterward, she had slept soundly in his arms. Over the past couple days, in the wake of Dicky's death, she had seen a glimmer of hope in all of this darkness. Joe was clearly shaken by everything. She would be there for him and would give him the love and support he needed.

Joe looked pale and gloomy, sitting across from her, sipping his coffee, and reading the paper. What he needed was a good day out in the sun, some sunshine to warm his spirit. Her mind drifted back to the first summer they had dated. They had always been outside, whether it was walks through the park, swimming out at Fremont, or canoeing down the Wapsi. She remembered how the sunlight had bathed them in their new love. Sunlight, it was exactly what he needed—what they both needed. A day outside, with the sun shining down on them and warming their hearts, would ease the tension of the darkness closing in on them.

"Joe, honey, I was thinking. Maybe we could get out, get some sun." Sally stood up and walked around the table to get Joe's coffee cup.

"Umm hmm," Joe grunted, not necessarily disagreeing, but acknowledging her idea might be a good one. He kept his eyes down, focused on the newspaper.

"It's going to be beautiful today, over 90 degrees and sunny. A great day to be outside." Sally poured him a fresh cup of coffee and set it down next to his hand on the table.

"Umm hmm," Joe grunted again, this time in a tone indicating he was not thrilled with this idea. His eyes still remained on the newspaper.

"I was thinking maybe we could get out on the river. You know, like we used to. We could put in a canoe up at Stone City and float down to Anamosa. A peaceful, beautiful day on the river." Sally stood behind him, gently rubbing his shoulders.

"Umm," Joe grunted again, and Sally knew he was thinking.

Finally Joe turned in his chair and lifted his eyes to meet Sally's. "I suppose a day on the river would be a nice break from the bar and all the ugliness going on downtown." Joe took a sip of his coffee.

Joe needed Sally. He needed her to keep loving him. She was still a valuable resource to use. What did he used to say? *Every chess piece on the board has a purpose in every situation.* In his mind, she was still on the board, still a part of his game.

Things had not worked out as he had envisioned. The plan had been dependent upon others, dependent upon weak individuals who lacked courage—weak individuals who couldn't pull the trigger, couldn't close the deal when needed, and in the end, couldn't be trusted.

Joe thought about the entire plan and how it had been executed. Its success had been based on the concept of others working together toward a common purpose. He felt a jolt of anger at himself for his own naiveté. He should have trusted what he knew. He had always known that the team concept was flawed. In the end, everyone worked for their own gain. Success in life was all about the survival of the fittest, and nobody could be trusted. Nobody.

Perhaps he was being too hard on himself. His dependency on flawed individuals was not necessarily a bad thing. They were slow in their thinking. Slow in their reaction. He was always five moves ahead of them and was able to bend them to his will. Sure, Billy West was still in the picture, but Joe believed he had inflicted enough damage to keep Billy from ever meddling in his affairs again. In his mind, Billy West may not have been destroyed, but he was defeated.

Joe smiled. He had done it all through facts and motives. He covered his tracks well. He knew there might be a few loose ends with Ronnie Wilson's gun, but Sheriff Barton was too distraught with his own emotions to be focused on other random events loosely tied to Joe's plan.

Joe's smile broadened. Barton had too many pieces to the puzzle or not quite enough. The sheriff was too stupid to figure it out. Joe had kept in close contact with Margie Pitts over the past couple of days, and he knew Jim Barton could not see how everything fit together. Joe had, in fact, covered his tracks well. He thought about chess. One pawn had been sacrificed, but the king remained well protected.

Joe's mind focused on Sally's proposal to get out on the river. He contemplated the possibility of a few loose ends with Dicky's death and the need for her support with his alibi. He had no need to burn bridges with Sally right now, and he was too exhausted to argue or fight with her. A day on the river would be good, away from Main Street and Anamosa. A day away in the sun would give him time to let things settle down.

"Really? We can go?" Sally asked eagerly, and Joe nodded, still smiling.

Sally couldn't believe Joe agreed to her invitation. He even smiled for her. Maybe there was hope. She hugged Joe while he sat in his chair and kissed him on the side of his cheek.

"I love you, Joe Matsell. I do love you," Sally said, kissing him.

Joe continued to smile and looked down to read his newspaper.

"How about some breakfast before we get going?" Sally asked as she turned to open the cupboard. Buried deep in his paper, Joe didn't respond. "I could make some poached eggs and toast?" Sally knew that was his favorite breakfast.

Not looking up, Joe nodded. He had read and re-read the article about Dicky Moss' death three times. Joe couldn't find any indicators in the article about anyone else involved in the incident. He smiled and congratulated himself. He had played the game well.

ꕤ

"Good morning, my love," Billy said as Anna hobbled into the kitchen. Billy glanced up from the stove at her and smiled. Her hair was in a large snarled ball on her head, and yet, she looked absolutely stunning. *God, I love her*, Billy thought as he leaned forward and kissed her forehead. "Honey, I brewed a fresh pot of coffee."

Still waking up, she didn't reply. She reached up and fumbled through the cupboard then pulled out a cup and filled it. Anna held the mug in both hands and brought it to her nose as she sat down at the kitchen table.

The kitchen was filled with the wonderful heavy smell of fried bacon and coffee. Billy's back was to Anna as he feverishly worked over the stove. "Just finished the bacon, coffee, and toast, and I'm frying the eggs now. Breakfast will be ready in ten minutes," Billy said over his shoulder as he focused on draining some of the grease out of the skillet. "How do you want your eggs, darling? Sunny side up like yesterday?"

"That would be great." Anna set her mug down. "How long have you been up this morning?"

"Well, got up with your pa and did chores. Guess that would've been about four, maybe four-thirty in the morning," Billy answered.

Anna looked up at the clock above the sink. It was five minutes to eight. He had been up for almost four hours. She smiled at him and wondered where he got his energy.

"We got everything done by seven, so I thought I'd come in here and whip you up some breakfast." Billy cracked an egg into the cast iron skillet. The sounds of the sizzles and pops filled the kitchen as the eggs fried in the grease.

Anna watched Billy as he stacked the toast and bacon on a plate while simultaneously tending to the eggs. She wondered what he would be like in ten, twenty, even thirty years from now. Would he still be making her breakfast? Probably. She wondered what in the world he ever saw in her. How had she become so blessed with his love?

Billy broke into her thoughts of the future. "I know last night when we talked you were hesitant about getting out today."

Anna took a sip of her coffee. She could feel the caffeine almost instantly enter into her bloodstream. She was just beginning to wake up, and Billy was already starting off with the same discussion they had last night before she went up to bed. She wasn't ready to talk yet and looked up at Billy with undecided eyes.

"Come on, honey. It'll be good for us. We need to get away from all of this," Billy said as he turned to the kitchen table and held up the newspaper. The story of Dicky's death was on the front page.

"Can't we just stay out here today?" Anna asked as she looked down and took another sip of coffee. It was starting to have its effect, and she was becoming more awake with each passing second.

Since the event three days ago, other than the time at the sheriff's office, Billy and Anna had remained on her family farm. The Jacobs had over four hundred acres of rich, productive farmland. In the center of the farm stood their house, a structure built in the 1890s when Anna's great grandfather started farming. Since then, the land had been passed down through three generations of her family. The farmhouse evolved with each generation. Originally it was a two story, two bedroom home with a kitchen, a small parlor, and storm cellar. Now it had three bedrooms, two bathrooms, a larger kitchen, a living room, and a large porch that wrapped around the front. The Jacobs' home was a constant work in progress as each generation changed it to support their family.

Her father, Sam Jacobs, was the head of the household and running the farm. He had lived on the farm his whole life. As a boy, he had lost his arm in a tragic farming incident and was lucky to survive. However, other than preventing him from serving in the military during WWII, the injury hadn't slowed him down for a second. In fact, it really did not have much of an impact on his life. He married, fathered four girls, ran a successful farming business, and was strong as an ox. During chores, Billy had been surprised at how active he was with only one arm.

Being around her mother and father was what Anna had needed. The farm was a safety blanket for her. She was surrounded by family and nothing could harm her here. The world could not touch her. She knew Billy had saved her. She could trust him. But for the first time in their relationship, she had mixed feelings of anger for him.

She thought back to that night and could clearly see his face in the dim light in that bedroom. Serious and sad. Leaning forward with that gun and not a hint of fear in his body, he'd been steady, completely calm and ready to meet the challenge coming for them from the other side of the door. He'd been ready to kill. It was almost frightening how relaxed Billy seemed when she thought about what was actually happening.

Yes, he protected her. He always protected her. But that wasn't the point. She was angry because he let the world in. He let the world threaten their safety. Billy challenged others for what he knew was right, but she had been at his side and was affected by the consequences. She was angry at him for letting it happen. She knew he was too proud in what he believed. What was all the more frustrating was that he was so much like her father—men of principles unable to compromise for what they knew to be right.

Billy would challenge the world if he knew something was wrong. And he would be right to do so and would come out on top every time.

Anna was the problem, and she knew it. She loved him. She loved him for everything he was, and that made it all the more frustrating. She was not ready for the world. But she would always be at his side to suffer the consequences the world would bring. It was his convictions for what was right and his character that attracted her to him, and this frustrated her even more. She wondered what the costs would be.

Anna could hear her mother's words in her head. "To truly love is to truly know pain and disappointment, but we love anyway because that's what our hearts do."

It was such a pessimistic view of love and life that had never made sense to Anna, and she wondered if it did now. Anna thought about the army and felt the same flash of anger. It was the same issue. The army brought the world to their doorstep. It brought the world between them. It was doing it again when Billy would leave in three days.

"Back to Benning," he would say. She was so tired of hearing that phrase. He only had four months of service left. She wanted him home—back in Iowa for good. Four months would not be that long. She could make it. She would be here on the farm, waiting for him, and they would be married. Just four months and all of this would be behind them.

"Darling, I really think it would be good for us. To get out and get a little bit of sun. Just be together. Away from the farm, away from your family, just the two of us together." Billy topped off her cup with hot coffee. "We can't stay out on this farm forever."

He knew he struck a chord with Anna. He didn't want to argue with her, but he knew what was best for them. After the incident, she had insisted on staying out on the farm. He knew it brought her a sense of safety, and she needed that. She was surrounded by her family, in the home she grew up in. It was a refuge for her, a refuge from the darkness of the world.

But it had been three days. Three days of farm work, of pork chops, meatloaf and mashed potatoes, and of listening to the radio. Billy didn't mind any of these things—in fact, he loved them—but he felt restless. They couldn't stay on the farm forever. He only had a few days, and he needed to wean her from the farm as much as possible before he left.

Billy carefully slid a spatula under each of the eggs and put them on a platter with the bacon and toast. "Anna Darling, you need to do this. It's been a hell of a week. You need to step out a little."

"But honey, I just…" Anna started to cry.

Billy wrapped his arms around her from behind. "Anna, the world can be a hard place. And it'll leave its scars, but we can't just hide from it all."

Leaning down and kissing her neck, he whispered in her ear. "I won't live my life hiding from it. I'm going to live in this world, and I'm going to do it with you at my side. You can't hide forever. I won't let you. I can't imagine not going through this life without you at my side."

Anna turned and looked up at him with tears streaming down her cheeks. "Oh Billy, oh Billy, why did he have to do that? Why did he have to…?" Leaning forward at the table, she held her hands up to her face and wept. "Oh Billy…why…why did he have to…Billy, why?"

Billy squatted down at her side, wrapped his arms around her and pulled her into his chest. "I know, Anna Angel. I know. But I took care of it. I took care of you. I'll always be here for you. Always." Anna's body convulsed in his arms as she sobbed. Billy buried his face into her neck, and her hair spilled down over his face. "Now, now, my love. I'm here, I'll always be here…"

They held each other for at least five minutes until Anna's father walked into the kitchen. "You kids need to get out today. With Billy's help these past couple of days, I'm way ahead on chores, and it's going to be a beaut of a day."

Anna lifted her head. Her eyes were red and puffy with

tears.

Anna's father picked up a piece of toast and took a bite. "I mean it. Get out of here. Go into town. Get away from us for a while. Besides, Billy's only got a few days before he has to get back to Benning. You don't need to spend all this time working out here on the farm." Anna looked at her father and struggled to force a smile. "Going to be a peach of a day. Crops are looking fine, but we'll need to get some rain this week."

Neither Anna nor Billy answered. An uncomfortable silence filled the kitchen. Sam poured himself a cup of coffee, aware he was interrupting a conversation. He stepped out to sit in a chair on the front porch.

"Did you put him up to this?" Anna pulled away from Billy.

"What? No. Honest, no. I didn't say a word." Billy lifted his hands in the air to declare his innocence.

"Not while you were out doing chores this morning?" Anna asked with a suspicious expression.

"No. We didn't say two words the whole time. I swear."

Anna got up from her chair, and looked out the kitchen window. "Well, it does look like it is going to be nice enough," she resigned. Then she took a deep breath and let it out slowly. "Okay, I'll go. But just the two of us. I don't want to be with anyone but you. Not Josh, not Charlotte, no one."

"Thanks, darling. I really think this will be good for you today. What we both need. Time together, in solitude." Billy stepped forward and grasped Anna's hand.

They both looked out the window. "It does look like it's going to be a beautiful day," Anna said, gaining confidence about her decision.

"It sure does. Just the two of us alone together. It's going to be a great day out on the river." Billy leaned over, kissed Anna's temple and smiled.

X

JOE PULLED THE fifteen foot aluminum canoe through the sand down to the water's edge. The launch area at Stone City was empty, but he didn't care. He liked it better this way. Joe didn't want to be around people today. He needed some rest—he needed rest from all the lies. The game had gotten so twisted, and he had to pay attention to all of the details. Winning was in the details. That was what he used to tell people after he would beat them in the game of chess.

Sally lugged the cooler across the sand. Joe turned around to see if she was close behind him. She wasn't. He had moved the canoe a good two hundred feet from the parking area to the river, and she was about halfway to river bank. He didn't want to walk back to help her, but he would. He didn't care about the damn cooler, but Sally insisted on it. She had spent a good hour pulling together everything for a large lunch. He would eat, but only to make her happy. All he cared about was the full bottle of whiskey he had in the canoe.

"Damn, it's hot today," Joe mumbled to himself. He thought about opening the bottle for a drink. It was eleven in the morning, and he sure could use one. But he'd wait until they were on the river. Joe sighed and walked back toward Sally. "Let me give you a hand with that," Joe said, taking the entire cooler from Sally and swinging it up onto his shoulder. He balanced it there as they walked toward the river.

"Looks pretty quiet out here. As beautiful of a day as it is, I'm surprised there isn't anyone else on the river." Sally glanced around with her hands on her waist.

"The river's high and fast. Guess folks don't want to risk it." Joe wiped the sweat from his eyes with his free hand.

"Is it safe?" Sally's voice cracked with fear.

"Sure. It'll be fine, honey. Current's maybe a little faster, but it'll be like any other time we've been out," Joe said, but he really wasn't sure if it would be safe for them.

Joe and Sally reached the water's edge, and Joe lowered the cooler into the center of the canoe beside the two life jackets wadded up on the floor next to Joe's bag.

Sally was about to ask about the bag, but she didn't. It was his bottle. He had been drinking too much, and she couldn't stop him. Nobody could. *No need to fight today*, Sally reasoned. She didn't want to ruin the day.

Sally was hoping for a beautiful float down the river. She looked out across the rippling water. The current was strong, moving quickly along the surface. Small pockets whirled, sucking whatever was on the surface down below. Sally couldn't remember ever seeing the river like this. The immensity of it was overwhelming. It had an unstoppable power, and a shiver ran through her, thinking about it. Sally's eyes were drawn to a log floating rapidly away. "Are you sure this is safe?" She looked over at Joe with a wrinkled brow.

"Sure it is." Joe saw Sally's worried expression. "We've been on this river a dozen times. I know every deep hole, every bend, everything there is to know. We'll be fine."

Joe's comments were as much for her as they were for him. He looked out at the river—it was almost unrecognizable, looking like some strange transfigured monster. The current was swift, and he knew it was deep. *To hell with it*, he thought. Couldn't he get a break? He wouldn't let the river stop him. He needed to rest today. He needed to free his mind and get away—away from downtown, away from Billy West and Sheriff Barton, away from Dicky, and away from all of his lies.

Joe put a paddle in the front of the canoe where Sally was going to sit. There, on the front of the canoe, the previous owner had carved his name into the aluminum. "D Moss" was permanently inscribed into the boat. Sally immediately saw it, and a cold current of fear shot through her body. She believed it was an omen of something to come.

Joe recognized her reaction and ignored her feelings. "Come on, honey. If we're going to be off the river by four we need to get going."

Several years earlier, Joe had won the canoe at the poker table with Dicky. It was a nice aluminum canoe Dicky had received from his parents for his sixteenth birthday. Joe smiled and thought about Dicky Moss and his canoe. He remembered how Dicky had been a loner. He would take the boat out alone on long overnight fishing trips, sometimes spending a whole week on a river.

Joe remembered how he used to give Dicky crap about not having a girlfriend, and he openly wondered what Dicky had been doing on the river for so many days. That fool had loved this damned canoe. Joe always knew Dicky was lost. He had taken better care of this hunk of metal than any other possession.

Joe smiled and thought about the inscription, "D Moss." Dicky had always been in over his head. He should have never sat down at the poker table. Joe had won the canoe fair, but Dicky should have known better than to wager his canoe. Damned fool. The cards almost always went in Joe's favor.

Joe's smile broadened as he remembered the summer after he won it. They would all go out as groups on the river. Dicky never had gotten back into his old canoe, though. He had always ridden with Ronnie or Tom or someone else. But he would always look it over as if he was going to eventually get it back. Joe knew it had bothered Dicky that he lost it to him. In fact, he had made it a point to beat the canoe when Dicky was around, taking it over large submerged rocks and logs. Sometimes it would sound as if the whole bottom was going to rip out as the current drug it across those obstacles.

On one occasion, Joe remembered looking over at Dicky in a nearby canoe, seeing tears streaming down his cheeks—all over a goddamn boat. Dicky had been a fool. Joe smiled again. Yes, he had been cruel, maybe even too cruel at times. Fuck it. Dicky Moss had been a man and responsible for his actions. He got in too deep and couldn't get out.

Sally looked down at Dicky's inscription again. Maybe this would be a positive sign for them. Maybe it would be exactly what they needed. One more float on the river, a ride in memorial to Dicky. Her thoughts turned to him. She never knew

Dicky very well. Nobody really did. He had friends, but no one was close to him. It made her sad. Damn pride. She wondered why men did what they did. What would drive Dicky to go after Billy West the way he had. None of it made sense to her.

She looked up at Joe. He had a strange smile on his face. Maybe he felt the same way about Dicky, gone far too early from this world. This time on the river, in Dicky's old canoe, might be therapeutic for Joe. She figured it must have torn at him to see Dicky's name, to see this reminder. She wondered how Joe was handling it. She knew he felt responsible, felt guilt for everything that had happened.

She wondered how long it would take for Joe to recover from his grief. He would drink today, and she would let him. He would be drunk, and she wouldn't say a word. She couldn't imagine what he was going through and hoped the booze would help him deal with all of it.

"It's going to be a beautiful day out on the water," Sally said in an attempt to lift Joe's spirits.

"Go ahead. Climb in and move to the seat in front," Joe said, ignoring Sally's comment. Sally obediently positioned herself, and Joe pushed the canoe out into the water. "There. That wasn't so difficult, now was it?" Joe asked. Sally nodded but was afraid and forced a smile.

They were off. Joe was surprised at how fast the current was as he steered the canoe out toward the center of the river. The current was swift and moving them much faster than he had anticipated—almost at a dangerous speed. He countered and steered with the paddle. He quickly gained control of the canoe and guided it across the water.

Positioning the canoe out in the middle of the river away from any visible obstacles, Joe paused for a break from paddling. He took his shirt off and felt the hot sun on his shoulders. The heat felt good. Sally had been right. They did need to get out. They needed a day in the sun. Time. He needed some time away from all the lies, from all the noise in Anamosa. He needed time to sort everything out and to think through his next moves.

Joe thought about Barton and how he was reacting to everything. Joe had kept his distance from the sheriff's office over the past couple of days, but he would have to make contact with Margie Pitts. Maybe tonight, no later than tomorrow. Joe looked up into the sun, and the heat warmed his face. He smiled. Yes, he would make contact with old Squirrel-Face. He needed information before his next move. It would require another engagement in the woods with Margie, but it would be worth it.

Joe reached down and rummaged through his bag until he found it—the safe, reassuring, hard glass bottle. It felt better than anything in his hands. He screwed off the lid, lifted the bottle to his lips, and smiled. It was going to be a hell of a day. He tilted the bottle up and took a long, deep drink.

ꕥ

"Are you sure you really want to go out on the water today?" Anna asked Billy as he loaded the canoe at the launch site.

Billy looked out at the river as it swiftly flowed by. "Must have gotten a good six inches of rain up north over the past couple of days. River's swollen today."

"We could use some of that rain down here. Papa says the crops sure could use it." Anna shielded her eyes from the sun and looked down the river alongside of Billy.

"The river will be fine. I know you're worried. I've been on these waters plenty of times when it was this high. We won't be swimming much today. Current's moving pretty fast, but it'll still be a nice day on the river." Billy handed her a life jacket, and Anna stared at it skeptically. "They aren't attractive, but we should put these on, just in case."

Anna knew Billy wanted to get on the river at least once while he was home. This was the last chance they had. He would be visiting his father at the hospital tomorrow, and he needed the last day to pack and get everything in order. The pain of him leaving pierced her heart again. She didn't want to think about it. It was too much to accept. Too hard to think about. If she did, it would eat away at her and ruin their day. "We better get going if we're going to meet Papa in Anamosa by five," Anna said, forcing a smile.

Billy positioned himself on the bank behind the canoe. "You move up to the front, and I'll push us off."

Getting ready for the trip took longer than Billy had anticipated. He had to go alone back to the house to get the canoe. Anna was not ready to revisit where it all happened. After loading the canoe, he returned to the farm to get her. The whole process took several hours. It was almost noon, and they would have to do some paddling to make it to Anamosa by five.

As the canoe floated out into the river, it was immediately

grabbed by the current. Billy anticipated it with his paddle and quickly gained control, steering the canoe toward the center. Billy's mind flashed back to Vietnam for a brief moment.

In a strange way, something about the feel of the river made him think about that dark corner of the world. It was the way the current pulled him into the river—it reminded him of how things could slip in the jungles of Vietnam. The ugliness of war could definitely grab him. If he didn't have something to ground him, he would slide down, backward, out of control.

He leaned back with his paddle and dipped it into the water. The canoe veered over to the left of a log protruding up ahead of them. Billy gripped the paddle firmly in his hands. Without a rudder, there was no way he would ever have control.

Billy smiled. His mind flashed back to even earlier times when he and his father would be in that same canoe and on the same river. They had gone several times as a whole family, but after his mother was gone, he and his father had spent a lot of time on the river together. Billy savored those memories—just the two of them together on the river.

They were both dealing with the loss of a mother and a wife. That time was healing for them, and it had given them what they needed. Time. Solitude. Friendship. Sometimes they would go an hour or two without saying a word. Other times, they would talk about history, sports, the outdoors, even girls. His pop would drink beer after beer as they floated from Stone City to Anamosa, but it never seemed to affect him. He seemed to have control. For Billy, it didn't matter. All he had cared about was the time they spent together—father and son in a canoe, enjoying the day, and letting the river take them to their destination.

He looked at Anna, in her swimsuit, sitting in the front of the canoe. It was an image that would be forever etched in his mind. The sunlight flashing on her long, blonde hair, the curves of her shoulders and her hips…her smile and the sparkle in her eyes.

She had the beauty poets dreamed of with their words. But there was a depth to it. Words could not be bent to touch it. It was her heart. Her beautiful, kind heart and her patience for others. She was simply the most selfless person he had ever met. She was everything he would ever want in a woman. God, he loved her. She made him so proud to be her man.

"Anna Darling, could you hand me a beer?" Billy asked as he calmly steered the canoe through the current.

Anna turned and opened the cooler. Inside was something wrapped up in brown paper. "What is this?" Anna asked, surprised. As she looked up, she was startled. Billy had quickly moved forward in the canoe and was kneeling down on a knee while balancing the canoe in the current.

"Anna Angel, make me the happiest man in the world. Will you marry me?" Billy pulled the package from the cooler and placed it into Anna's trembling hands. She slowly lifted out a small wrapped box. Opening the box, she found a gold band with a small diamond mounted on it.

"Oh Billy, oh Billy, yes, yes, yes…" Anna lunged forward into Billy's arms. The canoe wobbled and almost tipped in the fast current, but Billy regained control as he held her in his arms.

"Yes, Billy. Yes. Yes..." Anna buried her face into his shoulder. He could feel waves of convulsions in her body as she cried.

"Come on, Anna Darling. This is supposed to be a happy moment for you, for both of us." Billy tried to console her, holding her close to him.

Anna stopped and kissed Billy on the cheek. "Oh Billy, it's...it's just...I never thought I would wear this ring. I thought you were going to wait... that you were going to wait until I came down to Fort Benning."

"Well, I was. But after the week we've had, after everything that's happened and all that we've been through, I decided why wait? You thought I had spent the last couple of days at Sheriff Barton's office. Well, I was, but the truth is I was also shopping around at the jewelry stores in town. I couldn't find the ring I was looking for, at least not on a sergeant's pay. It had to be special. I saw a couple that were close, but not quite what I was looking for—not the right ring. This one. This ring...this was my mother's ring." Tears welled in Billy's eyes.

"Oh Billy, oh Billy, you shouldn't have, I couldn't..." Anna's hands trembled as she looked at the ring in the box.

Billy took the ring out and slid it onto her finger. "I love you, Anna Angel. I'll always love you."

Anna's lips quivered as she held her hand up and marveled at the ring on her finger. "Billy it's perfect...just perfect...it's the ring I always imagined." Anna fell forward as she wrapped her arms around Billy. "I love you, Billy West. I'll love you forever."

Billy held Anna for what seemed an eternity. Eventually he pulled away and grabbed the paddle to steer away from a rock.

"I drove up to Independence to see my pop. He wanted me to give it to you. In fact, he insisted. I know it isn't much, but it means so much to me and to my pa that you have it. That it be your ring. Don't mean anything to anybody just sitting at home in some box. You bring life to it. It belongs on your hand. Anyhow, it's the best I can do right now on my pay. I figure it'll have to do until I can get a job, making an honest living." Billy smiled as he steered through the swirling current.

"It's beautiful. We don't need anything else. This ring is perfect. I'm so proud to wear it…to wear it for you…for us…it's everything we need." Anna erupted in tears again as she tucked her head into Billy's chest. "I just never thought. I never thought this day would come. I know you proposed before, but those were just words…words I wanted to believe, but something was holding me back. But now, now I have my ring. Something so permanent, something forever. I never thought…I never thought it would happen." Anna leaned away from Billy, smiling, and wiped the tears from her cheeks.

"You know what this means? Looks like you are going to have to put up with me a little bit longer." Billy smiled and then he kissed her. "I've been trying to figure out where and when the best place would be for me to give you this. I thought about last night when we were sitting out on the front porch. I had the ring in my pocket the whole time, and I really wanted to give it to you. But you were so sad, still shook up from everything that happened—it just didn't feel right. I talked to your parents about it yesterday. Even formally asked for their permission." Billy smiled as a sheepish expression formed on his face.

"You mean they knew about all of this?" Anna asked with a surprised, accusatory expression.

"Yes, actually during chores with your pa, he recommended that we needed to get out, get away from the farm, and go someplace special…" Billy tried to explain and was interrupted again by Anna.

"He had a role in all of this?" Anna slugged him. "You men!"

"Hey, your ma knew too! Anyway, this river has always been a source of joy for me. It's a place full of wonderful memories. It seemed like the right place for us. Come on, my love. I'm going to sit in the back of the canoe. You can sit at my feet and recline between my legs." Billy moved to the back of the canoe.

"You sure you don't need me to paddle up front?" Anna asked.

"I can control the entire canoe from right here." Billy said, motioning for her to come with him. "Besides, I want to see how that ring looks on your finger." Billy smiled, and he meant it.

Sitting down on the floor of the canoe, she could feel the warm sun on her face, and she grinned. She held her left hand up and looked at the ring in front of her. It was perfect, like it was always meant to be on her hand. Anna felt joy, a joyful wholeness she had not felt in a long time. The ring proved he did love her—more than the army, more than the world itself. It had been years, probably since before Billy had left for the army, that she felt this way. She didn't know just how much she had been missing until now. Today, everything was right. Everything was whole again.

ജ

Joe was drinking hard, harder and faster than Sally could remember. She watched as he neared the bottom of the fifth of whiskey. With each passing minute and sip from the bottle, his eyes grew heavier and his speech became more slurred. Poor Joe. Sally thought about the burden he was shouldering with Dicky's death. She wanted to help him. Over the past couple of days, she had tried to console him. In some ways, he had reacted positively to her. A glimmer of hope, she'd thought, but she couldn't compete with the bottle. Whiskey was Joe's closest friend.

Sally looked out across the river. The current was swift. She was not a strong swimmer and didn't know if she could control the canoe on her own. She worried and watched as her concerns began to play out in front of her.

"I'm going to be sick." Joe slowly attempted to lean over the side of the boat. Vomit spewed from his mouth onto his chest and into the canoe.

"Oh my God! Oh my God, Joe! Joe…oh God!" Sally blurted out as she was repulsed by the sight and smell of six poached eggs and toast mixed with several quarts of whiskey. The putrid concoction splattered everywhere and floated in an inch of accumulated river water on the floor of the canoe. Sally gagged, and for a brief moment, she was sure she was going to throw up, too.

"Oh, no..." Joe moaned as he lurched forward on his hands and knees from the rear of the canoe to the center. "Oh God, I don't feel…" Joe's words were cut short as he convulsed forward on his knees and vomited again into the canoe. "Ohhhh. Oh, I don't feel so good." This time, he fell face forward into the pile of life jackets in the center of the canoe. He laid there, motionless.

"Joe! Joe! Joe?" Sally reached forward and nudged him to get a response. "Joe, are you okay?"

Finally Joe lifted his head and turned his face over the side of the canoe just in time to puke again, this time into the river.

"Oh God…the whiskey…and the eggs…I feel…I feel horrible." Joe looked up at Sally. There were chunks of eggs on the side of his face and down his front. She gagged again and started to vomit but was able to fight off her reflexes and force down the bitter contents in her throat.

"Oh, Joe. We got to get you home, honey. We got to get you out of this sun and into bed," Sally said.

"Get me to bed. Take me…" Joe slurred his words as he drifted in and out of consciousness.

"Come on, Joe. I need your help. I need you to help me get you home." Sally pleaded with Joe as he curled into a fetal position in the center of the canoe.

"Help. That's what we all need. You'll help me. Help me with Barton. Tell me about Sheriff Barton," Joe mumbled.

"What?" Sally asked. *Barton?* She was confused.

"Dicky…it should never have happened. But I made him do it. He was in over his head. Weak. He was always so weak. He had to be sacrificed. Some have to be sacrificed…only the strong survive…"

"Joe, what are you talking about?" Sally was afraid. She didn't want to know. She was afraid of the truth, but she knew she might have to face it.

"And Eddie…what a fool to think he could back me into a corner. But he paid…" Joe mumbled. "And it was so easy…nobody even suspected..."

"What are you saying?" A combination of confusion and fear washed over Sally as she began to comprehend the weight of his words.

"Take me home, Margie. I ain't feeling so good, baby. Take me home," Joe slurred and then collapsed in a heap of vomit in the middle of the canoe.

Margie. The words hurt. More than pain, she felt her heart ripped from her chest and a vast emptiness filled the void. Margie Pitts. She was stunned and didn't want to believe it. Sally thought about her relationship with Joe. All the time, all the work, all of this, her youth…everything she had given to him…he took and took and used her up, and now he couldn't even remember her name.

She hated him, and she would hate him forever. Somehow he was involved with Eddie's and Dicky's deaths. She saw him for who he was, a no good, lying, son of a bitch. But a murderer, too? She didn't want to believe it. Sally could see now that he never loved her. He never loved anyone. He loved power—the power to manipulate and bend and control. But murder? Yes. It was in him. Along with all the lies and hatred, it was just another phase of his control.

And now he was there, passed out drunk in the canoe, leaving it all up to her to get them home. And she would. She would take him home and put him to bed. And tomorrow he wouldn't remember any of it. And she would still be there for him. She would go on as if nothing had happened. This was what bothered her the most. This was what she hated. She didn't have any way out. She hated herself for it—for giving everything she had to this sorry excuse of a man, for giving up her youth, her innocence, and her life for a liar and a murderer.

Sally looked down at him. He was snoring. She could hear him even though his face was buried in the life jackets. All at once, she was disgusted by Joe. He was pathetic. He was a hateful man. He was a monster. Deep down she knew it was there, but she never had the courage to accept it.

Sally started to cry. She felt pity for herself. She was trapped and had to do something. Suddenly a burst of anger filled her thoughts. She felt a burning, hateful rage for Joe start to tremble deep inside—a flash of hot anger cutting to the core of everything she was.

She had an idea. She looked out across the river. They were still moving fast in the swift current. She took her paddle and pushed it down deep into the water. She couldn't touch the bottom. It was at least six feet deep. Now, if she could just move him.

Sally leaned forward and tried to lift the 270 pounds of dead weight, but she couldn't budge him. Nor would she be able to lift him over the side of the canoe.

He moaned as she shoved him. His heavy body rested in over an inch of water in the bottom of the canoe. She had another idea. She calculated that if she pulled the life jackets out from underneath his head he would lay face down in the puddle and might drown in it. It could work.

Reaching forward, Sally tugged and tugged at the life jackets. Pulling and pulling, but they wouldn't give. He was too heavy. And then, with her whole body into it, she yanked the life jackets free. The momentum almost sent her overboard, but she regained her balance. However, she flung the life jackets into the water, and they quickly floated away.

Joe's head smacked face down into the canoe with a dull metallic thud. He let out a groan and turned his face to the side, just above the puddle, and continued his heavy snoring.

"Damn!" she said under her breath. It didn't work. Sally's mind raced. She had to do something now. This was her only chance. It might be her only opportunity ever for a clean break. That was all she needed, a new beginning in her life. This was her time, and she had to seize it.

As she looked out at the river bank, she had another idea. If she could get to the bank, she could overturn the entire canoe and walk home from there.

ᜐᜑ

"Pop used to say that this stretch of the river was a little slice from heaven." Billy gazed up into the massive ancient trees, towering over the river. He and Anna had not moved in the canoe. Billy leaned back with his paddle dipped in the water, serving as a rudder, guiding them downstream. Anna sat between his legs, her head tilted back on his stomach. They drifted for what seemed like hours. Anna had not felt more at peace, more full of life, more complete with love, then she did with Billy in the canoe.

"Heaven…I feel it too." Anna leaned over and kissed Billy's thigh. Cuddling into him, she smiled, brimming with new confidence. Everything seemed true and more permanent than they were before.

They drifted for a while without saying a word. Anna gazed up at the clouds and felt as if she were floating with them as they went downstream. The water lapped against the side of the aluminum, and she felt Billy's muscles underneath her, shifting, countering, and controlling the canoe with his paddle. Minutes passed. Anna lingered dreamily into a relaxed safe sleep.

Billy smiled. The sun beat down on them, but it didn't matter. The warmth and the blinding brightness was what they needed. He turned his paddle, and the canoe glided under several oaks arching over the river bank. He wondered about their age, and figured they had been there for decades. Nothing had changed. The same trees were there all those times when he and his pop had made this journey.

Billy thought about his mother, about Anna, the direction his life was turning, and the future. He looked down at Anna. She was breathing heavily now, and Billy thought she might even be asleep. Good. She needed her rest. His Anna Angel. So beautiful. So right. His one and only love. He looked at the ring on her finger. Perfection. She would be his truth, his foundation, what he needed to find purpose in this world.

The current guided the canoe around the bend. About a quarter of a mile downstream, something caught Billy's attention. Anna's slumber was broken when she was startled by Billy's voice.

"Hey, there's another canoe up ahead." Billy pointed it out to Anna as they rounded the bend in the river.

"Can you see who it is?" Anna asked, yawning and rubbing the sleep from her eyes.

"No. Looks like it's just one person in the canoe." A perplexed expression formed on Billy's face.

"What? What is it?" Anna asked.

"That's strange. There's only one person in the canoe, and they're in the front. That ain't no way to control a canoe, especially on a river like this today. Looks like they're trying to pull something up from the center. Maybe even struggling. I think they're in trouble."

"Maybe we should help them?" Anna said in a concerned and questioning tone.

"I want you to move back up to the front of the canoe and start paddling," Billy said. "It should only take us a few minutes to catch up to them."

ꙮ

"Just got to get this canoe over to the bank. From there, I should be able to…I should be able to do it," Sally muttered. She nervously talked to herself as she tried to maneuver the canoe with the paddle.

The river narrowed, and the current moved faster now. She looked up ahead and saw the entrance to where the Buffalo flowed into the Wapsi. It was a dangerous stretch of the river, and the currents could be unpredictable. "Damn! I can't seem to get a break."

Suddenly, the current grabbed hold of the canoe and rapidly turned it sideways then backwards. Sally tried to maneuver with the paddle, but it was useless from the front of the canoe.

She was floating backward out of control now. Sally looked over her shoulder, and up ahead she saw a tree trunk partially breaking the surface of the river right in her path. The current moved faster, but she was able to turn the canoe a quarter of the way around. She was still floating sideways headlong into the quickly approaching obstacle.

Sally looked down at a snoring Joe, absolutely unaware of the peril that awaited them and absolutely worthless. She felt nothing but anger for him. But her anger quickly gave way to fear. Fear for the large tree trunk that jutted up from depths ahead of them.

Sally watched the currents swirl and collide around her. She wasn't a strong swimmer and probably wouldn't make it. Damn life jackets. She never thought she would need them. Now it was too late. The canoe floated sideways in the current faster and faster. Sally panicked and had no control. All she could do was wait. She held tightly to the sides and braced herself for the collision.

KERPLANNGEEEECCHHHHHHEEE! The canoe slammed into the log and hung there as the water built up around it. The roar of the submerged tree trunk scraping up against the aluminum sounded as if the entire bottom of the boat was being ripped out.

The canoe was caught up on the log, and in a matter of

seconds, it would likely capsize in the dangerous water. Sally was certain the end was near and had all but given up when she heard a man's saving voice clear and direct. Startled by the voice, she jumped and for a brief moment, thought she had imagined it.

"You folks need some assistance?" Billy asked. He immediately recognized Sally and saw a wild look of panic in her eyes. "Just hold it right there. I'll get you out." Billy grabbed a hold of the rear of Sally's canoe. Grasping the tip in his hand, he tugged with everything he had and was able to pull the canoes together. Securing Sally's canoe to his, the momentum of his boat in the current slowly towed Sally's off the log.

Billy held both canoes together and steered them downstream. "That was a close one. A few more seconds and this river would have completely overtaken you and pulled you under." Billy secured her canoe to his. Sally looked as white as a ghost, and then Billy saw Joe Matsell lying in the middle of the canoe.

"Is he…is he okay?" Billy asked with genuine concern.

"He...he isn't feeling well. Guess he drank a little too much and the hot sun's gotten the best of him." Sally felt anger at herself for protecting Joe.

"If you can steer us over to the bank, I think…I think I can get him under some trees in the shade." Sally had not given up on her plan as she pointed over to a grove of trees several hundred feet downstream.

"We got about a half a mile to Anamosa. If he ain't up to paddling today, I think it would be best if we stay together on this final leg," Billy said. "Besides, these currents are awfully hard to read, especially with the river so high right now."

Billy was interrupted by a voice from Sally's canoe. "Who…who…is that?" Joe stirred from his drunken sleep.

An uncomfortable silence fell upon them as Sally, Billy, and Anna watched Joe rise up to his hands and knees. All three hoped he would go back to sleep.

"What? What happened? Who…who is that?" Joe said in a confused, louder, angry voice. Up on his knees now, Joe tried to focus his eyes on the man in the other canoe. "You! It's you! West! Billy West! Billy West, you son of a bitch, no good bastard!" Joe shouted as he realized who he was looking at. "You no good bastard! I'm going to get you! I'm going to finish all of this. It's time to finish the game!" Joe shouted in anger as he struggled to get to his feet in the canoe.

"Joe, Joe, no!" Sally reached out to Joe to restrain him.

But it was too late.

Everything happened quickly when Joe grabbed a paddle and cocked it back. With all his might, he swung at Billy. Joe's full stroke was stopped with an immediate, dull thud. Instead of Billy, the paddle struck Sally in the back of the head.

Sally fell face forward into the canoe while Joe swung his arms wildly, trying to regain his balance, but he fell backwards into the water with a loud and distinct pop of his knee as it snapped and ripped out of joint. His left foot remained in the canoe, tangled up in the straps of his bag and the aluminum crosspiece that spanned across the middle. Joe's immense weight pulled the entire canoe over onto him in the water.

"Aaah! My knee! My knee!" Joe screamed as he fought to

keep his head above water. "Oh my knee, oh my God, my knee is, oh…" Joe writhed in pain. He cleared himself from the entanglement and the overturned canoe, moving freely with the current. "I can't…my knee…can't make it…I can't swim." Joe screamed, struggling to keep his head above the surface of the water. "Help…help me…I can't swim…"

Billy ripped his life jacket off and threw it to Joe, who drifted further from the canoes with the swift current.

"Grab the life jacket! Grab it!" Billy shouted.

"I…I can't seem to…I can't." Joe stretched out his hand, splashing and reaching in vain for the life jacket. Billy saw Joe was going under and wouldn't reach it so he immediately dove into the water.

"Billy, no!" Anna screamed.

But it was too late.

Billy had already committed himself to saving Joe.

Letting the life jacket go in the current, Billy swam to Joe, who desperately fought for his life. Billy was too late. Joe went under.

Diving down and swimming under water, Billy searched for him.

"No, Billy. No!" Anna cried out as she helplessly watched him disappear under water.

The water was a dark, brownish green. Billy could barely see. Deeper and deeper he swam. He was on the river bottom, desperately searching for Joe, but he was running out of time. He couldn't go much further without oxygen. A few more seconds and Billy would have to swim to the surface.

Suddenly he felt something large in front of him. It was massive. At first, he thought it might be a submerged log, but then it moved. It was Joe. Billy attempted to wrap his arms around him. Joe pushed against Billy and tried to fight him off. Very little time was left for either of them.

Billy cocked a fist and slugged Joe across the jaw. He had to get control of him if either of them had a chance. Billy struck him several times, and it seemed to work as Joe surrendered to his will. Now, with his arms wrapped tightly around Joe, Billy planted his feet in the mud. With every ounce of his strength, he thrust his body upward and projected them both toward the surface.

They were moving up but not fast enough. Billy started to get dizzy. They slowed more and more in their assent. Billy's head grew foggy as if he was going to blackout. With everything he had left, he kicked his legs to propel them to the surface. He could see the sun shining down through the green water above them. Billy's mind raced. Five feet, three feet…just a little further, and they would make it.

Then, everything went black.

The darkness closed in around Billy. His body became weightless and floated underwater. He was not going to make it.

So close to the surface…but not close enough.

His vision dimmed and his eyes closed. He thought about Anna. What would she do without him? Then he drifted into unconsciousness.

ᘓᘐ

Sally's overturned canoe was sinking into the current. Anna couldn't hold onto it any longer and tried to maintain control of her own canoe. Where was Sally? Anna looked around, desperately calling out for her. Nothing. Seconds passed. The river and the sun beat down on her and left her in the company of an eerie silence.

A shock of panic hit her. She wailed out and cried. "Billy!" Billy!" she frantically screamed out.

No response.

Anna was losing it. She was crying and had to get control of herself. Grabbing the paddle, she maneuvered the canoe over to where Billy had gone under. More time passed. She couldn't remember how long it had been since Billy had gone down. A minute, three minutes? She didn't know. The current moved so fast. With everything she had, she fought it with the paddle to keep the canoe in the same area.

"Billy! Billy! Billy?" She called out to him, refusing to surrender to her doubts that he might have been swept away.

Anna put her head down on her lap in her hands, sobbing. Then, in anger, she raised her hands up to the sky as if she was appealing to God and wailed out in pain. "Why? Why? Why have you done this to me?"

A few more seconds passed. A hopeless emptiness filled her. She looked into the dark river. She would dive into the dangerous waters to find him.

Nothing else mattered now.

She would die, trying to find him.

Even if only to hold him in her arms one more time before

she surrendered her own life.

She leaned over the side of the canoe to slip into the water. Suddenly she saw some large bubbles coming up a couple feet from the canoe. She thought her eyes were playing tricks on her. Could it be? She hoped against hope. She didn't want to trust her eyes. She saw motion just below the surface. Grabbing the paddle, she pushed it into the water, and she felt a tug. A hand grasped hold of it and exploded on the surface. Billy. In his arms was Joe Matsell. Both of them coughed and gasped for air.

Billy reached out and gripped the side of the canoe with one hand and held Joe with the other.

"Anna," Billy said, gasping for air. "Give me your life jacket. Joe needs it."

Anna nodded, unable to say anything as tears ran down her cheeks. She couldn't believe her eyes. Her Billy. He made it.

"Don't let go of the canoe," Billy ordered Joe as he strapped the last life jacket onto him. Both Billy and Joe held onto the canoe as they floated downstream.

"Thank God you were there with that paddle. I don't know if I would've made it if I didn't have something to pull me up to the surface," Billy said to Anna as he coughed to clear his throat.

Joe hacked up water and then started to writhe in pain. "My knee. Oh my knee…"

Ignoring Joe, Billy wondered where the other canoe was. "Where's Sally?"

"Her canoe…I couldn't hold on. It…it sank," Anna tried to get the words out but couldn't. It didn't matter. Billy knew she didn't make it. She was probably unconscious when the canoe overturned. The current was so strong he was surprised he and Joe made it.

Billy looked out across the surface of the water for signs of the other canoe, for signs of Sally. Nothing. It was as if the river swallowed them up and they never existed.

"Hey, where's…where's Sally?" Joe finally asked.

Neither Anna nor Billy knew what to say.

"Where's Sally?" Joe called out again, this time with an angry tone.

Anna and Billy both looked away. Neither could face him now.

"Sally!" Joe tried to holler out but coughed up more water.

"Sally!" Joe shouted at the top of his lungs. "Sally?" Joe shouted again, not as loud. "Sally! Sally? My dear? Sally?" Joe's shouts whimpered down, and he started to cry.

"Sally!" Joe shouted again, this time in sheer anger. "You…you! West…you did this! It was all you! It's always been you!"

"No, Joe. It was you. You did this. And we all know it," Billy said in a calm and direct tone. Looking into Joe's eyes, Billy saw a hint of panic. The game was over for Joe, and they both knew it. He had backed himself into a corner and run out of options.

With his life jacket on, Joe pushed off from the canoe and swam toward the river bank.

"Joe, what are you…" Anna started to ask but stopped when she saw Joe's head turn toward her.

"I'll be seeing you, West." Joe grinned a sinister smile. "I'll be seeing you…"

"Let him go, honey. Just let him go," Billy said, sighing heavily. "He's all used up, and he knows it." Billy laid his head on the side of the boat, exhausted.

"But he just…and Sally is…" Anna tried to reason with Billy, who was still clinging to the side of the canoe.

Billy was dizzy with exhaustion as he coughed to clear the water from his lungs. "I know, but we got to let him go. There's nothing we can do for him. Got to let him go. A man is the sum of his choices. And Joe has made his."

"But he's going to go back to town and…" Anna ran her fingers through Billy's hair and comforted him, looking out at Joe swimming for an undeserved freedom.

"No, he won't. The cards are stacked against him, and he knows it. If he makes it back, he'll probably leave town. Maybe for good." Billy was numb with fatigue as he coughed again and spit into the water.

The sun began to set and a breeze cooled off the hot day as Anna and Billy drifted in the swift current toward Anamosa. Anna could hear the siren of the cicadas in the trees on the river bank. Several turkey buzzards circled overhead and further down the river a fish broke the surface of the water. She scanned the river for Sally's canoe. It was nowhere to be seen. Anna laid her head on Billy's, holding onto him with all of her life.

Thoughts of Sally came to her, and she cried. So much loss. It was so awful; such a horrible, terrible loss. She couldn't believe everything that had happened and how quickly it all occurred. She looked down at Billy clutching the side of the canoe, and she cried for him—she thought she had lost him, lost him for good. She didn't want to even think about the possibility of this, but she did. The fear of losing Billy violently ripped through her emotions and shattered her heart. Anna cried uncontrollably. She briefly wondered if she was losing her mind and then released herself and sobbed hysterically. Just moments before, she had been completely ready to die when she thought Billy was gone. She had never felt so much emptiness in her soul. She would have ended it all. She was hopeless, hopelessly in love with Billy.

Wiping the tears from her cheeks, Anna watched in silence as Joe Matsell grew smaller in the distance as he struggled to reach the river bank.

XI

JUDGE SWANSON ENTERED the United Methodist Church that Sunday morning with a stern look on his face. He was annoyed. Not just annoyed; he was angry at himself for letting things slip away from him. Things had gone too far, and he should have interceded sooner. Prairieburg, Dicky Moss, and now Sally Mayfield. He wished he had stopped by Sheriff Barton's office after Moss's death. He should have. Judge Swanson had returned from Washington and had a lot of work to catch up on, but that was no excuse, and he knew it. Too many people were already involved. He liked to keep a lower profile, fix things behind the scenes, and keep things moving in the right direction without making waves.

His longtime nemesis in the community, Earl Brown, was already entrenched in an effort to protect Sheriff Barton. The whole affair with Dicky Moss's shooting was a mess and now this?

What was needed was truth, and he was not sure he would get that with Earl Brown involved. Brown had influence, but the Judge didn't respect him. Brown was lazy and tended to twist the truth to his advantage.

Over the years, their paths had crossed often. The former sheriff had gotten things done, but he had also cut corners. On more than one occasion, Judge Swanson had questioned his integrity. Brown was simply not a man who could be trusted.

With this situation, things were moving fast and had too many people involved—too many of the wrong people.

Judge Swanson glanced around the congregation scurrying to find their usual seats and worried about the future of Anamosa. It seemed to be drifting without a rudder. He was born here in 1910, had attended college, law school, and worked in Chicago. Then he had returned and opened his own practice in Anamosa.

He had watched the small farming town grow through the Industrial Revolution, survive a world war, the Great Depression, and a second world war. He remembered horse-drawn carriages on Main Street and the advent of the automobile. Electricity, plumbing, and new streets, he watched the town evolve, grow, and change. It was always improving. It was always moving forward.

But now he was concerned. Moss and now Mayfield. Inside he felt a slow, sinking sensation. The Judge worried these recent events were indicators of a large scale decline in the community. He speculated if something was slipping. He wondered if growth had plateaued and if they were now sliding down the backside. Young men and women grew up here but few stayed. Even less went out into the world and returned. Something was changing. Things moved faster, and people were becoming more transient. Judge Swanson wondered what this town had to offer young families and what it would be for future generations.

The transformation was more than people leaving, and it scared him. He shuddered to even think about the character of the youth, the community, and the country. No question, things were changing. In his fifty-six years on this earth, the one thing he knew was that things were always changing. The question was, what was his role in it all? As a leader, he believed he had a responsibility to shape and guide the community toward a better future. Right now, they seemed to be drifting off course, and the current was swift. He would guide them away from the obstacles.

The fact that bad things happened was not necessarily the problem. How people reacted to them was what mattered. That was what defined the community and the future. Reactions. He would guide the reactions—he believed that was his role. He had let things get away from him with these recent incidents, but now he would take action.

Walking down the aisle, Judge Swanson nodded his greetings as he led his wife and three daughters to their usual seats, the second row of pews in the center of the sanctuary. As the Swanson family sat, the Judge turned and saw Sheriff Barton in the back corner. He immediately got up from the pew and walked back to meet him.

Barton was falling asleep when Judge Swanson came up behind him and bent down to whisper in his ear. "Let's go downstairs and get a cup of coffee."

The startled sheriff jerked up from his sleep. Rubbing his eyes and yawning, Sheriff Barton turned and was surprised to see Judge Swanson standing behind him.

"Come on, Jim. Let's get a cup of coffee."

Barton got to his feet and moved out of the pew to follow the Judge to the basement.

ꕤ

"You've had a heck of a week," Judge Swanson said as he took a sip of coffee.

Sheriff Barton nodded but did not say anything. He'd known the day was coming when he would have to face Judge Swanson. He was surprised it hadn't been sooner. After Dicky's death, he had expected the Judge would have come by to talk about it.

Between shooting Dicky Moss and the aftermath that followed, the sheriff considered it the worst event of his life. That day had been a whirlwind of people and questions, and Barton had thought it would never end. It was probably a good thing Judge Swanson hadn't stopped by.

Just because Barton expected it didn't mean he liked it. He loathed meeting with the Judge. He knew Judge Swanson would have questions he would have to answer. It was not that he had to subordinate himself to the Judge that bothered him; it was that he would have to subordinate himself to the truth, and facing that truth would be painful.

More than anything, what troubled the sheriff most was Judge Swanson's demeanor. The Judge was the kindest man the sheriff had ever met. Not just in his words and actions but in his eyes. They had a level of genuine compassion. Judge Swanson cared. It didn't matter who the person was or what they had done, the Judge had compassion for them. The sheriff could not remember ever hearing him cuss or speak ill of anyone—Judge Swanson kept himself above it, and it made Barton feel uneasy.

Judge Swanson's virtues also made the sheriff feel less of a man and full of guilt and shame. Something in Judge Swanson's caring eyes let the sheriff know he wasn't judging him, but he also knew he didn't measure up. Something in his approach made people want to tell him everything, to give him the full truth, no matter how painful. And that was what Barton dreaded the most.

Over the past couple of weeks, so much had happened and things had gotten far out of control. Barton had not reacted well to any of it, and now he had to face the truth.

"We're going to continue dragging for her body this afternoon." Barton reached for a cookie on one of the trays set out for the reception after church. "The river's so high, and the current swift. It's like trying to find a needle in a haystack."

"Where exactly did she drown?" the Judge asked, although he already knew the answer.

"Right where the Buffalo enters into the Wapsi. You know the currents there. It's a dangerous section of the river, especially when it is this high." The sheriff shoved a cookie in his mouth and chewed nervously. Judge Swanson sipped his coffee and didn't respond.

Swallowing the cookie, Barton took a drink of his coffee and cleared his throat. "A lot of rocks and trees on the river bottom in that area. I figure the body's caught up on something."

"What happened, exactly?" Judge Swanson's eyes were direct and penetrating.

This was the question Barton didn't want to be asked. He could brush off most folks with an excuse about an investigation being underway, or that something was confidential, but not with Judge Swanson. He had to have the truth. If he didn't give it, he would find it eventually from someone else and come back, confronting Barton about it.

Judge Swanson believed in accountability, especially when it came to facts. After becoming sheriff, Barton quickly learned the Judge had an incredibly analytical mind. If something didn't add up, he would make you explain your logic. He could remember everything and would pinpoint the flaws in your thinking. It drove Barton crazy. There was no bullshitting Judge Swanson.

But this morning in the basement of the church, Sheriff Barton noticed something different in Judge Swanson's tone. It was the way the Judge asked the question. The fact he added the word 'exactly' made it all the more frustrating. It meant he probably already knew everything, didn't trust Barton, and wanted him to come clean.

Barton reasoned that the Judge probably knew he muddled up the Prairieburg investigation by dragging his heels—and that he was initially trying to pin it on Billy West. The Judge probably also knew he had missed critical evidence and not followed proper procedures with the theft out at Wilson's Farm.

He was certain Judge Swanson knew he should have had a flashlight that night behind West's house when he shot Dicky Moss. If he had only remembered his flashlight. He played the night over and over again in his mind—his actions and why he had forgotten his flashlight on his desk. In his years as sheriff, this had never happened before. He had been distracted by Margie Pitts. It was an uneasy distraction that made him not want to trust her. He thought something was missing in the paperwork she was filing, but he couldn't put his finger on it. He despised her constant smoking and her air of insubordination. But more than anything, he was bothered by the way she watched him as if she was tracking his every move.

Barton took a sip of his coffee and tried to block out Margie and his paranoia. Dicky's death was his fault, and he knew it. If only he had remembered his flashlight. Without his light, he put himself in a position where all he could do was fire his weapon. It was a hard lesson he would think about for the rest of his life.

And then there was Joe Matsell.

The Judge probably knew Matsell was behind all of this and would want to know what he was doing about it.

Barton looked up into Swanson's fatherly eyes and responded. "Well, I don't know everything for sure. But it sounds like Joe Matsell took a swing at Billy West with his paddle and accidently struck Sally Mayfield instead." Jim's voice cracked as the words came out. He was not sure if even he believed what he was saying. His response to the question had no effect on the Judge, and Barton was sure he was telling him something he already knew.

"Where's Joe Matsell?" Judge Swanson asked directly.

Barton did not like this question. The words stung. It was the question of questions because it cut to the truth.

Sheriff Barton took another sip of his coffee and paused for a moment, hoping the Judge would say something. He didn't want to answer this question because it illuminated his own incompetence. The Judge waited for an answer.

An awkward silence filled the room until Baron finally spoke. "That's a good question. I really don't know. Billy West claims that Matsell made for the riverbank about a quarter of a mile from Anamosa. But we don't know for sure."

"What do you mean, you don't know?" Judge Swanson had a hint of frustration in his voice.

"Well, I'm not sure I can trust Billy…" Jim coughed and turned his eyes away from the Judge.

"Jim, trust is something you have to earn for yourself. It comes with character." Judge Swanson, well over six feet in height, stepped forward and towered over Barton as he looked down at him.

The words hurt because Jim knew they were true. He couldn't trust Billy or other folks in the community because they didn't respect him. His own reputation had hindered the development of positive relationships in the town. And without relationships, he couldn't ever get close to them. He couldn't trust anyone, and in turn, they didn't trust him. They barely tolerated him. He felt hopeless. For a fleeting moment, he wished he never would have gone into law enforcement. Barton tried to say something, but words wouldn't come out.

"When you get on the slippery slope where you can't trust most of the members of this community, you're the problem," The Judge sipped his coffee slowly and kept his eyes trained on Barton. "You can trust Billy West. If he said it happened, you know it did."

Judge Swanson's words cut Barton to the core and set the tone for the rest of their conversation. Barton knew the Judge was aware of the flaws in the investigation and would keep picking and picking at him to expose them all.

"Was there evidence of any fresh tracks on the riverbank?" The Judge set his cup on the table.

"Yes. It looks like somebody did come up out of the water where Billy and Anna said they did…"

"And have you stopped by Joe's bar?"

"Yes."

"Well, what did you find?" Judge Swanson crossed his arms as he extended his line of questioning.

Barton paused. He felt as if he was stuck deep in mud. The more he moved, the faster he sank into the thickness. Finally he replied, "The bar is cleaned out and locked up. Looks like Joe Matsell skipped town."

"Have you put out a warrant for his arrest?" The Judge picked up his cup of coffee and took another drink.

"Well, I was getting to that, but I was waiting…" Barton sensed the thick mud, sucking him down, and felt tightness in his chest.

"Waiting?" Judge Swanson's expression transformed to anger, and he crossed his arms. "What the heck are you waiting for?" He raised his voice, and the sheriff looked down at his brown shoes. "You have a possible murderer, a dangerous man out there, and an exposed community. What are you doing to protect them? You need to see to it. Now."

Jim Barton had never heard Judge Swanson raise his voice before. It was painful. There was no question the Judge was disappointed in him. He wished this would all end, but he knew it wouldn't.

"Now, the shotgun that Dicky Moss used at the West

residence. Whose gun is it?" Judge Swanson asked, and Barton knew he was going to get into more details.

"It was Ronnie Wilson's shotgun. We have some solid evidence that the gun, as well as a pistol, was stolen from his farm," Barton answered, knowing full well the direction the questioning was going.

"When were they stolen?"

"Umm, I think it was last Tuesday," Barton replied and prepared his mind for the next question.

"When did Moss get out of the hospital?" The Judge sipped his coffee but kept his eyes focused on Barton.

"I'll check the records, but I think he was released on Wednesday, the day after the gun was stolen."

Judge Swanson moved in closer to the Sheriff, towering over him. "I'm not saying that Moss wasn't responsible, but there's no question he wasn't acting alone. Somebody stole those guns when he was in the hospital. You may not be able to prove it, but I'd wager it was Joe Matsell."

"But Billy…" Barton tried to reply.

"Sheriff Barton, stick to the facts. Billy West had nothing to do with any of this, and everyone knows it." Judge Swanson's words hurt Barton and wouldn't end. "If anything, you should be supporting him with whatever he and Miss Jacobs need. They're the victims in this. They've had one heck of a week."

Barton didn't respond. His shoulders hunched forward. His eyes were on the ground, and he couldn't raise them to meet Judge Swanson's. Barton felt alone in all of this. He had made mistakes. People were dead, and the community was looking to him for answers. They expected leadership. He didn't know if he had it in him to do the job.

Judge Swanson knew his rebuke had impacted Barton, so he lightened his tone. "You know, Jim, leading isn't easy. If it was, then everyone would do it. Sometimes I don't know if I'm leading or being chased." Judge Swanson smiled reassuringly and placed his hand on Barton's shoulder. "I believe in you, and I know you can do this. You've had a heck of a week, too. Now it's time for you to pick yourself up and move on." Judge Swanson didn't know if he believed his own words, but he knew he had to lift up the young sheriff. Barton nodded, but kept his eyes on the ground. "Stick to the facts, stay above the drama, and you'll get through this."

The Judge paused for a moment and cleared his throat. "Jim, try to reach out to folks in the community. There are a lot of good people in Anamosa. Many were born here, grew up here, live here, and will die here. Many folks believe in what this town is about. They're not the enemy. They're good people, trying to make a living and raise their families. It's your responsibility to serve them. You want their trust? You want their respect? It starts with straightforward communication, and it can start today."

Barton felt the tears well up in his eyes. He was hurting inside. Just a week ago, he killed a man. He had never thought that would happen, not in Anamosa. He had not prepared himself for it. The act disgusted him. He felt a thick wave of shame and wanted to cry.

Judge Swanson stood in front of him, and talked about

trust. It was hard for Barton to hear. The Judge was right, and he knew he needed to hear it. Barton needed someone to tell him, to point him in the right direction. No one had ever done that before.

"Now let's take care of this Matsell situation. Process the warrant and continue to sort through the facts. Ronnie Wilson should be out of the hospital by now. I know his father well. If you go out and talk to him first, you may get more information on what Matsell was up to."

Barton kept his eyes on the ground but nodded again. It was a solid lead, and he would start there.

"I've got some free time on my schedule on Wednesday. That'll give you a little time. Why don't you stop by that afternoon, and we can follow up on this situation." Judge Swanson had an amicable approach, but in reality, he was holding the sheriff to a tight timeline.

The organ played upstairs in the sanctuary, and both men felt it vibrate through the ceiling. Barton glanced at his watch. They had been talking for fifteen minutes, but it seemed like hours. Funny thing though, he felt better. A load had been taken off his shoulders. For the first time in a long time, he didn't feel alone. He felt he might even smile. He couldn't remember the last time that happened. Judge Swanson had that way about him. He somehow walked that line where he could be direct and could even chew you out, but in the end, somehow made you feel good about yourself. Somehow the Judge gave him hope.

"Sounds like services are getting under way. We probably should get going. My wife will have my hide if I miss church because I'm down here drinking coffee," Judge Swanson said with a warm smile.

Sheriff Barton wanted to shake his hand but couldn't find the courage. He was exhausted, but he also felt better. He felt a bond with the Judge. Something he never had before—a relationship. Maybe even the chance for some kind of friendship—not a close one, but possibly a developmental relationship. This was something he needed, something he yearned for.

Jim Barton was hurting inside. His wounds had not started to heal. He killed a man. He killed an unarmed man that was caught up in something he probably had no desire to be a part of. He killed a man that was already wounded, unable to communicate, and helpless. The guilt was as painful as if he had been the one wounded and was bleeding out. He played the event over in his mind again and thought about the flashlight that was left on his desk.

The whole event haunted him. There would be hard days ahead, and the pain would get worse before it would ever get better.

Years would pass, and his wound would eventually heal but would leave an ugly scar. The years would pass, years of service and understanding of his own redemption. Through it all, he would always remember this day with the Judge.

Judge Swanson reached out to shake Jim Barton's hand. Barton grabbed it and a smile spread on his face. Nothing more was said.

ꙮ

Andy leaned back in the pew in a subtle stretch and grinned. The church service was almost over. Pastor Jones often liked to end things on a high note. June Miller banged away on the organ while Ginny Ford and Laura Lee Meyer sang in a tug-of-war wrestling match. Andy looked over at the people next to him as they sang the last stanza of "Joyful, Joyful, We Adore Thee."

The words rang out from Andy and his family. "Hearts unfold like flowers before thee, hail thee as the sun above. Melt the clouds of sin and sadness; drive the dark of doubt away. Giver of immortal gladness, fill us with the light of day!"

This was one of his father's favorite hymns. For one, Andy's dad claimed the music was a masterpiece, the last artful strokes of a musical genius. It consisted of the last notes of the last melody of Beethoven's last symphony. Secondly, it was a joyful song. His dad always said it was a hard song to sing without smiling, and he was right.

Andy looked up at his mother and father, his Uncle Dave and his friend, Nancy, and Billy West and Anna Jacobs. All were singing. All were smiling. This was a magical moment, and he wondered if anyone noticed.

He captured this image in his mind. Three men who stood firm for what they believed, and standing next to them, the three women who loved them.

The hymn ended and so did the church service. John turned to Billy and Anna. "So what do you folks have planned today?" John knew it was their last full day together before Billy would be leaving in the morning.

"We're going to drive up to Independence to see my pop,

and then I've got to finish packing," Billy said as Anna wrapped her hands around Billy's arm and pulled herself close to him. She was already tearing up and couldn't say anything.

"How's your father doing?" Maggie asked, changing the subject.

"As well as can be expected. He has his demons. They've been chasing him for years. Now that they've caught up to him, he only has few options left. He's putting up a fight though, I'll give him that. He's sober, and that's a start." Billy forced a smile.

"No question he's a fighter, much like his son," John replied, and Maggie nodded. "It sure has been quite a summer. I still can't believe everything the two of you have been through. As horrible as it was, somehow there has to be something positive that will come from it all."

"Right now I'm not sure what it is. Only time will tell." Billy pulled Anna closer to his side.

"I overheard Sheriff Barton before church. From the sounds of it, Joe Matsell skipped town. If nothing else, maybe all of this exposed Big Joe Matsell for who he is and everything he has done. This town will be a better place without him." John confidently reassured Billy.

"I sure am glad we were all able to spend some time together," Maggie said to Anna, once again changing the subject to something lighter. "Those biscuits you made for the picnic were to die for. You still have to get me that recipe."

"Oh, they're easy to make. My mom's recipe. I'll write it down and stop by later this week. Maybe we could meet for coffee?" Anna said, surprised at her own invitation. She was exhausted. Even with the horrible events over the past few weeks, Billy leaving her was the most traumatic. Over the past month, everything had been leading up to this dreadful moment—his last day.

Anna didn't know how she was going to bear him leaving her again. But today, for the first time, she was able to see beyond it. She planned something for after he left. It was just coffee, but it felt good. Even if they were small steps, these plans would lead to their future together. *Four months*, Anna thought. Small steps. She could do this.

"Maybe we'll see you over Christmas when you get back." Maggie smiled and glanced at Billy.

"That would be great. I should be out of the army and home sometime before then," Billy said, and Anna glanced away, trying to return a smile.

"Well, we sure would like that. Wouldn't we, honey?" Maggie looked up to John.

"You kids need to get going. You've got things to do, and we don't want to hold you up." John stretched his hand out to Billy.

"Thank you, sir. It's been great seeing you, Maggie, and Andy. Thanks for all you've done for me. It was great spending time together." Billy shook John's hand.

"Billy, you be careful traveling back to Georgia," Maggie said to Billy in a motherly tone and then gave him a hug.

"He'll be fine, Maggie. Billy's a man. He can handle himself just fine," John said, correcting Maggie.

"Will you let me be a mom for a second? A little motherly

advice doesn't hurt anyone," Maggie replied to John in an exasperated tone, and then she turned to Billy. "You take care of yourself in your travels, and don't let any of those sergeants down at Fort Benning fill your head with any of their nonsense."

"Yes, ma'am." Billy grinned.

"Now you kids get going." John shook Billy's hand one more time.

"Thank you. Thanks for everything," Billy took Anna's hand and walked out of the church into the bright August sun.

XII

THE HOSPITAL SMELLED like a strange mixture of ammonia and antiseptics. It was a different odor, not quite like the military hospitals Billy was used to. The hospital was clean, and the staff was very helpful and polite, but something was missing. There was something deceptive to it, something less transparent. Billy thought it was almost too clean, if that was possible. It was as if the staff was attempting to cover up the hurt and misery living inside its walls.

Billy's heart hurt, but he forced a smile, reaching forward across the table to hold his father's hand. His pop looked tired, but he seemed much healthier than he had weeks ago when Billy had found him at Gus's Tavern.

Over the past weeks, Billy had visited his father on multiple occasions. Each time, he seemed a little better. This would be the last time they would see each other for a while, and they both knew it. Billy counted the months in his mind and how long it would be before he would be home. Four months. Then he would be back. They held hands in silence in an attempt to hold onto the moment, to slow down time.

Finally Butch broke the silence. "Been one hell of a summer." Billy nodded, unable to speak. Butch lowered his head in shame. "None of this would've happened if it weren't for me. Gus's Tavern, Joe Matsell, Dicky, Sally, and this whole mess. It's all my fault."

"No, Pop. It wasn't about you. It wasn't even about me, or Dicky, or even Sally. It was all about Joe. Some live in the dark, and when the light shines on them, they'll do whatever it takes to flee from it."

Butch knew his son was right but couldn't shake his guilt for everything that had happened. "Sure wish I could've been able to spend more time with you."

Butch's words settled on the table and reminded them both of how far he had fallen. Here in this hospital, fighting to remain sober, fighting for his own life, he was beyond being embarrassed and beyond shame. His pride had been stripped away long before he had been admitted to the hospital. Here he was unable to take care of himself. He had hit rock bottom and was trying to find his way out.

Billy tried to lift the conversation. "It's okay, Pop. I'll be home in a few months."

Butch leaned forward, and his face turned serious. "You'll never be back, Billy."

Billy disagreed, but Butch put up his hands. "This will never be your home." Butch cleared his throat and leaned forward in his chair. "In your heart, you may think of this as home, but it'll never be your home again." Billy shook his head in disagreement, but it had no effect on his father's words. Butch raised his voice. "In your heart you may call this home, but to those who live here, you're an outsider. In their eyes, you're from somewhere else."

Butch paused for a moment and let his words sink in. "In

your heart, this place holds those special moments remembered, and it's good that you have them. The memories, they're a part of what makes you, you. The strength and courage of the land, of the river that gives this land its character. It's on you now to take this character to the world. It's up to you now to leave your mark on the world. This is your chance to make a difference."

Butch coughed and cleared his throat. "This place is the home of your heart. It's a special place of memories of loved one's voices that can no longer be heard, of holidays and laughter, of ball games in the front yard, of barbeques in the summer, of first kisses and fast cars, of talks on the front porch, and of a boy's bedroom that's now a small dusty reminder of the man he has become."

Butch's eyes filled with tears. "You can always come back, but it'll never be your home again. You've outgrown it. The world's your home now, and there's so much out there that needs to be changed."

Billy cleared his throat and tried to speak up. "Pop, I've seen enough of this world to know that everything I'll ever need is right here."

Butch shook his head. "Everything you need may be right here, but not everything the world needs. This is your time. You can't let it slip away."

"But Pop, we can be…" Billy tried to disagree with his father.

"Time is what we make of it, Billy. And not all time is equal. There are periods in all of our lives where opportunities present themselves and define who we are. You're nearing one of these crossroads. We're the sum of our choices—choices that may only come around once in a lifetime. For better or worse, the sum of our choices. Remember that."

Billy didn't know what to say. He had heard these words before. His father had given him this same advice when he was a boy. There was a heavy silence at the table.

Butch grinned and turned the direction of the conversation. "Now what did that pretty young girl decide? Was your mom's old ring big enough for her?" Billy cracked a smile and nodded. The mere thought of Anna brightened up the darkest of moments. .

"Good. That's good. A man has to have a good woman at his side if he is going to amount to much in this world." As the words left his mouth, his mind drifted off to a happy time with his wife. There was a quiet stillness again as both men thought about a mother and a wife—the woman who had made them both who they were.

Butch reached across the table and held his son's hand. "You best be going, Son. You're burning daylight on this broken down old man."

"Pop, don't say that. Please don't say that. You've taught me more about being a man than anyone in this world." Billy glanced away and then turned his eyes back on his father and collected his thoughts. "Lord knows you've had your fill of it, but like you said, we can all change." Butch forced a smile through his tears and squeezed Billy's hand. He was unable to speak. "There are good days ahead of us, Pop. Days of laughter and sunshine for you, for me, for Anna, for our family."

Butch West forced a smile. That was just like his son, always the optimist. It was what made him special. He was always seeing the best in others, always able to see and challenge others to be better than they thought possible. It was a good trait to have, one he would need, one that would make a difference.

XIII

"I FEEL A lot better leaving the truck on your farm. Let your pa know I really appreciate him making room for it in the barn," Billy said to Anna with an air of sadness in his voice. In his mind, he was finalizing everything for his departure.

"You know it's not a problem for us." Anna came up behind Billy and wrapped her arms around him, laying her head on his shoulder.

The two snuggled in the back of Billy's truck out on the eastern edge of the cornfield of the Jacobs' farm. It was past ten o'clock in the evening. Instead of the farmhouse and Anna's family, they opted to spend their last evening alone in the solitude of the fields and stars above.

"I know, honey." Billy squeezed her hands, and for a moment appreciated her not seeing how hard this was on him. "It means a lot to me that you'll be there for my pop when he gets out of the hospital. Should be another month, but he'll be so surprised when you show up with his truck. And anyway, I feel better having it out here on the farm safe rather than in town."

"Can you believe Jim Barton stopped by today?" Anna asked, in an attempt to change the subject.

Billy rolled and faced Anna, her arms tightly around him. "I honestly couldn't believe it." Billy rested his chin on top of her head. "When he showed up on your front porch, that was quite a surprise. I figured I would be going back to his office for another round of questioning. Said it was just to check up on us, to see how we were doing. That was kind of odd. Never expected him to care." Billy gently ran his fingers through her hair as thoughts of all that transpired washed over him.

"He seemed so uncomfortable when we answered the door. Never expected him to go out on a limb for anyone, but I figured something had to give with all of this. Matsell and all his scheming. Eventually, cooler heads would prevail and folks would make sense of things. Light always finds darkness." Billy kissed the top of Anna's head and held her close at his side as the summer evening enveloped them.

A light breeze flowed over the corn. August. Crickets chirped in a soothing rhythm as the corn lightly swayed in the breeze with a light scratchy sound. A glow shone from the farm house a half mile across the field, beyond the rise in the corn where they were parked. It was all so peaceful and safe. Summer was taking its last stand, holding on a little longer before a crisp coolness in the air would blow in and the leaves would start to change.

Billy wanted it to always be this way. He wondered what lie ahead for them, what challenges they would face. He was certain he could take care of Anna. In the end, he always did. Billy smiled and thought about how everything worked out. He thought about how Barton finally came through. Somehow Billy knew he would.

Anna didn't respond. She shivered in the coolness of the late night and leaned into Billy. He pulled her closer and wrapped her in the warmth of his side. The day had gotten away from them. Church, Barton, the trip up to the hospital, and packing for Fort Benning.

Anna shuddered with a sense of desperation as time slipped away. It had been eight o'clock before Billy was done packing. Everything had gone so fast, and now it was getting late. He would be up early in the morning to catch the bus at seven. Anna hated buses. A sharp pain of stress plunged in her stomach. She couldn't bear to think about Billy leaving her in the morning.

Time, she thought. She wished she could stop it. It had gone too fast. The last seconds slipped through her fingers. In the morning, he would be gone.

Earlier in the evening when he had finished packing, Billy suggested they go for a ride—one last drive through town, through the park, and then back out to the farm. It had been good for them to get out and get away—away from his bags and uniforms, from the ugly reminders that told them he was leaving.

Now, the two of them sat in the back of the truck and held each other. This would be their last evening together. Neither of them spoke much. They didn't want to spoil the time they had left with words

Billy's mind wandered as he thought about their drive through town earlier that evening. Tragically, home pulled him closest when he was about to leave. One more drive down Main Street. One more drive through the park. He savored every corner, every tree. The town was thick with memories even though everything was smaller than he had remembered it to be when he was a boy. Even so, it was all the more dear to him. The memories wrapped their arms around Billy in a lasting embrace that wouldn't let go. He remembered riding his bicycle to the store and buying candy, fishing down at the dam, hiking in the park, ice skating on the backwaters of the river, going to the movies, getting ice cream at the Dairywhip. The memories came in waves, and he wanted to savor every one of them.

When they had driven north toward the prison, Billy recalled the warm days of summer before his mom was gone. His father had worked at the prison, and he and his mom would walk to the front steps to meet him at the end of the day. The stone lions—two magnificent statues—guarded the front entrance. As a boy, he would sit on them and imagine many adventures in a world where he lived amongst the beasts of the jungle. When Billy drove past the lions earlier that evening, they still stood on guard in front of the prison. They were unchanged by time or the world. His mother was gone and all of his boyhood memories seemed like a pleasant dream from so long ago.

At the end of their drive, they had stopped by his house one more time. Anna had waited out in the truck while Billy went in. The house he had grown up in seemed so small. He remembered the happy times, like a Christmas tree in the living room in front of the picture window and opening presents in the morning. He had remembered his mother, in her last moments in the bedroom at the back of the house. She had been so frail and sad, and his pop at her side, crying like he had never seen any man cry before.

Billy remembered when his mother had asked his father to wear his old Marine Corps uniform one more time. It had been such a horrible moment in Billy's life that he did not think it odd at the time, but now he wondered about their past together and why the uniform had been so important to her as she lay dying. Now it hung in the closet, collecting dust. The uniform was never worn again—a sad reminder of something in his parent's love that was gone forever.

So much had happened in that little home that was a part of who Billy had become. Not wanting to leave, he had slowly walked through each room and absorbed all the memories and all the love. Each room had defined so much of who he was.

Anna kissed Billy's neck, bringing him back to her and away from the memories of his childhood. "Which star is ours?"

Parked in the cornfield, Billy and Anna gazed up in the night sky. Billy studied the stars for a moment and then turned to Anna. "I want you to find it. Remember how I showed you?"

Anna tipped her head back and went along with him. "Let's see. I need to find the Big Dipper first. Is that it right there?"

"Yep, you've got it. Now where is our star in relation to it?" Billy's face was animated in the moonlight as he looked up at the stars.

"Okay, I think I take the edge of the cup, and go five spaces off in that direction." She couldn't quite remember and looked to Billy to see if she was right, but he just looked at her with a blank face, not indicating if she was right or wrong. He could be so frustrating sometimes. He challenged her, and she would prove to him that she could find it. "Some help you are," she said, looking up into his eyes.

They were wet with tears that Billy was trying to hold back. To keep herself from crying, she quickly focused her attention back on the sea of stars above them. "So back to the Dipper. If I go five hand lengths from the edge in that direction, I'll find it," she said confidently.

Anna outstretched her hand up to the sky and calculated the distance and direction to their star. Billy remained silent and watched her in the moonlight. She was so beautiful. For a few seconds, he could see a little girl flash in her expressions. He remembered that girl all those years ago as his mind raced back to that first dance where they'd met. He smiled and wondered how he had been so blessed to have the privilege to love this woman. And the true wonder of it all was that she loved him, too.

Billy thought about the stars that would have to align for them to find each other in this crazy universe. The probability they would grow up in the same town at the same time and that they would find each other was truly astronomical. It was all too hard for him to get his mind around. From the moment they met, they just were. It was as if they were always meant to be.

Billy smiled. It wasn't her outward beauty. It was something deeper. Her inward beauty. Her heart, her beautiful heart. A heart that radiated through her and manifested itself in her actions. It brought a spark to her eyes and an easy smile. But more than that, it was her selfless example, her care for others, and her compassion. She made him a better person, a better man. She rounded his sharp angles and made him more tolerant of others and even brought a sense of humility that Billy didn't know he had. Billy looked at the massive blanket of stars stretching out above them and was in awe at the wonder of their love.

"I found it! I found it!" Anna shouted triumphantly. "Look there. Just about five hand lengths from the cup on the dipper. There. The star is right there. Kind of dim, but it's there. Do you see it?"

Billy smiled. Her face shone in the moonlight. She looked like a little girl. He nodded, acknowledging that she successfully found it, but didn't say a word. He couldn't. He was too emotional to speak. If any words were to come, she would know immediately he was afraid. Afraid of the future and what would come. He didn't know for sure, but what he did know was all that mattered was right here, right now under the stars together—this moment to remember for an eternity.

"Our star, our North Star. No matter what happens. No matter where we are. We'll always have the North Star to remind us of our love, to guide us…" Anna's voice cracked as a wave of sadness overwhelmed her, but she would continue, she had to continue. "It's our true north. The world will keep spinning and spinning, but it will always be there. Changes will come. At times the sky will be full of patterns of stars that will keep moving. They won't make any sense, but this one, our star, will always be there."

Tears streamed down Anna's cheeks. Billy was leaving. They were engaged, and the future seemed bright, but something was lacking. He had something in him she couldn't quite touch. He wanted the world, and she couldn't give it to him. Four months and he would be home.

It all seemed too good to be true. Anna looked down at the ring on her finger and wondered if he would find the world he wanted. Would he be happy? Could she feed his heart with the world he needed? She looked up at the stars once again. She had to remember his words that night at Prairieburg. She had to remember what he had said.

"Right there, where it's right now. Holding strong, unmovable, it'll always be there for us. Our truth. Before the break of day in the very early morning, and in the deepest and darkest of nights, it will always be there for us. It's our true north. Our love. Always there, always guiding us, no matter what this world brings…" Anna broke down and sobbed. She had remembered his words from that night at Prairieburg. She had done it. Billy was leaving, but she would remember his words.

"I love you, Anna. You're my Anna Angel," Billy pulled her close and softly kissed her lips. Nothing more was said as they held each other and gazed at the endless waves of stars above.

Part Three

Samuel

Present

THE DOOR SWUNG open and there stood Sheriff Barton. He motioned for Andy to come in and then retreated back into his office. Andy had not seen him in decades, but he could tell over the years, the sheriff had lost considerable weight. When Andy was a boy, Jim Barton seemed so large and massive. All these years later, he looked like any average American. He stood at six feet, just an inch taller than Andy. The sheriff had greyed significantly, and his shoulders slumped, but all in all, he looked good. Andy figured he must have been in his mid to late sixties.

"Mr. Crawford, I'm truly sorry about your father." Sheriff Barton's hand was outstretched, and Andy gripped it. Despite his age, Barton had a firm handshake.

Andy looked into his eyes. They were tired. For over forty years, Barton had served the community as sheriff. This was nothing short of a lifelong, honorable commitment, overseeing and protecting a community, watching families develop, grow, and eventually break apart as the children moved on to start their own families. Sheriff Barton was there, ready during the good times, and fully involved in the times of trial.

Watching over the living and dying of the members of this community had its effect. Yes, Sheriff Barton's eyes were tired, but there was something more—a sense of sadness, too. He had grown close to so many people and had been there for them when they had needed him.

Over the past decade, Andy's father had kind words to say about Sheriff Barton. Early on in his career, the sheriff didn't get along with anyone, and Andy remembered that his father had sharp words with him on more than one occasion. But based on his father's more recent feedback, Sheriff Barton had overcome personal challenges and changed.

"I appreciate that, sir. And please, please call me Andy," he replied as he sat down in the chair in front of the sheriff's desk.

"Andy, I want you to know how hard it is to believe that your father's gone." Sheriff Barton sat down behind his desk.

Andy didn't respond. Hearing those words were difficult for him. He still hadn't come to grips with his loss. Sheriff Barton realized he had struck a chord with him and quickly reacted. "I'm sorry, I didn't mean to…"

"It's okay. Really, it's all right. I'm just…I'm trying to believe it myself." Andy kept his eyes lowered but lifted his hand to the sheriff in response.

"Are you up to talking about this?" the sheriff asked in a compassionate tone.

"I am. I just arrived in town, and I know you had some things you wanted to tell me. I thought I'd stop here first," Andy said, preparing himself for what the sheriff had to tell him.

"Are you sure? Because if you'd like to wait a day or two, we can do that," Sheriff Barton offered. Andy recognized a warm kindness in his eyes.

"No. No need. It helps for me to start with the truth about what happened. I want to know everything before I coordinate funeral arrangements." Andy's voice cracked, and he gripped the arms on the chair as he started to come to terms with his loss.

"Okay. Okay, if you're up to this, I'd like to share some things." Sheriff Barton cleared his throat and looked down at a folder on his desk. Andy glanced up and realized that the sheriff was emotional as well.

"Before we get started, would you like a cup of coffee?" Sheriff Barton asked.

"You know, a fresh cup of coffee would really be great," Andy said, nodding.

With that, Jim Barton went over to his office door and peered out toward Margie Wilson's desk. "Margie, could you put on a fresh pot of coffee for Mr. Crawford and me?"

Andy could hear Margie's squeaky voice. He couldn't make out everything she said but understood her say something about her husband, Ronald, coming to get her for lunch. Andy waited as the two chatted for a minute, and then the sheriff returned to his desk. Andy could tell he was frustrated with his secretary.

"She's putting a fresh pot on." The sheriff sighed as he took his seat. "It'll probably be about fifteen minutes." Andy sensed a resigned annoyance in his voice, but Sheriff Barton regained his composure and then blurted out, "This really is the end of an era."

Andy wasn't sure how to respond and just looked at him.

"Your father and all. The end of an era. Dave and now John. And Maggie and Nancy, too. Just hard to believe. It's the end of an era in this town." Sherriff Barton cleared his throat as his face turned red with emotion. "There just aren't men like them. They only come around maybe once in a lifetime, you know?"

Andy just nodded. He was getting choked up, and it was difficult for him to talk.

The sheriff knew this was hard for both of them and tried to change the subject. "You know, your father and I didn't get along when I first started as sheriff. In fact, I would say he probably hated my guts." Sheriff Barton chuckled and temporarily broke the somber mood. Andy nodded and forced a smile. "You probably don't remember. I would guess you were ten or maybe closer to twelve at the time. But one summer, we had some real trouble. I was new at the job, immature, and never faced anything like it before. Well, I made my share of mistakes. Mistakes I'll regret for the rest of my life, but afterward, when the dust settled, your dad came by to see me."

Andy knew Sheriff Barton was talking about Billy West, Dicky Moss, Joe Matsell and everything that had happened during the summer in 1966, but he never knew his father had come by to talk to him.

"That summer I killed a man," Sheriff Barton said. The words still pained him, and he took a moment. "It was, and will most likely always be, the most traumatic event of my life. I never thought I'd have to deal with something like that. And afterward, it was nothing I would have ever expected. I felt so alone, so lost. I sincerely hope no person ever has to go through what I went through. I was completely torn up inside and desperate for some kind of acceptance."

Sheriff Barton coughed and cleared his throat. "Probably the lowest point in my life, and it all came to a head one day." He looked over at Andy for a brief moment then looked away. "I woke up one morning feeling so empty. I couldn't go on. That morning, I had decided that if nothing changed by the end of the day, I was going to take my own life. With that decision made, I felt at peace. Not just peace, I felt joy. I had finally found the answer to stop my pain and was looking forward to ending it that day."

Barton leaned forward with a serious, contemplative expression. "I remember it as if it was yesterday. I was sitting here at my desk, staring at the clock as the seconds ticked off. The hour hand got closer to four o'clock in the afternoon. The clock ticked as if it was in my chest, counting down. I wanted to push time forward and get on with it. I didn't want to wait."

Sheriff Barton paused a moment, glancing off to the side. He had deep sadness in his tone and a brokenness in his eyes. "But I did. I had some strange sense of obligation to myself and the deadline I had given myself. Looking back, it didn't make sense." He shook his head and stared blankly as if he was back there in 1966 and didn't want to stay. "Anyway, when the hour hand reached four I was going to take this revolver from my holster and end it all." Sheriff Barton took a deep breath and let it out slowly.

Andy had no idea what to say. He had not expected anything like this when he walked in the sheriff's office.

Sheriff Barton exhaled again and gripped the arms of his chair. "As God is my witness—at no less than one minute before four, your father walked into this office. My loaded revolver rested on this desk in front of me." He shook his head in disbelief. "I still can't believe someone came for me. And of all the people, the one I never expected, the one I never thought would even care, was your father." Sheriff Barton had tears in his eyes and struggled to speak.

Andy cleared his throat and tried to say something but was at a loss for words.

Sherriff Barton spoke in an even, direct tone. "Somehow he knew I was hurting, and he talked me out of it. After that afternoon, we met just about every day for a while. Step by step, he let me open up and share the pain. And as time went on, we met every week and then about once a month. We'd meet at Buddy's Café for coffee. Sometimes your Uncle Dave would join us, sometimes he wouldn't. As I remember, he was courting your Aunt Nancy at the time."

Barton smiled at the memory. "Anyway, I'd like to think we'd become friends. It wasn't like we were buddies. It was more than that. We shared a bond. He understood what I was feeling, what I was going through. I never expected it, but I wouldn't be here today if it hadn't been for your father. To put it simply, he cared. He cared for me when no one else did."

"I never knew he did that," Andy replied, and an awkward silence filled the room. Andy could hear the clock ticking on the wall, and it now made him feel uncomfortable. He immediately changed the subject. "So whatever happened to Joe Matsell?"

Sheriff Barton smiled. He realized Andy did remember that summer back in 1966. "Ah, Big Joe Matsell. Now that's an interesting and twisted story." Leaning back in his chair, the sheriff rubbed his chin, "After the death of Sally Mayfield, Joe locked up his bar and skipped town. In fact, he never came back. About three years later, I got a call from a sheriff down in southern Missouri. Apparently late one night, Joe got drunk and decided to wrap his car around an oak tree. Killed himself and some girl he was seeing. Just a shame. Wherever that man went, he left a path of destruction in his wake. Eventually it caught up with him. It always catches up in the end," Sheriff Barton said in a somber tone.

"Anyway, enough old history. Joe Matsell isn't worth anyone's time." The sheriff raised his voice and pushed the conversation in a new direction. "Let me tell you about yesterday."

"Do you have a notepad or something I can write on?" Andy rubbed his eyes. "In my state right now, I don't know what I'll be able to retain unless I write it down."

Sheriff Barton reached into his drawer and pulled out a spiral notepad and a pen, then slid them across the desk to Andy.

"So yesterday, I'm out on my patrol, and I decided to drive through Riverside Cemetery. As I'm driving, I saw something lying in the grass, up on the hillside above the river. Didn't make any sense, so I dismounted from my patrol car to investigate. Walking up, I immediately recognized your father." Jim Barton paused for a moment with a somber expression. "He was curled up on Maggie's grave. He looked peaceful, like he was sound asleep. But he was gone."

Andy nodded and diligently wrote down what Barton said. Tears streamed down Andy's cheeks, and he couldn't look up. It was easier if he focused his attention on his writing.

"But that's not all. There was a red rose on your mom's headstone. I looked around the cemetery. There was more. Over on your Uncle Dave's stone, there were two empty beer cans. From the looks of it, he drank one and poured the other over his brother's grave." Andy held the pen in one spot, struggling to write but unable to look up.

"Then I looked down the hill and saw something blowing in the breeze. I walked down. There were papers everywhere. I gathered them up and brought them back to the office. Not sure what to make of it. It all seems kind of random. From what I gather, it's information on seven or eight different families. Looks like one's from West Virginia, one's from Texas, another from North Dakota, Alabama, and Arizona, and another from Vermont."

Barton had a puzzled look. "All kinds of information about graduations and marriages, and children being born. One of the families runs a farm, another owns a car dealership, and another has their own law practice. One of the men in the families is the mayor of his town, another is in jail. Two families are black, and four are white. And one, I think, is Hispanic. One of the kids graduated from Stanford, another from Michigan, and another from West Point. There's information dating back to at least the 1970s. I tried to make heads or tails of it all, but quite honestly, it doesn't make any sense."

"Are you sure this has something to do with my dad?" Andy asked with a quizzical expression.

Sheriff Barton nodded. "After we moved your dad up to the hospital, I immediately called the care center across town where your father was living. They were absolutely frantic. They said his pneumonia over the past twenty four hours had taken a serious turn for the worse. They were preparing to evacuate him to the hospital when he disappeared. The staff had been searching for him all morning—seems he just walked off the premises."

Andy was dumbfounded. When he had spoken with his father for the last time he knew he was sick with a cold, but Andy didn't know it had become such a dire situation.

"There's no question he planned this, but it doesn't add up. From what I gather, he stopped by the gas station and picked up a six pack of beer. Then he stopped by the flower shop to buy roses."

Sheriff Barton looked puzzled. "Hard to believe he did this in the condition he was in, but that's not all. Based on the report from the care center, he had been on one of their residential computers, going to all kinds of websites and pulling up information on these families. He must have printed out at least fifty pages over the past couple of weeks. The folks at the care center thought it was dementia. Several times, they tried to convince him to give up all of the papers he was collecting, but he had made such a fuss they had figured it was best they let him keep them."

Sheriff Barton opened the folder on his desk. "Here are the documents. From what I gathered, there are at least six, maybe eight families in here. Names are James, Murphy, Leonard, Thacker, Gomez, Andrews, and Brown. There might even be more. I don't know for sure. There's contact information in there for some of them, but I'm not sure if any of it makes sense. The folks at the care center thought his senility was the onset of Alzheimer's. None of this probably means anything."

Andy reached out and pulled the folder toward him. "Thanks, Sheriff. I know this hasn't been easy for anyone. Not for you nor for the folks at the care center."

Andy knew his father. He had talked to him almost every day. He knew that physically, his health had been slipping. His father may have been suffering from the onset of pneumonia and his body may have been failing him, but Andy knew his father's mind had still been sharp. Andy didn't believe in their assessment that he was suffering from Alzheimer's. It really didn't matter, but Andy was curious. He would look into the information the sheriff provided.

Standing up, Sheriff Barton walked over to the wall where a number of plaques, certificates and pictures were on display. The sheriff lifted one of the frames from the wall and walked back to his desk and sat down. "Here." He handed it to Andy.

Andy looked down at the frame and started reading. He paused and looked up at the sheriff. "I've never seen this before."

"I know. Most folks haven't. When the courthouse was remodeled, I found it back in one of the closets. They didn't think they would have a need for it and let me have it. I've kept it posted in my office for years. It serves as a reminder, you know?"

Andy nodded and didn't answer with words.

"You remember that day in November?" Sheriff Barton asked.

"I do," Andy responded, as tears rolled down his cheeks.

November, 1967

I

"BOTH HANDS ON the wheel, Andy," John Crawford said, correcting his son in the driver's seat. "You keep drifting toward the shoulder and jerking the car back to the center. You've got to feel the road," John instructed his fourteen year old son as the car swerved back to the right side of the highway. Andy briefly glanced at his father and noticed he was pale. He also noticed his father's hands were firmly planted on the dash board. Andy found it funny and wanted to laugh as his father held on for his own dear life next to him in the passenger seat.

"I'm doing my best, Dad," Andy replied, suppressing the smirk forming on his face. He was frustrated with his father's continual corrections. Andy knew his father was shaken by his driving, but Andy was tired of his overbearing directions. They had been driving together every weekend for the past three months, and he still couldn't get a good "feel" for the road.

"I want you to look out further beyond the front of the car. Look out to the horizon of the road. I know it's hilly here, but try to look out a few hundred yards. By doing this you'll start to rely on what you feel in the road, not necessarily what you see," John explained.

The two continued their drive north on the two lane highway out of town. Andy struggled as they occasionally drifted to the center of the highway, or to the shoulder, and then swerved back between the lines.

John Crawford had broken out in a sweat, and he honestly wondered if they would make it home alive. He also wondered if his son would ever figure this out. It scared the hell out of him.

John felt helpless in the passenger seat and would quite often reach for the steering wheel to correct the direction the car was moving. The thing that scared him the most was that they could actually die out here on the road. One wrong turn, the slightest mistake, and it would all be over for them.

John was even more apprehensive because of the increased traffic on the normally quiet road. It was a beautiful fall day in November, and the farmers were busy bringing in their crops. In addition to the fall harvest, pheasant hunting season had opened and hunters from across the state were pouring into the countryside.

"Slow down, Andy." John had a nervous edge to his voice as he corrected Andy.

It was the fall of 1967. Andy had recently turned fourteen and had finally gotten his driver's permit. This was a new phase in his life, and he was struggling. His father knew Andy was no longer a little boy, but despite Andy's own feelings about it, he wasn't a man either.

Andy openly questioned everything and rebelled against his parents. It upset his mother, but John knew it was a natural progression to manhood. John was confident Andy would be fine. He had his mother's heart. Despite all the changes going on in his body, he was obedient and would make it through adolescence. John smiled. The struggle for manhood was going on right there in the car, and John remembered how he had rebelled against his own parents years ago.

After five miles of fatherly correction and a son's increasingly frustrated reactions, they were almost ready to turn around. John got the strange sense someone was following them and looked over his shoulder to find his instincts were correct. A look of anger flashed across his face. "How fast are you going?" He immediately attacked his son in an accusatory tone.

"I'm only going fifty. I haven't gone any faster than that the whole time," Andy defensively explained.

"Couldn't have been. Sheriff Barton just pulled up right behind you and is flashing his lights." John's face was pinched with anger. He glared at his son with disbelief.

Andy didn't believe him and immediately looked in his rearview mirror only to see his father's words were true. Barton was right behind him.

A look of panic instantly overwhelmed Andy, and his father recognized his son didn't know what to do next. "You need to slow down and carefully pull off onto the shoulder and stop the car." Andy obeyed his father and guided the car to a stop on the side of the road. A look of pure fear now spread across Andy's face. "Just stay calm and roll down the window. He's walking toward your side of the car now," John said as his son did as he was told and then slumped down in his seat. His worst fears were becoming a reality.

Stepping up to the driver's side of the car, Sheriff Barton leaned down and looked into the window. "John, would you mind coming back to my car for a moment." His tone was cold and ominous. Andy tried to imagine what he had done wrong and started to think about serving time in prison. His mind raced. He had homework due the next day and wondered how he would get it turned in if he was locked away in a cell.

John got out of the car and walked back to the police car with Sheriff Barton. He immediately noticed there were several other men sitting in the car. The Sheriff handed John a document and gave him a chance to read it.

John's face grew pale. He looked back up at the Sheriff but couldn't find any words.

"I've been driving around for over an hour trying to figure how to do this. You see, these men needed directions and stopped by the office. I've never done this before and I…I just started driving…driving around town, trying to find courage. When I saw your car, I figured it was more than just..." Sheriff Barton paused for a moment. "Would…would you mind…would you mind coming with me?"

John's head started to spin. He felt dizzy, and then he looked up into Sheriff Barton's eyes and realized the man needed his help. "I will," John said, and Sheriff Barton reached out and shook his hand.

Andy watched his father and the sheriff in his rearview mirror. He couldn't hear what they were saying but could only imagine. He watched as his father shook the sheriff's hand. He couldn't believe it. His father actually agreed with the sheriff, and now it looked like he was coming back to the car to get him. Andy started to gather all of his things—his wallet, his coat. Suddenly the thought came to him that he wished he had brought a deck of cards or a book. He figured he would need something to pass the time in jail.

John stepped up to the driver's side and directed Andy to get in the passenger seat. "What? What did I do wrong this time?" Andy asked in a dejected voice.

"Nothing. You didn't do anything. I need to drive now," John said as he slid into the driver's seat. Andy noticed his father's face was flushed, and he really didn't know if he was angry or sad. He just seemed upset.

Andy immediately forgot his thoughts about jail as they were replaced with anger at his father. "What was that all about back there? Where are we going?" Andy asked, but his father didn't respond. This frustrated Andy even more. His father never told him anything. He always felt left out and excluded from the conversations between his mother and father. Andy wanted to tell him he was no longer a little boy; that he was a man and was up to whatever challenges the world had in store for him.

His father started the car and wouldn't say another word the entire drive. Andy crossed his arms and proceeded to sulk as his father turned onto the highway and followed the sheriff's car north.

ﻮ

The two cars turned right onto a farm lane and continued for about a half mile until they arrived at a white farmhouse with a large wraparound front porch.

"What are we doing here?" Andy asked. He was puzzled. He had never been at this farm before.

But his father was already out of the car. He didn't respond to his son's question. Andy again felt dejected and continued to sulk in the passenger seat of the car. He was growing more and more angry at his father for treating him like a little boy. Andy quickly began to wonder what was going on as he watched his father, Sheriff Barton, and two men in military uniforms walk up toward the house.

Andy didn't know what was going on but realized it wasn't good. Sheriff Barton stopped about halfway to the house, and his father made it to the base of the front steps where he stopped. The two men in the military uniforms continued forward and stopped at the front door where they paused for a moment and then knocked.

John could not find the courage to take another step. His feet simply froze to the ground, and he couldn't move. He started to get dizzy again. He heard the sound of a baby crying from inside the home. To gain his composure, he focused on the officer and the army chaplain in front of him as they knocked on the door. He heard the footsteps of someone coming to the door, and he didn't know if he would have the courage to go on.

Anna saw the silhouette of a man in a uniform in the window by the door. Her heart jumped with a moment of strange excitement. That image. She had seen it before when Billy came home to her.

But it didn't make sense this time.

She didn't want to believe her eyes, but she felt an incredible surge of wonder. Could he be home again?

With her baby in her arms, she excitedly opened the door.

She saw the men in uniform. An immediate flash from excitement to confusion to disbelief came over her eyes. She looked beyond them and saw John Crawford, and further beyond him, Sheriff Barton.

In less than a second, John watched the flood of emotion in her eyes go from hopeful joy to disbelief, to realization, to anger, and then to pain.

"Mrs. West, it is with my deepest regret that…" The army officer attempted to console her with his well-rehearsed script.

"No! No! No! Not my Billy! No! No! This isn't happening! Not Billy…they can't take my…no, not my Billy!" Anna let out a horrible, pain filled cry.

For the rest of his life, Andy would never forget that terrible sound. Andy immediately felt paralyzed. He couldn't move from the car—he didn't want to move. Sitting in the passenger seat, he felt protected from the world. He couldn't get out of the car to face the challenges of the world. All he could do was watch with a painful realization of what had happened.

Anna crumpled up in the door way. She fell to her knees with her baby in arms and screamed at the men.

John ran forward and wrapped his arms around her.

"Get out! Go away from here! John, make them go away! Make them go!" Anna sobbed hysterically. John held her with everything he had. He tried to comfort her. "Get out, you bastards! All of you! Get off of my farm! Get off! Make them go away!" Anna pounded her fists on John's chest, and she even tried to kick the officer standing at the door. "Not my Billy! You can't have him! You can't have my Billy! No! No…."

Anna suddenly drifted off and fainted in John's arms. From the car, Andy watched his father and how he struggled to hold her and her baby in his arms. Anna's mother had heard the screams and quickly ran in from her garden. Seeing that Anna was unconscious, Sarah Jacobs took the crying baby from her arms and tried to console him. John picked up Anna and carried her into the front sitting room.

"Jim, give Doc Murphy a call. Tell him we need him out here right away," John shouted over his shoulder at Barton while searching the sitting room for a place to lay Anna.

"Please put her down on the couch." Sarah cradled the baby close to her body, trying to maintain her composure.

Anna abruptly regained consciousness as John lowered her onto the couch. "No! Not my Billy! You! You bastard! You bastards can't have him! You can't have him! You can't have my Billy!"

Anna's mother came to her side and held her in her arms. "Oh, Anna…oh Anna…I'm so… oh Anna…" Sarah rubbed Anna's back. "There, sweet girl…there…there…"

"No! No! Not Billy! Mama…Mama, they can't have him. Mama, tell them…please tell them…they can't have my Billy…they can't take my Billy away…" Anna's voice tapered off as she faded into unconsciousness again. Sarah gently rocked her daughter in her arms.

John Crawford looked around the sitting room. He felt

useless and empty. He could not do anything. Nothing he could say would bring comfort to her.

"Where's my baby? Where's Sammy? Where's our boy, Sammy?" Anna suddenly awoke and asked in a frantic, panicked voice.

"He's fine, dear. He's just fine." Sarah continued to console Anna as she drifted off again. "Shh, sweet girl, Shh…shh…there, sweet girl…there…" Anna's mother held her close as she too silently wept.

John felt so helpless. He didn't know what to do next. He watched Sarah Jacobs gently rock Anna on the couch. In the background, the baby cried.

Billy West was gone.

He couldn't bring himself to think about it. It was all too much to accept. He was dizzy with the thought of it all and steadied himself as he stepped out onto the front porch.

Andy was still in the car. He watched his father as he stood on the front porch and smoked a cigarette. The two men in uniforms said something to him, but Andy couldn't hear them. The uniformed men went into the house, and Sheriff Barton moved back to his police car. Andy watched as his father sat down on the steps and buried his face into his hands. His father was crying.

II

BILLY WEST DIED on November 11th, 1967. Veteran's Day.

It took several weeks for his body to be transported back to eastern Iowa for the funeral, and now that day had arrived. It was a cold rainy day in early December. Andy would always remember it. Not for what was said, or for even who was there. He would remember it for the cold empty faces, the gray sky, everyone dressed in black, and the steady freezing rain.

Andy sat in a pew with his mother and father, his Uncle Dave, and Dave's new bride, Nancy. They sat three rows behind Butch and his daughter-in-law, Anna West.

Butch West looked horrible. He seemed to have aged twenty years over the past couple of weeks. Andy heard his parents talking about him that morning. Butch had a steady job working as a janitor at the courthouse. They were hopeful he would somehow remain sober through all of this, but they didn't know how any man could. Butch looked withered and worn out, as if the world had taken everything from him. As Andy thought about it, it had.

Andy looked down the pew toward his father, his mother, his Uncle Dave and Aunt Nancy. His mind went back to the last day he saw Billy, sitting right here, in the same row of pews with them. He remembered all of them singing "Joyful, Joyful, We Adore Thee." The image was etched in his mind.

Billy's casket lay at the front of the church on the altar with an American flag draped over it. Massive bouquets of flowers surrounded the coffin, and a large lone framed portrait of Billy in his military uniform stood on display to the right of him.

Andy sat numb in disbelief. He looked at the flowers, the picture, and then his eyes settled on the casket. This funeral was for Billy West. The great Billy West was somewhere inside that box on the altar. He wondered how it had all come to this. He wondered how it could be possible. Not Billy West. Not the hero of his childhood dreams. He found it so hard to get his mind around. Billy West not in this world was too hard to accept; it was all too permanent.

Billy West was gone.

Andy had never been confronted with death, and he couldn't accept that Billy was gone. A terrible wave of sadness overwhelmed him all at once, and he thought he was going to cry.

Andy tried to hold in his tears as he reached over and held his father's hand. John Crawford's eyes moved with the procession as he watched people slowly fill the church. Josh Sanders was in the second row right behind Butch and Anna.

John watched Josh as he came around and gave Anna a hug and then sat back down. He had recently read about Josh in the newspapers. Josh would finish school at the University of Iowa that spring and immediately start pitching for the Pittsburgh Pirates. John was happy for him, and he knew Billy would be too. Josh had made it to the majors.

Josh rested his hand on Anna's shoulder from behind. She

reached up with her hand and held his for several minutes. John observed as Josh leaned forward and whispered something to her. Anna slowly let go of his hand, and Josh leaned back in the pew.

Anna sat lifeless and empty.

John and Maggie had brought dinner out to their farm several times over the past couple of days, but they never saw her. She remained upstairs in her room, unable to face any visitors, unable to see anyone that reminded her of Billy. This was the first time John had seen her since that day in mid-November. She seemed cold and empty, as if a large part of her was gone, as if she had died with Billy. There was simply nothing there—she didn't have any expressions left. Her emotions had been completely drained out from her.

John and Maggie worried for her. She was young. She had so much life ahead of her. They knew some wounds might never heal. It could take years, but the scars would always be there.

The United Methodist Church was full. People stood in the back of the church. John Crawford knew most of these folks never really knew Billy. They knew his name, and the things he had achieved when he lived in this town, but they didn't really know who he was. The hypocrisy frustrated him. Today they would say wonderful things about Billy, things they had never said when he was alive.

Folks came out in droves for funerals, but they never had the time of day for a person when they were alive. John thought about the irony of it all. The previous summer he remembered many of the people in the church speaking negatively about Billy.

Some of them even wanted him put in jail. It didn't really matter now. None of it mattered. John wondered what did matter. He looked at Maggie. He knew he would always love her. Always. He reached down and held her hand. She was all that mattered in his life. It was the horrible times like this that made it all so clear. The pain was so real. They would need each other on this day.

ཨ

"Samuel William West was a man who could do anything he set his mind to. I mean that. Anything." Pastor Jones started the memorial ceremony.

Anna West sat in the front pew, unable to focus on the pastor's words. She didn't want to. She didn't care what he said. None of it mattered to her. Other than the pain, she was completely empty inside. She knew folks would say kind things today. That was all well and good, but it didn't matter. She stopped living. Billy was gone. So much of him was a part of her—now she had nothing left.

Over the past couple weeks, she had cried so much she didn't know how to live without tears. Not a minute went by that she hadn't thought about ending her own life. Even sitting in the pew, she thought about it. Ending the pain. Her eyes darted briefly to his portrait, but she turned away when she caught a glimpse of the casket. The pain was too much. She would do whatever it took to hold Billy in her arms again. And she was certain she could do it. Just thinking about it made her feel strangely better—end her own life to look into Billy's eyes one more time and feel his love. It was the only solution that would stop the pain.

Anna looked down where she held little Sammy in her arms. Samuel William West, Junior. He was perfect. Already six months old, she could see so much of Billy in him. His eyes, his confident smile, and the expressions on his face were mirror images of his father. He was all she had now. She would do whatever was necessary to protect him. She tucked his head against her chest and kissed him. He was the only thing holding her back from taking her own life.

Anna lifted her eyes up as Pastor Jones spoke. "The trophies, the high school records…he's at the top of so many lists in this community. It's hard to keep track of everything he did in such a short lifetime. But he believed in so much more. Few understood him."

The pastor was right. Nobody understood Billy. He was so gifted, so confident, and so committed to truth…to his country. It was his commitment to a much greater purpose, to something far nobler than most of the people in the church understood. A devotion that was so complete that it left its scars, and in the end, it took everything.

Anna didn't want to listen to that pastor's words. To try to put words to Billy's life was impossible, and they would certainly fall short of the truth. She wanted to cling to the memories. That was all she had now. Little Sammy and memories of Billy.

Since Billy's death, she had locked herself up away from the world. Coming to the memorial was the first time she had left the farm. Most days, she wouldn't leave her room. She had spent her time in her mind, trying to remember everything. Every moment, every detail, everything he ever said to her, how he made her feel, everything he did, all of it. She had to remember all of it. It was all she had left of him. It was the only way she could keep loving him. She had to honor him by living and reliving their love in her memories.

Anna looked down at her purse. In it were two letters from Billy that had arrived with his personal effects. She didn't have the courage to open them and wondered if she ever would.

She clutched the letters in her hand and held them. She let her mind drift into her memories, to the security of her mind, to the safety of Billy's arms. She floated to an earlier time. She felt herself being lifted up from the memorial service, away from the church, and to her memories when they were together far away from all these people who never knew him.

October, 1966

III

IT WAS MID-OCTOBER in 1966, and the leaves were changing. Anna had ridden twelve hours on a bus from Cedar Rapids, Iowa to Columbus, Georgia. Although scenic, it didn't matter to her. During the trip she couldn't focus—a desperate panic distracted her from everything. Pulling into the bus stop, Anna looked out the window. Billy stood tall in his uniform, waiting for her. He looked so handsome and confident. He finished his cigarette and flicked it to the ground. He seemed so relaxed. She wondered how he could be so calm when their world was about to change forever. *He didn't know.*

He didn't know she had a baby growing inside her. His baby.

As Anna sat waiting to get off the bus, she wrung her hands. Her head spun and her mouth went dry. Her chest tightened. She gasped to get more air and thought she would faint. Her mind raced with so many thoughts. She was going to have a baby. She had so many questions about their future, and she had no idea where to start. She needed Billy. She needed to be with him. She needed him to tell her they were going to be all right. She needed him to tell her what they were going to do.

She ran from the bus and threw herself into Billy's arms. Before he had the chance to catch her, she blurted out the news of her pregnancy.

"Pregnant?" Billy said in surprise, and then took Anna into his arms and swung her around. "Honey, that's wonderful. It's absolutely wonderful." Anna wept as Billy held her. Billy lifted her off the ground in his arms and kissed the tears off her cheeks. "Anna Angel, why are you crying, darling? We're going to be fine. Everything's going to be fine."

They held each other for several minutes. A soft drizzle rained on them while soldiers exited a bus and scurried around them with their duffle bags. Neither Billy nor Anna took notice of them.

"Billy, what are we going to do?" Anna whispered softly. Billy heard the panic in her voice and saw the fear in her eyes.

He held her face in his hands. "We'll figure it out, darling." He kissed her lips, reassuring her everything would be all right. "We've got the weekend to talk about it and figure everything out."

These were not the words Anna wanted to hear. After twelve hours on a bus, she was impatient. She was more than impatient, she was pregnant and afraid. She was desperate and needed answers. She needed comfort. She needed to know how everything was going to be all right. She needed more, and she expected Billy to know the right thing to do right then and there.

Anna looked up at Billy with terror in her eyes. She wondered how her mother and father would react. How others in the community would look at her. She could not bear to face the judgment in their eyes. Anna buried her head in his chest and sobbed uncontrollably. She felt a hollow sense of disappointment in Billy. She had expected more.

Billy pulled her tight into his arms and gently swayed back and forth as the rain came down harder. “Now, now, Anna Angel. Now, now…”

Billy kissed the top of her head and then whispered in her ear, “I'll make this right. I'll make everything right.”

ℬℭ

“Let’s just go down to the courthouse and get married.” Billy lit a cigarette and leaned forward in his chair at the restaurant.

“Married? In a courthouse? Today?” Anna asked in disbelief. Her hands trembled as she sipped her coffee.

“Yes, the sooner the better. If we’re married, I’ll be able to support you through the military with medical benefits.” Billy grasped her hand on the table and squeezed.

Anna loved Billy. She always knew he was the man she wanted to spend the rest of her life with. But as long as she could remember, she had envisioned a beautiful wedding with her family in their church at home. She never expected her life to unravel this way. Anna pulled her hands away from Billy and covered her face as she cried. “I never dreamed this would happen to me.”

Billy wasn’t sure what to say. This was one of the only times in their relationship he didn’t have all the answers. “Oh honey, it’s going to be all right. We’ll get through this…”

"Get through this? Get through this? I don't just want to get through this!" Anna slammed her fist down on the table as her face reddened and transformed with anger.

"But honey, we'll get married, and I can help you take care of the baby." Billy reached out for her hand again and caressed it.

"Billy, the baby isn't due until May. You get out of the army in December! Getting married for a couple of months of medical support doesn't make any sense," Anna snapped at Billy in frustration as she pulled her hands away and crossed her arms.

Billy reached across the table with both hands and pleaded with her. "But I love you. Just being together is all that matters. This is our life. Sure, it's not what we expected, but we can handle this. This is the beginning of our life together."

Anna didn't respond. Billy's words felt empty to her. She didn't know what she wanted. She expected more. She wanted to be protected from the world, but now she was suffocated by it.

"I'll get out and get a job," Billy said. Although he hadn't thought through this option.

"Get a job? Where are you going to find work?" Anna asked in a skeptical tone. For the first time in their relationship, she didn't believe Billy. His future was now unpredictable, and she could see the disappointment in his eyes. He could find work, but she wondered if he would give up everything for her.

"I'll come home. I'm sure there's work as a guard at the reformatory, or I can work in one of those new stores in Cedar Rapids. I could always help out as a farm hand until something else comes along." Billy didn't have a plan, and it frustrated him.

He hadn't expected this. He knew it was possible, but he

never expected it to happen. He loved Anna and was ready to marry her. He had no question about that. After he returned to Fort Benning, he was confident he was ready to leave the army. He would go back to Iowa, attend college, play baseball, and get married. Those plans were gone now. He had to do what was best for Anna and the baby.

"I hate Iowa," Anna blurted out. The comment was unexpected, and Billy didn't know how to respond. He looked down at his coffee cup on the table. "I mean, I hate the way everyone judges you. The way folks look down their noses with ridicule. Always judging, always talking behind your back. I hate it."

"Ah honey, you're just being…" Billy slid his chair over to her side and tried to put his arm around her, but she pulled away.

"No, I'm serious. It's such a small town, and everyone talks. Just earlier this week we were at Buddy's for breakfast. I could feel people's eyes on me. Looking into me and passing their judgment. Like they knew I was pregnant and were looking down their noses at me. Later that day, we were at H&Js buying some groceries, and I heard a couple of the ladies in the next aisle over talking about me. I actually heard them." Anna's lip quivered, and she fought back the tears.

"I don't want to go back, Billy. I don't want to go back to Anamosa. Take me away from there. Take me away from that small town and all the judgment and hateful talk. I don't know what I'll do if I go back. I don't know how I'll be able to…" Anna started to cry.

"Honey, it will be okay. It will…" Billy put his hand on her back and began to slowly rub her shoulders.

"I'm pregnant! Do you know what they'll say? What they'll say about me? About you? About my family? I don't know how I'll be able to face my family. The disappointment. The look in my mother's eyes. The silence of my father. I don't know how I'm going to face all of this."

Billy put his arm around Anna and pulled her close. He didn't have all the answers. In fact, he had none. He only knew he would do anything for her. He held her close and whispered his promises. "We can do this, darling. We will do this. I'll protect you, Anna Angel. I promise. Whatever it takes. I'll protect you."

ꙮ

Anna had been home from Fort Benning a week and still didn't know what to do. When she had left Billy, he was determined to get out of the army, come back to Iowa, and find work. He never said it, but she could tell by his eyes that he was disappointed with the direction his life had turned. She knew he loved her, but she had heard the hope slip from his voice. Before all of this, he was excited about coming back, going to college, playing ball with Josh. Now with the baby on the way, this option was off the table, and he never mentioned it again.

Anna couldn't stand to see a broken man. Billy had a look in his eyes she had seen before. It was the same look in Billy's father's eyes when they drove him to the hospital in Independence. Billy was feeling lost, as if his life, his plans, his dreams slipped through his fingers. And this broke her heart.

For some time, she was certain he had wanted to stay in the army, that he felt a calling to lead soldiers. But in the past month, he seemed to have grown away from the army and was now interested in the prospect of going to college. She had been happy he felt this way, even though deep inside, she knew he was doing it for her.

Anna wondered if she kept him from his dreams, what would the consequences be? Billy was special, and he could change the world. She felt guilt, as if she was actually holding him back. She couldn't see him settling in a small town in the Midwest. It might destroy him. It might destroy both of them.

In Anna's last discussion with Billy at Fort Benning—against her own desire—she tried to convince him to stay in the army. She encouraged him to go to officer candidate school and become the leader of soldiers he had always wanted to be. He had already been propositioned multiple times about staying in and becoming an officer but had turned them all down because of her.

But now things had changed. She tried to convince Billy they could get married, and she could live with him in the officer housing at Fort Benning. She could have the baby in Georgia, away from the gossip and slander of a small town.

Now, a week later, it was a cool Saturday morning late in October. Anna sat in the front room of the old Jacobs farmhouse. She rehearsed how she would to tell her parents about the baby. She wished Billy was there to protect her and to take her away from all of this.

At that very moment, Anna heard someone walking up the

steps of the front porch. She leaned over and peered through the window and saw the silhouette of what looked like a man in uniform. Her heart jumped for a moment, but her mind told her it didn't make sense. Pulling away the curtain to the front window, she couldn't believe her eyes—it looked like Billy at the door.

Slowly opening the door, she was overwhelmed with disbelief and then incredible joy. Anna's eyes were wide. Her hands trembled as she held them up to her mouth and took a step backward. There on her front porch, in his army uniform, was Billy West.

"Nobody's going to call our child a bastard." Billy stepped forward and took Anna in his arms.

"What are you…what are you doing here?" Anna tried to come to grips with what was happening.

"Pick out your prettiest dress, my love. Today you're getting married." Billy pulled Anna into his arms and kissed her deeply.

"But Billy, I thought…how are we going to?" Anna pulled back and tried to ask more questions.

"Anna, I have my dress ready for you." Sarah Jacobs' voice startled Anna as it came up from behind her in the entryway.

Anna looked over her shoulder and saw her mother holding up her own wedding dress on a hanger. "You…you knew?" Anna questioned in disbelief.

Anna's mother nodded. "Billy called us earlier this week and told us everything."

"Everything?" Anna started to cry.

Anna's father came down the steps wearing a tie and a navy

sport coat, the only one he owned. He put his arm around Sarah, who was crying, too. She nodded. "Now we've got to get you ready. You're getting married this morning."

"Anna Darling, you need to listen to your ma. I've got Judge Swanson waiting for us down at the courthouse. Get your dress on. In a couple of hours, we'll be husband and wife." Billy smiled proudly.

Anna was stunned. The world was spinning around her, and she couldn't find any words. She stood numb in the doorway with Billy.

"Anna, your ma and me went out and bought you some luggage for your wedding present," her father said as he reached into the closet and pulled out suitcases.

"But…but I…"

"When you get back from your wedding today, we need to get you packed. You'll be leaving in the morning for Fort Benning," her father explained.

Anna turned to Billy. He looked so handsome on the front porch in his uniform. The image would be forever etched in her memory. She threw herself into his arms. Billy would take care of her. He would always be there for her.

IV

ANNA PULLED THE two letters out of her purse and lifted her eyes up to Pastor Jones who led the service from the pulpit. His mouth moved, but she couldn't focus on his words. She felt like she was spinning; faster and faster, and falling downward, deeper and deeper.

It was all so hard for her to get her mind around. If she had only been stronger. Her silly pride. She let it take over. If she'd only stayed home and had the baby…if she had agreed with Billy about leaving the army, he would be here now. He would be working at the prison, taking care of her and their son. Even still, she knew he wouldn't be the same. He would always wonder about what could have been.

When she had opened the possibility for him to become an officer, he took it with no hesitation. She would always regret that decision, but she knew in her heart it was what he wanted. It was probably what he always had wanted. She felt dizzy as her mind spun in circles. If she had just stood up to him. If she had just let him take care of her.

No one could stand up to Billy West. She knew that. What frustrated her most was that he was so good at leading soldiers. He led from the front and was always setting the example. He had a special way of engaging people that made them want to be better, to do more, to follow him. He had always been that way.

She had known the risks. She had heard the ugly stories about Vietnam from other wives, but she had pushed them out of her mind. Not her Billy. Nothing would touch him. She had convinced herself of that.

The days at Fort Benning had been good, maybe the happiest of their life. They had lived in the tiny one bedroom quarters on post while little Sammy grew inside of her. Billy threw everything he had into officer candidate school and graduated with honors at the top of his class. After graduation, he went through Airborne and Ranger School, again proving to be the leader she knew he was.

Everything had moved fast. Only days after Ranger School, he had his orders. He had been assigned to the 173rd Airborne Brigade and would be leaving for Vietnam within weeks.

She remembered their last days together. She was seven months pregnant. In her third trimester, little Sammy was growing into a very active little boy. She wished she had been happier when she was pregnant, but the fact was, she had been miserable. Her back had hurt, her feet were swollen, and she had felt as though she had ceased to exist as a woman. She was a life vessel for this being inside of her. Sleeping, walking, and just about every other aspect of her life had become difficult.

Her mind drifted to the memory of their last kiss. It was very early in the morning and still dark. Billy wore his uniform and carried a large green duffle bag. They stood in the rain, spending what would be their last moments together. They had waited as long as they could before Billy had to get on the bus for the airfield.

They were soaked in the cold spring rain. Holding her face in his hands, Billy looked deep into her eyes and reassured her. "We'll see each other soon. Just six months. We'll meet in Hawaii halfway through the deployment." Anna was unable to speak and nodded as tears rolled down her cheeks. "I love you, Anna Angel. I love you so much. I'll always love you." Billy leaned down one last time and kissed her.

Anna remembered how his lips were so cold against hers. Their last kiss. Billy turned and got on the bus. And that was it. The last time she saw Billy. He looked over his shoulder once more as the bus sped away. She could read his lips as he said, "I love you, Anna Angel."

Sitting in the church, Anna was overcome with a queasy feeling like she was going to be sick. She looked down in her arms again. Sammy was sound asleep, nestled up to her side. He had so much of Billy in him. Another wave of sadness washed over her as the tears clouded her eyes. Other than pictures, Billy had never looked into Sammy's eyes. Anna pulled her son closer to her. Billy would never hold Sammy in his arms.

Anna looked at the two unopened envelopes. Billy never mailed them, but he wrote a date on each envelope—one was dated November 1st, the other November 2nd. Nine days before he had died.

She ached to hear his voice. She needed something, anything to give her strength to go on. Anna's eyes focused on the envelopes when she felt an unbelievable and overwhelming presence of him next to her. An indescribable wave of serenity washed through her entire body. For the first time since Billy's death, she could breathe. A deep yearning for his love burned within her, and she was overcome with an urge to open the letters.

When Anna found the letters in Billy's belongings, she tucked them away. They were Billy's last words to her, and she couldn't bring herself to open them. But now, at the memorial, she felt it was the right thing to do.

Anna softly caressed the envelope dated November 1st with her hands. She gently loosened the flap ever so carefully with her fingers, knowing he had sealed it for her. Inexplicably, she felt as if his hands were guiding hers as she lovingly pulled the letter from the envelope. Holding the letter, she was ensconced in his love. She closed her eyes, savoring the moment, before she began to read.

My Anna Angel,

Hello, my love. I'm sorry it's been a couple of weeks since my last letter—have been busy on this end and finally got back to camp to a shower and hot chow. This is the first chance I've had to write. No worries, I'm OK, just been busy.

How's Sammy? Thank you for sending the pictures. Whenever I have a free moment, I find myself looking at the two of you together. I lay back on my cot and dream of the day when I'll be back in Iowa and we'll be together. Our little family under one roof—it seems too good to be true. Hard to believe we're halfway done with this deployment. Sometimes the days drag on and on, and then I look at the calendar and realize that months have passed.

The platoon is doing well. As I've said before, we got off to a bumpy start. I don't think they were expecting somebody to push them as hard as I do. But I've whipped them into shape, and I think we're the best platoon in the battalion. The battalion commander was out with us last week, and he said so himself! Amazing how far we've come. I just have to keep setting and enforcing standards so the team remains focused. The men have learned so much and have seen what I've been teaching work in action. Trust and respect are hard to earn and easy to lose. But I feel like we've turned a corner, and they believe in what I'm doing. Leading soldiers, taking care of them, feels natural for me. It's what I do. It's what I have to do. I think you've always known that.

I caught a little of the news today. More riots. It seems that back in the states, folks are turning against what we're doing. I can see how some feel that way. So much misinformation in the news. It can be confusing. Things at home are different from when I was here before. But from my perspective, we're still facing a communist tyranny that is lost in its hatred and pitted against everything that we as Americans stand for. Pure evil. I never thought I would see so much evil in my lifetime. I've seen it here, and if we don't stand firm, who else will?

Sorry darling, I didn't mean to take this letter that way. Just seeing the news and what Americans are saying at home…it's hard to swallow when I know the sacrifices our soldiers are making every day over here.

On a positive note, I finally found a West Pointer I liked. You know I don't trust the CO and LT Robinson, but the other platoon leader has completely surprised me. Jim Leonard is his name. He's a natural. He doesn't give a damn what other officers think and speaks his mind when something doesn't make sense…so he probably won't make it too far in this army. He doesn't suck up to the CO (like Robinson does), and he doesn't take unnecessary risks with his men. He's smart, humble, and caring, and his men love him. He reminds me of Josh in a way. I like him. He's probably the <u>*second*</u> *best LT in Vietnam. He and I really hit it off, which is good—you know I needed a friend over here.*

Enough about me, how are the parents? Probably about harvest time. Hope things are drying up so your pa can get the crops in. Got a letter from Pop. He's doing well. Really likes his job at the courthouse and seems happier than I can remember. Said he was out for dinner and that Sammy is growing like a weed. What do you think, is he going to be taller than his old man? Probably be pitching for the Cubs by the time he's twelve.

Well my love, got to get going, another long and unproductive meeting with the CO in about five minutes. I'm sorry this letter was more about me than about us. I'll write more later.

Did you get your tickets for Hawaii yet? Next month and we'll be together. Hard to believe. Counting the days, my love. Counting the days.

I love you, Anna Angel.

Always,

Billy

Anna smiled. It was the first time she had smiled since that day of days, weeks ago. She wiped the tears from her cheeks. He wanted her to smile. She sensed it. She could almost feel his arms around her, pulling her close to his chest. He'd be looking down at her, smiling, and then kissing her. He'd lean down and wipe the tears from her cheeks with his lips as he had done so many times before. Yes, she could almost feel him with her. Somehow she knew he was there with her now.

Anna looked up at Pastor Jones. His face was somber and serious. She peeked over at Butch West. He looked absolutely horrible. It was as if his life was draining out of him by the second—so much sadness, so much loss to endure. She worried about how this would affect him. Then she thought about herself. She couldn't begin to think about how she would be affected. She didn't care. She looked back up at the pastor. His words meant nothing to her, and she couldn't listen to them.

Anna suddenly felt herself lifting up and becoming removed from it all. She had the most extraordinary realization she was being held in Billy's arms and floating with a current, above the pain of the world. But it wasn't water. It was so much more than that. It was safety. It was joy. It was love. A sense of love she had never known existed, and she didn't want it to end.

Anna looked down at her ring with a smile, then closed her eyes. She surrendered to an indescribable, surreal tranquility. It reminded her of that day she and Billy were swimming at Fremont with Josh and Charlotte. She had leaned back in the water, feeling weightless as the stream lifted her up and the clouds had floated overhead. But now it was much more than that. It was peaceful and safe. She didn't want it to end, but in a split second it was over. She opened her eyes and found herself sitting in the hard oak pew, confined once again to the rules of the world.

Anna held Billy's last letter in her hands. She was not sure whether she should open it. She ran her fingers over her name on the outside. Once again, she sensed Billy's presence. She let go of all her fear and sadness and relished in his strength around her. Suddenly her hands were moving. She wasn't thinking anymore. She had given up and was reacting to him as if his hands were guiding hers. Opening the letter, she started to read.

My Anna Angel,

Last night I had a dream. It was that day on the river, with Joe

Matsell. But this time, as I swam upward, I reached out for your paddle, but you weren't there. I never made it to the surface. It was the strangest sensation I've ever had. I don't know what death is, but I felt myself drifting freely and completely surrounded by love. I think my mother was there. It was like I was a baby wrapped safely in her arms, and she was walking, taking me somewhere. It was the most peaceful sense of joy I have ever felt, so much so, that I didn't want to wake up.

I've never had a dream like this before. I wonder if this was a gift, or a sign, or maybe it wasn't anything at all. Whatever it was, I felt compelled to share it with you.

My love, we're moving out tomorrow, back to the Central Highlands. It's a dark corner of the world—full of shadows and ugliness. If I'm not able to write to you again, I wanted to give you a few words that would live with you when I am no more.

Anna Angel, my love for you is timeless. It always has been and will always be. It is without beginning or end. It just is. It's always, my love. Always.

You're so much a part of me that I honestly don't know where I stop and you start. My love for you is interwoven into my heart and soul. I think we're both this way. It's truly a wonder, and I often ponder how I was so blessed to have it for most of my life. That I would find and love only one woman in this world…a woman who would make my life complete.

I know these words are hard for you to read right now. But I send them to you with only love and all the compassion within me. Be strong, my love. You must find your courage. You must be strong for Sammy. And know that when you hold Sammy, you will be holding a part of me. He's part of both of us. He's such an amazing gift from God—in the brightest days, and the darkest nights, you'll always find me in him. Always.

I know you're angry and may even feel guilt for the decisions we made. Please don't. Please rid yourself of these feelings. They dishonor both of us and what we are. I only want you to love me and feel pride that I lived my life doing what I believed. I made this decision to serve my country with my own free will. I know the costs. I know the risks, and they're worth it to me. I know some would consider it a selfish endeavor…please don't. You're a part of me, and I love you, but being a leader of soldiers is also so much of who I am.

You know me better than anyone. You're so much a part of who I am and only you truly understand this. I love you, I love my country, and I love serving soldiers. I was born to love you, and I was born to do this. If I should lay down my life for it, you have to know it was not in vain. Please don't diminish my sacrifice with your anger and sadness.

I do not regret losing our love. Because that will never happen—our love will always be. My only regrets are that I won't be there to help you as you face the challenges of the world and that I won't be there with you to see our son become a man—to play catch with him in the front yard, to teach him to drive, to guide him as he courts and marries a woman, and starts a family of his own. I won't be there, but know this. I will be there.

When the morning breaks and the birds sing, I'll be there. When you awake from your slumber, I'll be there. When you take a sip from your first cup of coffee, I'll be there. When you hold Sammy in your arms, I'll be there. When you face the challenges of the day and settle in the evening, I'll be there. And when you drift off to sleep at night, I'll be there. My love for you will always be there. And where it is, I am also.

You're young, my love, and have your whole life ahead of you. Know that I love you. But I love you so much that I don't want you to be alone. I wish for you to only have joy as you walk through life.

Look to the stars, my love. I am there. I will always be there. Remember what I said—no matter what happens, no matter where we are, we will always have the North Star to remind us of our love, to guide us. It's our true north. The world will keep spinning, but it will always be there. Changes will come, and at times, the sky will be full of patterns of stars that will keep moving, that won't make any sense, but this one, our star, will always be there. Right where it is right now. Holding strong, unmovable, it will always be there for us. Our truth. Before the break of day in the very early morning and in the deepest and darkest of nights, it will always be there for us. Our love. Always there, always guiding us, no matter what this world brings.

My dear Anna Angel, in my last breath as I leave this world, know that I will only be saying your name. That you will be in my last waking thought. And my love, don't think of me as gone. I'm simply waiting for you. Not far away...I'm just around the bend in the river...you will find me in the warm summer sun...I will be there waiting, and no matter what this world brings, I will hold you in my arms again.

I love you, Anna Angel.

Always,

Billy

Anna closed her eyes and held the letter. A small smile spread across her lips. She felt Billy's love. She felt his arms around her. She wanted to cry. She wanted to be angry. She wanted to shut herself off from the world, but she knew he wanted her to be strong and courageous. Somehow she would find a way to go on. Somehow he knew exactly what she would be feeling, right then and there in the church. With his words, he gave her the encouragement she longed for.

A sense of peace came over Anna. Billy would always be there for her. Somewhere nearby, just out of sight in another room, waiting for her to enter and be with him.

She looked down at Sammy. Billy was right. He was a gift from God. There was as much of her in him as there was of Billy. He was their legacy. He was their gift. As long as Sammy was in her life, Billy would be there, too.

Anna looked up to Pastor Jones. For the first time of the service, she listened to his words.

"As I think about Billy and his sacrifice on the altar of freedom, I think about Jesus' sacrifice for all of us. Just before his own death, Jesus shared these words of love with his disciples."

Pastor Jones cleared his throat and then began to read from his King James Bible. "If ye keep my commandments, ye shall abide in my love; even as I have kept my Father's commandments, and abide in his love. These things have I spoken unto you, that my joy might remain in you, and that your joy might be full. This is my commandment, that ye love one another, as I have loved you. Greater love hath no man than this, that a man lay down his life for his friends."

Pastor Jones paused for a moment to let these words resonate within the walls of the church and even his own heart. "Samuel William West gave his life so others might live. He did it with the fullness of life with everything at stake. If he were here today, he wouldn't want sadness, or anger, or frustration in trying to find meaning in all of this.

"Billy lived his life doing what he was born to do. He was

serving his country. He was leading soldiers. He wouldn't want you to mourn his death, but celebrate his life, his sacrifice. One day, everyone in this room will go and be with the Father. Billy was one of the few people in this world who did it while doing what he believed."

Anna's mind drifted again to Billy and happier days of warm, caressing sunshine, and the indescribable love when they held each other. Time had slipped away, and she didn't want to come back, but somehow she had to. Something stirred her conscious, and she was alert again. She did not know how long she had been gone, but when she looked up, Pastor Jones was no longer speaking. Music, beautiful music, filled the church. She recognized the song. It was one of Billy's favorite hymns, "It is Well with My Soul." The words pierced her heart as they rang through the church.

"When peace, like a river, attendeth my way. When sorrows like sea billows roll. Whatever my lot, thou hast taught me to say, it is well, it is well with my soul…"

As the music enveloped her, Anna looked down at the baby in her arms. Sammy woke up, and in his eyes, she saw Billy looking back at her, and she knew somehow she would make it through another day.

Epilogue

ANDY WIPED THE tears from his cheeks.

"I'm going to get another cup of coffee. Would you like one?" Sheriff Barton asked as he got up to leave his office.

Andy looked up from the framed document he was reading and nodded, acknowledging that he would.

He was amazed. He had never seen this before. Looking down at the framed document, he read it again.

Medal of Honor Citation

Rank and organization: Samuel William West, Second Lieutenant, U.S. Army, Company B, 1st Battalion, 503d Infantry 173d Airborne Brigade. Place and date: Dak To, Republic of Vietnam, 11 November 1967. Entered service at: Anamosa, Iowa. Born: 2 September 1946, Anamosa, Iowa.

Citation: For conspicuous gallantry and intrepidity in action at the risk of his life above and beyond the call of duty, 2LT West distinguished himself by a series of daring actions and exceptional heroism while engaged in combat against hostile forces.

Serving as a platoon leader in the Central Highlands on the morning of November 11, 1967, another platoon in B Company was inserted west of Hill 1034 to search and destroy large enemy formations occupying the area. The platoon became engaged by a much larger enemy force and suffered heavy casualties. Four helicopters attempted to extract the platoon but due to intense fire were unable to reach all of the soldiers. Second Lieutenant West was at the forward operating base when the first aircraft arrived with survivors from the platoon. Lieutenant West voluntarily boarded an aircraft to assist in another rescue attempt. Arriving at the pickup zone, the aircraft was immediately engaged by small arms and RPG fire. Two of the helicopters were shot down, and the other two were unable to land due to the intense enemy fire.

Lieutenant West was in one of the aircraft that was shot down but was the lone survivor of the crash. West suffered lacerations to his left hand and face during the crash. Running across the pickup zone through continuous enemy small arms fire, he was wounded again with shrapnel to his back from an enemy rocket propelled grenade. 2LT West found the squad leader and the survivors of the remaining squad. He discovered that the platoon sergeant was dead and the platoon leader was missing. All of the soldiers in the squad were wounded and Second Lieutenant West immediately began rendering aid. Shielding the wounded from the enemy fire with his own body while providing medical assistance, West sustained a gunshot wound to his left thigh. Having stabilized the severely wounded, West set up a perimeter, redistributed ammunition, and began directing fires against three major enemy attacks on his position. 2LT West coordinated a series of air strikes and artillery fires on the enemy positions and momentarily mitigated the threat for one helicopter to land. He dragged and carried multiple dead and wounded soldiers onto the aircraft. While lifting the wounded onto the aircraft West was wounded again, this time a gunshot wound to the shoulder.

Despite these injuries, he repositioned the remaining four soldiers in a tight perimeter and continued to search for dead and wounded while directing fires against an oncoming enemy. Moving to the edge of the pickup zone, he found the platoon leader wounded but conscious. He lifted the platoon leader and while running back to the perimeter was met by two enemy soldiers. He immediately shot and killed one of them and after his weapon malfunctioned, he fought off and killed the second in hand-to-hand combat. Suffering additional lacerations to his arms and face from the enemy's bayonet, through his unconquerable spirit, he lifted the wounded lieutenant and carried him back to the security of the perimeter.

Second Lieutenant West continued to tend the wounded and coordinated indirect fires on another attack from a much larger enemy force when another helicopter crashed on the north side of the pick-up zone. 2LT West immediately moved to the crash site to assess casualties. All of the soldiers on the aircraft were killed in the crash, and West was unable to remove them from the wreckage. 2LT West could see at least ten enemy soldiers assault from the tree line toward the four man perimeter, and with no regard for his own safety, immediately attacked them in a frontal assault. Firing his rifle, he killed half of the men before he was wounded again. This time, a gunshot wounded his hip and his right calf. Despite his serious wounds, he crawled forward and killed two more of the enemy soldiers and thwarted their assault. Unable to walk, Second Lieutenant West crawled back to the remaining soldiers as another aircraft was preparing to land.

Under increasing automatic weapons and grenade fire, 2LT West mustered his strength and coordinated additional airstrikes on the enemy positions. Seriously wounded and facing a buildup of enemy forces with his team of soldiers, he was able to direct fire from gunships and suppress the enemy threat momentarily to allow a helicopter to land for extraction. In dire condition, West continued to fire his rifle and killed three more enemy soldiers assaulting their perimeter. He was wounded again with a gunshot to his left arm and chest. Mortally wounded, he collapsed and was pulled onto the aircraft.

Through his fearless leadership, unshakable courage, and extremely valorous actions in the face of an overwhelming enemy, Second Lieutenant West saved the lives of at least eleven men. 2LT West's extraordinary heroism, and intrepidity at the cost of his life, are above and beyond the call of duty and are in the highest traditions of military service and reflect great credit upon himself, his unit, and the United States Army.

When Andy finished reading, he lifted his eyes from the document.

Sheriff Barton was again filled with emotion. "Something, isn't it?" Barton said, and Andy felt an immense weight in the room. He couldn't find the right words to respond. "Every now and then, I take that frame down off the wall and read it. I read it so I might be reminded of all of those who have gone before us. Who have sacrificed for us so we might enjoy our freedoms. Freedoms that are so uncommon in this world." Barton's tone was serious and direct. "I wonder what we would be if it weren't for the Billy Wests of the world," Barton concluded.

Sheriff Barton's words triggered a memory and Andy's mind raced back to 1966. He remembered that summer evening on the porch with Billy, his father and his uncle. He thought about the confrontation between his mother and his father.

And at that moment, in the sheriff's office, he finally understood.

Both of them were right. Billy was created for greater things. He was born to lead. He had a calling in his life to change the world. He was destined to do something that would change the lives of those around him, leave a legacy, and pave the way for something bigger than him. Yet, his mom was right too—about the cost, the loss, the sacrifice, and the scars on those left behind. He could clearly see how they were both right and somehow their conflicting views intertwined and had a profound effect on the man he was today.

Andy looked down at the framed document. His mother, father, uncle, and Billy were gone. They were all gone, but their message, their hearts, their legacies lived on. He finally got it. He understood how they all lived in him now.

Andy lifted his eyes from the document and cleared his throat. "I remember that day in November. I remember the funeral. But whatever happened to Anna?"

"Anna West? That's a darn good question." Sheriff Barton took a sip of his coffee and set his cup on his desk. "After Billy died, most never saw her again. She stayed out on the family farm for a couple years. There were rumors, but no one really knows for sure. I heard she locked herself into her bedroom. Locked herself up and away from the world. From what I heard, she even stopped taking care of her son, and her mother had to tend to him. She became a recluse, some even said she went crazy. Sadness can do that to you. It can eat you from the inside out and leave you as a shell of your former self." Jim Barton paused for a moment.

"Word is that one day something mighty peculiar happened. This young man came calling for her. He was a ball player. As a matter of fact, he was one of the best this county ever produced. Josh Sanders was his name, and he played for the Pirates."

Sheriff Barton took another drink of his coffee. "Anyway, one day he showed up at the farm to see her, and the way I heard the story, that very same day, she took her little boy and left with him. As far as I know, I don't think she's ever returned. I suppose memories will do that to a person. When you lose someone you love, too many memories can be just that—too many memories. And if you live in your memories for too long, well, they get the best of you."

The air in Barton's office was thick and warm. Andy could hear the annoying tick of the clock above the door and Margie Wilson pounding on her keyboard outside the office.

Barton glanced down at his watch and a look of surprise formed on his face. "I've got a meeting over at the courthouse and I need to…"

"That's okay. You've given me enough of your time and more than enough to get the funeral arrangements started." Andy stood up from the desk.

"The end of an era…your father…his generation. Him and his brother. They don't make them like that anymore. I sometimes wonder what this world will become without men like them." Sheriff Barton stood up and stretched out his hand to shake Andy's.

"Yes, sir." Andy gripped Sheriff Barton's hand.

"Please let me know if there's anything you need," Sheriff Barton said.

"Funeral is on Saturday. I just have to pull everything together with the funeral home. My wife, Susie, had to stay back to finalize a case with her law firm. She'll be here tomorrow with the kids, and we should be fine," Andy explained.

"Okay, but I mean it. Let me know if there's anything I can do for you," Sheriff Barton repeated, and then realizing Andy had forgotten his father's papers, added, "Oh, and don't forget all of these papers I found at the cemetery."

"Thank you, Sheriff." Andy took the large folder and shook the sheriff's hand one more time. "If anything comes up, I'll let you know," Andy said, and he turned to leave the office.

ꕥ

"This may sound strange, but did you know my father?" Andy heard a click, and the phone went dead.

Spread across his bed in the hotel room were stacks of papers organized by their last names. Gomez, James, Murphy, Leonard, Thacker, Andrews, and Brown…but none of it made sense. They did not seem to be connected in any way.

Andy was initially excited to dig into this. Many of the phone numbers were circled in red ink as if his father was guiding him to discover something profound. But after calling three of the families with no results, he wondered if his father had been growing senile and in the process of losing his mind.

These were families spread all across the United States with diverse economic and ethnic backgrounds. It didn't make any sense. Andy picked up the phone to make another call. He would not give up. He convinced himself there had to be a link.

Andy found a circled phone number to a Thacker residence in Alabama and dialed it. He heard a woman's voice on the other end of the line.

"Hello, my name is Andy Crawford. My father recently passed away and left information about the Thacker family in his belongings at the care center."

There was silence on the other end of the line and Andy tried again. "His name was John Crawford. Does this name sound familiar to you or to anyone at your residence?"

An angry voice shot back at Andy. "Is this a telemarketer? I thought I blocked all of you. I'm on a do not call list! How did you get this number?"

"No, ma'am. My name is Andy Crawford, and I'm calling about my…" The phone went dead before Andy could finish his sentence.

"What did all of this mean?" Andy sat alone in the hotel room with stacks of paper spread all over the bed and was talking to himself. "Dad, what are you trying to tell me?"

Andy turned on the television and went to the mini-refrigerator. He found the cold beer he had put in it earlier in the day. Opening one, he started to sift through the piles again. There were notes about weddings in at least five of the seven piles. Several young adults graduated from colleges. One went to Stanford and another to West Point. He found clippings about babies being born, and there were several obituaries.

Andy compared two obituaries—one for Benjamin Andrews and the other for Maurice Thacker. One was faded and difficult to read, but his father circled something on both documents. Looking closely, Andy realized both had served in the army during the 1960s. In fact, both had tours in Vietnam at the same time.

Andy fisted his palms in the air with a fresh surge of excitement. He had not caught this connection before. Could this be the link? Were these all veterans? Had they served together in Vietnam? What was his father telling him? Andy thought about his dad as he sifted through each of the piles again. Gomez, Murphy, Brown, and Leonard. In several of them, there was information about service in the military, but in others, he couldn't find anything. He wondered if this theory was leading him to another dead end. Exhaling, Andy picked up the phone to call another number.

A man answered. "Hello, this is Jim."

Hello, Mr. Leonard?" Andy paused. "My name is Andy Crawford, and I'm calling you to get information about my father. His name was John Crawford." There was silence on the line, and Andy took a deep breath. "My father recently passed away. I'm calling about information he had in his personal belongings about you." Andy sighed, waiting for the phone to go dead. But it didn't.

The man on the other end replied, "Well, I'm sorry to hear about your loss."

Andy thought the man seemed older. There was a kindness in his voice that was welcoming in comparison to the reactions he had received in the other four calls he had made. The man continued, "Hmm, let me see, Crawford…Crawford…John Crawford, did you say?"

"Yes, sir. He was seventy-nine and lived in a small town in eastern Iowa," Andy replied.

"Nope, never heard of him," the man answered.

"Okay, sir. I appreciate your…" Andy started to respond.

"Where in Iowa did you say you are from?" the voice on the other end of the line interjected.

"Oh, it's a really small town. You've probably never heard of it," Andy said.

Mr. Leonard spoke up confidently. "I once had a very close friend who was from Iowa. He was also from a really small town. Guess they're all pretty small out there. Let me see...it was umm…I think it was called Ana… Ana something… Anamoze… Anamosa, that's it. He was from Anamosa. Ever hear of it?"

There was a long silence on the phone. Andy didn't know how to respond.

"Sir…sir, are you still there?" The man on the other end asked.

Andy finally found the strength to continue.

"What was his name?" Andy asked, but he was sure he knew the answer.

"His name was West. Samuel William West. But I knew him as Billy," the man replied.

Andy's mind began to spin, and he suddenly felt dizzy with nausea. The palm of his hand was sweaty as he gripped the phone tightly in an effort to gain control of his senses. He looked down at the all the papers spread across his bed and tried to focus on the voice on the other end of the line.

"Ssss…Sir…Sir, did…did you say Billy West?"

There was silence on the line, and Andy thought he lost the connection. "Sir, were you at Dak To in November, 1967?" Andy focused his words as he tried to remember everything in the Medal of Honor citation from Sheriff Barton's office. There was a very long pause on the phone, and Andy could hear the man on the other end take a deep breath.

"Dak To." The man hesitated, and Andy heard a heavy sigh. "Dak To…I haven't heard that name in so many years. Such a dark and dangerous place. I've never talked to anyone about Dak To." The man's voice was sad and ominous.

Andy knew he had struck an emotional chord, but he had to go on. "Were you there with Billy?"

There was another long, silent interval on the other end.

"Billy? Dak To? Yes. Yes, I was there," the man answered. "We were all so young. So young back then. We could move mountains…and some did, and we all paid for it. Some of us are still paying for it." Andy didn't know how to respond, but he didn't have to as the man continued to talk on the other end of the line. "I was just a snot-nosed lieutenant, trying to do what was right. Trying to take care of my men. Trying to accomplish our mission. Balancing it all on a razor's edge. Those were sad and amazing days. I never lived more and never had so much been taken from me…it was so horrible…so much loss…too much loss…"

Andy remained silent and tried to write down everything he said. The man's voice cracked on the phone, and he stopped for a moment. He was crying.

"Dak To? Yes, I was there. I was with Billy when he died. He died in my arms as we flew out of that damn place. Billy saved my life…he saved most of my platoon that day. I've never seen anything like it, and will probably never see it again. So much sacrifice, so much love."

"Sir, I really appreciate your…" Andy tried to thank him but was interrupted.

"He came back for me. I wouldn't be here today if it wasn't for Billy. Not a day goes by that I don't think about him. About what he did for me. Every day I wonder if I have lived my life in a way that honors him. Did I meet his expectations? I know I've made my share of mistakes…that sometimes I'm letting him down. But I wonder if I have earned the life I was given?"

The tone of voice on the end of the line reminded Andy of his uncle. He thought about his childhood and all their long talks while fishing, camping, or just sitting on the porch together. Andy didn't know how to respond to Mr. Leonard and tried to turn the discussion in another direction. "Can you tell me about Gomez, Murphy, Brown, Andrews, James and Thacker?"

"I haven't talked to them in years. They were all there with me when Billy came and saved us. There were others, too. Brackers, Lawson, Frenchy, and Pender. God, we were all tore up. The enemy seemed to come from everywhere. I don't know how anyone could've survived. But somehow we did. We never would've made it if it wasn't for Billy."

As Mr. Leonard talked, Andy thought about Billy, and he thought about his own father. This was just like Dad. A quiet man with a heart of gold. Andy thought about how his dad died at Mom's grave. He had planned all of this…the beer with Uncle Dave, the rose for Mom, and all of this information at Billy's gravesite. Andy realized his father wanted to somehow let Billy know he had not given his life in vain—somehow, he had to help Billy see the goodness he created in this world.

"Mr. Leonard, I want to thank you for your time today. You shed some light on things for me," Andy said and there was suddenly a long pause on the other end of the phone.

Mr. Leonard finally broke the silence. "Is it beautiful?"

"What?" Andy was confused. "Is what beautiful?"

"The cemetery Billy's buried in. Is it beautiful?" Mr. Leonard asked again. "So many times I've convinced myself I was going to drive up there to see him, and every time, I talked myself out of it. I guess I still can't find the courage to face him." There was another long pause on the phone, and the man was crying again, but somehow, he continued. "I just wanted to know if where he was laid to rest is beautiful."

"He is buried at Riverside Cemetery on the hillside overlooking the river." Andy took a deep breath, realizing he didn't answer the question. "Yes, sir. It's beautiful."

"Good," he replied. "That's good. He deserves it. He deserves beauty. He deserves everything this world can give him."

ʊɑ

"I'm going to take the kids and get lunch. Do you want to come?" Susie asked Andy as they found their departure gate at Chicago O'Hare.

Andy was not feeling well. The past week had been a roller coaster of emotions. His father's funeral, all the family and friends, lots of laughter and tears, and too many memories. Now, as he sat down at the gate, he was exhausted. The flight from Cedar Rapids had been bumpy, and he didn't have much of an appetite. The only thing he wanted to do was to sit for a while.

Susie took the kids toward the food court while Andy sat at the gate and looked through his carry-on bag. In it, he had the documents from the families he had received from Sheriff Barton, and he also had a book he had found in his father's belongings at the care center.

He took out the book. It was a compilation of letters that had been left at the Vietnam War Memorial in Washington, D.C., published in 1993. Andy thought it odd that it was one of the only books his father had with him.

After five minutes, he was restless and couldn't focus on the book. It had too much emotion for him after all he'd been through. Closing the book, Andy decided to get a cup of coffee instead.

He made his way through the busy crowds toward the coffee shop.

"I'll have a caramel macchiato and a skinny vanilla latte," the woman in front of Andy ordered with a pretentious and annoying voice. Andy had no idea what a macchiato was and wondered what made a latte skinny. For a brief moment, he speculated if he might be in the wrong line. All he wanted was a cup of coffee, just a large cup of strong black coffee to help him focus. In a brief moment of panic, he looked up at the drinks on the sign and couldn't understand or find anything close to what he wanted.

"Just tell them you want a cup of their house blend. That's what I usually do." There was a direct and clear voice right behind Andy that startled him.

Andy must have looked as lost as he actually was, trying to figure out his order. He turned and standing behind him was a man in a light greenish-blue, digitally-patterned, military uniform.

"Is it that obvious?" Andy asked as a grin formed on his face.

"I have the same problem. Too many choices. I don't even know what they are. When did ordering a cup of coffee require learning a foreign language?" The man in uniform smiled.

The two men nodded and looked up at the menu on the board.

"So, are you coming home or going out?" Andy asked.

"I'm on my way back. Was just home for a couple of weeks for leave."

There was a long pause, and Andy wanted to ask him more

questions but didn't know what to say. He didn't have to say anything.

"This is my second deployment to Iraq. The first one was back in 2004. Now this one…we've already got word we'll be back again in 2008," The soldier said.

Andy did the math—that would be three year-long deployments in five years. He couldn't imagine the toll this commitment had on soldiers and their families. Andy looked at the soldier closely. He was young and reminded him of a little boy. Andy thought about his own kids. This young man couldn't be too much older. Andy was surprised when he saw the black bar on the soldier's chest. He was a first lieutenant.

"What branch are you in?" Andy asked, realizing he was an army officer.

"I'm in the infantry," the young man replied.

Andy thought of Billy and stretched his arm forward to shake the soldier's hand. "Thank you for your serving our country."

Andy didn't know what else to say. He suddenly felt less of a man. Here he was, on his way home to Baltimore, while this man going on a completely different path—to an ugly place that was so far removed and foreign to anything close to Andy's own home.

Andy unexpectedly was in awe for this soldier and the others he had seen in the airport that day. This feeling was replaced by gratitude for those who served. His uncle, his father, Billy, and this young man buying a cup of coffee, on his way to God knows where.

"Take this $20. Whatever this young man wants, give it to him." Andy leaned forward and whispered to the attendant behind the counter.

Turning back to the soldier, he spoke again. "Thank you for what you do. Safe travels and Godspeed."

Andy felt awkward, almost ashamed of himself for what he said. He was in the presence of someone who was making a difference in the world. He felt oddly insignificant for what he had done with his own life. Andy shook his hand one more time and walked back to his departure gate for Baltimore.

ꕤ

Andy pulled the book from his bag and sat back to sip his coffee. The first fifty pages of the book were horribly sad—letters from loved ones to lost soldiers placed at the Vietnam Wall. It was too much, too heavy to take in. Too much to read. Andy was again surprised that his father had this in his possessions.

Andy set the book down on the seat next to him and took another sip of his coffee. He looked out across the corridor that led to other gates. He watched all the passerby's. There were so many people coming and going and moving in so many directions.

Andy enjoyed people watching, and the airport was one of the best places to see so much diversity. A woman in a tight miniskirt walking a Chihuahua on a gold chain leash. A businessman hurrying by with his briefcase. An elderly man in a wheelchair. A little girl walking with her mother. Several pilots and flight attendants walking briskly to catch their next plane. Andy saw the lieutenant from the coffee shop walk past with a drink and a sandwich.

Taking another sip of his coffee, Andy glanced down at the book and noticed something he hadn't seen before. One of the pages toward the end was folded down. He picked up the book and opened it to the marked page. He almost dropped his cup in his lap when he read the first words.

"My Dearest Billy,

In 1982, they dedicated this memorial to you and put your name on it with all the others that gave their life in that awful place. It's been four years, and I finally decided to come and find you.

I didn't want to come. Not because it's a long drive from Pittsburgh or because I didn't care. It took me so long because I do care. I still care. It took me four years to find the courage to come and see you here.

I still cry for you. Not openly. The tears have dried up, and there are none left to shed. They're all inside now. It's my heart that cries for you. I know you would be angry, but there's a hole in my heart that nothing in this world can heal. In the first couple of years, I cried so much I didn't think I would go on, but somehow I did. Even now, the tears of my broken heart don't help. Almost twenty years later and the pain is still real. But at least they remind me of the love we had.

Sammy has been my rock. I think you knew he would be. There's so much of you in him. You would be proud. He's definitely your son. He has your drive and your strength, but I think in many ways he's even better. I know you would agree. It's his heart. There's something so pure and noble in it. I cannot believe he's almost twenty, and a young man, ready to face the challenges of this world. It scares the hell out of me. He seems so young. Were we really this young?

He's decided he wants to be a pastor. He wants to serve others and lead them to God. I support him, and I know you would, too. He has the heart for it. He's a good man. I know you would be so proud of the man he's become.

Josh is a good husband and father. Somehow you knew he would be. He loves me and has been a wonderful father. But there are times, even now, when Sammy, Josh, and I are together, and it feels like it is the three of us again from all those years ago. The interaction, the laughter, and the love. Maybe you're there with us.

I'm sorry for all of the tears. Sometimes I feel so alone and so empty, and I just want to feel your arms around me again. Josh understands. There are times when he misses you too. He has never had a closer friend. That war took something from all of us, and nothing will ever replace it.

I often find myself gazing up at the stars, searching for our star. I find it and feel you with me. Holding me, wiping away my tears, and whispering sweetly in my ear that you love me, that you'll always love me.

I find comfort there and know that someday you'll hold me again. Someday soon, I will come around the bend in the river, and I will find you in the warm summer sun waiting for me, and we will hold each other again. Until then, my love, I will wait for you, I will wait for you to fill the hole in my heart and make me whole again.

I love you. Billy,

Always,

Always Your Anna Angel

Tears burned in Andy's eyes, and he wiped them away. He felt numb, as if he had just traveled back in time. He was there again, with Billy and Anna and his family, enjoying a summer day at a picnic, in the park, along the Wapsi. The men played horseshoes, the women laughed, and not far away, the river slowly drifted by.

Andy would reach out to her. Anna might still be in Pittsburgh, and he would find her. He would finish what his father started. Somehow he would show her Billy's death had not been in vain. Murphy and Gomez, Thacker and Leonard, and all the other families. Andy would tell her. He would show her the truth. She would know Billy's sacrifice saved others. She would see the impact Billy had on the world. Andy would heal the scars from all those years ago.

"I got you a sandwich." Susie startled Andy as she sat down next to him. Andy didn't reply. He closed the book and looked away to hide his emotion. "Are you okay?" Susie asked.

"Mom, can we go over to the bookstore and check out the magazines?" their son, John, asked, interrupting his mother.

"Yes, but take your brother and don't go anywhere else. We'll be boarding in about forty five minutes."

"Aw, Mom, do I have to take Davey?" John asked with a pout.

"Yes. Yes, you do. Or you can just sit here and stay with

us." John was thirteen, and his younger brother was eleven, an age when everything his younger brother did was annoying.

"Okay. Come on, knucklehead. Let's go," John said to his little brother as he got up and walked toward the bookstore.

"John, can you pretend you like your brother?" Susie said in an exasperated tone.

Davey got up and ran after his older brother, leaving Susie and Andy alone at the gate.

"Andy, are you sure you're okay?" Susie asked, knowing something was on her husband's mind.

"Susie Darling, look at that man in uniform over there. And there's a woman on the other side of the terminal in uniform too." Andy jutted his chin and looked toward them.

Susie followed her husband's eyes and found the soldiers. She could not imagine what their lives were like and suddenly felt a wave of sadness for them.

Looking to her husband, she asked, "I wonder if these wars will ever end?"

Andy didn't respond immediately. Susie's words settled over them. They watched the soldiers for a few more minutes.

"Susie, where did we get such men and women?" Andy asked. She didn't know how to respond and just nodded. "Sometimes I wonder what our country would be if not for them. I wonder what we would be if not for what they do for us every day."

Tears welled up in his eyes. Susie didn't need to say anything. She knew he was right. She took his hand in hers and put her head on his shoulder. They quietly watched as the soldier picked up his duffle bag, swung it over his shoulder, and boarded the plane.

The End

Acknowledgments

This never would have been possible if not for the unyielding love and support of my wife and best friend, Amy Beth. She, and she alone, knows my heart and why I had to tell this story. The debt of gratitude I owe her is without limit. Putting up with me as I stomped around the house in the darkness early in the morning in search for a pencil…supplying me with soothing tea late into the night as I wrestled with words when I should have been nestled at her side in bed…and of course, my countless imperfections. My only hope is that she truly knows how much I love her. Always.

To my legacy, Emily and Will. As a father, I know there were times when I was there, but I wasn't really there. I was lost in my mind on the Wapsipinicon, on a battlefield in Vietnam, or somewhere deep in Anna's heart. I hope that somehow, in this story, you will find a part of me that will live in your hearts when I am no more. I love you.

To my family and friends who provided helpful feedback on the early drafts of the manuscript. Although there were times you may have thought me crazy for writing this story (and your feelings were probably justified), you also provided the love and support I needed to see it through. Thank you.

Lastly, I cannot express how thankful I am to my editor, A.L. Zaun. When we started this brutal process I think we both had expectations. Thankfully, we were probably both wrong. The fact that she believed in the story is what made it ring true with all of its texture and color. If this novel touched your emotions and carried you deep down the river with Billy and Anna, it was because of her efforts to make it shine and truly special. Thank you, Ana.

On a final note, if this story is worthwhile it is due to two events in my life. Growing up in Anamosa, Iowa and serving in the United States Army. Anamosa is a very special place, maybe the best of places for a boy to live, grow and dream. Sometimes I wonder if one has to leave to appreciate the surroundings, the people, the river…and the joy they bring to a childhood. Anamosa will always be my hometown. As for the Army, I was fortunate to serve on the greatest team in the world. It made me the man I am.

About The Author

Jay Soupene was born and raised in Anamosa, Iowa. He graduated from West Point. After twenty years of service and multiple combat tours, he retired from the Army. Jay and his lovely wife, Amy, live in Iowa with their two children Emily and Will. This is his first novel.

To learn more about Jay Soupene, he can be contacted at:

Website: http://wapsipiniconsummer.wordpress.com/.

Facebook: https://www.facebook.com/wapsipinicon.summer

Email: Wapsipinconsummer@gmail.com

Made in the USA
Middletown, DE
12 December 2014